# OFF THE MENU

# OFF THE MENU

## OFF-LIMITS LOVERS
### Book One

## LORE TOWNSEND

*For anyone playing their cards close to the chest...*
*You'll know when the time is right. You got this.*
*We're all rooting for you!*

## Before we begin...

This love story leans a bit to the kinky side, especially when it comes to the bedroom scenes. I mean, that's why you're here, right? All the wild and crazy spice that some of us can only dream about.

Just wanted to note that, while I've done my best to include safety and consent wherever necessary, this is a work of fiction and should not be taken as a guide or manual for the BDSM lifestyle. The characters in this story get up to hijinks that may not be safe or recommended to try between your own sheets without preparation and conversations about safety.

That being said...if you have fun on this wild ride and want to join the rest of us who enjoy similar fantasies, you can find us in Lore Townsend's Romance Club on Facebook.

Love you!

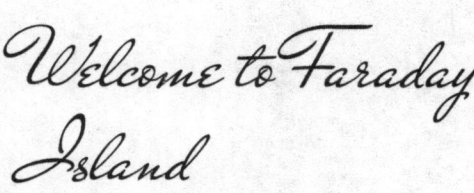

# Welcome to Faraday Island

If this is your first time checking into The White Sands Resort, you've started at a great place. Dominic and Reina's love story is first in the series, so you'll get a nice, easy introduction to the world of Faraday and the cast of characters who will become familiar throughout the series. Here's a little cheat sheet, just for fun.

The owners of The White Sands Resort:

- **Dominic:** The chef
- **Sam:** The general manager
- **Ben:** The lawyer
- **Avery:** The wild card

Places you'll go:

- **Faraday Island:** a fictional tropical island with the climate and geographic features of a small island off the coast of Belize (where I was when I started writing this book).
- **Saubry Village:** The town on Faraday Island.

- **Merit Island:** The small island next to Faraday where the guys own a house.
- **The White Sands Resort:** The four guys purchased the abandoned resort over a decade ago and reopened it as a high-end beach destination.
- **Raft:** The restaurant located inside The White Sands Resort.

# OFF THE MENU

# Rule #1

STICK TO THE PLAN

REINA

After burning my life to the ground and escaping to a tiny tropical island with my tail between my legs, I can't decide if I should attend the first staff party looking hot...or humble.

Fuck it. No one here knows me. This is my chance to reinvent myself. To start over.

I decide to go with casually hot, pulling on a short denim skirt and strappy pink tank.

A bit of sparkle for my eyes and a bit of gloss for my lips is all I can get away with in the heat and humidity of my new island home, but I'm satisfied with the girl I see in the mirror—even if she doesn't look much like me.

It's not like I have anyone to impress at this party anyway. I already have the job, one I'm wildly overqualified for, and the likelihood that one of these island-dwelling staff members is going to be the love of my life is laughable. To say the least.

Slipping my phone into my back pocket, I head for my door. It feels freeing to not need a purse. No need for a wallet or keys, or anything really. I walk down the path through the palms that leads away from the staff apartment building with a spring in my step.

The air is warm with a gentle ocean breeze, and I can hear the gulls calling out overhead. Instead of car exhaust and over-flowing garbage cans, I smell coconut sunscreen and blooming flowers. I'm actually feeling excited about the future, something I haven't been able to say in quite some time.

The staff clubhouse is only a short walk down a sandy trail toward the beach. It's much larger than my little studio, with enough room to accommodate a crowd. The big common room is air-conditioned, thank goodness. Several rattan sofas and chairs all situated around an enormous television fill the space. A large, open doorway to my right leads to a kitchen and dining room area with one round table and chairs.

I see Sarah, and she waves me over to the sofa where she's sitting with a few other women. I met most of the other staff at orientation a few days ago. Sarah and I hit it off and are becoming good friends already.

"Did you grab a drink?" Sarah asks when she spots my empty hand.

"Oh, no. That's okay. I'm not a big drinker."

She smirks at me. "It's the season's kickoff party, Reina. Everyone will be having a drink. Let's get you one."

I follow her into the kitchen where she kneels in front of the mini fridge.

"I could make you a vodka cranberry?"

"Sure, that sounds good." I made enough vodka crans at my last job to kill a horse, but at least I can water it down over the evening.

Once I have my token cocktail in hand, I settle into the party. I watch as people arrive, some smiling, some looking a little lost. I know the feeling. That *"what am I doing with my life"* feeling. I introduce myself to everyone I can, and before long, I know almost the whole room.

"The staff here are all really nice," I say to Sarah over the reggae beat coming out of a nearby speaker.

She nods enthusiastically. "The locals are really chill. They seem to love working here. As for us imports, to take a job like this, on an island in the middle of nowhere, you have to either be running from something or trying to solve some kind of a problem. So, people tend to be pretty humble. We're all in the same boat."

I consider that for a moment. I know that my desire to get away from that soul-sucking city and finally free myself of credit card debt prompted my move to Faraday, but it hadn't occurred to me that anyone else might be in a similar situation.

"You?" I ask, hoping Sarah will understand what I mean.

Her smile tells me she does, and that I'm not the first person she's told this story to. "Definitely. I was married back home in California to a jerk who treated me like crap. When I tried to move out, he got violent. I found this job online while staying in a women's shelter. I spent my last thousand bucks on a plane ticket, and I've never looked back."

I know Sarah's in her second season at the resort, which means she has had over a year to recover from her ordeal, but I can't help my heartbreak for her. I lay my hand on her arm and give her a kind smile. "Damn. That's tough, Sarah."

She shrugs. "Maybe. Or maybe it's the best thing that ever happened to me. I mean." She glances around the room full of smiling, chatting people. "Look where I ended up. Paradise."

It really is paradise here. I haven't had the chance to see the rest of the island, but from what I've heard, there's a small town with a weekly local market. I know some of the other staff spend their days off enjoying the beach and heading out on boat trips to snorkel and swim. Maybe this place really will be just what I need to get back on my feet.

With the party in full swing, the clubhouse is pushing capacity. I stick close to Sarah's side as we make our way through the crowd. I can feel everyone's happiness and excitement. It's really refreshing. Back in the city, anyone I met was either jaded about the industry or struggling so much to survive that conversations tended to revolve around problems and complaints.

I could hardly blame them. I was living the same life. It's one of the reasons my parents were so insistent that I move back to the small town of Ottawa where I grew up and take a job at the local public school where they both work. The stress of trying to pay rent and get around on buses in those harsh winters was starting to show on my face, and I couldn't hide my struggles from my family any longer.

But I also couldn't give up on my dream of making it on my own.

I made my decision, one that upset my parents so much we haven't spoken since I told them.

Regardless of what they think, I'm really starting to feel like I made the right choice, something I haven't felt in years. My confidence level rises with every smiling face I encounter.

I can do this. I can do the job they hired me to do, and I can do it well. I have a great little apartment to live in, and I have all these nice people around me.

When I walk into the kitchen to refill my drink, however, the vibe instantly feels different.

I've been noticing a different group of people congregating there throughout the evening. They don't stop in the great room to say hello or introduce themselves. They just walk right through without a glance in our direction.

Now that I'm in the entryway to the kitchen, I see them sitting around the table and standing against the walls, playing some kind of card game. No one looks my way as I stand awkwardly in the doorway, waiting for someone to say hello, or offer a smile.

No one does.

With a curious frown, I finish making my drink and turn to head back out to the main room to ask Sarah about them.

And I run smack into a solid wall of muscle.

Luckily, I'm holding my glass to the side, and I manage to swoop it up and away to level out the liquid so that I don't spill a drop—a little trick I picked up in my years of waitressing. Once I know I'm not going to be doused in red cranberry juice, I manage to take a breath and look up to apologize for my clumsiness.

But all the air gets sucked from my lungs, quite possibly from the entire room, when my eyes settle on the man in front of me.

I can't bring myself to blink as I gape at Mr. Tall, Dark, and Broody with his dark, loose hair hanging low over one dazzling hazel eye. He's sex on long, lean legs tucked into designer looking jeans and a gray tee that stretches tightly over what I know would be a rock-hard chest if I dared to reach out and touch it.

He seems to be older than just about everyone in the room, but in a sexy, somebody's older brother kind of way that makes me feel like a little girl at a slumber party.

When my gaze finally makes it back up to his painfully gorgeous face, our eyes lock, and a shock goes through my system. It's like he's pure electricity, and I'm the conductor. I stand frozen to the spot, unable to move or look away from those mysterious, searching eyes that have been watching me as I checked him out from head to toe.

*Oops.*

"Excuse me," he says finally, his low, deep voice painted with a hint of humor. The tiniest little smile reaches the edge of his eyes.

I snap back to attention. "Oh, yeah, sorry. I…" I can't help but blush terribly and glance down at the floor.

"Dominic!"

I hear the shout behind me and glance back to see all the people at the kitchen table now looking right at me. At us.

"Sorry. Excuse me," I mumble and make my escape back to the sofa where I last left Sarah surrounded by chatty coworkers.

5

"What's got you all riled up?" Sarah asks, leaning over to whisper conspiratorially in my ear. "Someone catch your eye?"

"What? Oh, no. I'm fine." I try to steady my breath and get the color down in my cheeks, holding up my now full drink. "Vodka catching up with me, I guess."

Alcohol is an easy scapegoat for my fluster, but it couldn't be further from the truth.

The truth is…I'm not fine at all.

I think I just ran smack into a god of some kind. Demi-god at least.

*Who the hell was that guy?*

Never in my life have I felt that kind of energy emanating off a person. Never have I found myself struck quite as dumb as I was back there, faced with him. I'm a master of banter, trained by my years running a dining room to be able to talk to anyone, to not ever lose my cool because of a celebrity, or an angry, intimidating customer.

But I fell flat on my face back there—stuttering, speechless, and shamelessly staring.

"Hey, ladies!"

I look up to see a tall, blonde man with a huge smile in full aloha gear making his way toward us.

Sarah jumps to her feet and hurries around the sofa to pull him into a hug. "Reina, this is Charles. He runs the spa and also the resort gossip mill. He's a good friend to have around, if you know what I mean."

Charles gives her an exaggerated eye roll but offers his hand to me. "The pleasure is all mine. You are a doll!"

I accept his hand and smile. "Nice to meet you, Charles."

"Reina's from Chicago," Sarah goes on, taking her job of introductions seriously.

"Ooh, the big city, huh?"

I nod and offer a tight-lipped smile. I don't particularly want to get into my life story right now—or ever—but I do want these people to like me, so I offer what I hope is enough to satisfy him.

"I lived there for about five years, went to college, and worked in restaurants. I'm so happy to be here, though. The weather is amazing."

I'm timidly taking steps toward accepting people as friends again after my crash and burn in the city. The people at my last job seemed like my friends, seemed so trustworthy—until I trusted them. Then it became very clear that they were only looking out for themselves. I know not everyone in the world is like that, but for now, I'm going to play it a bit closer to the chest.

I try not to let myself sink into dark thoughts about the past and instead focus on Charles's cocktail-induced chatter about how amazing the island is and how much I'm going to love it here. I'm just getting the rundown of which tour boat companies give the best discounts to resort employees when movement catches my attention across the room.

It's the man from earlier.

His dazzling eyes and chiseled features don't turn in my direction as he makes his way through the crowded great room toward the kitchen. As his hand touches the molding of the entryway to the next room, however, he glances back as if he could feel my gaze on him.

"Hey." A slap on my shoulder yanks me back to the present. I turn to find Sarah giving me a knowing glance.

"Ignore that one, okay? He's...not available."

Not available? I could have sworn he just fucked me with his eyes. "What do you mean?"

"I mean, he doesn't play nice with the staff, and he's kind of an asshole."

"Oh, come on. He's not an asshole," Charles cuts in defensively. "He's simply...broody. Handsomely aloof. Keyword there being handsome." Charles gives me a little wink.

I'm dying to probe for more information, but Sarah's too quick.

"Don't waste your time thinking about him."

It's far, far too late for that. I don't think I could stop the thoughts if I tried. The way his dark stubble highlighted his lips. His long lashes framing eyes so deep and bright I could sink into them and be lost forever.

"Who is he?"

Sarah rolls her eyes. "I'll tell you, but only because you'll find out soon enough anyway. But you've got to promise me that you won't bother, okay? This place is crawling with beautiful men, and one of them has your name written right on his cock. Just not that one."

"Okay," I breathe out. I would say anything to get his name from her.

"That's Dominic Fuentes."

I snap my mouth closed and look at her in surprise. Dominic Fuentes. As in the famous chef-owner of the restaurant where I'm newly employed? Holy shit. He's some kind of rich trust funder who works all the time, even though he doesn't need to, creating his own culinary empire and winning all sorts of awards for his cutting-edge food. "I pictured him a bit more... old?"

Sarah snorts out a laugh. "He's older than we are."

"How old?" I'm hardly a teenager any longer at the ripe old age of twenty-six. That man could have been in his late thirties. Forties maybe.

*Not too old for me.*

"Reina, stop! I'm not talking about him anymore, okay? He doesn't date staff, he's a jerk, so just forget you ever saw him. I don't know why he's even here. He never comes to staff stuff." She turns back to the group, clearly done with our conversation.

"Maybe he finally noticed me and came to sweep me off my feet." Charles gazes toward the kitchen with a dreamy look in his eyes. "But in all seriousness, girl, she's right. This resort is stocked full of sexy new meat. And I include you in that state- ment." Charles gives me a knowing look that has me shaking my head and laughing. "You have your choice of the bunch, don't get bogged down with an old bore like Dominic." He tosses another glance at the kitchen doorway where Dominic disappeared just moments before. "Besides, that one is mine."

Now it's Sarah's turn for an eye roll. "Oh my god, Charles. You are delusional." She turns back to me. "Dominic doesn't have a single friend. That has to say something about a person."

"He has friends," Charles continues his defense. Clearly this crush runs deep. "He has three of them, at the very least."

Sarah snorts out a laugh and rolls her eyes.

"What do you mean?" I ask. It seems like I should have spent a bit more time on Google before I moved to this resort.

"You really don't know anything about this place, do you?"

I shake my head impatiently, urging her to go on.

"Seven years ago, four childhood best friends bought the decrepit resort from the development company that built it and ran it into the ground. Those friends are Dominic, Sam, the GM, Avery, who shows up sometimes to party, and Ben, the lawyer who no one has ever seen out of a suit—even in this heat," Charles explains. "They all pooled together some of their trust fund money to buy the resort, then they fixed it up and opened it. Dominic and Sam live on the island full-time running the place, while the other guys just pop in on occasion."

I take a moment to process this new information. "That's pretty cool, I guess. That they went into business together."

"They're all hotties, but Dominic takes the cake," Charles adds with a wink.

I laugh out loud and shake my head.

"Speaking of hotties, there are some serious ones at this party, and we need to be over there." Sarah motions with her head toward the center of the crowded room. "Tonight we lay the groundwork for the action we will be getting this season. We will not spend the evening drooling over some guy who will never even acknowledge our existence."

Charles gives me a conspiratorial smile and a shrug.

I follow them to a few open seats where a lively group of people just started laying out a card game. I'm disappointed to find out that it's some kind of drinking game, but I don't want to spoil the fun, so I take my turn when it comes around and, of course, have to drink. As Sarah takes her turn, I lose myself in my thoughts.

Dominic Fuentes. Why hadn't I thought about looking the guy up before? I certainly have experience working at nice restaurants, but I've never seen a chef who looks like that. Chefs are usually overweight, over-boozed, stressed-out old men. Not this one. He's more of the chiseled-by-the-gods type. I would be more than happy to make the necessary sacrifice if it meant he would bless my bed.

The hairs on the back of my neck stand up as my awareness prickles, and I turn to find him looking over at me again. He's leaning against the doorway to the kitchen, bottle of craft beer in hand, giving me a slightly amused look, as if he can read my dirty thoughts.

*And he knows my every thought is about him.*

I hold his gaze and give him a small smile before a shout from the group pulls me back in to take my turn. When I glance up a minute later, he's gone.

# Rule #2

## ALWAYS CARRY A FLASHLIGHT

### REINA

"I'm going to go grab a drink, do you want anything?" I ask Sarah quickly as I get out of my seat. I've got to get into that kitchen before I lose my nerve. I can't wait another second to say hello. Or say something. Anything.

As I make my way through the crowd, the sane half of my mind tries to talk me out of it. It's too soon to be chasing after a guy.

Too soon to be thinking about anyone but myself.

When I finally escaped the city, maxing out my already very overdue credit cards to fund the trip to this island, it was for a fresh start. Away from the drama of the city and the skyrocketing costs of rent and food and cabs.

I planned to live in the cheap company apartment, work as a breakfast server, and dig myself out of the personal and financial hole I'd dug while chasing my big city ambitions. The last thing in the world I need to be doing is running headlong into a relationship, fling, whatever, with the chef at my new restaurant.

Or anyone for that matter, regardless of what Charles said.

I kneel down in front of the mini fridge and grab the cranberry juice, planning to just top off my drink. I'm plenty tipsy. It's been a hot minute since I had so much booze.

I add a splash of juice to my drink and scoop in a bit more ice. Then, I turn to the table of people where Dominic is sitting. I try not to look too eager as I close the distance between us, sliding my hand across the counter for balance.

"What are you guys play—?"

I don't even get the words out before the guy sitting in front of me stands, whoops and yells, turns and knocks into me... hard.

I buckle forward at the elbow in my gut, my finely honed waitressing instincts failing me as the hand that isn't braced on the counter for support sends the full glass of bright red juice shooting across the table.

Time slows down to quarter speed. The glass flies forward with a wave of cranberry extending from it, people quickly scoot their chairs back to avoid the splash. The red juice seeps into the white cards, turning the whole table into a sodden mess.

I just stand there, still slightly hunched over, hand braced on the counter, my mouth hanging wide open for what feels like an eternity.

"We *were* playing poker." The annoyed voice brings me out of my stupor. I stand up straighter and take a breath to apologize, but no one is paying any attention to me in their scramble to control the mess.

"What the actual fuck."

"Fucking newbie."

"Waitresses."

I can hear their muttered insults as I try to make my feet move from the spot. Try to flee. I know my face is as bright red as the cranberry juice, especially once I realize that the hot chef I came over to try to flirt with is probably listening to his friends make fun of me.

When I glance up, though, he's on his feet, heading toward me.

"It's not a big deal. We'll clean it up." His voice is kind, but I can't get over the fact that these are the first real words he's speaking to me.

It's more than I can take. I turn and hurry out of the kitchen, back to the sofa where Sarah and Charles are still sitting.

"I gotta go." I grab my sweater from where I draped it and turn toward the door, not stopping to explain.

"Wait," Sarah calls behind me. "Are you okay?"

I can't imagine how ridiculous I must look—flushed beet red and running from the party. But I have to get out of there...now.

"I'm fine," I call over my shoulder.

But, of course, I'm not fine. I'm a little drunk and a lot upset.

As soon as I walk around the corner from the clubhouse, I realize my mistake.

It's really dark out here, and even darker on the path through the palms. The guest paths are all perfectly lit with solar lights, but I need to take the back way, up an employee-only path from the clubhouse to staff housing. I hadn't thought to bring a flashlight when I left my apartment earlier, so now I'm stuck trying to follow the trail with nothing but the light from my phone.

I think I'm doing pretty well, all things considered, when I suddenly trip over a root I didn't see jutting up from the ground.

There's no way that root is in the middle of the path though.

I stop and look around as best I can in the tiny beam of light, noticing with horror that I'm indeed no longer on the path. I try to retrace my steps but only seem to get more lost. My phone is now flashing the low battery alert at me and unhelpfully dimming the flashlight as the remaining percentage drains toward zero.

*Do not panic.*

I'm walking around at a resort, no doubt within feet of the staff apartment building and my own new home. There's no actual danger.

But good luck convincing myself of that when I'm alone in the dark, half drunk. After a few minutes of only getting myself deeper into the brush and more lost with sounds that I'm convinced are alligators or serial killers coming from all sides, I'm in full panic mode.

"Lost?"

A deep, amused male voice from behind makes me jump in surprise. I spin and shine the light from my phone into his face.

Dominic grimaces and holds his hand up to shield his eyes.

*It's him.*

He came out to the woods to rescue me, even after I made an ass of myself in front of his friends. My heart swells, and my tipsy emotions start to spill out of my eyes in the form of grateful, embarrassed tears.

"Yes," I manage through my sobs. "I thought I could follow the trail, but my light isn't very bright, and I..." I trail off as Dominic slides his arm around mine, pulling me close to him.

"Let's get you home."

He makes short work of getting us back to the trail in the pitch dark after my phone finally gives up and dies. The man sure knows his way around.

I was just a few feet to the left of the path, wandering around in circles. My embarrassment burns on my cheeks, and I'm grateful for the pitch dark now so Dominic can't see me.

We approach the staff building, which, in my defense, is sorely lacking in the exterior lighting department. "I'm on the second floor."

I follow him up the stairs and unlock my door, pushing it open as he stands aside. Reaching in, I click on the porch light which I didn't think to leave on for myself.

"Thank you," I manage, trying to break the awkward silence.

Dominic says nothing but reaches up and uses his thumbs to wipe the tears from under my eyes, pausing for a moment with his huge hands on either side of my face.

"Do you want to come in?" The words are out of my mouth before I even realize it.

"Better not."

My traitorous hand reaches up and touches his shoulder, the warmth of his body causing my own to burn with desire.

*What am I doing?*

My brain and body clearly aren't on the same page. I know I shouldn't be touching him, but my hand continues to slide down the sleeve of his T-shirt until I reach the skin of his bicep. His arm feels solid and warm under my fingertips—the contact sending a shiver down my spine.

My heart beats almost painfully hard in my chest, and I close my eyes for a brief moment to try to catch my breath. When I open them, his face is mere inches from mine.

I rub my thighs together, and his gaze darts down to the movement. Just that slight dip of his eyes down my body makes me throb between my legs.

I know he knows, but right at this moment, I don't care.

His hand touches down on mine, and I stop breathing, the anticipation of his next move is too much. But before I can even think about where I want him to touch me first, he removes my hand from his arm and steps back.

I look down at the porch, desire turning to embarrassment at the rejection.

"It's going to be a long season, love. Plenty of time for mistakes."

The sultry tone of his voice, the way he says the word *love*, and no doubt the alcohol coursing through my veins, makes it too much for me to handle. I want this man right now. I need him.

"No time like the present." My own daring shocks me.

Dominic's mouth curls into a snarl, and he steps forward until his body presses against mine. Then he steps forward again, and I'm forced to step back, until I'm in my apartment, standing with my back pressed against the wall, with Dominic's rock-hard chest firmly against mine. I can feel his warmth on my nipples as they harden behind my thin tank top. I nearly whimper with desire at his closeness.

He leans down until his lips graze my ear. I can feel his hot breath on my skin as he speaks. "You know, when I saw you on the couch at that party, I said to myself, now that looks like a good girl. You aren't going to make me a liar, are you, love?"

"No," I whisper.

"Good." Dominic keeps his face pressed to my ear as he slides a hand down my arm to my hand and keeps going. When his fingers graze over my hip and curl around to my ass, I actually whimper a little bit.

With a breathy laugh, he slides his finger to the seam of my shorts and traces it over the roundness of my butt and right down between my legs. When his hand reaches my center, he gives my throbbing sex a little squeeze before releasing it and sliding his hand down my inner thigh.

I'm putty in his hands, holding my breath, waiting to see where he will touch me next.

"You *are* a good girl, aren't you?"

His raspy whisper in my ear shakes something loose, and before I know it, I'm reaching for him, hands on his shoulders, sliding around his back, wanting nothing more than to pull him closer and to make him touch me. I try to press my hips forward into his, but he pulls away and takes a step back.

Once again, I'm left cold and rejected. Flushed and desperate for the touch it seems I'll never receive.

He lets out another little laugh. "Get some sleep. Work starts tomorrow."

And then he disappears into the darkness.

# Rule #3

## PICK YOUR BATTLES

## DOMINIC

I like early morning meetings as much as any chef, which is to say not a damn bit. I stayed up later than I meant to because of the staff welcome party, but I thought it was important to make an appearance this year. The staff I brought on board this season is next level, with a few choice steals from high-end properties in Europe and the US. If we ever had a shot at winning the prestigious Pendleton award, it's this season.

I never expected to find myself nose deep in the neck of some resort newbie after rescuing her from the woods during a late-night stumble home. I don't know what it is about that girl, but I can't stop thinking about her. When she ruined the poker game in a not-so-subtle attempt to talk to me, she not only embarrassed the hell out of herself, but she gave me an excuse to exit. I knew I shouldn't have followed her out, but I had to make sure she got home safe.

She's gorgeous, first of all, and has the look of someone who knows what they're doing, even if her adorably tipsy self can't handle a drink. Whichever department was lucky enough to make that hire will be all the better for it. Seasonal workers often come with more problems than brains, but you have to take what you can get when you are running a business like this, so far from the real world.

I gave up trying to find that special someone years ago. It became clear very quickly that she wasn't just going to show up here on my tiny island.

*But maybe she just did…*

I shake off the thought before it can sink in. I've learned my lesson the hard way about trusting other people with my heart.

What does exist on this island is my very own fine dining restaurant, Raft. I've made the success of this restaurant, and the resort, my purpose in life. Raft will be where I make my mark on the world, the legacy I leave behind.

Much less complicated than a relationship.

I'm the last to arrive at the meeting, and the impatient looks aren't lost on me. Avery and Ben must have flown in last night for this meeting and are likely flying out again right afterward.

When we signed those papers seven years ago, after months of negotiations with the previous owners, I know they had high hopes of getting to spend more time here in paradise, but that hasn't been how it worked out. As Ben's career progressed up the ladder, so did the time commitment it required. I'm not sure exactly what Avery's excuse is, but the man never seems to be able to stay in one place long—even if that place is a paradise he owns. Sam and I are lucky to see them once a quarter for this check-in meeting.

All those years ago when the deal went down, I was still sous chef at Normaste, working my way up the ranks. I had my sights set on New York City, where someone would surely give me my own kitchen after the career I had in Europe. I had a plan. My life was all mapped out.

Instead, Sam came to us on our annual buddy trip with this crazy idea.

He was a decade into a career managing upscale resorts in

tropical places, and he thought this one had real potential. One look at the abandoned kitchen and dining room was all I needed to get on board.

The other guys were harder sells, but in the end, they agreed. After all, the millions each of them needed to put up for their share is chump change to guys like that. Luckily for Sam, I didn't bat an eye at the figure I needed to put up to cover both my and his shares. He doesn't come from a family with a bottomless bank account, so he's putting in labor and expertise as his share.

That didn't bother me a bit. I got my own restaurant, located inside an insanely upscale resort on an island that you have to be bleeding money to even set foot on.

If there's anywhere on the planet where I can build the kind of exclusive, high-end, award-winning restaurant of my dreams, it's here at The White Sands. If there's any group of guys on the planet that I want to be doing it with, it's these guys.

"Gentlemen."

"Fuck, Dom. You look like hell."

I take my seat with a smile. If any of us guys had concerns about what owning the resort together would do to our lifelong friendship, we needn't have worried. Our bonds are as tight as they were on day one. "Yeah, I stopped at the staff welcome party last night and might have had a few too many."

"Ooh, checking out the new meat?"

"Jesus, Avery. No. I would never screw around with the staff. That's just asking for a lawsuit." I level a hard gaze in his direction. "And you should do the same."

He shrugs me off. "Any pussy lucky enough to get a hard-on out of me knows how good she's got it."

"Charming, Ave. I bet they fall all over themselves when you tell them that."

"Whatever, Dom. Just because you like to be an old stick-in-the-mud doesn't mean the rest of us have to. I fly in four times a year, and when I do, I like being surrounded by bikini-clad titties. Employees or not, I'm not picky."

I rub the bridge of my nose and sigh. "Ben, tell this man he's a lawsuit waiting to happen."

The man to my right chuckles. "He's made it this far paying off his own scandals, Dom."

I shake my head. "Whatever. Let's get on with this. I need to get back down to the kitchen."

"Do you ever leave that kitchen?"

"Only when you assholes make me. I have a lot to do to get ready for the new staff."

"We'll make it quick." The sudden businesslike tone to Ben's voice gets my attention.

"We want to have an open dialogue about the restaurant menu," Ben says plainly, his hands steepled in front of him like the high-powered lawyer he is.

I nearly shoot out of my chair. "What about the fucking menu? The menu is my territory. Raft is mine. End of discussion."

Beside me, Sam sits up a bit in his chair. I turn my glare in his direction. If he's a part of this coup, I'm going to kill him.

"Dom, we've been getting a lot of comments, as you know." He holds his hands up to stop me as I start to interrupt. "From our guests who come stay with their families. They're surprised to find that the restaurant on the property doesn't serve kid-friendly options. It makes it hard to advertise The Sands as a family destination when the kids end up eating whatever the parents can scrounge from the bodegas in town. We need to figure out a way to make food available for the whole family, as well as maintain the standards of the fine dining dinner menu," he adds quickly when he spots my look of rage.

I take a deep breath and try to keep my voice level as I offer them the same answer I've given every time this comes up. "We are working toward a Pendleton award in that restaurant. Do you know what that kind of publicity could do for this property? It would put the island on the fucking map. We wouldn't have to slum ourselves out offering deals to fucking families." I spit the word out as if it's poison. "If we win that award, we can raise all the prices, and people will stand in line to pay." I look around the table at the same weary expressions I always get when this subject comes up. "This is our season. The staff I managed to poach for the dinner shift are next fucking level. You guys have got to trust me on this. I know what I'm doing."

I don't look over at Sam as he takes a deep breath to answer. I already know what he's going to say. "Dom, it's getting harder and harder to keep our current guests happy with the dining situation. The people who are at the resort *right now* need to be our priority, not—"

"This is the last season of your fancy shit," Avery cuts in, and I swing my glare in his direction. If looks could kill, the man would have holes burned through his skull. "We all voted, and we have the majority. You can have this season to try for your award, but in the offseason, we are going to come to a compromise on the menu, and it will go into effect next season."

I don't bother to answer him as I swing my head back around to Sam. He's not meeting my eye, his gaze fixed on the pen he's fidgeting with.

Sam has always been the one on my side through all the bullshit problems the big city guys try to bring on us. It's Sam and I who are on the property year-round, running this place with the sweat off our backs.

And I paid Sam's share. If these guys try to pull majority, I could easily play that card. I actually own fifty percent of The White Sands, even if that's not how we choose to look at it on a daily basis.

It's my one trump card, the only way I can leave this meeting on top. But I can't do that to Sam. Not after everything he's been through, and everything he and I have been through together.

Sam didn't grow up with the kind of money we did, but it didn't matter one bit. From that first day we all met when he transferred into our fancy prep school, he's been part of the crew. He spent his childhood hanging out on our estates while his single mother worked three jobs. He spent every vacation jetting off with one of our families.

He always shows gratitude in whatever ways he can, but I know his place in the group wears on him. Even as an adult, with his prestigious, skyrocketing career as GM for the most exclusive resorts in the world, he never managed to catch up to any of us.

Generational wealth is a head start that no one can beat.

When I agreed to front his quarter of the money, I made a pact with him and with myself. That money left my hands at that moment and would be his share in the property for as long as we owned it. It was a deal we made on the down-low but a deal nonetheless. I am nothing if not a man of my word. To call him out as not an actual investor now, in front of the other guys, would mean the end of our friendship as well as our working relationship. Both of which I need to make my life worth living.

After a moment of staring, Sam meets my eye. I can see the apology there, the regret. He got bullied into this by the other guys.

I sigh and shake my head. "Whatever. It doesn't matter. We're winning that award this season, so there's no point in even having this discussion." I stand and push my chair angrily back to the table. "Was there anything else?"

No one speaks so I leave the conference room, slamming the door behind me.

It's true that this isn't the first time those guys have tried to bully me into turning my five-star masterpiece of a dining experience into a fish and chips joint. I've seen the comment cards and reviews complaining that there "isn't a single menu item served for dinner that my kids will eat." I've never wavered for a moment. Breakfast and lunch are family-friendly.

Dinner is mine.

It's possible that in the future, we could have a separate kitchen and dining room making burgers and mac and cheese, or whatever those yuppies think their kids will eat, but I can't do that alone.

I have been trying since day one to find a restaurant manager who can help me run a second shift, but I've yet to find that person on this island. As it stands, I'm already working every waking hour trying to keep my one restaurant operating for all three meals, seven days a week. If I take on anymore, I know it's going to kill me.

The elevator lets me off on the kitchen level, and I walk quickly down the hallway that leads to my office. The shades are still drawn, no surprises there. It's far too early for even my most eager of dinner cooks to be reporting for work.

The office is a pass-through room—one door opens to this hallway, where the elevators and laundry facilities live. The other door leads straight into the prep kitchen where the a.m. crew is busting ass to get the menu ready for our official opening.

I toss my bag down on the desk and head straight for the door opposite me. I'm going to need a big cup of coffee to get this day started. Luckily, brunch service should be in full swing. The restaurant is in soft opening week, serving meals to the resort staff as the restaurant staff gets trained. Next week, it's game on, as the first guests of the season arrive.

I walk through the prep kitchen and turn to head toward the server station when I spot her. The woman from last night.

Shit.

If I had thought for a second that woman was a restaurant employee, I would've kept my hands to myself.

There's nothing in the universe that could have prevented me from imagining stripping those little shorts off her and licking her from head to toe while I manhandled my cock in the shower after I left her apartment, but what I do in the privacy of my own home is my business.

I am not the kind of chef who screws waitresses.

That's the quickest way to get shown the door in this business. The last thing I need is to lose the respect of the culinary industry by getting caught up in a scandal with a server. And a breakfast server, no less.

I guess I have some backtracking to do…and quickly.

I head over to the coffee station and pour myself a cup. I'm leaning on the counter when she finally comes back from the table she was waiting, and our eyes meet. That adorable blush I remember from last night hits her cheeks immediately. I offer her a smile, hoping we can put the misunderstanding behind us and move forward in a more professional manner.

"Hey," I say, setting my coffee cup on the counter. "I'm Dom."

"I know who you are," is her sassy answer. She slides the menus she's holding onto the shelf and starts typing her table's order into the computer.

I smile to myself at her boldness and walk over to lean on the counter right next to where she's working.

*Crossing another boundary, Dom.*

"You know who I am, do you?" I hear the flirt in my tone, but I can't help myself. This woman is a walking temptation with her long, wavy auburn hair and big blue eyes.

She looks up from the computer, nods, and then goes back to the screen.

"And did you know who I was last night?"

That gets her attention. I would be willing to bet she didn't think I'd bring that up. She meets my eye, and her blush nearly brings me to my knees.

"Maybe."

I've got a full-on grin now. I love a girl who can dish it out. "Maybe, huh? Well, I bet, based on the fact you didn't look a bit surprised to see me here this morning, you knew exactly who I was last night."

"And if I did?"

"If you did, then you spent the eve of your first shift downing cocktails and trying to seduce your new boss."

She's holding her breath now. I can tell by her stillness. I wonder if she's waiting to see if she's in trouble, or if I'm going to tell everyone what happened.

Only one of those things is true.

This girl is in a world of trouble.

"What do you say you tell me your name, and we call it even?" The gratitude and hope that rushes into her eyes gives me instant savior complex.

"Reina."

"Reina." *Queen. My fucking queen.* "Well, it's very nice to meet you, Reina."

"Likewise."

"I guess you better get back to work." I gesture with my chin at a new group of housekeeping employees seating themselves at a booth in the corner.

"Yes, sir."

My mouth drops open, and my dick takes notice of her words, but she walks away before I can respond. It's probably better that way. I'm not sure my response would have come in the form of words.

*Yes, sir...fucking hell.*

Shaking my head, I grab my coffee and head back toward the office. The last fucking thing I need right now is this kind of distraction, but I know myself well enough to know that this is far from over.

When I open the door to my office, shifting my junk a bit to try to hide the growing arousal in my pants, Sam is waiting for me.

"You busted out of that meeting pretty quick," he says as I set my coffee cup down and flop into my chair.

"Yeah, well. I didn't have anything else to say."

"You know I had no choice with those guys. I'm on your side."

"It sure as shit doesn't look that way when you vote with them on something like this." I'm pissed, but also disappointed.

I thought Sam had my back. The last thing I need is to be worried that my closest ally, the person I work with on a daily basis, will vote against me in secret partner meetings.

"You've known about this problem since day one, Dom. Don't put this shit on me." Sam is apologetic but clearly isn't about to let me get away with any prima donna chef shit.

I need Sam to call me on my BS, I count on it, so I lift my head and try to shake off the fog of anger that's been following me since the meeting and hear what he has to say.

"We need to find a way to make everyone happy, not just you. When we signed those papers, we committed to making this resort a place where guests can relax—a paradise for vacationers. You've lost sight of that. I know you've got your reasons. You've got your own shit going on, but seriously, man. We need to start talking about solutions, not just awards."

I sip my coffee and take a long, slow breath, spinning the gold ring on my right middle finger around and around, a habit of mine when I'm stressed. "I can't work any more hours, Sam."

"I know. I'm not asking you to work anymore. I just want this line of dialogue to be open between us, okay? I mean, we made it work with pizza night, right? And look what a success that is." My glower must be evident, because Sam gives a small chuckle. "I know it's not winning any awards, but we make a lot of people happy with that service. Families, locals, staff. Everyone loves it."

"People love our tasting menus." I can't help but defend my service, even in the face of my logical, kind, best friend.

"I know they do, Dom. I love your tasting menus. They're the best on the planet. Anyone who gets to eat your food walks out of this place blessed. You are the absolute master of your craft."

But it's not enough. I can hear his unspoken words.

"Sam, I already gave up one night for *fucking* pizza. I know it's great pizza. People love it. But judging season is almost here, and I can't control which night those people will show up. I already have Monday pizza night hanging over my head. What if the Pendleton judges show up on a Monday expecting a five-star tasting menu, and it's fucking pizza?"

Sam has heard all of this before, and he doesn't bother answering. "You gotta decide what your priorities are, Dom. I know this award is important to you, but is it worth all this?"

"If I win that award—"

"Then what, Dom? All your problems go away?" A bit of Sam's smile has worn off in the face of my stubbornness, but his big heart still shines through. "You will still be the same person, with the same job, and the same shitty family back in the States. You will still wake up in your house on that hill alone." His hand is on the doorknob now, clearly not expecting a response from me. "I know you're searching for something, man, but I'm not sure this award is going to give it to you."

The door clicks softly behind him, and I can't help but shake my head at the unrelenting kindness of that man. Even when he disagrees with me, even when he just dropped what amounts to a mic drop of a statement, he won't slam the door behind him. He won't give up on me.

I know I'm lucky to have a friend like him. Lucky to have three of them actually. Those other guys know me better than I know myself and have loved me since I was a snot-nosed kid. I know they mean well. I just can't give up this dream. Even if I come out the other side as the same workaholic miser who has given up on love. Even if my family doesn't even send a text when news of my achievement hits *The New York Times*.

I'll still have that award hanging on my office wall. Isn't that good for something?

# Rule #4

## DON'T COME TO WORK HUNGOVER

### REINA

*I'm never drinking again.*

The morning is just as tough as I knew it would be. I make it to the restaurant on time, but I'm not feeling my best. Sylvia, the manager training me, doesn't look her best either, so at least I'm not alone.

The restaurant is gorgeous. Blonde wood covers the walls, which accentuates the large windows overlooking the ocean. The tables are a similar light wood and gleam in the morning light. The large windows give the place a boat-like atmosphere. It's otherworldly and so beautiful.

The state-of-the-art kitchen, with gleaming copper pans and stainless-steel appliances, wood countertops, and handmade ceramic dishes, make this place truly incredible.

Honestly, it looks a bit like the Michelin-starred property I ran in Chicago before the city became too much for me, and I had to get out of town—or risk having a nervous breakdown.

I get the flow of service pretty quickly, but I know I'll need to do a bit of studying to learn the menu. It's filled with local ingredients I'm not familiar with.

I ask for a printed copy to study at home, and one of the other waitresses tells me I can grab one from the office. She points in the direction of a closed door at the far end of the kitchen. I have to walk through a line of prep cooks to get to it.

I tap lightly on the door, and when there's no answer, I turn the knob and open it. I'm hoping there will be a stack of menus, and I can just grab one. I take two full steps inside before I realize I'm not alone.

I catch movement out of the corner of my eye and look up to find Dominic there. With no shirt on. "Oh, sorry!"

After our short banter at the server station an hour before, I was feeling confident and sassy, like my old self. Now, faced with him here, alone in this small room, my self-conscious fears start to creep in.

As I watch, unable to take my eyes off him, he sets down the shirt he just took off and pulls on a white tee. Then he chooses a black chef's jacket from a hook on the wall and pulls it on over the T-shirt. He buttons the front slowly, never taking his eyes off of me.

When he's fully dressed, he finally speaks. "Can I help you, Reina?"

I'm so surprised by his choice of words, how different they seem from when he introduced himself an hour before, that I feel myself blush and look away as I stammer, "I was just going to grab a menu to look over at home."

Dominic takes a few steps in my direction and looks over some papers scattered on the desks in the office. "I think I might have given them all out yesterday."

"Okay." I turn to leave the office, but his voice stops me.

"How's your first shift going?"

I turn back to him. "Great. Everyone is really nice, and the restaurant is beautiful." It's all true, but it feels strange to be saying the words to this man, who was front and center in my fantasies all night, as if he's nothing more than my new boss, who I'm trying to please.

*He is your new boss, and you are trying to please him!*

"Glad to hear it," he replies shortly. "Stop by after your shift, and I'll give you a menu."

"Thanks." I just want to escape, so I do, closing the door behind me and scurrying back to the server station.

The rest of my shift proves to be much harder than the first half. I know he's here. I can feel him watching me. And it's not just my imagination running wild. Every time I glance in the direction of the kitchen, his eyes are on me.

In my wildest dreams, I return each of his smoldering glances with a sultry, flirty stare of my own, but I've never been quite that suave. Each time our eyes meet, I feel the blush rise in my cheeks, and I have to look away.

It's all very distracting.

Somehow, I make it through brunch service without totally screwing anything up and head to the back to hang up my apron and get my bag. On the way out, I stop by the closed office door once more. This time, I can hear voices behind it. I tap lightly on the wood, and the voices stop. The door swings open so quickly I jump back a bit in surprise.

Dominic is standing just inside the doorway, hand still on the knob.

"Sorry to interr—"

"It's fine." Dominic turns and steps back into the office, leaving the door open behind him. I can hear the door on the other side of the office open and close, so I assume whoever he was talking to just left.

I follow Dominic in and stand a few steps inside the door, unsure of what to say or do.

"Close the door, please." His words hang in the air for a moment before I realize they were meant for me.

I turn and push the door closed. I pause. The silence stretches like time standing still. When I finally turn around, there's nowhere to hide. I'm alone in a small, dim room with this man. Goose bumps shiver over my arms as I take in the small office, and the enormous presence standing just a few feet from me. The walls seem to be closing in as I find myself locked in a heated stare with my fantasy come to life.

I wait, holding my breath, to see what will happen next.

He leans against his desk, holding a printed menu in his hand. "How did the rest of service go?"

"It was great." I know there's something else going on here, and I'm preparing myself for it. "I was up kinda late last night, but I made it through." All I want is for him to acknowledge our little encounter the night before. I realize my mistake almost immediately.

"You know, I don't like it when my employees show up to work hungover."

"Oh." I cast my eyes downward, surprised by the sudden scolding. I'm a grown woman, used to making my own choices and dealing with the consequences. Somehow, though, all I want right now is to please this man.

"I expect them to arrive in my restaurant ready to work." He takes a step closer, still holding the menu in one hand. "And that means well rested and well fed."

I can't think of a single thing to say, so I stay quiet, still looking at the floor in front of me.

"Reina."

I look up at the sound of my name.

"Did you eat anything this morning?"

"Oh, not yet. I was just about to sit at the bar and—"

"You told me last night you were a good girl, Reina."

"I—"

"Do good girls show up to work hungover and hungry? Do they wait tables all service looking like they were up all night partying?"

I thought I looked just fine when I left my apartment earlier,

31

and every time I checked my face in the restroom since, but I'm not about to say that now. He's clearly unhappy with my performance, and I'm burning with shame.

Dominic tosses the menu on the desk next to me and takes a few more steps, until he's pressed right up against me. He takes my chin in his hand and turns my face up to meet his. "I would be angrier, but that little blush you have is fucking adorable."

I feel my blush get brighter as I try to hold his gaze. Tears start to swell at the corners of my eyes.

"I want to let you off with a warning since it's your first day." Dominic's voice is low and gravelly. "But I don't think you would learn your lesson that way."

I'm frozen in place, terrified of what's about to happen.

*Am I going to get fired?*

I don't have to wait long. He spins me around so fast I hardly even realize what's happening before my hands are on the door, and he's pressed up behind me. I can feel his hardness pressed against my ass and a jolt of electricity shoots through me.

"I think I'm going to offer you a different kind of punishment. What do you say?"

"Yes." It's all I can do not to scream it. Whatever he wants to give me, I'm taking.

"Yes, what?"

"Yes, you may…punish me. You can do whatever you want."

Dominic slides his hand over the swell of my ass, his body pressed tightly to mine, his face tucked into the crook of my neck.

He gives my ass a sharp slap, and I respond with a tiny yelp.

*Is this really happening right now? In his office?*

"Are you going to be a good girl and show up for work prepared from now on?"

"Yes." I don't want whatever this is to stop, but I do want desperately to please him.

"And how are we going to make sure of that?"

"I promise?"

He laughs softly in my ear. "Not good enough."

"I—" Whatever promises I was about to spew are cut short by another slap on my ass.

"That's two."

This isn't a fantasy I ever imagined coming true, but here I am.

*Give me another, please. I'm a bad girl.*

Dominic pulls me away from the door and positions my body in front of one of the desks. He places my hands flat on the wooden surface and pulls my hips toward him. He stands behind me rubbing both hands over my ass now.

I should be prepared for what comes next, but my mind hasn't caught up with the action.

Smack.

"Dominic!" I hiss out, trying to keep my voice down, very aware of how many male cooks are on the other side of that thin wall.

"It's Dom."

Smack.

"What?" My mind is all over the place, shooting wildly from pain to pleasure. I'm struggling to track one thought to the next.

He steps close and pulls me up so my side presses to his chest. I can barely breathe with the closeness, the anticipation of the moment. My shame over how much I seem to like being spanked like a child melts away as he slides his hand down the front of my tight skirt.

"My name is Dom," he says as his palm finds my lace panties, fingers pressing against the fabric-covered entrance to my sex.

I know he can feel how wet I am.

Then he slaps my ass again, harder than before.

"Dom, that hurts!"

"Say it again," he growls in my ear, still holding my pussy hostage in his tight grip.

"That hurts!"

33

He brings his hand down on my ass again, hard. "Not that. Say my name."

"Dom!" I cry out as quietly as I can.

Smack.

"Dom!"

*When did his hand get under my panties?*

As the next slap claps across my bottom, I feel his fingers slip inside me. His palm roughly presses against my clit. The friction of his hand, coupled with the adrenaline from this spanking, threatens to send me over the edge.

"Again."

Smack.

"Dom," I squeak out breathlessly. I'm unable to stop my hips from grinding against his hand, craving more and more. He presses another finger deep inside me as I ride him.

"Girl, you want it so bad, don't you?"

Smack.

The spanking sends my mind reeling. I can only focus on what I really want, which is more pressure on my clit, more movement of his fingers deep inside me. I arch my back to give him better access to the fire between my legs, and he does not disappoint.

Keeping his fingers inside, he slides his thumb around my clit, giving it a little flick at the very same time he lands a hard spank on my bottom.

"Dom!" I'm coming now, there's no stopping it.

I grind my hips into the pressure from his hand as I buckle at my core, the pleasure shooting through my body. He holds tight to me, landing three more hard smacks on my ass as I convulse and try my hardest to keep quiet.

When I'm finally still, we stay frozen like that for what feels like forever. He has his hand deep inside of me, his other hand smoothing over my smarting ass. My upper body is buckled over his arm, and his face is pressed into the side of my neck.

"Good fucking girl."

Dom slowly slides his hand out of my skirt and stands me up. I lean on the desk, not trusting my legs to support my weight just yet. I watch as he takes a towel from a stack on his desk and wipes his fingers off, all the while holding my gaze with those deep brown eyes.

"Did you learn your lesson?"

"Yes," I reply instantly, sure it's what he wants me to say.

"And you'll never show up for work hungover again?"

*If this is the punishment, I might become a bit of a lush actually.*

"No." I would say anything right now to please this man, even if all I want is more punishment.

He gives me a half smirk and turns to lift the printed menu from where he tossed it on the desk. Holding it out to me, he waits.

I struggle to gather my composure, smooth down my skirt and hair, take a few deep breaths, and then take a step forward to take the paper from him.

"Thank you," I say, which only makes his smirk deepen. I feel my blush explode over my cheeks.

"Be sure to study up," he says, gesturing to the menu with his head. "There will be a test."

I can hardly breathe, my thoughts racing through my mind like a tornado. I want to say something witty, something smart and sassy, but I only manage, "I will."

He doesn't move or speak for a long moment, and I realize too late that I've been dismissed. With a fresh rush of embarrassment, I turn and hurry out the door. I don't know what the guys working just outside of the office heard, but I don't look up to find out as I make my way quickly back to the server station.

"You got your menu?" Sylvia, my manager, asks casually as I lean on the coffee counter, trying to catch my breath.

*What just happened? Did I really just get spanked and finger-fucked by my boss in his office? With all the other employees mere inches away?*

Keep it together, Reina.

"Yeah, got it." I hold up the paper. "I'm just going to sit at the bar and order some food."

Really, I should run from the building, but I haven't eaten all day, and I don't have any food back in my apartment. I find an empty barstool, and Sarah comes over to set down a cup of coffee.

She's dressed just like me, in all black, and has her apron tied smartly around her waist. She's a lunch server, and her shift just started.

"How was your first day?" she asks cheerfully.

"It was really great." I want nothing more than to spill about what just happened, but I know she won't approve. She was the one who told me flat out to stay away from Dominic.

*Dom.*

She places a lunch menu in front of me and gives it a tap. "I'll be back in a sec to take your order."

As soon as she's gone, I take a large drink of the black coffee and grimace. I take cream and sugar, but I'm not about to complain right now. I need the caffeine to calm me down.

A sharp tap on the bar startles me, and I look up from my coffee cup.

Dom is standing there. He just placed a small pitcher of cream and a ceramic pot of sugar on the bar next to my menu.

I flush bright red, of course.

He grins.

*For once in my life, I'd like to be able to play it cool.*

"Thank you," I say and pour cream into my coffee, grateful for the activity to distract me from the fact that he's *right there*. I can practically smell myself on his hand as it hovers inches away from me.

As I'm stirring the cream and sugar in, my menu slides away. I look up in surprise, but he's already placing a plate in front of me.

It's the French toast from the brunch menu, one of the most

delicious looking meals that I had the pleasure of delivering during my shift. My mouth waters at the aroma of the crispy, egg-soaked bread, griddled in melted butter and topped with whipped cream and blueberries.

I look up to thank him again, but he's reaching under the counter to grab a silverware roll and placing it next to the plate.

"Thank you." It comes out as a whisper this time. I'm under his spell, and he hasn't even said a word.

"You've been saying thank you a lot today."

I look down as I feel the blush rise.

"Look at me."

I obey, my eyes meeting his over the bar. I can't quite read the look in his deep brown eyes, but the familiar sly grin still plays across his face.

"Adorable." His voice is barely a whisper. "Enjoy your breakfast." He turns and disappears back into the kitchen.

Sarah appears as I'm taking my first bite. "Oh, you already ordered?"

I awkwardly chew and swallow before answering. "It was left over in the kitchen," I offer stupidly.

She wrinkles her forehead at me but lets it go. "It's pizza night tonight. The one night of the week they lay off the fancy dinner service, and all the employees and some people from town come to eat. We've got to go. Everyone will be there." She's leaning on the bar next to me, staring dreamily off into the distance. I wonder if she's thinking about anyone in particular.

"Okay, that sounds great. I just can't drink tonight."

She gives me a knowing look. "Hard morning?"

I nearly choke on my French toast but manage a nod.

"It sucks to work brunch when everyone else comes in later. That's what I was doing last year and trust me—I never got any sleep. But don't worry, you'll still get to have fun on your days off." She heads off to take care of her tables.

I finish my meal and slip out without another Dom sighting,

which I'm grateful for. That man does all sorts of things to me that I've never experienced before. I mean, I'm usually a pretty confident, independent woman. But when he turns that devilish stare my way? I melt into a giggling, blushing puddle. It's ridiculous.

But I love it.

# Rule #5

## STAY IN YOUR LANE

### REINA

As soon as I get back to my apartment, I crawl into bed and sleep for the entire afternoon. When I finally wake up, the sky is starting to turn golden. I can see the fading light through the tiny window over the desk on the other side of the small, square room, and I crawl out of bed to peer out. From this angle, I can almost see the water at the bottom of the hill. The lovely golden color of the sky is peaceful and beautiful.

I walk over to open my door, wanting to step out into the fresh air, but when I go to push the door open, something drags across the porch. Peeking around the half-open door I see a small brown paper bag, folded at the top. I lift the bag and open it, peering in at the black object at the bottom.

I pull out a flashlight, and a fancy one at that. Mid-sized and sleek black, it's heavy enough that I know it can double as a weapon if I need it to. I turn the bag over to see if there's a note, but there's nothing.

I know who left it, though. The same man who rescued me from the dark woods where I was wandering without a light.

My body reacts immediately to the thought of him outside my door while I slept. It's hard not to sink into the fantasy of him opening the door, pulling back my covers to find me in just a tank top and panties, sliding his hand—

"Hey Reina!"

The shouted greeting jolts me from my fantasy. I look up to find Sarah and Jess, one of the other lunch servers, coming down the walkway toward my door.

"Hey." I try to sound casual, reaching back to set my new treasure on the desk inside.

"You about ready to head down to the café?"

*Pizza night.*

I nearly forgot all about that.

"I fell asleep after work. What time is it?" I'm feeling a little groggy after my long nap.

"It's a little after six," Sarah answers. "We wanted to get there early so you could get to bed on time tonight."

I smile gratefully. "Give me ten?"

The girls settle into the deck chairs I have set up outside my front door and begin chatting about their own first shifts as I quickly throw on a short-sleeved green dress that shows enough of my cleavage for me to feel sassy. My hair is a lost cause, so it goes up in a messy bun. My usual makeup routine of a little sparkle on my eyes and lip gloss only takes a second, but at the last moment I decide to add a bit of mascara.

*Who are you getting all dolled up for, girl?*

Now that's a silly question.

I laugh to myself as I toss my wallet and phone into a denim purse, along with a light sweater. It has been a very warm day, but the nights tend to cool off. Before I head out the door, I grab my new flashlight and add that to my bag as well.

Pizza night is in full swing on the patio of Raft when we arrive.

I recognize some of the other resort staff from the orientation as well as casually dressed people who must be locals, all mixing with the resort guests. The guests are easy to spot in their brand-new, high-end resort wear and giant floppy hats.

We settle at the bar and choose our pizzas from the night's selection of specials written up on a large chalkboard. I go for a white pie with roasted garlic, butternut squash, and prosciutto. The girls order wine, and I settle on a house-made peach soda.

I feel his gaze before I see him. The hair on the back of my neck stands up, and the butterflies in my stomach immediately take flight. When I turn my head, I'm not at all surprised to find him watching me from the doorway that separates the dining room from the beach patio seating. I give him a small smile, trying my hardest not to immediately look away, even as I feel a blush start to rise in my cheeks. He returns my smile, his eyes never leaving mine.

"How's your pizza?" Sarah asks.

It takes me a second to realize she's talking to me. "What? Oh, it's great. Do you want to try a piece?"

We are all swapping slices, gushing over how delicious the food is, when a shadow falls over our small section of the bar. We look up in unison and find Dom standing there, watching us.

"How's the food, ladies?" His tone is calm and casual, like he's the king, bestowing his attention upon us.

*I suppose that much is true.*

"Oh, so good. I got the sausage pie, and it's my favorite yet." Sarah is quick to take the lead in answering.

Dom's expression doesn't change as he takes in her words. "Will I see you three at the party later?"

Sarah and Jess nod enthusiastically.

"Definitely," Jess responds with a smile.

"And you?"

I don't need to look up from my pizza to know that he has turned his full attention back to me.

I bite my lip and shake my head. "No, I have to work early. I think I'm going to skip the party this time."

He gives a little nod and a barely perceptible smile. "You ladies enjoy your dinner." And then strolls back to the kitchen.

"What the actual fuck was that?" Jess hisses at Sarah. "He has never spoken to us before. I'm not sure he's ever even looked at me in my whole time working here."

Sarah nods in agreement. "That was crazy. But one thing I know for certain—we are not missing that party." Her head turns quickly to me. "Girl, you have got to come. That was a personal invite from our mysterious overlord."

With a small laugh, I turn back to my pizza. "Nah, I gotta get some sleep for the early shift."

And besides, Dom will be at the party. If he goes and doesn't see me there, he'll know that I'm home in bed.

I allow myself to drift into the fantasy. One where I behaved and tucked myself into bed with my book at a reasonable hour. Dom went to the party and saw that I wasn't there, so he came to my apartment to tell me what a good girl I am.

I nearly choke on my food as the thought becomes over-whelming.

"You okay over there?"

I take a sip of soda and nod. "Yeah. Just swallowed wrong."

"Well, I don't know what caused the shift in that man's atti-tude, but I don't know if we should trust it."

She has my interest now. "What do you mean?"

"I mean that he doesn't talk to waitresses who don't work dinner shift. He barely talks to anyone as far as I can tell. And offering invites to parties? That's just insane. The man is practi-cally a hermit, sitting alone in his big house at the top of the hill, doing god only knows what. When he isn't here, of course, which is rare. He's a workaholic and a recluse."

"And freaking loaded," Jess chimes in.

"Loaded?" I ask, falling for the bait.

Jess grins at me. "Word is that he's the youngest son of some rich old family from back east. He was supposed to join the family business, but instead he ran off to train at restaurants all over the world. They say he only agreed to buy the resort with his friends when they convinced him he could use this restaurant to make a name for himself."

I take another bite, considering her words. If Dom is so wealthy, why would he work all the time?

As if Jess can read my mind, she answers my question. "He's obsessed with winning awards and has almost all of them—but not the big one. He's been trying to get this place nominated for a Pendleton but hasn't succeeded yet."

I'm familiar with that award, and all the rest of the prestigious culinary awards that exist in this world. My last property had most of them hanging on the wall as well. I take a moment to think about the menu here, as well as the service style, looking for little improvements that would catch the eye of the mystery judges who will pose as guests at some point this season.

*No, no, Reina. That's not your job. You are here to relax and pay down your debt, not to push yourself to get this place up to par for award season.*

Not that anyone asked me. I'm just a first-season brunch server, the lowest member of the restaurant staff. I altered my resume so that no one would know the truth about my actual work history. I gave myself enough experience that they would hire me, but not enough to raise questions about why I want to serve breakfast.

My mind drifts to the place it has been almost constantly since my unexpected encounter in the office.

*Dom.*

The mystery of the man deepens, and I struggle to keep my mind from swirling with thoughts of him touching me, kissing me, whisking me away to that giant house and making me his.

*Stop, girl. You are racing toward heartbreak.*

My friends have said plenty of times that he doesn't date waitresses or interact with brunch servers at all. What we did in the office must be some kind of fluke.

*But what about the flashlight?*

The thoughtfulness of the gift has me stumped. I desperately wish that I could ask my friends for their opinions, but it doesn't feel right. What Dom and I shared was so private and against so many rules, that I can't imagine confiding in anyone about it.

"Ready to head back up? I need to change into something much sexier for the party tonight," Jess asks as we finish our drinks.

"Not thinking you'll catch the eye of a certain chef, are you?" Sarah teases her as we climb off our bar chairs.

"Of course not!" Jess tosses Sarah a scandalized look. "But there will be plenty of other guys there to impress."

I smile at their banter, pulling my new flashlight out of my bag. I'm ready for the dark palm trail now. I glance around one last time, but don't see Dom before I disappear around the corner.

# Rule #6

## YOU REAP WHAT YOU SOW

### DOMINIC

As much as I put on a show about tolerating pizza night, there's no denying that it comes in handy. When you operate an establishment like Raft three meals a day, seven days a week, you are always playing catch-up. Monday night has become the evening my dinner crew gets to do extra prep, plan, and elevate their dishes. The breakfast and lunch guys can handle pizza.

I'm just coming back from a visit to the dining room—a nightly ritual when we serve our regular tasting menu to dinner guests, but not something I generally do on pizza night. I could just feel her out there, and believe me...I know that sounds crazy. But it's the truth.

I just can't stay away from that girl.

After completely losing control in the office earlier, I've been searching for a time to pull her aside and make sure everything is okay between us, but she's never alone.

*She's going to be home alone tonight while all her friends are at the party.*

I shut that idea down right away. There's no way I can show

up at the poor girl's apartment without first knowing for sure that she isn't just bending to my will because I intimidate her. Because I'm her boss, and she's scared not to. Both of those things have their place in the bedroom—mine especially—but not until agreed upon by both parties beforehand.

I'm so distracted by the thoughts of her blushing cheeks, both on her face and under her little skirt, that I don't notice my sous chef Marcus until he's right behind me.

"Chef," he says, and I try to hide my startle.

"What do you have for me?" I ask.

The dinner cooks are working on something back in the prep kitchen they have been trying to keep secret—not that anything is a secret from me in this place. Still, if they have all teamed up to create a new dish and want to wait until it's perfect to share it with me, I'll allow it. The menu is so well crafted right now, and they're executing it perfectly night after night. I'm happy to let them get a bit of their creativity out in other ways.

"The crew has something they want you to taste."

I nod and follow him back to the prep tables where my core dinner crew, three men and three women, are all hunched over one of the long stainless-steel tables.

They have grown close over the last two weeks since arriving on island, and I'm happy to see it. It's too often I see the opposite —cooks competing with each other for attention or promotions.

Not this crew. They have flowed together seamlessly from day one. It's one of the reasons I think we have such a good chance of placing on the Pendleton scale this season.

Only three of the six chefs are carryovers from last season, and two of those have been with us for two full seasons already. It's tough to find people willing to give up everything and move to a place like this, and the people who do decide to venture to a tropical paradise often leave after one season. I get it. You really are a world away from everything familiar—family, friends… Amazon.

To make matters even more complicated, the weather

patterns on this island dictate tourism patterns, and we only run our seasons from October to late April. That's six long months to wait for the season to pick back up. Even though we will keep employees housed and employed in one way or another throughout the offseason if they choose to stay on island, most folks leave for their hometowns when we pack it in for the season and never make it back.

As I approach, one of the female cooks glances up and smiles.

"Chef." She steps back to reveal the plate they have all been working on.

Half of a cauliflower, seasoned and garnished, fills the center of a large white dinner plate. I smile and nod to myself, happy to have a mystery solved. I've been eyeing the cauliflower plants up in the rooftop garden, knowing damn well I didn't ask for them to be planted. These cooks must have gone to the trouble of having cauliflower grown for them to create this special dish. I'm even more impressed.

"Looks good. Tell me about it."

The female cook takes a step back and allows one of the other females to step forward. This must be the leader of the project.

"Half roasted cauliflower, grown right in our garden, turmeric tahini, and pistachio gremolata. Fresh mint, also from the garden. The turmeric root came from one of the local farmers in town."

She's hitting all the right notes. I love to see our ingredients come from as close to the island as possible—full points if they were grown right here on Faraday. The dish itself is pretty large, it would have to be a shared item, which isn't something we currently do on our tasting menu. I don't have full confidence sending a family-style dish out to the guests—not when the judges could arrive any day. I've gone the route of all individual servings for the full tasting menu. It's a safe choice, but one I have confidence in. We take our risks in other areas.

"Smells great. I'm very impressed that you got Ely to grow you cauliflower for a secret dish."

The woman flashes me a smile. "Wasn't that hard, honestly."

I take the fork and knife offered to me and step up to the plate.

The dish smells amazing, and I'm excited to taste the flavor profile my cooks have come up with.

One of the most challenging things to get used to as a head chef is people watching me eat like their jobs depend on it...even if sometimes they do.

All day long, I walk through the kitchen, and people hand me spoonfuls of sauce or custard or soup, pieces of bread or cookies, sometimes even seared scallops or slices of sashimi. As I put the food in my mouth, they watch intently, trying to read the verdict from my face before the words leave my mouth.

If you're a self-conscious person, this would never be the job for you.

I cut into the cauliflower and take a bite. The first flavor that hits my tongue is the turmeric. They used the whole root, rather than a dried powder, so the flavor is subtle—in the best possible way. It mixes with the sesame in the tahini to create Asian fusion in my mouth. The crunchy pistachio gremolata, complete with lemon zest that I know damn well came from our house lemons, adds to the exotic feel of the dish.

The cauliflower itself has been left whole to preserve the interior flavor and texture of the vegetable. All too often, cauliflower is cut up so small that it turns to mush. When it's seared off whole like this, it allows the cook to make sure it's tender all the way through without having the gorgeous outside florets lose their integrity.

"Great job on the cauliflower. It's cooked perfectly." I take another bite and chew thoughtfully, seven sets of eyes watching my every move. "The turmeric tahini tastes incredible. Who came up with that?" A young cook from the back of the group lifts his hand, and I nod in his direction.

After I chew and swallow one more bite, I set down the fork and knife. "This is really great work, you guys. I'm impressed. It's a little big to go on the tasting menu, as you all know, but let's see if you can adapt it to be a single serving. Let me know when you get that ready to taste." Nods all around. I'm sure they expected my comments, even if they were holding out hope that it would go on the menu the following night. "Let's keep the whole dish prepped starting now, though, we can use it as a special to send out to VIP tables and larger parties." More nods. "Great work, everyone."

*Now get back to work.*

I don't say the words aloud, but I know they're implied. These cooks have a ton of work to be doing, and god only knows how much time they spent on this little project. Not that I want to stifle anyone's creativity, but we have a damn kitchen to run.

They gather the plate, dirty utensils, and all of the scattered ingredients and head toward the front kitchen, leaving me and Marcus alone.

"Damn fine crew you put together this season, Chef."

I nod in agreement. "It's those guys who are going to win us the Pendleton this year."

"It's your food that will win us the award, Dominic."

"It's those people cooking my food that will win," I reply, and we both smile.

Marcus is in his third season at Raft, and I don't know how I ever ran the place without him. He's the steady, silent type, running a tight ship with looks and eyebrow raises. He has never failed me, not once, in all three seasons he's worked in my kitchen.

We reward that kind of loyalty and talent at The White Sands. We have a hard enough time getting and keeping people in general—an uber talented, highly specialized cook like Marcus could waltz into any restaurant in the world and get a job. I have to make it worth his while to stay. He has a house to himself just off resort property, as well as many other perks.

I've never flat out asked if he has his eye on my job, or if he's just résumé building for a power move somewhere else on the globe, but it's going to have to come up soon enough. The last thing I want is for him to leave because he feels like there isn't anywhere for him to move up. I would gladly create a new chef position for him before I let that happen.

Once we get that Pendleton on the wall.

In meetings with the owners, and to the rest of the real world, my fixation and endless work toward this award looks crazy. I know that because I've been told plenty of times. In the kitchen, it's anything but.

No one understands what it means to get this award like these cooks do. It's one thing to work at a place with a Pendleton, it's quite another to have worked the line the night the judges ate the winning meal. Each and every person in this kitchen wants this as badly as I do, and they're willing to follow my orders to a T, trusting that I can get us there.

I can't let them down.

# Rule #7

## LEARN THE DAMN LESSON

### REINA

Turns out a four-hour nap after work was a bad idea. It's nearly midnight, and I can't sleep. I tried all the usual things that help —I took my melatonin, made sure to shut the blinds so the building lights didn't shine in, and turned the A/C down a few notches.

I even went a round with my favorite vibrator. Nothing.

It seems my mind has no interest in going back to sleep and has decided to torture me instead.

The first hour or two, I get to listen to it worry about money. I just got my first paycheck, and while it was pretty nice, I now have the ability to do some math and learn exactly how many of those paychecks it will take to get me out from under this mountain of debt. The number is higher than I want it to be. Far higher than I'm going to accomplish this season. Or the next.

I pull out my journal and make a list of everything I'm grateful for, including my two-hundred-dollar rent on this apartment, my five-minute walk commute to work, and the sunshine I get to enjoy in my new home.

Something about that word, though, sends me into a whole new tailspin.

Is this really home?

It could be. I know I could work at the resort for as long as I want, and I'm pretty sure there isn't a time limit on how long employees can stay in staff housing, as long as they're still employed.

I could live here. I could make a life that included the ocean, sun, sand, and the weekly market. I could learn to live without phone reception and consignment clothing stores and Starbucks. I already feel myself relying on the internet less for information and entertainment, considering the fact I've only had a signal strong enough to stream anything between the hours of four and six a.m.

I already know what my family will say. They'll tell me that I'm running from something. They'll tell me that I need to quit messing around and move back "home" to start teaching. To get my career started.

I try to block the words out as they float through my mind. That's their home, not mine. Just because I've arrived at the ripe old age of twenty-six without a career, a big house, a husband, and kids doesn't mean I'm messing around.

I'm just living my life my own way.

Running, though…they'll have me there.

This move did feel, and still feels, a lot like running. The way I left, piling almost all of my belongings on the curb, giving one week notice at work before hopping on the plane—there isn't anyone out there who wouldn't called that running.

But deep down in my heart, I know the truth. I may have been running, but it wasn't running away so much as it was running to. I was running toward a better life.

I knew there was more out there for me than the city, its dreary fall and spring, the scorching summer in my cramped, one-window apartment, and the subzero winter that stretched on month after month. More than lugging plastic shopping bags on three buses to get my groceries home or carrying mace and a keychain rape whistle everywhere I went.

That's not the life I want. That place never felt like home.

Could it feel like home here on Faraday Island?

*Dom could make it feel like home.*

With a laugh, I toss the sheet off and flip my pillow to the cool side, the A/C suddenly not managing to keep the temperature down.

*Dom.*

What was that in the office? It happened so quickly, it almost feels like I dreamed it. But my behind still smarts from the smacks, so I know damn well it happened. Dominic Fuentes, chef of The White Sands Resort, my freaking boss, took me in his office and spanked me.

Not that I'm upset about it. I was more surprised than anything in the moment, but having the chance to look back on it now, it may have been the hottest thing that's ever happened to me.

I've worked for a handful of chefs, and exactly zero of them could have pulled such a stunt—hand deep inside me, ass bared, counting the slaps—without my having called the police.

But Dom? He can spank me anytime he wants.

He must have enjoyed it as much as I did, right? I mean, there's no way he makes a habit of that sort of thing. I would certainly have heard about a spank-happy chef who's always doling out punishment to the waitresses. As a matter of fact, Sarah told me flat out that he doesn't interact with waitstaff, especially not a.m. waitstaff.

So, it's just me. He was so overcome with the desire to punish me for showing up at work hungover and sleep deprived, that he spanked me until I came.

And then asked if I was coming to the party tonight.

The thought makes me sit straight up in bed.

What exactly did he say when he strolled out of the kitchen to chat with Sarah, Jess, and me—something the two of them assured me had never happened before. He asked if he would see us at the party later. I know he met my eye longer than the other two when waiting for an answer, and I read that to mean that he was making sure I knew that I better not come.

What if he was inviting me to play the same game? My mind reels with the idea.

I'm sure that's what was going on, now that I think about it. How could I have gotten it so wrong? He's probably sitting at that party right now, wondering where I am.

*He knows where you live. He could have come over.*

But that's not the game. The game is, I show up, have a few drinks, and then he punishes me for it in the morning.

I'm out of bed and flipping on the lights before any kind of logic can sneak past my fevered thoughts.

I've just pulled a tiny red dress off its hanger when I hear a noise outside my door.

*Oh my gosh, maybe he did come over.*

I slip the dress over my head quickly and rush to open my front door. When I fly out onto the patio, I nearly collide with a man...who is not Dominic.

"Charles?"

"Oh, honey, sorry to wake you," a very drunk sounding Charles says in his drawl before pulling me into an embrace.

I can see over his shoulder that Sarah caused all the noise, having dropped her keys while trying to relock her apartment a few doors down.

"What are you guys doing?"

"Your girlfriend over there needed to grab her phone charger and made me stumble all the way home with her."

"You're going back to the party?"

"Sure thing, sweetheart."

"Hang on. I'm coming, okay?"

Sarah appears by Charles's side, charging cable in hand. "Hooray!" she shouts before clapping her hand over her mouth and bursting into a fit of giggles as Charles and I both shush her. "Sorry, sorry," she mumbles through her fingers.

"Give me ten minutes, okay?"

I'm ready in five.

The party tonight is at the home of one of the dinner cooks, rather than at the staff cantina like the company-sponsored one I went to before. It's a short walk off resort property and down the same road I drove up when the taxi brought me from the ferry.

We walk for about ten minutes, the two of them filling me in on who's at the party, who said what, and who each of them has their sights set on for the night.

I have to fight the urge to laugh as I listen to the tipsy ramblings about their crushes and planned conquests even though I'm on a similar mission—dead sober.

The house is a one-story bungalow style, set back from the road a bit with a large, sandy front yard and the ocean as a backyard. I wonder briefly how a cook manages to rent an oceanfront house, but loud music, loud voices, and bright light quickly grab my attention.

The party is nothing like the awkward, meet-your-new-coworkers gathering from the night before. Half-naked resort staff members getting increasingly tipsy and intimate cover the front porch. I can hear loud reggae music coming from somewhere inside. Beer pong is set up in the sand, and it's fairly obvious the players are not on their first round.

We make our way through the crowd to the kitchen, where one of the bartenders I recognize from the dinner shift has set up a full bar.

"What'll it be?" he asks with a smile as we approach.

The way Sarah leans over the counter toward him, biting her lip and perusing the lined-up bottles with her fingers, lets me know this is the guy she's chosen for the evening.

I smile back at him. "You even bartend in your free time?"

He shrugs, and his smile softens. I can see why Sarah has this one on her radar. The man is adorable. "I get some of my best ideas for the cocktail menu at parties like this. I can try new combos out, and it doesn't matter if they suck." He glances down at Sarah, who is still leaning on her elbows and watching him like he hung the moon, giving her a kind smile. "People don't seem to care."

"Well, I'll have tonight's special," I say.

"Me too," Sarah chimes in. "And one for Charles, too." She glances around for her now absent companion.

"I call this one Midnight Malibu," the man says as he passes us clear plastic cups. "Let me know what you think." He delivers the last line to me with a little wink.

I offer a tight-lipped smile in return, lifting my glass in a little salute before following Sarah off through the crowd so she can find Charles and deliver his cocktail.

When I step through the sliding doors out onto the ocean-front deck, the warm, salty breeze off the ocean stops me in my tracks. I close my eyes and inhale.

*I really do love my new home.*

When I feel the tingle start from my toes and travel to... everywhere else, I know immediately who it is.

Damn. I was hoping to get at least halfway through my glass of liquid courage before having to interact with the man. I quickly take a large sip, then another.

The drink tastes incredible, the sweetness of the tropical fruits perfectly masking what I'm sure is a lot of alcohol. I'm swallowing my second gulp when I realize that Dom probably just watched me chug half of my drink.

Off to a great start.

I glance around the yard, and it takes me exactly one second to lock eyes with him. He's sitting in a padded deck chair by a metal fire pit just off the deck. A few other guys sit with him, a couple of whom look closer to his age than mine.

I smile and offer a little wave, immediately chastising myself.

*Cue the blush.*

My feet move on their own volition, walking across the

deck toward the stairs that will lead down to where he's sitting. For some reason, I can't talk them out of it. Before I know it, I'm approaching a large group of men, who are all talking loudly over each other, not paying any attention to me at all.

Except for one. Dom has been tracking my approach since I took my first step, and I don't stop walking until I'm right next to him.

"Hey, Dom."

My words cause a hush to descend over the rowdy group of men. All voices stop, their heads turn toward me, and suddenly I can only hear the beat of my own heart.

I try to ignore them, forcing myself to wait silently through the seemingly endless seconds while I wait for Dom to say something. Anything.

He's going to say something, right?

"Hey, you gonna spill that drink on us, or what?" one of the other guys says.

I turn my head away from Dom. One of the younger dinner line cooks starts laughing across the fire. I recognize him from the party last night. He was one of the scowling people cleaning cranberry juice off the cards.

I'm embarrassed. Mad. And blushing furiously, dammit.

"No, I'm not going to spill it on you," I say, before tilting the glass to my lips and chugging the whole thing. "I'm going to drink it. And then I'm going to drink another."

I spin on my heel to storm off, nearly colliding with Sarah, who has come up quietly behind me. "What are you doing?" she hisses so softly only I can hear it. I don't answer, but I do grab the full cocktail that was meant for Charles out of her hand, replacing it with my now empty cup.

And then I chug that one as well. I can hear laughter behind me as I toss the cup into the yard and storm back up the stairs.

Once I'm safely through the sliding doors, Sarah finally manages to catch up with me.

"What the hell, girl? You are pounding drinks like you don't gotta work in five hours."

I groan and pull out my phone, glancing down at the clock.

What am I doing here?

Did I really expect him to be glad to see me?

No, that's not what I was doing at all. He promised me punishment if I didn't obey him, and for some reason, punishment is all I want from him. Whatever he has in mind for me, I want to deserve it.

Where the hell are these thoughts coming from? Never in my life have I been the type of girl to act up for attention. No, I'm the good girl—the actual good girl. Good grades, nice friends, worked a part-time job to save up for my own used car, my own gas, and insurance. I just followed the rules without question.

Until I couldn't anymore.

Until graduation rolled around, and I was faced with following those rules straight back to Ottawa, Illinois to accept a job as a junior teacher in the same tiny district where both of my parents teach. Those rules would have had me moving back into my childhood bedroom until one of the nice guys from church finally chose me and put a ring on my finger, moving us into a house down the street from my parents and knocking me up.

No, there came a point where I couldn't follow those good girl rules anymore, so I just stopped. I stayed in the apartment I lived in for college. I went full-time at the job I worked weekends while attending school. I stayed in that state of limbo for nearly five years, pretending that it was a life. Pretending that I wasn't just avoiding deciding what to do next.

Pretending that I could afford it once my parents' contribution stopped coming, which happened a few months after graduation, when they realized I wasn't packing my bags to come back home. They probably assumed I would fail without their money and be forced out of the city. And they would have been right. If it wasn't for credit cards.

Speaking of which...

The reality of my current situation falls on me hard.

I'm so deep in debt.

Most days, I try not to think about it. I leveraged my last dime to get to this island, this job, and now here I am, purposely disobeying a direct order from my boss and getting drunk at a party before my morning shift.

What the hell am I doing?

I need to get home now.

"I'm going home," I say to Sarah, who is still looking around for the elusive Charles.

"What? You just got here."

"I really shouldn't have come."

"I saw you out there with those guys, Reina. I'm going to figure out which one of them you have your eye on," Sarah says with an evil grin. "I know what gets a girl out of bed in the middle of the night to walk down to a party she shouldn't be at. And it's not her best island girlfriend. It's the call of the cock." She bursts into giggles at her own ridiculous joke.

I smile despite myself, shaking my head. She's not wrong, but I'm not about to admit that. There's no way I'm going to tell her who I really came to see.

"It's okay, you don't have to tell me," she says, like a mind reader. "I'll figure it out. It's my favorite game. Ooh! There he is." She grabs my arm and drags me across the room toward Charles and another man.

The sudden motion does something jarring to my brain, making the room spin a bit.

*Goddamn tropical cocktails.*

I'm drunk again.

"Charles, Reina needs to go home, can we walk with her?"

"Girl, we just got back here. And I'm a little busy, can't you see?" Charles hisses, tossing a glance over his shoulder at the handsome man lounging against the wall behind him.

Sarah's glare is unrelenting. "You are not going to make us walk alone."

Charles growls at her. "This is literally the safest place on the planet."

"Not if you stumble drunk into the ocean and drown," she says, hands on hips.

Charles lets out a sigh and an eye roll so perfectly dramatic that I have to smile. "Fine. Give me ten." He turns back to his date.

"That's perfect," Sarah says to me. "I have to pee so bad. Meet us on the front porch in ten?" She stumbles off before I can answer.

As I make my way to the front door and settle on the last porch step, I weigh the likelihood that they're actually going to materialize in ten minutes. With a sigh, I check my phone clock again, deciding I will give them fifteen before I just walk home alone. It's really not that far.

I wait a full eighteen minutes before dragging myself to my feet and heading down the remaining steps, clicking on my flashlight.

Only to find Dom standing right in front of me.

"What are you doing here, Reina?" he asks in his deep, husky voice.

"I..." I shake my head and sigh. "I don't know. I'm sorry."

Dom crosses both arms across his chest and considers me. "It wasn't even twelve hours ago that I told you there would be consequences for partying before your morning shift. Do you remember that?"

My cheeks burn with shame. I can't believe he's going to do this here, where any of the partygoers can hear him. "Yes, I remember," I say softly, not meeting his eye.

"I bet you do," he says with a chuckle. "That's why you're here, isn't it?" There's a hint of curiosity in his voice that makes me glance up at him. He has the tiniest shadow of a smile on his otherwise stern face.

"No. I mean, maybe? I'm not sure why I came, I just..." My own arms cross tightly across my chest as I fight back the urge to cry. "I said I was sorry, okay? This was clearly a huge mistake. Can you just move so I can go home?"

"You want me to move so you can walk home, alone, in the dark, at two in the morning."

"Yeah."

"Not going to happen."

"Well…" I'm not sure what to say, but I'm feeling feisty and a little bit annoyed that he won't just let me disappear into the dark with my shame. "What is going to happen?"

"Exactly what I told you would happen in the office. Consequences."

I don't know which part of me emits the little moan without permission, but whichever one it was, is going to be in so much trouble later.

Dom lets out a small, breathy laugh. "Not the good kind."

"There's a good kind?" I know there is, and my panties do too, but for some reason, the only defense mechanism still online right now is attitude.

"Oh, I think we both know there is."

I stand statue still and hold my breath as Dom's arm snakes around my shoulders, pulling my body next to his with a sharp tug. I don't want to stumble, but my feet didn't get the message fast enough, so I do. I don't fall, luckily, but it's so obvious that I'm half drunk. Maybe all the way drunk.

As if it wasn't before.

"I'm going to give you a little dose of the bad kind, just so you're clear on the difference." With his arm still around my shoulders, he starts to walk around the side of the house.

I should be thrilled right now. This is exactly what I wanted, right? I mean, sure, I didn't expect him to take me around the side of the house and pull up my skirt where anyone could see, but sometimes you have to take what the universe offers you. The man has his arm around me. He's talking to me in a way that could totally be considered flirting.

This is going great.

When we make it around the corner, though, the truth becomes very clear.

I'm standing in front of an off-road style golf cart—black with green trim. The cart itself has a bench seat for two or three up front and another in the back. This one happens to have a wagon attached that is nearly the size of the cart itself.

And the whole vehicle is filled with drunk line cooks.

"What?" I stop short, planting my feet so firmly that Dom has to stop to keep from losing his grip on me.

"This." Dom tightens his grip on me, pulling us forward toward the cart. "Is how drunk restaurant staff get home from parties. Get in."

The seats up front are all filled, except for Dom's driver's seat. I can only fit in the wagon with four guys, but he can't possibly expect—

"Nick, scoot," Dom calls to the guys in the cart before turning to me. "Hop in."

I turn my face back to the wagon just so I don't have to see his smug expression for a second longer. Swallowing any remaining pride, I climb in.

The guys shift over, hardly missing a beat in the drunken version of "Billie Jean" they're belting out into the night air. The guy to my right, a cook I recognize from the lunch shift, slides his arm around my shoulders and tries to pull me into the chorus. I offer a tight-lipped smile and remove his sweaty limb.

The cart clicks on, and we drive off.

If I thought the golf cart taxi ride was bumpy, being in the back wagon is insane.

There isn't really anything to hold on to except my new drunk, sweaty friends, so I'm bounced and flung with every pothole and unnecessarily sharp turn the cart makes. To make matters worse, it's pretty clear this wagon has a day job on the landscaping crew. The bed is full of sand, dirt, and plant pieces. By the time we get to the first stop, I'm already sweaty from trying to hold on in the hot night air, and filthy from all the dirt sticking to my sweat.

Dom stops at my building last.

There are two other passengers who live in the same building as me, and they're both up front. For the last leg of the journey, I'm alone in the wagon, which I was grateful for when the last loud, smelly man finally got out, but I soon learn is far worse. Now there isn't enough weight in the wagon to hold it on the road. I'm riding in a dirty, bouncing kite.

By the time the vehicle stops in front of my building, I'm not sure I could get myself out of the back if I tried. The two guys also getting out must notice my state because they come around back and haul me out of the wagon like a corpse, setting me on my feet and bracing me from both sides.

"See you in the morning," Dom calls without a glance backward as he drives off.

I tell the guys my apartment number, and they deliver me to my door.

I now have to add a shower to the list of things to do before I collapse into bed for a little sleep. My shift starts in four and a half hours, so I huff off to the small, shower-only stall in my bathroom.

Stripping off my dress, I let my thoughts drift back through the events of the night, and doubts about Dom take over.

What the actual hell was I thinking going there like that?

I don't know what came over me. It was like I was pulled by an invisible string. I pride myself on being a responsible, stable adult. One who supports herself, takes care of herself, and makes good decisions.

*Oh, like the decision to live off of credit cards you couldn't pay off for five years?*

As I stand naked in front of the mirror, that thought catches in my throat.

*What if my parents were right?*

What if I fooled myself into believing that I was self-sufficient for all those years, when in actuality, I was nothing more than an irresponsible, overgrown teenager, running wild with far more credit than I was capable of managing.

It's more than I can bear. Hot tears roll down my cheeks as I step into the weak stream of lukewarm water. It does little to wash away my existential crisis, but right now I don't know what else to do.

By the time I'm toweling off, my tears have stopped. And a new resolve has begun.

I'm going to make it this time...on my own. No crushes to distract me.

I'm going to put my head down, work hard, get promoted, and pay off all my debt while living in this tiny apartment.

I have to. I have to prove to myself that I can be trusted. That I'm a responsible adult.

I crawl into bed for what will be a short nap before work and smile at my new steel resolve.

Tonight was exactly what I needed to get this Dom thing out of my system. I learned my lesson, and I'm back on track.

# Rule #8

SHE'S MINE...

## DOMINIC

I can see her struggling, but she manages to push through. I'm actually impressed by the way she cleaned herself up and put on her cheerful smile for this shift.

It's busier than usual for a Tuesday brunch, all the tables have been full since the doors opened. I'm sitting in a booth with Avery, who stayed on island after the meeting for a few days to "take care of some business," as he calls it.

Business being—getting his dick wet.

I love the guy, but his escapades are well known on this island. As a matter of fact, everything about everyone is well known on the island. It's one of the main reasons why I set my desires aside when I decided to make it my home.

It's one thing to casually date in an American city of two million people. It's quite another to do so on an island full of tenth-generation locals and my employees.

Avery is partial to a third category of people on the island, one that is all but invisible to me. The vacationers. He's happy to stroll into a bar, spot a beautiful lady, and have his dick in her ten minutes later.

That just doesn't work for me. I need a warm-up period, a period of banter and tension build-up before anything of the bedroom variety happens in my relationships.

And that seems to be what's going on right now, against my better judgment, with a woman I should be leaving the hell alone.

When I spotted Reina that first night at the party—her luscious round ass, flirty ponytail, and big, bright eyes—I just knew she was my type. She's done nothing to prove me wrong so far, with her adorable blush, sassy attitude, and affinity for getting into embarrassing situations that lead to trouble.

She's perfect. The timing and circumstances are just all wrong.

This season I have to prove to the world, and myself, that I'm good enough to stand among the top chefs. That I am what I say I am—an amazing, dedicated chef. Not just some rich kid who bought himself a fancy kitchen but couldn't hack it. It has to be now before my partners force me to give it all up and flip burgers.

If I start adding in distractions that will take my attention away from where it needs to be—my kitchen—things will go south real fast.

But this one distraction is just so...distracting. I'm not sure I've ever wanted to go south more in my entire adult life.

*Get it together, man.*

I already know I fucked up royally with that stunt in the office. I was out of my mind to have touched an employee like that. She's just so beautiful, and she wanted it as badly as I did. She needed it like I did. I could tell.

It's the first time I've ever lost control at work, and I can only pray that it doesn't cost me everything.

I offered her a taste of my other side last night, the one I show to the rest of the world, and I hope I convinced her that pursuing me is not what she wants. There are a lot of easier catches on this island, and a girl like that could get any of them.

"Good morning, gentlemen." Reina's sweet voice brings me out of my rumination. I look up from my coffee cup to see her smiling brightly down at our table as if we are two perfect strangers that she's delighted to be serving.

"Morning, Reina," I answer, not breaking eye contact.

To her credit, the cheerful server impression doesn't falter for a second. "I see Julie already got you coffee. I'll have to thank her for that. Did you have a chance to look over the menu?"

"Don't bullshit us."

I feel Avery's eyes shoot to me as the words fall out of my mouth. I only meant to say them in my head.

"You know we know the menu by heart." I try to make the line a bit softer, as if I was making a joke the whole time, but I can feel the tension in the air. I've ruined whatever good cheer was there, even if it was pretend.

Good. I want to ruin it. I want her to stay away from me.

"Ave?" I ask, eager to get that feminine, flowery scent away from me before I reach out, grab it, and take a bite.

"I'm going to have the polenta and greens with poached eggs." He looks up and gives Reina a million-dollar smile before turning to me.

"Just tell them to make me something," I say gruffly, holding my menu out for her to take. Those cooks better come up with a perfect fucking breakfast, or there will be hell to pay.

"I'll get those orders right in for you guys." Reina's syrupy sweetness is still intact. "Can I bring any juice, cocktails, maybe an order of our mini scones to go with your coffee?"

I open my mouth to send her off, but Avery is too quick. "You know, love, I would take a shot of Baileys for my coffee, and those scones sound lovely."

His smile is genuine, his tone so warm and kind, I want to punch him in the mouth.

Reina returns his favor, offering up one more of those erection-worthy pursed-lip smiles before heading back to the server station.

"Jesus, Dom, why do you have to be such a dick?"

"That is an employee, Ave."

"Yeah, and so was the blonde in my bed last night, but that didn't stop her from swallowing my cock." His tone goes up a bit on the last word, and he glances around with a grimace and a laugh.

I shake my head. "I have to live here. I can't be screwing employees."

"I didn't ask why you weren't screwing her, Dom, although I will never understand. I asked why you were being such an asshole."

"Hard morning." It's not a full-on lie. This morning has been hard in all sorts of ways. One of which is hiding under the table in my pants.

"Well, I won't tell you how to run your restaurant," he starts, but I'm in no mood for this conversation after the meeting yesterday.

"Perfect. Don't."

Avery leans back in the booth, stretching both arms across the backrest and grinning like I'm a child acting up in the most adorable way. When Reina appears a moment later with his drink and a plate of warm scones, he sits forward and clasps his hands in front of him on the table. "Thank you so much. Was it Reina?"

Predictably, Reina smiles at him. "Yup, Reina. And you're Avery, right? Some of the other girls told me you're one of the owners. It's nice to meet you. I've met three of the four now."

"The pleasure is all mine, Reina." Avery purrs her name, drawing the syllables out. She leans closer.

"I need another cup of coffee." My demand is sudden, and they both look abruptly at me. Reina recovers first, smiling.

"Of course, Mr. Fuentes, I'll be right back with the carafe."

Then she tosses Avery a smile and a look I can't see before walking away.

I grind my teeth and glower. I hadn't meant to sound so harsh. I just needed to get her away from Avery's deadly charm. I've seen it work on too many unsuspecting females in the past. Reina will not be one of them.

Why not? She's not going to be mine.

The word sticks in my mind. *Mine.*

*She is mine.*

Avery starts chastising me again for my behavior, but I'm not listening. For the second time this morning, words just come out of my mouth without my permission. "She's mine."

Avery stops mid-word, his mouth hanging open. "Excuse me?"

"My employee. She's my employee. You will keep your hands off her."

"I...I never said anything about pursuing her. I have my companion for the week all picked out. You okay, man?"

"I'm fine."

Avery tosses me a knowing look. "Well, you don't look fine. What you do look like is a man who has gone far too long without getting laid."

I glance furiously around to make sure no one is eavesdropping on our conversation. "That's so easy for you to say. You just parade around the world, never working a day in your life, screwing anything that—"

"Oh, come off it, Dom. You have more money than any of us. If there's one person who doesn't need to be putting in eighty hours a week in a fucking kitchen, it's your rich ass. You choose this life for some unknown goddamn reason, so don't get all high and mighty about my lifestyle. You could use a few years of vacation and fucking. It does amazing things for your attitude." The look he gives me tells me that he's not at all impressed with my current attitude.

"There are more important things in life than—"

"Than relationships with other humans? No, Dom, there isn't."

I flop back in my seat and cross my arms. I know he's right. I've been working so hard for so long that I'm beginning to forget who I was before I started this whole thing. I used to like things besides work. I used to have friends. I used to have a vision for my future that included a family and vacations on the beach like the ones I remember from my own childhood.

Now all I have is a million-dollar view of the beach from a giant house that I never have time to be in.

Luckily, I'm saved from having to bare my soul by Reina reappearing with our breakfast.

"This looks amazing." Avery has switched off the judgmental best friend act and switched on the handsome, single, independently wealthy one. Reina beams under his attention.

I grind my teeth again. "Mine looks really good."

They both turn to me, barely masked surprise on their faces.

"Tell the cooks it looks good," I say.

"Sure. I'll be happy to tell them that, Mr. Fuentes."

I don't know why she's started calling me that, but it does nothing to improve my mood. "It's Dominic. Dom."

I know she knows my name. She screamed it just the other day as I spanked and finger-fucked her in my office not twenty feet from here. But somehow, between then and now, I stopped being Dom and became Mr. Fuentes.

*Just like my father.*

And I'm trying to drive her away just like he does with everyone.

"Dom," she repeats, holding my gaze.

The world stops, time stops, as we stay in that locked gaze for far longer than is appropriate. I don't know how long passes before I hear Avery say, "Okay, then. I guess we're all set."

Reina jumps and looks at him, recovering quickly and offering a smile. "Perfect, yes, well, enjoy your breakfast." And she scurries off without another glance in my direction.

I turn my full attention to my food, but I can feel Avery's gaze on me. I glare up at him. "What?"

The sly, mischievous smile on his face gives him away. The man could never manage a poker face. "Nothing."

"Oh, fuck off, Avery."

"What? I didn't say anything."

"Just eat your damn breakfast and stop looking at me like that."

"She seems really nice—"

"Avery, I swear to fucking god."

He laughs and pours the shot into his coffee, shaking his head.

"It's nothing."

"Yeah, looked like nothing."

"Let it go."

"I will if you will."

I pick up my fork and dig into the plate of eggs and fried potatoes in front of me. I will let it go. This conversation that is.

The girl? That might be a bit more complicated.

# Rule #9

## THERE'S A FIRST TIME FOR EVERYTHING

### REINA

Waiting on Dom at breakfast the morning after he humiliated me with that wagon ride is just as fun as I expected it to be. Not at all.

I tried everything I could to get someone else to take their table when they strolled in with no luck. One of the younger girls actually cried when I suggested she go over and get their coffee order.

I can't really blame her. I remember being a new waitress, working my first job. Each and every time I picked up a tray of drinks, I said a prayer.

Avery, the other owner who joined Dom for brunch, is quite the ladies' man. I could tell just from our interactions, but I've also heard plenty of stories—and I've only been on the island a week. It's a good reminder that nothing stays truly private in a place like this. Not only is the island small, but I live in close quarters with the same people I work and socialize with. It's the kind of place where you need to choose your behavior carefully.

Which makes me all the more embarrassed over my display

of naïveté the night before. I'm going to need to act with a higher level of discernment in the future in order to maintain a reputation I'm proud of—and one that will get me promoted. No one will make the "drunk girl" breakfast manager.

Luckily, I'm so busy that I hardly have time to worry about Dom and Avery. Unlike the newbies, who would be fawning over their table constantly, trying to keep the owners happy, I know that my priorities are the real guests. I can say with one hundred percent certainty that Dom would rather me focus on the customers, and if Avery knows anything about business, he feels the same. They can find the saltshakers if they need them. I have drink orders to deliver to fussy resort guests.

I do manage to stop and ask if they enjoyed their breakfast as they're getting up to leave, and Avery assures me that breakfast was lovely. Dom is already halfway to the kitchen as if it's calling to him, and he can't stay away a second longer.

As I'm setting their plates in the dish area, I catch a bit of his conversation with the brunch line cooks, who have all stopped their frantic egg flipping to give him their full attention.

"Really, really nice sear on the pork belly, Franz. And those poached eggs, who was that? Nice, James. They were perfect. I'm very impressed, guys. Keep it up."

The faces of the young guys working the brunch line are beaming with concealed pleasure and pride. They all grunt out thanks, but it's clear that they're overjoyed by the praise.

It's not the first time I've witnessed such a display in my short time here. The way Dom interacts with the kitchen staff may appear harsh and gruff to someone unfamiliar with the industry, but the respect and devotion his staff feels for him radiates off them.

He commands respect, and he works just as hard as any of the lower members of the staff, which makes him deserve it. It's easy to see why these cooks turn out such good plates time after time. They're well taken care of and have a great leader.

Dom turns abruptly from the cooks and nearly collides with me where I'm standing, watching him.

"Sorry," I say quickly, turning to flee, but he catches my arm.

"No, Reina. I'm sorry."

I open my mouth to say something about how I was standing in the way or otherwise deflect his words, but I don't get the chance.

"I'm just…sorry," he repeats, his intense stare locked on me.

After a pause so long I realize he isn't going to continue, I stammer out a reply. "Sure, yeah. It's fine." I know we aren't talking about our near collision, and I'm really not sure what to say, especially right here, surrounded by the eyes and ears of the entire café staff.

"Stop in my office before you leave."

He turns and heads back into the kitchen before I have a chance to reply.

The whole rest of my shift, I'm distracted by the thought of being back in his office, alone, with him. Last time I went in there and closed the door behind me…

I have to stop thinking about that. Whatever it was, it's over now. I'm going to march in there and tell him that it's fine that it happened. I'm not mad or going to file a complaint with HR but that it really can't happen again. I have too much on the line to be taking such a risk.

I rehearse my speech in my mind repeatedly until the moment my knuckles hit his office door.

It opens almost immediately after my first knock. Dom is standing there, so close, and his scent envelopes me in pine and citrus.

*Shit.*

I glance down at my feet, steeling my resolve and restarting my mental rehearsal.

*I'm not interested. I need to focus on myself right now. It was fun, but—*

"Come in." He steps back and leaves the office door open.

I walk through and close it behind me. The click of the latch is loud enough to wake the freaking dead. It's almost as loud as my heart hammering away in my chest.

*Breathe Reina.*

"Dom, I—" I start out strong, but my words come out at the same time he says, "Reina, I'm sorry."

I stop short, my perfect speech slipping from my mind. "Why do you keep apologizing?"

Dom leans back against his desk and crosses his arms. "Because I acted like a jerk last night."

"And this morning."

A little twitch at the corner of his lips tells me my words had the intended effect. "And this morning."

"Okay, well, thanks. I accept your apology." I take a deep breath and look up, preparing to deliver my speech. "And I just wanted to let you know that while I had fun yesterday, it's not really something that I think is in my best interests to continue. I'm not mad, but I need to focus on myself right now."

I'm not sure how many of the well-prepared lines I manage to speak, or if they came out in the right order. That man's eyes are just so mesmerizing. He watches me speak as if I'm telling him I'm going to take my clothes off. As if I already have and am standing naked in front of him.

He licks his lips and lets his gaze drift down.

"Dom!" I snap, and his eyes come back to mine. "Did you hear me?"

He pushes off the desk and takes a few steps closer. "I heard some over-rehearsed bullshit about how you don't want this."

He's far too close to me right now for me to be able to think clearly. "Why are you so rude?" I can tell my cheeks are bright red, and tears are starting to form in the corners of my eyes. This is not going as planned.

"I'm not rude." He's less than an inch from touching my

body now, and I glance down to make sure I'm not going to accidentally brush the tips of my nipples against his chest.

He uses one finger to lift my chin back up.

"I'm commanding. I'm tough. I've been told I'm a hard ass and that I ask too much of people. But I've never been called rude."

His face is so close, I could lick it.

"There's a first time for everything, I suppose," I whisper.

That earns me a full-on smile. And it's freaking glorious. I can't hold in my tears when he smiles at me like that.

"What are you doing to me?" His own voice is just above a whisper. Soft words, spoken only for me.

"I'm not trying to do anything." It's not a lie, not anymore. I may have been trying to do something last night, but that's all over now. At least, it was when I walked into this office. Now, I'm less sure.

"You're not, are you? Not trying to do anything. Just doing it naturally. Distracting me from my work, driving me crazy with your sweet little ass." He reaches around and gives my very sore butt a little squeeze as he says the words, eliciting an involuntary squeak and what I'm sure is a very bright blush. It only makes that swoon-worthy smile grow wider.

"And those pink cheeks." His voice is an actual whisper now as he slides the words down my neck, his lips millimeters from my skin. "I, too, have my own things to worry about. But now, all I can think about is the sound you made when you came on my fingers. The feeling of your pretty little ass under my palm."

He has my butt in his grip again, pulling my hips forward against his body. Between that and the way his lips graze down my neck, I'm in no state to be speaking words. But what choice do I have?

"Sounds like we agree, then. We should stay away from each other. Focus on our own things," I manage to get out.

Dom lets out a short exhale and releases me, taking a step

back and refolding his arms across his chest. "I agree that's what we should do, yes."

I hold my breath tightly, willing my face not to betray any of the ways those words crush my soul completely. I nod and turn to leave.

"But I don't think for a second that's what you actually want."

I pause, sigh, and lean my forehead on the door. "What I want is...complicated."

I want to pay off my debt. I want to feel confident that I'm a responsible adult. I want to know that I'm making the right choices in life. I just can't see how sleeping with my boss is going to give me any of those things. In fact, it could ruin everything.

"I'm going to make this very simple for you."

I don't turn around, in fact, I don't move at all. It would be wiser to do so, to run from whatever he's about to say and never look back, but I'm frozen to the spot.

"There's another staff party tonight, like there is most nights. You have to work breakfast tomorrow, as we both well know. You have three choices. First, you can show up at that party hoping to inspire some kind of punishment from me like you did last night. If you choose that, it will turn out even worse than it did last night."

I'm grateful I didn't turn around because the shame I feel about last night sends more tears down my cheeks.

"Your other two choices involve keeping yourself home tonight and getting to bed at a reasonable hour. You can lock the door and turn your porch light off. If someone sees that, they'll know that you're not interested and that would be that. You could also leave the light on and the door unlocked. That might lead someone to believe that whatever this is...is still on the table."

I'm stunned by his words. I wipe at the tears on my face but still don't turn around.

He's leaving this completely up to me. I have to choose, and he'll act accordingly.

Which means…

*He wants me.*

I force myself to take a long, slow breath through my nose to prevent myself from going into full panic mode. I need to get out of here and get somewhere quiet where I can think alone.

I wipe my eyes quickly with my hand again and turn the knob.

The bright light and noise of the prep kitchen hit me like a slap. I take a deep breath and hurry through, trying to keep my head down.

Unfortunately, a server making a quick exit from the closed door of Dom's office with a tear-stained face will not go unnoticed. Almost every one of the prep cooks has something to say.

"Oh, Reina, did he make you cry?"

"Damn! He's such a dick."

"Don't pay any attention to him, girl, you are killing it."

I'm laughing by the time I make it through the prep kitchen and into the server station. I'm so grateful for the cooks on my shift for standing up for me like that. Restaurant staff can be thick as thieves, and it fills me with joy to have been accepted into the fold.

The last place I worked was too high stakes for this kind of camaraderie, at least it was on the dinner shift. I always felt like I was in competition with everyone around me, even the people I thought were my friends. I make a silent vow to appreciate how good I have it on the a.m. shift. There's no reason to submit myself to that kind of pressure again.

As a matter of fact, I think I could be happy working brunch forever, with these people. Training complete newbies to wait tables and make lattes. Having my afternoons free and seeing the sunrise. This is a whole side of the industry I never knew existed. I finally feel like I've found my place.

My elation fades pretty quickly as I remember the conversation I just escaped from. What Dom is suggesting could put all of my newfound joy and freedom on the line. If I start up with the boss and things go south, how long could I still work here?

The reasons to walk away from this could fill a book. On the other side, the leaving my porch light on and throwing all caution to the wind side, there's only one reason. But somehow, that broodingly handsome reason feels weighty enough to tip the scales.

# Rule #10

## PRAY FOR DARKNESS

### DOMINIC

I feel like a fucking grandpa at some of these staff parties. It's not exactly a boost to my ego. I usually stay away, but one of my cooks is celebrating his birthday tonight, so I said I would make an appearance.

Three parties in one week. It's a personal record for me.

I made a pact with myself this season that I would work harder to bond with the people working dinner shift. It's them I'm relying on to work their hardest and ultimately win us the Pendleton.

My mentor, Jean Paul, spoke often of the importance of being one with your crew. If they see you as a peer, someone they can emulate, the person they want to become in their career, they're more likely to give it their all.

It's not likely that any of the young hotshots I have working the line this year dream of growing up to be a lonely workaholic chef, single into his late thirties, hoarding a fortune but never taking the time to enjoy life. I mean, who wants that? I need to walk the walk if I'm going to inspire greatness from these kids.

Hence, my presence at this loud party when I would much rather be in my own home, quietly sipping whiskey and listening to records while planning out next week's menus.

Or obsessing over a certain waitress's porch light.

I find my crew quickly. It's not hard to spot them. They tend to separate from the rest of the crowd, as if their position at the restaurant creates a forcefield around them. They're different from the hordes of seasonal staff who come and go each year. These men and women are culinary professionals, hand selected by me to work dinner service.

"Dominic!" One of the younger guys from dinner shift spots me first and waves me over. He's a good kid, a rising star in my kitchen and the culinary world. I was lucky to snag him at the beginning of the season. He could have gone anywhere in the world.

I walk over and take a seat at the table where they often congregate to play poker.

"Deal you in?"

"Sure," I respond. I'll only stay for a few rounds, but playing the game is a good way to make them feel like I'm one of them.

The cards fall, and I try my best to pay attention to the hand, but my mind is elsewhere.

*Reina.*

It's not like me to get so hung up on a woman, but this one has me in her claws.

And I know she didn't mean for it to be that way.

Maybe that's the most endearing part of her. I'm so used to being pursued, having women make up excuses to talk to me. Reina just fell into my lap. Literally.

Well shit. Just the thought of her name has me aroused and impatient to get out of here.

It's not that I'm expecting to find that light on.

*Am I?*

It's just that...I want to.

It'll be reckless, something that I pride myself on never, ever

81

being. If someone caught me in the apartment of a brunch wait-ress with my cock buried deep in her sweet pussy...it could be the end of everything I've worked so hard for.

I've seen other chefs go down that way, and I'm not going to let it happen to me. Not only do I have my eye on a different prize, I could never face my family after such a scandal.

No, I need to keep whatever this is under reins.

*Reina...*

I slam the rest of my drink and rise to find another. I cannot afford to lose myself in a crush like a teenager. Seriously, I have a fucking hard-on just thinking about her. I may as well be sixteen, not thirty-nine.

I have too much going on right now, trying to get the restau-rant back up to speed after the winter break. Trying to get us up and running at peak performance before awards season starts and the scouts make their way to our little island to secretly dine and judge us.

But there's no denying it. When I should be focused on tasting lobster étouffée and coconut paletas, all I can think about is getting my tongue deep inside that woman. Tasting her sweet-ness as she moans through her orgasm. When I should be showing my new bakers how to shape dough, all I can do is imagine my hands slapping against her sweet ass. The thought of her bared before me as I pull up her skirt and bend her over my knee...

My cock stiffens in my pants, a-fucking-gain, and I chastise myself for letting my mind wander so far down that path.

Luckily, or possibly very unluckily, I left the choice up to her. When I should have shut it down entirely, I opened myself up to letting her decide.

In the moment, it seemed like the perfect plan. If I show up and her door is dark, I walk away. Easy.

But what if it's not? What if I walk through that door? There will be no coming back from that.

I let out a long sigh and rub both hands down my face.

I am so fucked.

If that light is on, and I go inside, I'm fucked. If that light is on, and I manage to talk myself out of going inside, I'm still fucked.

But the light could be off. I should be praying right now that the light is off. I try to summon a prayer, but it doesn't come. Finally, the suspense of the moment is too much for me to bear.

"I'm gonna head out, you guys. Happy birthday, James. See you all at work tomorrow. I want to see well-rested, well-hydrated cooks by the afternoon, got it?"

Good natured groans and complaints mix with the goodbyes, and I'm grinning by the time I make it through the door of the kitchen. I have a great crew this year.

I only hope I still have their respect after tonight.

# *Rule #11*

## YOU CAN'T TAKE IT BACK

### REINA

I want to say that I agonized over the porch light decision for hours, weighing the pros and cons, before making a decision, but that would be a flat-out lie. I turned that light on the second I got home at three in the afternoon. You couldn't even tell it was on with the midday sun glaring down, but I didn't care.

I may have even checked it periodically throughout the evening to make sure the bulb hadn't burned out. It wasn't until darkness fell, and I could monitor its brightness through my closed blinds that I was able to relax into my bed.

It's nearly midnight, hours after I gave up on hearing a knock at my door when it comes. I've been drifting in and out of sleep, but with the nap I took earlier, as well as my uncomfortable staff apartment mattress, with its loose springs and sagging center, deep rest has been escaping me.

The first knock is so soft, I almost convince myself I imagined it. Then a few sharper raps come, and I'm out of bed in an instant.

*Oh. My. God. Is this actually happening?*

I force myself to look surprised as I open it a crack. "Dom?"

He's leaning on the railing of the porch, looking smolderingly handsome in dark jeans and a tight black tee. His muscular chest and arms, usually kept hidden under a chef jacket, are on full display.

When my eyes finally leave his pecs and drift upward, I find him giving me a knowing smirk. "See something you like?"

The question is so unexpected, especially coming from my boss, that my mouth drops open. "I...I..." I stutter, unable to think of anything to say for a moment. Then, my mind snaps back online. "You came."

"Don't look too surprised," he says with a twitch of a smile, glancing up at my porch light.

"I didn't go to the party," I say stupidly, so nervous I'm sure it shows.

"I know you didn't. Like a good girl." His hand cups the side of my face, his thumb tracing my bottom lip.

*Oh, god.*

Those words...his touch...send a flutter through me, and I nearly gasp for breath.

Dom notices, of course, his smile widening. "Are you going to let me in, or am I going to stand out here on the patio all night for everyone to see?"

"Oh, yes, of course." I stand back, opening the door wide.

Dom strolls into my apartment. As I close the door and lean against it, I'm unsure of what to do. In my fantasy, he just throws me down on the bed and tears my clothes off. There isn't much discussion. Now that he's standing in the middle of my tiny living room, looking around at my scattered clothing and unpacked suitcases, I'm terrified.

"Nice place you got here."

I search his voice for any of the nerves I feel, but I come up lacking. "Thanks. It's yours, I guess."

His eyes snap to mine at that comment, and for a moment, I worry I've said something wrong, calling out the fact that he's

85

the owner of this place and bringing attention to our severe power imbalance.

But he just smiles slyly and takes a step toward where I still stand, cowering against the front door. "And everything in it?"

He's flirting, and I want to flirt back, but I'm so nervous that I can barely make the words come out. "Well, the bed and the tables and the chairs are yours, I guess."

"What else?" He's slowly moving toward me, looking up and down my body. I can almost feel the heat radiating off him. One step more and he'll be touching me.

I know what he wants me to say, but I just can't make myself say it. "The lamps?" I squeak out instead.

His face is serious now as his eyes darken and roam down my neckline. "How about that adorable blush, Reina?" The way he says my name makes my knees weak. "Is that blush mine?"

"Y-Yes."

He takes the last step and crushes his chest against mine. One shift in either direction, and my nipples will graze across those rock-hard pecs through my thin tank top. I can barely breathe, and I feel my heart racing.

"What else?" he asks in his coarse whisper.

Slowly, I reach down and take one of his hands in my own. His skin feels so warm to the touch, his fingers calloused from years of kitchen work. I take his palm and lay it flat against my pounding heart. "This."

It's the right move.

His lips find mine in an instant, pressing my head back against the door as I continue to hold his hand against my chest. I close my eyes and part my lips as his tongue slides across them, brushing against mine.

Memories of the encounter in his office flash through my mind, the way he gripped my pussy and spanked me until I came, and my knees start to go weak as liquid heat swells between my legs. I press my hips forward and find that he's just as aroused as I am.

I boldly slide my hips from side to side, rubbing myself back and forth across his erection as he continues to press deeply into my mouth. The hand that's not on my chest slides around, and I feel his grip on my ass. It's still a bit tender, and I take a sharp breath.

Dom breaks his mouth from mine and slides his lips down my neck. "How's your sweet little ass doing?"

"It's a little sore," I admit with a small laugh.

"Hmm. And why is that?"

"Because you...spanked me." I feel the blood rush to my cheeks at the words. As if Dom can feel it as well, he pulls back and looks at my face.

With a sly smile, he presses a soft kiss to each of my pink cheekbones. "And why ever would I do that?"

I'm barely breathing now, held up only by his grip on my behind. "Because I was a bad girl."

The growl that escapes his lips resonates against the skin of my neck. "You were a bad girl, weren't you?"

"Yes."

"But you're a good girl now, right?"

"Yes, Daddy." I don't expect the words to come out. I've never in my life said such a thing, even though I've thought it plenty of times since meeting this particular man.

Dom's hips hit mine and press me harder against the door. "Say that again."

"Yes, Daddy," I call out confidently this time, the words acting like a spell and releasing me from the prison I hadn't even known I was in.

The spell works on Dom as well. No sooner has the word *daddy* left my lips than he has me in his hands, lifting me to his body. I wrap my legs around his waist and cling to his neck as he spins and crosses the room.

Finally, reality catches up with my fantasy. Before I know it, he tosses me on my back on the bed.

I stretch my arms above my head and look up at him, waiting

to see what will come next. I can feel the heat between my legs, and I let my knees fall open to the sides, aching for his touch.

"Look at you. Such a beautiful, good girl."

I bite my lip to hold back a scream of impatience. I want him to touch every part of me right now.

Dom takes his time crawling onto the bed, placing one knee on either side of my thighs until he's straddling me, looking down. He looks like a wild man up there, his eyes flashing in the dim lamplight, looking like he can't decide where to start.

I arch my back, bucking my hips up toward his.

"Tell Daddy what you want, love."

*If this is what it takes to get it, I guess I'll ask.*

"I want you to fuck me."

The response is immediate. He leans down and grips my chin in his hand, bringing his face close to mine. I can smell whiskey on his breath as he stares into my eyes. He's not smiling now. "Filthy fucking words coming out of my sweet girl's mouth."

I bite my lip and wait. It's clear I said something wrong. I want him to tell me how to fix it. It takes everything to hold back the tears.

"Why don't you find a way to ask me nicely for what you want?"

"P-please fuck me?"

With a growl, Dom is off of me, turning me roughly over onto my stomach. He's so strong that it feels like it takes him no effort at all. Before I know it, he has me on hands and knees. He stands next to where I'm on all fours on the bed. I don't get any warning before the first spank lands.

"Ah!" I cry out, more from surprise than anything.

"I don't want to hear words like that coming out of your mouth. Is that clear?"

*So, so fucking clear.*

I bite back a laugh, grateful he can't see my face.

"You are getting one spank for every letter of that dirty word that came out of your sweet lips. F," he spanks me hard, right in the center. I grit my teeth and bear it.

"U." A spank on the left cheek.

"C." A spank on the right.

"K." This time his hand drops a bit lower, landing his slap right on my aching pussy. I nearly scream at the contact I've been dying for.

"Oh, you like that, do you?"

"Yes."

"Do you think you know how to get more of what you like?"

"Yes."

"Hmm. Okay. I'll give you one more try." His hands run up the backs of my thighs until they reach the edge of my short shorts, then over my smarting cheeks. I can barely think over the screaming between my legs.

*Have I ever been so turned on in my life?*

"Please, Daddy...I want you to take my shorts off. Please." I throw another please in for good measure.

He chuckles behind me, hands still inside my shorts. "That was much better. Do you promise not to use such filthy language again?"

"Yes." I hope I can remember. Working in restaurants my whole adult life, I haven't had much reason to watch my mouth.

*Girl, you've got a hot fucking reason now.*

Dom's hands slide out of my shorts and grip the elastic waistband. He pulls them over my round butt in one smooth motion. The growl he lets out at the sight of me bared before him is so animalistic, I quiver in anticipation.

Once he tosses the shorts to the side, he takes his place right behind me. I can feel his erection rubbing between my legs as he stands on the floor, gripping my hips. "What's next?"

"I...I would love it if you got on your knees. Please."

Dom strokes my ass. "My girl's ordering me to get on my knees, huh?" He doesn't sound displeased, but I panic.

"Not ordering. Asking...nicely...please." I add a little extra sweetness to the last word, tilting my hips a bit more, so I know my wet pussy points right up to his face.

He takes the bait, just like I knew he would. I can feel him lowering himself until his face is level with my wetness. His warm breath blowing against my clit nearly sends me over the edge.

"P-please."

"Please what, little one?"

"Please lick me?"

It's like I let a wild animal off his leash. Dom's tongue lands down on my wet entrance, pressing so deep inside of me that I moan and fall to my elbows. When he slides that marvelous tongue all the way forward and circles my clit, I cry out and buck my hips into his face.

I can feel him smile against me as he continues to lick, adding his fingers to the game. One, then two fingers slide inside me, working their way up and forward until they're massaging the spot in my body that I thought no one would ever find but me.

"Oh my god, Daddy," The word falls freely out of my mouth now, as if I've been screaming them my whole life.

I've been thinking about this moment for days. Touching myself. Fantasizing. I'm going to explode into his mouth in mere seconds. As if Dom can tell I'm close, he picks up the pace, pressing his fingers deeper, making his tongue sharp as it flits back and forth across my clit.

My forehead slams into the mattress as I crash into release, pressing my body harder against his face as waves of pleasure break one after another. Dom continues to lick and stroke me as I come, humming his approval into my flesh, the vibration prolonging my orgasm.

When I'm finally still, he slides his fingers out of me and grips my hips once more. I feel him rise to his feet behind me.

"You came like such a good girl. What do you say to your Daddy?"

I turn my head to the side so that he can hear me loud and

clear. "Thank you." It feels so good to know I have the right answer to his question.

"I need more of you, little one."

I press my hips up and back in response. There's nothing I want more in the world at this moment than to feel his cock pounding inside me.

"But I want to see your eyes for our first time."

*Our first time? That sounds like there will be a second time. And a third...*

I'm breathless as he once again flips me over as if I weigh nothing. I stare up at him, taken aback by his beauty. His muscular form nearly glows in the soft light of my lamp, and I follow the path of soft chest hair all the way down his hard stomach to the chiseled V disappearing into his pants.

Maybe it's just the chemicals from my orgasm still lingering, but I'm pretty sure this is the most gorgeous man alive.

*And he's all mine.*

And with that thought, I'm officially getting way ahead of myself. I don't have time to consider the implications of this night together, however, because he's unbuttoning those pants and slipping them off.

Dom is naked underneath, as if he was anticipating this. The clatter of his jeans and belt hitting my hardwood floor can't distract me from the sight of him, naked before me.

I hear the familiar tear of a condom wrapper and hold my breath as he reaches down to take his cock in hand. Long, thick and rock hard, Dom rolls the rubber down his length never once taking his eyes off me.

He leans over me, stripping my tank top roughly over my head and attacking my breasts with his tongue and teeth. I cry out, spreading my legs even wider to give him room to climb over me.

After a thorough sucking of each nipple, Dom raises his head and looks me right in the eye. "Are you ready to get fucked, baby girl?"

I can't speak the word, but I pray I'm allowed to nod my head enthusiastically when he asks.

"Say it, little one," he growls.

"I'm ready."

"Good fucking girl." He sits back on his heels, taking his massive cock in hand once more.

My eyes go wide at this close-up view of him, totally naked. He is chiseled like a god, his muscular thighs leading my eyes right between them to that lusciously long cock. My mouth waters at the thought of running my tongue down that shaft.

Dom rubs his tip at my entrance, circling it around in the wetness from my orgasm. "You are so wet, baby girl. Who made you like this?"

"You did, Daddy."

How easily we fell into this role play. I don't let my mind wander into the reality of what we're saying just now. There will be plenty of time for that later.

All I can focus on now is the fat tip of his cock, slowly breaching my body and pressing an inch inside. I tilt my hips to allow him to slide easier, and he takes my cue, pressing deeper until he's all the way inside my body.

The stretch of my skin around his cock feels so perfect. So full. So...everything. I'm so wrapped up in the moment that I don't properly prepare myself for when he starts pumping.

I can feel his tip slide up and down my inner walls, the drag of it in my tight pussy is the greatest sensation of my life. I need so much more. And I need it now.

"Harder."

Dom grips my hips and obeys, pulling out nearly all the way and then slamming himself back into my tightness. I cry out as his body hits mine over and over. My back arches off the bed, and my eyes squeeze shut.

"Look at me, little one."

I open them and take him in. His eyes are nearly black with

pleasure, lips curled in a snarl as he attacks my willing body again and again.

"You like it when I fuck you like this?"

"Yes, Daddy." I don't recognize my own voice as it comes out, sharp and raspy.

"You are so adorable, sweet girl."

Something about the softness in his voice and the sweet term of endearment he uses while fucking my brains out sends me over the edge once more. I buck my hips forward to get more friction against his body as my eyes squeeze shut, and I cry out.

"I'm coming!"

Dom moans in pleasure as I spasm against him, pounding harder and harder. As I come, I can hear his own breath catch. I open my eyes just in time to watch his gorgeous six-pack abs contract as he releases into me with a few hard thrusts.

When his body stills, he's leaning over me, gasping for air.

The idea that I have as much of an effect on this man as he does on me makes my chest swell with a feeling I can't quite name.

*Pride?*

Whatever it is, I want more of it. All of it.

I grasp his shoulders and pull him down to the bed beside me, curling as his cock slides out of me.

"Dom." It's all I can think of to say in the moment.

My use of his name seems to break the spell. His eyes open, and he's staring right into mine. Into me. I almost shy away from it, unsure if I'm ready for this man to know me so deeply.

As if he can tell I'm about to bolt, Dom places a hand behind my head, stroking his thumb down my cheek. "So beautiful."

I close my eyes and feel myself blush.

Dom lets out a soft laugh. "I'll never get enough of that blush."

I open my eyes as he rolls off the bed. I watch him walk into the bathroom and close the door halfway. When he comes back, he sits on the edge of the bed, and I curl toward him.

"I'm not sure what I expected when I came here tonight, Reina, but this wasn't it."

I let out a small laugh of surprise. "You showed up on my doorstep at midnight, and you weren't expecting to end up in my bed?"

It's Dom's turn to look a bit sheepish. "Well, I expected that, yes." His look turns serious, as if he's trying to see into my mind. "I wasn't expecting you to be so...perfect."

Unsure of how to respond, I roll over and sit up. My tank top is beside me on the bed, so I slip it on and stand, searching for my shorts.

"Reina." His voice stops me as I pull my shorts up.

I turn and look at him, waiting.

"I don't do this often. I mean, I've never done this." He motions between the two of us, glancing down at my tousled sheets. "With a waitress before."

I'm definitely glad to hear that I'm not just another server who fell for his charms, but something about his tone has me hesitating.

"I just don't want you to get the wrong idea."

I roll my eyes and turn away. "It's fine, Dom. I'm a grown-up. You can leave."

He's on his feet in an instant, rushing toward me. "That's not what I meant at all." He grabs me by the shoulders and turns me around to face him. I avoid his stare for as long as I can, but he lifts my chin so I have to look at him. "I just...there's a lot of pressure on me in the restaurant. I have so much riding on this season." He hesitates, and I can feel him deciding how much he wants to tell me. "I just can't be seen as a chef who gets involved with waitresses. You know?"

I take a deep, steadying breath to hold off the tears I feel creeping in. "Sure, yeah. No worries. I mean, I'm brand new here, and I really like it. I don't want people to think that when I move up it's only because I was sleeping with the boss. Honestly, there's more on the line for me here than for you."

I struck the man speechless, and I nearly smile when I see his mouth hanging open momentarily.

"You, you want to move up at the restaurant? I mean, yes, of course, I know what you mean. This could look really bad for you. I hadn't even thought of that."

He looks genuinely taken aback in this moment, and I'm reminded of a word he keeps using for me.

*Adorable.*

"It's okay, Dom. This will be our little secret. It was a lot of fun. When I see you at work, I'll just smile and go on with my day."

"No, no, no." He's shaking his head vehemently, holding me by both shoulders now. "That's not what I meant either. I don't want this to stop...what we have together...unless you do."

After a pause, I shake my head too. No point in lying now. There's nothing I want less in the world than for this to stop.

Relief floods his features. "Okay, so we just play it cool and see where it goes. If anything bad happens, I will take all the responsibility. You are safe at work, I promise."

Even though I barely know this man, I find myself believing him. I do feel very safe in his arms. And who am I kidding? I would say just about anything right now to get fucked like that again.

*I mean, screwed. Not fucked. I wonder if screwed is a dirty word?*

My amusement must be written across my face because Dom relaxes and smiles. "What's so funny, sweet girl?"

I bite my lip shyly and look down at my feet. He raises my chin to meet his face once more. "I was just trying to figure out which words are dirty," I lift my gaze and look directly into his deep hazel eyes, "and which ones were okay for a good girl to say, Daddy." My tone is drop-dead sexy.

Desire spreads over his face. "What fun would it be if I just told you, little one?" He lifts one of my hands and brings it to his lips, placing a soft kiss on my knuckles. "You're going to have to figure that out for yourself, one punishment at a time."

After Dom leaves, I lay awake for a long time, playing the scene over and over in my head. It was all so unexpected, just like he said, but so freaking hot.

Who would have ever thought that I would get off calling a guy daddy? I never called my own father that—thank God—and wouldn't really say I was someone with daddy issues.

There's just something about Dom that inspires it in me. He is such a daddy. And I know he knows it. Hearing Dom's words play back in my mind, *you're such a good girl*, is nearly enough to make me climax. He knows just what he's doing, and that's fine with me.

Your daddy kink is my daddy kink, I guess. Sharing is caring, am I right?

Whatever this is, I know I'm already in too deep to walk away. I've only known this man a few days, but I'm willing to put my entire new life on the line for him.

I only hope it isn't a huge mistake.

# Rule #12

## PLAY IT COOL

### REINA

I thought I was nervous showing up to work before, but this morning is a million times worse. I take extra time on my appearance, of course, making sure I look my absolute best.

I only got a little bit more sleep last night than I did the night before, but I didn't have anything to drink, so I know I can keep it together.

At least, that's what I think until I see him.

Dom is getting a cup of coffee when I walk into the server station after putting my bag down in the back room. When he turns to face me, I feel my face explode into flames.

He laughs and shakes his head. "You're going to have to play it cooler than that, sweet girl." His hushed tone is a balm to my nerves, words spoken just for me as he passes by without a touch and heads to his office.

My shift actually goes really well. The breakfast manager, Sylvia, tells me over and over how happy she is to have me on her team. If she only knew how overqualified I actually am to be serving breakfast. She's damn lucky to have me.

All of my experience working at a swanky Michelin-starred property has instilled in me a keen eye for detail, and a deep knowledge of what works and what doesn't. I know it's not my place to be pointing out problems with service in my first week, though, so I keep my observations to myself.

The people on the a.m. shift are a breath of fresh air. After my years in high-end dinner service, I'm pleasantly surprised every day to be greeted with such fresh-faced, genuine smiles. The servers are mostly working their first waitressing jobs, some having moved up from hosting, some from other customer service positions. They're so enthusiastic about everything, it almost makes me feel like I'm new again as well, seeing things through their eyes.

Not once have I heard any of them complain, make fun of a person, or critique a dish from the menu. They happily help each other with table clearing and after-shift cleanup.

Deep down in my heart, I know that the industry will break most of them, leaving them jaded, sarcastic, and too cool to enjoy the simple pleasures of the job. For now, however, they're untouched, and I get to enjoy their innocence. I think some of it may be rubbing off on me.

The cooks on the a.m. shift are no different. They all have plenty of experience on restaurant lines, but most of them arrived here from more casual places. They can see the job for the incredible opportunity it is, rather than a chore they have to show up to every day.

The specials they create are fun and whimsical, and they work together to make them shine before jotting them down on scrap paper for one of the servers to add to the chalkboard. Even just a simple plate of eggs and toast will come through the kitchen pass looking like someone really took the time to make it perfect.

And that is the biggest difference between my job now and my job in Chicago. The people I work with here at Raft fully focus on the person receiving the plate. They want them to have a great breakfast, or coffee, or cup of tea. The high-end dinner servers I worked with in Chicago only thought about themselves.

It's only been a week since I started this job, but already my heart aches knowing it will be taken from me. I don't know how long I'll be able to hide the fact that I should be running the dinner shift, not playing waitress at breakfast. I probably could have made it through the whole season if I didn't have the hawk-like eyes of Chef Dom on me during almost every minute of my shift, but that ship has sailed.

As I'm sitting at the bar during the break between breakfast and lunch, drinking coffee and enjoying a plate of eggs, Sylvia leans on the bar next to me.

"Did you have a chance to study that menu yet?"

Damn! I completely forgot to even take the thing out of my bag. I have been awfully distracted, but I know that's not a good enough excuse. Luckily, I have years of culinary experience to fall back on, and I know I can probably slide through some questions about the breakfast dishes.

"Yeah, I did it last night."

"Good." Sylvia smiles at me, her relief clear. "Because Chef Dominic wants to see you in his office."

I don't know what expression sneaks onto my face before I can catch myself, but it must be bad because Sylvia laughs. "It'll be okay. I know he can seem intimidating, but he just wants what's best for the restaurant. I've already told him what a good server you are, and he knows better than to mess with my staff." Her tone is motherly, soothing. If only she knew what was really making my heart race.

I nod and try to smile, knowing my cheeks are probably still bright red. "Should I go now?"

"Best not to keep him waiting."

# *Rule #13*

## IF SHE CALLS YOUR BLUFF...CALL HERS

### DOMINIC

"Enter." I hardly look up from my computer as the door cracks open. I'm expecting one of my prep cooks to be bringing me a taste of whatever they're working on, so I'm pleasantly surprised to see bouncy auburn curls, a sparkling smile, and adorable pink cheeks peek around the corner.

"You wanted to see me?" Reina asks, all business.

This is the first time we've been alone at work since spending the night together in her bed, and I wasn't sure how it would go. My biggest fear, of course, is that she'll be too obvious, too clingy, and demand too much of me in front of others, giving away our little secret.

By the nervous look on that adorable face, however, I get the feeling Reina has chosen the opposite route. As if playing daddy's baby girl in bed wasn't enough, it seems that she also wants to play chef's little waitress.

I close my laptop lid and sit back in my chair. "Yes. Come in. Close the door behind you, please."

She does what I ask and then stands with her back to the

closed door. I don't think she's actually afraid of me, but she looks apprehensive now that we're alone in the office. I can hardly blame her—there are over a dozen male cooks in the prep kitchen just on the other side of that door, and she knows I'm not scared to bend her over in here.

"How was service?"

"It went really well. You have a good crew on brunch."

Something about the way she appraises the staff catches my interest. "Where did you work before coming to Faraday Island?"

"Oh, a little place in Chicago," she replies as if I wouldn't be interested to know the name. This conversation just got a whole lot more interesting.

"Just some little place, huh? Nowhere special?"

Reina shrugs and bites her lip. I want to push, but I don't want to scare her off. There's something going on between us that is fragile. I don't want to break it over a stupid restaurant name. If she's not ready to share about her past, that's fine with me.

*I can certainly relate.*

"Did you get any studying done last night?"

The flush in her cheeks is reward enough for my changing the subject. I can't help but grin at the way she squirms under my question, not wanting to admit to working her whole shift without studying the menu like I told her to, but knowing damn well that I'm aware how she spent last night.

"A little."

"So you are ready for a quiz on the menu?"

"Sure."

I lean back in my chair, folding my arms across my chest. If she's not going to back down, admit that she didn't read it, and ask for more time, I'm certainly willing to call her bluff.

"Please, have a seat then." I gesture to the chair across from me. Reina sits down. She can tell we're playing some kind of a game, and she's waiting to learn the rules.

*Hell, I'm making them up as I go.*

I have exactly zero experience with secret work relationships.

"I'm going to go over the menu, and for every question you
answer correctly, you get a point. For every question you get
incorrect, I get a point." My cock twitches at the thought of the
game I have in mind for later, once we know who has how many
points.

"Are you keeping score, or shall I?" she challenges me.

I toss a pad of paper in her direction and slide a pen beside it.
"You can."

I watch as she writes R and D at the top of the page and
draws a line down the center. Then she sits back and looks at me
expectantly.

*Girl might be calling my bluff after all.*

I grab my own copy of the current brunch menu and scan for
potential challenges. I grin as I spot one. "What are the six ways
guests can order eggs?"

"Easy, medium, hard, sunny side up, scrambled, poached."

She makes a mark under her name without even waiting for
me to proclaim her correct.

I'm going to have to try harder.

"What does it mean to have something sous vide?"

"Sous vide is a low-temperature water cooking method."

"And what sets it apart from any other cooking method?
Poaching eggs versus sous vide, for instance."

"The low temperature and longer cook time results in more
tender foods, and it's also possible to get the egg to a precise
cooked state that is difficult to achieve in a pan or in boiling
water."

I sit back in my chair and consider her answer.

"Was that one question or two?" she asks.

Her little smirk could not be cuter.

"Two."

Reina gives herself two points.

"Awfully sure of yourself."

"I told you I studied."

"Which wine would you suggest to a guest ordering a classic Benedict?"

"I would suggest the French Crémant d'Alsace but let them know that if it was my breakfast, I would choose the fresh orange juice mimosa."

Reina gives herself another point without waiting for me to answer.

"How would you prepare a cortado for a guest?"

"A cortado, while not technically listed on our brunch menu, would be prepared with two shots of espresso and equal parts steamed milk. Like a tiny little latte."

She puts a mark under her name.

"How quickly should food be taken out to a table when it comes up in the window?"

She bites her lip. I may have stumped her on this one. The answer to that question isn't on the menu.

"Well," she starts. "I've been trained here to take food to a table the moment it hits the window. Although, technically, I would say that the food should wait if all members of the party aren't seated, especially if there are only two guests. I find this practice especially troubling with eggs. I can't imagine coming back from the restroom to find my eggs getting cold on the table without me."

"Excuse me?" The words come out sharper than I expected them to, but her answer surprises me. To not only be telling me that the way we do it here is incorrect, but that she knows a better way—in her first week—should be infuriating.

But, deep down, I know she's right.

What she's suggesting is how it works at dinner. No one would ever take a course out if a guest left the table for any reason. We let the rules slide a bit at brunch. It's a more casual service, and we just try to get the plates out as quickly as possible.

"I mean...I just..." she stutters, backtracking quickly. "Just based on what I've learned in the past."

"At the little place in Chicago where you used to work."

Reina nods and swallows hard.

"That's a point for me," I say.

She looks up sharply, but decides not to argue, even though I can see the flare of injustice in her eyes. She makes a mark under my name.

"What's the tally?"

"Five for me, one for you."

"I wonder if that means you won."

Reina narrows her eyes at me. "I clearly won. Or passed. Or whatever it is we're doing here."

This girl is a firecracker who is not going to let me get away with any bullshit. And I love it.

*As long as she keeps saying "Yes, Daddy" in the bedroom.*

"What's your next day off?"

"Saturday."

Impossible. "After that?"

"The following Tuesday."

"Perfect." It will be easy for me to get away early on Monday night. "Do you know where my house is?"

Reina shakes her head.

"Okay, well you have some time to figure it out without looking suspicious. I expect you on my doorstep at nine p.m. Monday night. Bring your five points. You'll need them."

The flush and excitement paint her cheeks pink. My now-hard cock begs to throw her against the closed door and show her what I can do with one measly point, but I need to keep it together.

I agreed to keep her safe at work, and I can't do anything that could damage her reputation.

*Or my own.*

"Okay." She stands, clearly feeling dismissed. I should let her walk out the door, maintain some semblance of professionalism, but I just can't.

I reach her just as her hand touches the doorknob. My face goes straight into the crook of her neck like a moth to a flame. I take a deep inhale of her delicious scent and fight the urge to bite her.

"I need an office with locking doors," I growl into her skin.

Reina laughs. "I'd be in trouble then." Her tone is sultry and low.

Maybe my pulsing hard-on will win this battle after all.

"You're in trouble now, sweetheart."

"What did I do to displease you, Daddy?" she whispers.

"I know you didn't study that menu. And I know there's something about your work experience you're not telling me."

Reina whimpers as I press my hips into her ass, my cock jutting between her cheeks over her tight work skirt.

"And you just walk around the restaurant with this ass." I grind into her for emphasis. "Like you don't even know what it does to me. Do you know how hard it is to focus on work knowing you're in my dining room in this tight little skirt?"

She's panting now, wiggling her ass against me as I grind.

"And now you come in here and get me all worked up, and I can't do anything about it. I have to wait so damn long to sink my dick into your sweet pussy again."

"Why do you have to wait?" She's breathless, clearly as turned on as I am.

"I'm trying to be professional." I grind the words out against her body.

Reina laughs, the soft, tinkling sound melodic and light. "You're so professional."

"Fuck, girl." I can't take it. "Go into the staff bathroom in the changing room now. Close the door but don't lock it. You better be just as wet as I know you are now when I get in there." Using all of my strength, I pull away from her and walk back across the room. The sooner she gets out of here, the sooner I can have my reward. "Go."

With one last sultry look tossed in my direction, Reina opens the door and disappears, closing it behind her.

I sit on the edge of my desk and wait five agonizing minutes before storming out of my office and slamming the door behind me. The crew of prep cooks all glance up nervously, wondering which of them has caused my displeasure, each of them trying not to be noticed and called out. I pass by them without a word and disappear down the hallway.

When I enter the staff changing room, it's empty. I can see the light through the crack under the closed bathroom door. I'm out of my mind with want and need for her. Knowing she's just a few feet away, ready to take me, is nearly my undoing.

I cross the room and turn the handle. It's unlocked.

Reina is pressed against the far wall, hands in her apron pockets. Her cheeks are flushed, and her dark eyes are giving me the all-clear.

I lock the door and cross the room to meet her.

Our lips meet in a kiss so passionate, it feels like we've been separated for months, not hours. I can taste coffee on her tongue and smell the subtle scent of vanilla in her hair. I fist my hand in that long, flowing hair and bring her with me to the counter. I spin her to face the mirror, pulling her shirt up roughly to expose a red lace bra.

The growl that escapes my lips is automatic. I cup a lace-covered breast with one rough hand as the other pushes her skirt up. My fingers find the outline of the matching lace thong that runs along her wet slit. I slip under the fabric and find her so ready for me, I can barely stand it.

I wiggle her tight skirt the rest of the way up around her hips, until I have her smooth, round ass bared before me. Rubbing my hand in a circle around both cheeks, I press her torso down onto the counter with my other hand.

"You better keep it down, got it?" My voice is hushed but firm.

I hear her whimper out an agreement from her place face down on the counter.

In a near manic state, I bring my palm down on her behind with a sharp clap.

Reina cries out quietly, and I glance nervously at the door. If someone was on the other side of it, would they be able to hear everything that was going on in here?

I reach down and turn the sink on full blast just to be safe.

"Do you know why you're bent over the counter right now, naughty girl?"

Reina shakes her head vigorously.

I land two quick smacks on her bottom before answering. "You are supposed to be a good girl at work. You know that, right?"

"Yes." I can just make out her muffled reply.

"And yet you stroll into my office full of sass, trying to tell me how to run my restaurant. What did you think was going to happen?"

"I didn't think."

Slap, slap.

Reina cries out again, but leans into it this time, arching her back to give me a full view of the paradise waiting just below her red, round cheeks. I bare my teeth at the sight of her eagerness.

Without warning, I lean down and take a big, hard bite of one of her sweet cheeks. The move earns me a little shriek and a laugh.

"Oh, you think this is funny, do you?"

Slap, slap.

One smack lands on each cheek as Rena shakes her head again.

"Not funny. I'm so sorry. I'll never sass you at work again."

I can't help but grin at her answer.

*This woman is going to drive me crazy.*

I land a hard smack and let my hand linger, sliding over her tender skin and down between her legs.

"Are you on birth control?" It's not very smooth, but I have to ask. I don't carry condoms in my work pants.

"Of course."

Before I know it, my cock is in my hand, the smug bastard knowing it won the game.

I kick her feet out to the sides and pull her upper body up by her hair so I can see her face in the mirror. I only look away from her begging eyes for a moment so I can seat myself at her entrance, and then I press inside, gently the first time, and then harder as I coat my cock in her nectar.

I hold her hips and watch with barely restrained awe as she takes my cock, her beautiful breasts bouncing in the mirror with every thrust.

"God, fuck, girl. Look what you made me do."

"Sorry, Daddy." She doesn't sound a bit sorry.

"This can't happen every day, little one." My thrusts spin out of control, harder and harder. Reina takes it with muffled moans of pleasure.

This woman will be my undoing.

"You are going to have to find a way to be less sexy at work. Got it?"

"How shall I do that?"

Her breasts bounce so perfectly, I want to bite them.

"Don't call me Daddy at work for one thing."

"Yes, sir." Teetering on the edge of orgasm and still managing to sass me.

"You going to come for Daddy, dirty girl?"

"Yes!"

"Fuck, Reina." I can't hold back a second longer. As I watch her face contort with pleasure, I empty into her, my thrusts completely losing any sense of rhythm.

Again and again, I spill myself into her tight pussy, and she takes it all. When I can't move anymore, she gives my still-hard cock a little squeeze with her internal muscles, sending a jolt of electricity through my body.

"Girl."

"Yes, Daddy?"

I can't answer, I just rest my forehead against her back and pant. When I finally catch my breath, I pull out and slam the faucet down to turn the water off. Grabbing a paper towel from the dispenser, I gently clean her up before wiping myself off and pulling my pants back on.

I lean against the back wall and watch Reina straighten her thong, her skirt, and finally, her top.

She grabs another paper towel, but I lurch forward and take it from her.

"No."

She looks at me, confused. "But I—"

"You're going to go out there and work the rest of lunch with my cum dripping down your thighs." Just the thought of it makes me hard enough to go again. I consider it but decide it's not the best idea. We've already been in here too long.

"Go. Tell Sylvia I want you trained to bartend for lunch. When you feel me dripping out of you, I want you to think of how hard you just made me come."

She's flushed and embarrassed and so fucking gorgeous. I watch as she pulls a tube of lip gloss from her apron pocket and applies it in the mirror. Our eyes meet in the reflection, and she bats her lashes at me.

"Get to work."

"Yes, sir."

And she leaves me there, leaning against the wall, completely incapacitated. My mind is reeling with images of the things I'd like to do to her. Ways I'd like to fuck her. Things I'd like to order her to do to me.

How on earth am I supposed to get any work done?

With a sigh, I compose myself and head back to the kitchen. There are still a few hours before dinner service starts, and I need to check in with my cooks. Poor bastards are likely to get the short end of my frustration this afternoon.

# Rule #14

## EVERYONE'S WATCHING

### REINA

On Saturday morning, I wake to knocking at my door. I lay in bed for a moment after my eyes open, groggy from lack of sleep, and wonder who could possibly be knocking so early.

I climb out of bed and toss on pajamas, making it to the front door just as another loud knock lands.

"Okay, okay," I grumble as I pull the door open a crack and lean out.

I'm expecting to see Sarah there, or maybe Charles, but it's a strange man in a work polo. He's got a mattress propped up next to him on the porch.

"Can I help you?"

"This is apartment 202, and you're Reina Hansen?"

"Yes," I say, eyeing the mattress beside him. I take a step back and open the door the rest of the way. The warm, bright, tropical morning is glorious, even in my sleep-deprived state.

"We've got a delivery, and we'll be removing the old one." The man glances behind me into the apartment, no doubt taking in the disheveled state of affairs.

I consider his words and finally process their meaning.

*He's delivering me a new mattress?*

There's only one explanation for why I would have this kind of delivery showing up after one of the owners of the resort spent an hour in my bed.

*My bed wasn't good enough for him.*

No, no. I correct myself quickly.

*He got to lie in one of the beds he provides for his staff and found it sorely inadequate.*

Still, accepting a gift like this from Dom changes things. It was one thing for us to have gotten together as boss and employee. It's quite another for me to be accepting special treatment like gifts because of it.

"So, you gonna let us in? Or are we going to stand out here with this mattress all morning?"

"Oh! Yes, sorry, I just woke up…" I turn and walk back into the apartment, kicking my things to the sides of the room to clear a path for the men to enter. I quickly strip the sheets and blankets off the old mattress and pile them on my desk chair. "Come in."

I'm hardly in a position to turn down a beautiful, brand-new, pillow-top mattress. Not when my old one is an ancient, sagging, brownish abomination.

*I'll accept this one thing, and that'll be it.*

It's not even a gift, really. He still owns the damn thing. He's just allowing me to use it. And himself, probably.

Yes, he did this for himself.

The thought of spending another night on that old mattress was too much for him, so he bought himself a new one.

I'm still doing mental gymnastics over the whole thing as the men enter my tiny apartment and make quick work of swapping out the mattress. As I close the door behind them, I can't help but squeal with joy and take a running leap onto the gorgeous new bed.

Even though it still feels a bit like I earned this gift with my body, I'm too happy right now to feel exploited.

I laugh to myself at the thought as I remake my bed.

There are a lot of things about this new situation with Dom that I'm unsure about, and the possibility of gifts and special treatment is one that hasn't even had time to cross my mind.

I don't get long to think about it, sprawled on my decadent mattress, before another knock hits my door, followed by the sound of it opening.

"Girl!"

It's Sarah, and she's incredulous.

"I saw you getting a new mattress delivered and couldn't believe it. How on earth did you pull this off? Where did they even get it from? There's hardly a mattress store on the island."

Shit.

How am I going to explain this to her? And she raises a fair question. Where did Dom procure a mattress in only a few days on a tiny island in the middle of the Pacific?

"I complained to maintenance because I had a spring come through the fabric, and they said they had this extra one from the hotel available." I don't like spewing lies, especially not to my friend, but what else am I supposed to do?

"Well, I'm going to submit a maintenance request immediately. I've been sleeping on sprung springs for two years now."

There's a hint of injustice in her voice that I can't ignore. I feel like even worse of a friend.

*Would I even have told anyone if the delivery guys hadn't been spotted?*

I know the answer to that question easily. No.

As I watch her jealously eyeing my new bed, I make a snap decision. "They told me they're all getting replaced. They just had a...hangup with the delivery." It's another lie, but one I'm pretty certain I can make come true.

If I have this new power, why not use it for good?

"Really? That's amazing!" Sarah's on her feet now, jumping with excitement. "I'm going to go tell everyone."

She runs out of the apartment, leaving me wallowing in regret. Not ten minutes ago I was ready to draw the line about special treatment, now I have to ask Dom to buy everyone on staff a new mattress.

*What am I doing?!*

The one thing I know for sure right now—I need a cup of coffee.

I should stop at the staff cantina for a cup, but I'm craving espresso. I glance at my phone and see that it's nearly ten. The breakfast rush should be dying down by now, I rationalize with myself before heading down the hill.

It's not until I reach the gleaming beechwood front doors that I realize I'm going to have to face Dom in there. What will he think about me showing up at work on my day off and distracting him?

It's too late now, the servers have already seen me and waved. I head in and settle myself at the bar.

"Morning, Reina. Nice to see you on your day off."

"I really need a latte."

"Coming right up." Sylvia smiles and heads over to the coffee station.

I pull out my phone and open up my usual apps, preparing to scroll the feeds while I'm logged onto the much faster resort guest Wi-Fi. I hardly have time to process the first meme before a shadow darkens the screen.

"Morning."

Just the one word from him has me blushing uncontrollably. "Morning. You are always here," I say, trying to make a little joke to cover my nerves.

"Not always." The insinuation in his voice does nothing to help my blush.

I shake my head, unable to meet his eye. "I got your gift," I say, my voice low. "Thank you. But everyone else needs one too."

"Excuse me?" Dom is amused by my request, I can tell.

"They all saw the guys bring it in and wondered why I was getting one, and they weren't."

"There's only one bed in the staff building I care about."

"What am I supposed to tell people?" I'm trying to keep my voice low, but I'm growing frustrated. It's hard to have to ask him for this, and he's not making it easier.

"What did you tell them?" He's still amused by the situation, which only makes me more frustrated. This whole thing is his fault—he sent a huge, obvious gift to my apartment and got me in trouble. He should be apologizing right now, not teasing me about getting caught.

"I told them the truth." I say as defiantly as I can, meeting his eye.

"You did not." The laughter in his hushed voice breaks through my resolve, and I can't help but smile.

"No, of course not. I told them maintenance replaced it because a spring busted through."

His amused eyes sparkle down at me.

"And then I told them all the staff mattresses were getting replaced, mine just came early." I'm not sure exactly what I'm expecting from his expression at that statement, but further amusement isn't it. "You're not mad?"

"Why would I be mad?"

"Because now you have to buy, like, a hundred mattresses?"

"I'd buy you anything in the world, Reina. A few mattresses is nothing." He straightens up a bit and rolls his shoulders back. "Although, it was not a simple feat to get that one mattress for you so quickly. The other hundred are going to take more time."

But my mind is stuck on his first statement. *I'd buy you anything in the world, Reina.*

"I'm not...you know..." How to get across what I want to say without sounding like an idiot? Better just go for it, I guess. "I'm not doing *this* so you will buy me things."

"I know. That's what makes me want to buy you things even more."

I feel myself blush at the look he's giving me now, like he wants to throw me on the bar and ravish me.

"I hope you're not harassing my star employee, Dominic."

Sylvia sets down my steaming latte on the bar, causing Dom to have to step back from where he was leaning.

"Not at all, Syl. I was just getting a report on how the a.m. shift is going so far."

"And?" Sylvia looks from me to Dom and then quickly back again. It's amazing how scared people are of this man. He has been nothing but accommodating to me so far.

"And I was telling him how smoothly everything is running," I say quickly.

Sylvia relaxes visibly and smiles. "Well, that has a lot to do with you joining my team, Reina. I'm lucky to have you." She gives Dom another glance before heading out to seat new customers.

"Careful there, superstar. You're going to earn yourself a raise with all that good work you're doing."

"You wouldn't." I smirk at him.

"Try me." Dom gives me one more of those knee-buckling looks before walking back into the kitchen and out of sight.

I'm completely breathless, flustered, and far too turned on to be sitting at the bar at my place of employment. I take a sip of my coffee, relishing its magical soothing abilities.

"If I hadn't just seen that with my own eyes, I never would have believed that Dominic had so many smiles inside of him." Sylvia is beside me again, a heavy tray of cleared plates in her hand. "Whatever that was, keep it up."

"What? Oh, he's just...I mean, he seems nice. Nice enough for a boss, you know. I mean..." I stammer like an idiot, feeling a blush rise on my cheeks.

Sylvia rolls her eyes knowingly and heads toward the dish pit with her tray.

The woman is old enough to have seen everything in this industry, so I'm not surprised she picked up on whatever tension must have been visible in the air between us just now and how flustered I am after a five-minute chat with the head chef.

We are going to have to be a lot more careful.

# *Rule #15*

## NO SLEEPING ON THE JOB

### REINA

> **Dom**
> Hey Reina, it's Dom.

The text beeps just as I'm setting my bag down in my apartment. It's unusual to have such good service inside my place, so I grab for my phone and read the screen, in case I need to reply quickly.

I have no problem with him having my phone number, of course, but I know I haven't given it to him. Living on this island of spotty phone service and in such close proximity, we haven't had the need for phones yet.

> **Me**
> How did you get my number?

I hit send before I consider how rude of a reply it really is.

> **Dom**
> I got it from your employee file.

Dread sinks through my body and pools in my gut. He's been going through my employee file? I guess he has access to it, he is the freaking boss and all, but somehow, I never imagined that he would dig into my personal information.

I take a few deep breaths to calm myself down.

I have nothing to worry about in that file. My résumé conveniently skips over the fancy restaurant in Chicago where I was helping the chef win the very award Dom is trying to win, so he wouldn't have found out.

Just as I let my fear of him finding out go, a new feeling rushes in to replace it.

Guilt.

I could be helping Dom with his award season prep. I've been through plenty of them...and won the awards. I know I could offer some suggestions about changes to the restaurant service that would take the place over the top.

But I don't want to. Even if it would get both Dom and I closer to our goals.

I've spent plenty of nights thinking about the fact that dinner servers probably make more than all of the a.m. staff combined. I've done the math, estimating how quickly I could have this debt paid off with huge dinner tips.

But my gut thinks it's a bad idea.

I know some of my newfound happiness stems from the crazy hot secret affair with my boss, but there's no denying that some of it comes from my job.

I love the breakfast shift.

Everything about it makes me feel so light—a stark contrast to the dead weight I was carrying around every single day of my career in Chicago.

I made my way up through that restaurant chasing the money and respect, trying desperately to make myself fit in with the suave, cool people who were running that world, and look what I have to show for it. A mountain of debt and a psyche held together with Band-Aids, waiting for the healing to take hold.

There's no amount of money that would make me put myself in that position again.

I would rather spend the next ten years paying back credit card companies one minimum payment at a time than risk going back to that dark place.

Besides, the last thing my budding new relationship needs is the stress of actually working together. It's really hot to play boss/employee right now, but there's no denying the fact that we don't really work together. I'm busy with my breakfast guests, and he's fully enthralled with the world of dinner. We need to keep it that way.

I know this whole thing just started, but I'm head over heels. I want that man like nothing I've ever wanted before. I want to know him. I want to know what a future for the two of us looks like.

I want to let him know me.

*You aren't letting anyone know the real you with all the lies you're telling.*

It's one thing to lie by omission to my friends about a guy I'm secretly seeing, it's quite another to flat-out lie to the guy about something as important as this.

I make a decision. No more lying to Dom. If he asks me again, I will tell him. I will also tell him the reasons I don't want to work the dinner shift again. The whole terrible truth. Maybe I can do private consulting or something. Offer what help I can without actually setting foot on the dining room floor during that service.

With one last calming breath, I type out my reply.

> **Me**
> I would have given you my number.

> **Dom**
> Well, now you don't have to.

> Listen, I had an idea.

> **Me**
> I'm listening…

> **Dom**
> I feel like it would only be right for me to test out that new mattress. You know, to make sure it's up to par.

A blush and a grin spread across my face together as I shake my head and laugh.

> **Me**
> Is that right?

> Come on over then.

I hit send and hold my breath. It is a bold thing to say, especially when it's broad daylight and anyone could see him come to my apartment.

Everyone would definitely see him.

I don't even care. I'm ready to throw caution to the wind. I would do anything to get that man alone right now, even something completely reckless.

> **Dom**
> Not the best idea right now.

My heart sinks, but seriously—what was I expecting?

> **Dom**
> Come down to the resort main building, head through the lobby to the service elevator by the back doors that lead to groundskeeping. Take the elevator to the floor marked K.

Well, this just got a lot more interesting.

> **Me**
> Okay, I'm walking down now. My phone won't work.

> **Dom**
> See you soon.

I take the world's quickest shower and throw on a flower sundress with a matching set of lacy underthings hiding beneath. I take my time on the path down to the resort, not wanting to arrive a sweaty mess from hurrying through the heat of the afternoon.

I greet the front desk employee with a wave and pass through the lobby to the elevator hiding down a short hallway in the back. I hit the letter K and feel a jolt of surprise as the elevator starts to take me down instead of up like I expected.

When the doors open, I step out into another world.

The first thing that comes to mind is the Titanic. Specifically, how the Titanic's massive commercial kitchen would look after sinking to the bottom of the ocean.

Because that's where I am.

All around me is an eerie blue glow coming from emergency lights lining the walls. There is massive commercial kitchen equipment all around the room, cords pulled from the wall and dangling on the floor. Long, dusty, stainless-steel countertops extend in all directions. I can see the opening to a large dish room, as well as half-open doors to three walk-in coolers.

To my right, twenty feet away, is a set of double doors with round windows just at head height, which must lead to the dining room.

"Pretty amazing, isn't it?"

I jump a foot at the sound of Dom's voice coming from my left. I hadn't even realized I was holding my breath so tightly until it shoots out of me in a little scream.

"You scared me."

He's on me in an instant, warm, strong arms wrapping around my waist and drawing me into his body. "Sorry, little one."

"It's okay," I squeak out, melting into him. "What is this place?"

"It's the original restaurant from when the resort was built in the fifties. The restaurant upstairs, where we work now, is the one we put in when we bought the place. Or I put in, that is."

I shake my head in wonder. "This place is massive. Why don't you use it?"

Dom lets out a sigh and steps back from me, keeping hold of my hand and starting to lead me through the giant space. "We just don't have the staff for both, and I want to do fine dining. The guys, the other owners, initially thought we would open both so we could serve more casual fare in addition to the tasting menus, but I just don't have the capacity to run two places at the level I want to."

I look up at his face as he speaks, watching shadows pass over his features.

"So, this place sits empty, and I bust my ass upstairs. Ultimately, my vision is to win that Pendleton and get The White Sands on the map as a culinary destination, which should make attracting employees to this far-off island easier. But then we have to figure out housing for more staff, among other things." He lets out another sigh. "We'll get there, but it's a big project to take on."

We pass through the swinging doors and into the dining room. I stop short and shake my head, mouth hanging open as I look around in amazement.

If I thought the kitchen was like being in a sunken cruise ship, this room is a million times creepier. The tables are still set up with tablecloths and little bud vases with fake roses. I even spot a pair of half-empty salt and pepper shakers.

It's the most post-apocalyptic thing I've ever seen in real life. Like everyone just disappeared in the middle of dinner service.

At this point, I wouldn't be all that surprised if a ghost waiter came through the door carrying plates.

"This is wild."

"Right? I couldn't believe it when I came down here after we first bought the place. The property had been closed for nearly twenty years so the whole resort had this abandoned feeling, but this place has always been the creepiest. We pilfered what we could for the new restaurant, but for the most part this is exactly how it looked on the last dinner service in '96. I kind of love it, but I don't have time to give it the attention it needs."

It's getting more and more challenging to keep my mouth shut about the possibilities for this place. Even if it was just a staff cafeteria, the value it would offer to the lives of the nearly two hundred staff members is mind-boggling.

"But, my sweet girl, I brought you down here for a different reason."

My attention snaps back to him. I love daydreaming about possible new restaurant ventures as much as anyone, but I want whatever Dom has to offer me way, way more.

"Why did you bring me down here?" I let my voice go soft and sweet. It's not terribly difficult. I'm feeling an awful lot like I need protection in this eerie place, and I know just who I want to save me.

"Did you ever wonder how that mattress appeared so quickly on your doorstep?"

I nod up at him, waiting patiently.

"We have a stash of them down here in a storeroom. In case something terrible happens to one of the beds in a guest room, and it needs to be replaced before the next guests check in."

I like where this is going, and I happily take his offered hand and let him lead me through another door on the far side of the room and down a short hallway.

When he swings open the door, I laugh out loud. It's a small room, maybe ten by ten, with a row of mattresses leaning against the wall.

Dom walks over and grabs the last one in the line, pushing it so that it falls on the ground with a thump. There's just enough room for it to lay flat.

"Wow, it's so..." I almost say romantic, but I'm not sure if that is an appropriate thing to say in a secret workplace affair. Is he trying to be romantic right now or just looking for a convenient place to be alone?

"I know it's a little shoddy, to be down here in the basement, hiding in a storage room, but I thought it might actually be a little—"

"Romantic." The word flies out of my mouth, and I feel my cheeks flush, and Dom turns his head slowly to me, a smile growing across his face.

"I was going to say hot, but if hiding in a dark closet in the basement is your idea of romance, little one, I won't argue."

I can't even look at him, my embarrassment is so great. Luckily, he can sense my upset and pulls me in close, pressing a kiss to the top of my head. "Get over there."

I step forward and kick off my flip-flops, climbing on the mattress on my knees. Dom pulls the door closed behind us, and the room falls into complete darkness. I gasp, but he quickly turns on his phone light, which lights up the small space very well. All of a sudden, it feels like we're camping. It's just Dom and I, alone in the dark woods in our tent. With an epic mattress.

"I've been eagerly waiting to test out that new mattress in your apartment. Why don't we pretend we're there now?" Dom pushes me down so I'm lying in front of where he's kneeling.

"I'm pretending we're camping."

Dom lets out a surprised laugh. "Camping. Okay, that's good too. Let's pretend we're camping." He lowers himself over me, placing one hand on either side of my shoulders. "Out in the woods, just you and me. We can make as much noise as we want."

He brings his mouth to mine, and I lean up to press harder

into the kiss, my hands grazing up his arms and settling in his hair. When his mouth slides to the side and begins its descent down my neck, I decide to get brave.

"You know, it must be hard for you to really get a sense of the mattress from up there. Why don't you lie down, and I'll get on top."

"My girl gives orders now?"

"Not orders. Just suggestions."

Dom slides off me onto his side, pulling me with him as he rolls to his back. In one smooth movement, he has me straddling him.

I feel a rush of power and desire shoot through me as I gaze down at him below me and grind my body onto the growing erection in his pants.

"Look at you up there, little one."

"I'm on top," I say as I lean forward and take his wrists in my hands. I press them over his head, stretching my torso long over him as I lean down and press my lips to his. He invades my mouth immediately, and I follow suit, merging with him as I continue to move my hips up and down on his now rock-hard shaft.

I release one hand and reach between our legs to grip him. His hand follows, heading straight for the hem of my dress.

"No," I say, feeling emboldened by my position.

"Excuse me?" he says, pulling my dress roughly over my head and tossing it to the side.

With a small shake of my head, I grab his wrist and place it back on the bed behind his head. "In my camping fantasy, I tied you up. You can't move your hands."

Even in the dim phone light, I can see his eyes darken with desire.

"You tied me up, huh?"

I nod and reach back between my legs to find his cock. "You just have to lay there while I have my way with you."

"Laying on this mattress, tied up, while someone has their

way sounds pretty great," he starts, lifting his hips to thrust into my grip. But then before I can even react, he has us flipped over, and I'm pinned beneath him, my own arms held over my head. "But it's you who's getting tied up, and it's me who's having my way with you."

I didn't even have time to react before he flipped me. I catch my breath now as he holds my body firmly in place, his hips pressing down on mine, his hands holding my wrists tightly to the bed. "You don't want me to tie you up?" I ask.

"Not going to happen," he responds, landing his teeth on the edge of my lacy bra. "But you want to be tied up, don't you?"

I don't respond, biting my lip and waiting for whatever is going to come next.

"Answer me, little one. Have you ever been tied up before?"

I shake my head.

"But you think you might like it."

I nod, too embarrassed by his direct questioning to utter a single word.

Dom leans down and speaks directly into my ear, his voice low and gravelly. "Don't move."

Then he sits upright, releasing my hands. I stay still, keeping my arms above me and watch as he pulls off his black tee and rolls it into a long rope. He then ties it in a loose, bulky knot around my wrists.

"That'll have to do for now."

His words send electric bolts through my body. For now? What does that mean for later? I've never been one to get into anything really kinky. My sex life up to this point has always been pretty tame. I never took initiative, never spoke up. I just laid there and went through the motions.

Look at me now. Tied up in a closet in the basement at work —by my boss, no less. Calling him Daddy, letting him spank me and control me. I never could have predicted this for myself, but somehow, it feels so right.

"What do you think of the mattress?" I ask breathlessly.

Dom grins at me and takes a couple of bounces on his knees, causing both of our bodies to bounce. "Not half bad. Shall we put it to the real test?"

I nod eagerly, desire and anticipation mixing between my legs.

*I need him to touch me.*

As if he can read my mind, he unbuttons his pants and leans to the side to pull them off. His cock is finally free, and the thing is raring to go. I let out a whimper at the sight of it, my desire for the fullness overwhelming every one of my senses.

"Oh, my girl's eager, is she?"

"Yes, Daddy." I give him what he wants, desperate to make him respond in kind.

He grips his cock at the base and leans back, rubbing the tip of it around my clit where it hides under my black lace panties. I moan with my arms still held obediently overhead.

"Shall we take these off?"

"Yes, Daddy," I say again, this time with even more vigor. I cannot stand another second of this torture.

Unfortunately, Dom seems to sense that. I can almost see him decide to make it even worse for me.

He does slide my panties down ever so slowly, following their progress with his tongue. When he drags his tongue back up my legs after tossing the little lace garment to the side, I brace myself for his tongue between my legs, but he bypasses my yearning flesh, licking instead over my hip and up to my navel. I cry out in frustration, jutting my hips up to show him where I need his touch.

"Patience, patience, little one," he breathes against my stomach, settling his legs on either side of mine once more. He fists himself again, lowering the tip of his shaft to my now-bared clit, circling it around. I squeeze my eyes closed and toss my head back.

But then he pulls away.

I open my eyes to find the tip of his cock inches from my face.

"Open up."

I obey, and he dips his velvety head into my mouth. Closing my lips around it, I circle with my tongue. No sooner have I settled in for a round of this, however, when he pulls it back out, returning to my clit.

"That's nice. Wetter," Dom murmurs as he starts massaging my slit with his cock.

I hold my breath, teeth clenched tightly on my bottom lip, relishing the feeling of him stroking up around my clit and back down to my opening.

With my eyes squeezed closed, I don't see his cock until it's pressing against my lips once more. I take it in my mouth as far as I can, Dom's hand still guiding it as he slides over my tongue. Soon, he returns it between my legs.

After a few more rounds of going from my pussy to my mouth, I'm on fire. I don't care at this point whether he chooses between my legs or in my mouth, I just need him inside me now.

"Dom...p-please," I stutter as he continues his slow, delicious torture of my clit with the wet, velvety head of his cock.

"Excuse me?"

"Daddy! Please, I can't take it anymore."

"Well, because you asked so nicely..."

I'm so wet that the head of his cock slides into me with ease. I hold my breath, savoring the feel of him stretching me open, the slow, torturous slide, until I can feel him all the way inside. "Yes," I hiss out through clenched teeth.

"That's what my girl wanted? You should have said something sooner."

I can't even rise to his teasing right now, the feeling of him gripping my hips and slowly pressing in and pulling back out of me overtakes all of my senses.

"Shall we see what this mattress is made of?"

"Yes."

"Yes what, baby girl?"

"Yes, Daddy."

Once again, that word from my lips unleashes the animal inside him. He pumps into me hard once and pulls out only to thrust back inside even harder. Just as I feel his hips crash against mine, fully sheathed, I hear them.

"...all original flooring in the dining room, and the windows are..."

I let out a small gasp as the voices outside the door come closer. Dom claps a hand over my mouth, and with the other, he fumbles for his phone, turning off the light and leaving us in pitch darkness.

"It's really amazing, how come no one uses it?"

A woman's muffled voice replies. They seem to be stopped right outside the closet door.

Dom doesn't move a muscle, keeping his hand clamped over my mouth and his cock nestled deep inside me, his forehead resting on mine. I can feel his heart beating against my chest—and between my legs.

As much as I'm trying to be good and keep quiet and still—I'm well aware of the consequences if those people hear us and swing the door open—my body has other ideas.

As if it wants to mimic the heartbeat in his cock, it answers with a little clench of my muscles.

Dom responds instantly, his core tightening. "Reina..." The warning word is nearly soundless, uttered directly into my mouth.

Something about the rise I'm getting out of him, the power I have in this moment to disobey when there's nothing he can do about it...

I do it again, this time on purpose. I clench down on my muscles, giving his still-hard cock a nice squeeze.

"Reina, damn it, you better stop that."

But I don't stop.

I turn my short, jolting squeezes into a rhythmic, wave-like massage that I've been perfecting at stop lights my entire adult life.

There's nothing he can do to stop me. If he moves a muscle or says one word out loud, the people right outside the door will hear him for sure. The danger, the power, the thrill of it all—it's the most erotic moment of my life.

"You're going to be in so much trouble when we get out of here," Dom breathes as I continue to work him, silently and in complete stillness.

"If you don't like it, Daddy, you can pull out." My own words barely make waves in the air as I breathe them into his ear.

Dom slowly slides his face down to the side of my neck and latches onto the meat of my shoulder with his teeth. As I squeeze him rhythmically, he bites down harder and harder.

I can tell his teeth are going to leave a mark, but I don't care. I want him to leave a mark. I will wear this man's mark with pride.

"It's amazing that all this is just down here, and no one knows it."

"This resort has plenty of secrets. We discover more all the time."

There's a thump on the wall just outside the door, as if someone kicked it softly, or leaned on it. Dom and I both draw in sharp, silent breaths and hold them, anticipation of what could happen thick in the air around us.

I squeeze my eyes closed even though it's totally dark and really lay into him, giving his poor, tormented cock all I have left.

I don't have to wait long for my silent reward. His body buckles at the core, and I can feel him pulsing inside me, his teeth still latched onto my shoulder. When he finally stills, his jaw releases, and he's able to whisper once more.

"You are going to pay for that, sweetheart."

I bite my lip in silent response, even though he can't see me.

"Ready to head back down to the pool?"

The voices start to move down the hallway, in the direction of the elevator. We stay perfectly still, perfectly quiet until it has been silent for at least a minute.

When I can't stand it anymore, I ask, "Do you think the coast is clear?"

Dom sighs into my skin, the sound turning to a soft laugh as he pulls his face out of the crook of my neck.

A second later, the phone light turns back on, and I can see his face, but not well enough to read his expression.

"That was close," I say, still whispering as low as I can.

"You wanted to get us caught." Dom's voice is low, but not nearly as low as mine.

"What?" I respond incredulously. "No. I would never."

Dom sits up and slides out of me, folding his arms over his chest. "What do you think your punishment should be for this?"

"For making you come?"

"I think come might be a dirty word."

My mouth falls open in surprise. "Come is not a dirty word."

"And now you've said it twice."

I snap my mouth shut and roll my eyes. "How long do we have to wait until we can leave this stupid basement?"

"Stupid basement, huh? Not fifteen minutes ago, you were pretending it was a romantic camping trip."

"Yeah, that was before someone started calling perfectly fine words dirty and accusing me of trying to get us caught by giving you an orgasm." I roll away from him, trying to struggle to my knees on the soft mattress with my hands still tied in the T-shirt.

Dom is on me in an instant. He gets his arms around my waist and hauls me over his knees as he sits back on his heels on the bed. "There's no time like the present."

"Dom! Let me go!"

"What did you call me?"

"I called you Dom. I'm not calling you Daddy right now because I don't think—"

Smack.

His palm lands on my bare ass.

"Dom." I squirm, twisting and trying to get away. He holds me firmly.

"What's my name again?"

"Dom," I cry defiantly, already knowing what it's going to earn me.

Smack.

The pain of the spanking is a shock to my system, taking my breath away.

"One more time, little love."

"Daddy!" I give him what he wants almost unconsciously.

Smack.

I moan and try in vain to escape once more.

"Good girl. Next time I ask you for something, I'm going to expect you to obey sooner, is that clear?"

I say nothing, my shame and anger boiling together into a toxic stew.

Smack.

"How many was that so far?"

The calm in his voice only further infuriates me. I keep my head buried and say nothing.

Smack.

"Okay! It was..." I do some quick counting in my head. "Six."

"Six, huh. Well, you've got five more coming to you."

I immediately try to struggle away again, but he holds me tight.

"And if you don't behave, or if you make any more noise, I'm going to add ten more. Got it?"

I don't respond.

Smack.

I take the slap like a champ, letting it echo through my body.

The pain is calming in a way. It brings my mind into focus. Only four more to go.

Smack.

Dom lands this spanking right on top of the last one, causing my eyes to water. I can barely breathe through the sting of it, but I force myself to take one long slow breath after another.

Smack, smack.

The two in quick succession land on my thighs, a pain so sharp I cry out.

"What did I tell you about making noise, baby girl?"

I whimper out an apology, resigned to my fate.

Smack.

The last of the original ten lands between my legs, making more of a wet sound as Dom's palm hits right where his cum is still dripping out of me.

"Oh, my girl is extra wet right now, isn't she?"

It's a cruel joke, and I have to hold back tears at the humiliation of it all. Somehow, even with the spanking and the control, I'm still totally and completely turned on.

Maybe it's because of it. I've never felt this way in my life.

Dom slides my body off his knees and onto the bed, bringing my knees up and arranging my body over them in a curled position like I'm doing yoga. I let him move my body like a rag doll, all the fight gone from my system.

He settles himself on the bed behind me, and I feel his hand land between my cheeks, sliding down to my opening, and continuing on to my swollen, desperate clit. He got me so worked up before the interruption, and I never found my release.

Smack.

The blow is not unexpected but still takes me by surprise. I cry out, but catch myself halfway though, forcing my mouth to close around the sound.

"Good girl."

Smack, smack, smack.

He has a better angle on me now, and his spanks come hard and fast. In my child's pose position with my bound wrists out before me, all I can do is take it.

Smack, smack.

His hand strikes between my legs once more, slapping the drenched flesh. The feeling of his strike on my pussy is the most beautiful pain. It's unlike anything I could have ever imagined. I never would have thought to ask someone to hit me down there, but now that he's doing it—it's only a matter of time before I come from the blows.

Smack, smack.

Two more open-handed slaps to my pussy, and I'm moaning, grinding my hips backward toward his hand. I'm rewarded with a softer touch as Dom slides one hand through my wetness and nestles a finger in my aching opening.

Holding my pussy tightly with that hand, Dom brings the other hand down hard on my bottom for my last two spanks.

Smack, smack.

Tears pour openly from my eyes as I press my face into the mattress, clenching my teeth against the pain. Dom brings his thumb up to circle my clit, his fingers still deep inside me, and the pain morphs to pleasure.

When he withdraws his hand a moment later, I feel cold with its loss.

I don't know what's coming next. All I can do is wait to see.

Dom rearranges himself so that he can land his mouth on my clit, sucking it into his mouth and playing with it with his tongue until I can't breathe. When he adds his fingers back to the mix, two or more slipping inside and his thumb reaching back to penetrate my tight rosebud, I'm coming almost immediately.

He sucks and fucks me through my orgasm, not letting off any of the pressure or pace until I'm laughing and crying out for him to stop.

He releases me and lands one last soft spank on my sore behind before collapsing onto his side. I roll to curl up beside him, the adrenaline in my system covering my skin with goose bumps as I try to catch my breath.

Dom pulls me close and strokes my hair softly. I close my eyes and bask in the moment—the high of it, the passing low, the feeling of being so close and so cared for.

"You okay?" he asks softly into my hair.

The ability he has to go from alpha punisher back to being my teddy bear makes me smile. I know it's the reason I feel so safe during our little games. I can have this man back anytime I want him.

"Yeah. That was a lot...but I liked it."

"You like turning into a brat and making me punish you?"

I nod, my eyes boldly locked onto his. I want him to know how much I actually do like this, how safe I actually feel, so he won't be afraid to take me so far in the future.

"It might be my favorite part. Do you...like it?"

Dom's eyes turn molten as his lips tick up into a smile. "You know I do, little one. You're the most perfect woman I've ever laid eyes on."

The look on his face takes my breath away, sending a blush into my cheeks as I wriggle a bit to escape his strong arms and bring myself to a seat.

"That was a close call." He doesn't sound mad, just thoughtful.

"Do you know who was out there?"

"I have a guess."

"What would have happened if they found us?"

Dom lets out a soft laugh and rolls to his back. "Nothing. Honestly, he was probably down here for the same reason."

"Avery?"

"Yeah."

"He has a bit of a reputation around here."

"It's well deserved. He's one of the reasons I keep to myself mostly. Until I met you." Dom rolls back to face me. "Watching him blow through employees and locals like he doesn't have to live here hasn't been the highlight of my time on this island."

"He doesn't live here, though? Where does he live?"

"Here and there. Never stays anywhere or with anyone too long. He had it pretty hard growing up. Parents completely absent. Nannies and housekeepers raised him. It's done something to the way he trusts people. The way he thinks about relationships."

"That's sad."

"Money does not guarantee a happy childhood, that's for sure."

He pauses, still looking me right in the eye. I can feel the words bubbling up in my chest, the ones I want to ask about his own childhood, but the moment passes, and I don't ask. I'm too chicken. If I start asking questions, won't he ask some of his own?

"I should get back to the kitchen," he says finally, making no move to get up.

"Yeah, I should get back…" I have nowhere to be, so I just trail off, waiting for him to make the first move.

When he does, it's to pull me closer.

"This was the highlight of my day, Reina. Every time I see you, my day brightens."

"I…" There's nothing I can say that doesn't sound stupid in my head, but I have to say something. "I had fun, too."

"If anything ever stops being fun, you just have to let me know, okay?"

I nod, feeling the blush hit my cheeks once more. There were certainly moments during our little tumble in the closet that I felt ashamed for how much I liked being punished by him, but I never wanted it to stop.

"I'm serious. I may be the boss here, but that's never the case in the bedroom. You're always in charge."

"Okay." I manage to look up long enough to let him know I

understand before nervously busying myself locating all of my articles of clothing.

It's one thing to get freaky in bed, it's quite another to actually talk about it.

Dom pulls me back in to place a kiss on the top of my head before rising to his knees. When we're dressed and put together for the most part, we walk hand in hand back down the hallway.

I close my eyes briefly as we move through the dim rooms, allowing Dom to lead me. Allowing myself to pretend that we're walking somewhere public, holding hands like this. A soft ache starts in my chest and grows until I'm nearly in tears.

When did I start wanting so badly for this to be real?

I know without having to think about it that I've wanted it all along. Sure, I understand the secrecy and wanting to keep it quiet for a while. But there's no denying the fact that this thing, whatever it is, is fully and completely real in my mind.

I glance up at Dom as we reach the elevators and wonder if he feels the same.

"You head up first. If anyone asks, tell them you came in through the pool entrance and took the elevator up from the P floor."

"Okay," I respond breathlessly, in no hurry to part from him.

The doors slide open, but I don't let go of his hand.

"Reina," he says, pulling me in for one more tight embrace. "I'll see you Monday night. And probably every day until then, okay?"

"Okay," I say again, still not releasing him or walking into the elevator.

With a soft laugh, Dom kneels down before me and takes both of my hands in his. "I'm going to be thinking of you nonstop until I get to touch you again. Will you think of me?"

I nod, biting my lip.

"Go on, then. Let me miss you for a while."

Those words release me somehow, and I finally take a step

back into the elevator, just as it was giving up on me and closing its doors. I fight them back open and stand inside, eyes glued on the gorgeous man still kneeling before me.

When the doors slide closed and I'm finally left alone, I nearly sink to my knees with the pent-up emotion raging through me. I have to brace myself on the railing and take several deep breaths.

It's too much. He's too much. He's mine, but not quite. It's everything I've ever wanted, but also not. It's real, but not real enough. It's everything and nothing and perfect and terrible all wrapped into one delicious secret.

When I reach the lobby, I manage to walk through with my head held high. The afternoon sun is like a warm bath, washing away my fears.

I've got this. Whatever it is, however long it lasts. I'm going to just enjoy myself.

I hold my secret smile close to my heart as I make my way back up the hill.

# Rule #16

## WHEN YOU'RE OFFERED GOOD ADVICE—TAKE IT

### DOMINIC

There are times when I can forget my age.

When my team and I are in the flow of a busy service and everything is going well, flames are burning, plates are clattering, people are calling out orders and questions, and the din of the dining room is heady above the noise of cooking. Or even when I get myself up to speed on a treadmill downstairs in the gym that has become my refuge. One foot in front of the other, arms bent and pumping at my sides. One breath and then another.

Bumping over potholes and loose gravel in a golf cart on the white coral sand road to town is not one of those times.

"Jesus fucking Christ, Sam, slow down. You're going to kill me."

Sam just laughs, maneuvering the four-seater around yet another hole formed by the torrential tropical rains. This island was not meant for things like roads. Or five-story hotel buildings for that matter.

"Why did I let you drive again?"

"Because you couldn't get yourself out of the kitchen in time to bring the cart around, as usual."

Sam and I are taking one of our frequent trips to town to run errands and get lunch at our favorite beachfront café. I have a couple stops this trip that are bound to raise questions, so I'm preparing myself for storytelling.

Lying really.

It's not my strong suit.

As a white male raised in an extremely wealthy family, I'm well aware of my privileges in life. One of those privileges has been not needing to lie very often. But I feel the need to lie now. I feel it deep in my core. It's a protective feeling, an instinctual one.

Protect what's mine. Keep her safe so no one can take her from me.

This reaction to a couple of nights with Reina concerns me. Maybe that's one of the reasons I'm not ready to share the big news—even with my most trusted confidant.

If this was just a fling, a drunken mistake that I'd taken too far, I probably would have confessed to Sam already. This is something else entirely.

"I got a call from Mackenzie that he'll be back in the shop around eleven," Sam says, glancing over at me.

"Oh?" I reply offhandedly.

Mackenzie is the barge owner responsible for ninety percent of the stuff on this island that didn't arrive in someone's suitcase. He's my only option for getting mattresses imported, and I plan to talk to him today about bringing them over from the mainland.

"Yeah, he said you called him."

"I need to talk to him about a load."

"Got some furniture for your house coming?"

I grit my teeth and try to make the lies start flowing. It's impossible.

I'm screwed.

"I ordered new mattresses for the staff housing units."

Sam is silent. I glance over and find him watching the road, his face unreadable.

Like a nervous idiot, I ramble on, "It came to my attention that the beds in those units are completely unacceptable. I need my crew well rested if we're going to have any chance of making a good showing for the judges this year."

"Is that so?"

He doesn't buy my story for a second, but I'm not sure what else to say. I figure I'll just keep my mouth shut unless he asks me about it directly.

I don't have to wait long.

"You sure you didn't find out firsthand the state of the employee beds?"

I cough out a laugh. I hope that it comes across as indignant, but I'm sure I just sound like a fool. "You'd like that, wouldn't you?"

Sam looks over at me for a long moment, taking his eyes off the road just long enough for the golf cart to hit one of the legendary pits in the road, sending us both a foot into the air. I grab for my sidebar, trying to avoid hitting the dirt.

The tension of the moment is broken by the disruption, but the question still hangs. Luckily, Sam seems to have decided to let it go. We ride in silence for a few moments before we see a group of employees walking down the side of the dirt road.

They're easy to spot on this island, where there's a distinct difference in wardrobe between locals and our seasonal imports. They're all wearing flip-flops on their long walk for one thing, something a resident of the island would never have done. The amount of skin showing is another dead giveaway. Live on a tropical island long enough, and you swap sunscreen for loose, long clothes that covers your skin most of the time.

We're about twenty yards away, and approaching quickly, when I recognize my girl.

She's wearing short denim cutoffs and a red bikini top with

an off-white linen bag slung over her shoulder. I vaguely recognize her companions as one of the lunch servers and Charles, the spa manager.

She's got on flip-flops, of course, which must be killing her on the uneven, sandy dirt road. They're a good ten minutes out from the resort, which means they have another ten before they get to the village.

And then they have to walk back.

I grit my teeth at the thought of her suffering, but I'm not sure I have a good option. Glancing back, I register that the three of them could technically fit in the back seat on the way to town, but we need all the cargo room for our shopping on the trip home.

I'm just about to say something to Sam about stopping to pick them up, when she glances back and catches my eye.

Her eyes widen at the sight of me, those adorable cheeks starting to pinken as her lips part, and she takes in a surprised breath.

Suddenly, I'm struck with indecision.

It's well within my rights to stop and pick up a few employees, but now I'm worried I might be violating her privacy. Intruding on her personal time.

Would she want me to do that?

I'm fully prepared to deal with the consequences of Sam finding out about our relationship, but does she feel the same?

I decide to let her make the first move. If she waves or indicates in any way that she wants us to stop, I'll have Sam pull over. If not, we'll just keep on with our mission and let her go on with her day.

Our eyes stay locked as the cart approaches, bumping over rocks and swerving around potholes. When we catch up with them, I'm so close I could reach out and touch her.

But, of course, I don't.

She watches us approach and then pass by without so much as a flinch in her expression. When I can no longer keep her in sight without turning around in my seat, I have to let her go.

"Christ, Dom."

My head shoots to Sam. "What?"

"What the fuck, what? I can hear you thinking." He shakes his head and laughs. I lean back heavily in my seat, cursing myself for ever thinking that the person who has been with me since childhood would miss any of that.

"Whatever it is you've got going on, you better be smart about it." Suddenly, my friend has been replaced by the GM, the guy who works day in and day out with HR, handling conflicts arising from employee relationships.

"You know what, I don't even want to know." Sam lets out another laugh, shaking his head. "If you haven't told me yet, then you don't want me to know, so I'll let you have it. But fuck, Dom—"

"I've got it handled."

Sam laughs again but says nothing.

I'm saved from any more of this conversation by the cart approaching the large cement archway over the road that indicates the entry to the village of Saubry.

Sam parks in our usual spot in front of Mackenzie's. It's centrally located so we can do most of our errands on foot from here. We'll swing by the grocery store on the way out of town to grab the food items we like to stock in our own fridges for the few meals we eat away from the resort.

Sam, bless his fucking heart, saves me the awkwardness and waits outside while I head in to talk to Mackenzie about the transport of the hundred and thirteen mattresses that I ordered to be shipped to the port in Houston where his container ship docks.

It's a pretty straightforward request. I'm willing to pay extra to get them on the next ship, which leaves the day after tomorrow, and I'm just here to pay the man upfront in hopes of things actually going that way. Cash talks, and I constantly grease palms to get things done. I'm happy to play my part.

When I come back out, Sam and I walk down the narrow lane that weaves between shops, restaurants, bars, and dive tour huts on our way to lunch at the beach.

The village is a lively place, everything brightly colored and open air. Familiar faces are just starting to get tables of wares set up for the day, and we stop several times to chat as we make our way down main street.

"Hola, jefe," a deep male voice calls to me from behind a mountain of bananas and plantains.

"Morning, Carlos. You get any of those red mangos in this week?"

"Yes, sir. Just arrived. Perfectly ripe."

I nod in satisfaction. "Go ahead and send the lot over this afternoon."

The man nods enthusiastically and waves as we continue on.

"Mawnin', gentlemen!"

"Morning, Freida. How's the family?" I answer as we pass by the stand being set up by one of the island's local artists. Freida weaves the most incredible wool rugs. I have several in my house.

"Oh, good, good. Can't complain."

Sam stops at the next booth to purchase a few bags of fried plantain chips, and I wait in the street. I am, of course, included right away in a dusty game of soccer with the young children of the market vendors.

"Over here, Dom," they all shout as I dribble the ball between the kids. I give it a firm kick and watch it glide through the rectangle of small white stones that they have set up as the goal. Half of the kids cheer, the other half shake their heads in disappointment. I'm grinning when Sam joins me.

"Ready?" he asks, and I nod. It's harder to walk away now with all of the children calling after me, but I shout back a promise to play a full game with them next week, and they finally return to their own game and let us leave.

We arrive at Martha's Kitchen to loud greetings, as if we are heroes returning from war. I smile at the familiar faces in the open, breezy dining room as Sam and I make our way to our usual table.

I kick off my flip-flops and sink my feet into the sand, enjoying the contrast of the hot top and cool underneath as I sink them deeper. Our beers arrive, and plates of chicken and rice follow shortly after. There's no need to place an order at Martha's. She knows just what we want.

I'm just finishing sopping up the stewed chicken gravy with my last handmade fry jack when a shout from Sam beside me makes me look up.

"Hey, Charles."

*Just my luck.*

The three of them are strolling down the beach, carrying brightly colored bags. They all look up at Sam's shout, Charles lifting his hand in a wave.

We know Charles well. He's been with The White Sands since the beginning. He was a scuba bum living in the village when we arrived on the island and took a job folding towels in the spa. His talent for customer service, and keen eye for detail, shot him up the ranks quickly, and these days he's in charge of the entire spa.

"Come join us for a drink," Sam calls.

Dread sinks down my throat and expands in my chest. Why is he doing this?

Because he thinks it's funny to torture me, that's why.

Well, it's one thing to pull a stunt that will embarrass me, but I don't like the idea of Reina having to sit here and endure the uncomfortable half an hour a cursed drink will take.

"Sam, don't."

The look he gives me—so joyously entertained and excited for the upcoming torture he's about to put me through—I can only shake my head and sigh. There's no stopping this train wreck.

Sam leaps up to grab an extra chair when the three of them get to the table. It should have been me to notice that, but I have my head up my ass so that didn't happen.

She seems calm, though, as she says hello to me, accepts an introduction to Sam, and settles into a chair. The waitress takes their order and brings out three cold cocktails quickly.

I notice she doesn't have any shopping bags of her own. The haul piled in the sand next to the table all belongs to the other two. She just has her linen bag, which looks about as empty as it was when I saw her on the road.

"How are you enjoying your day off?" Sam, ever the people person, chats easily with everyone.

Sarah pipes up first. "We're loving it. It's Reina's first time in town, so we were just showing her around."

Sam's gaze travels slowly from Sarah to Reina, who offers him a friendly smile. Something in me yells out to lunge for Sam and steal that smile back or punch him in his stupid, smile-accepting face.

Luckily, I do neither. I manage to maintain my glowering, silent presence, grateful all of a sudden for the years I've spent honing it.

"The town is really cute," Reina says simply, taking another sip of the mocktail she chose.

I watch as Sam glances at Sarah and then back to Reina.

Perfect.

He hasn't quite decided which of them it is. I wonder if I can manage to keep my shit together long enough for him to not find out right now.

"So, Reina. You're in your first season? Have much experience doing seasonal resort work in paradise?"

Another smile and I want to rip the guy's face off.

*That's your best friend, man. Chill the fuck out.*

But I can't. Something inside me has gone into beast mode, and it's all I can do to keep my mouth shut.

"No, first time doing anything like this. I'm from Chicago. Well, I moved to Faraday from Chicago. I'm from Ottawa, Illinois."

"Ottawa, huh? A country girl," Sam offers good-naturedly. "What did your family think of this move?"

Reina looks down at her hands, and I want to jump across the table and comfort her. "They weren't exactly thrilled." She meets Sam's eye once more, a sad smile on her face. "My parents think I should move back to Ottawa and teach at the local public school, like they both do."

My breath catches in my throat as my jealousy toward Sam and my concern for Reina sour into complete and utter revulsion. But this time, I want to punch myself in the face.

How could I not have ever asked her about her family? Her parents? Or her friends for that matter. How does Sam know more about my girl in three minutes than I do? The answer is pretty clear—she grazed over her work history once when I asked, so I assumed she wasn't comfortable talking about her past. Well, I guess I read that totally wrong.

I wonder if she has been waiting for me to ask her more about herself or for me to offer more of my history to her. That's what people do, right? I kick myself for my sorely lacking social skills. I spend so much time behind a kitchen range that I seem to have forgotten basic human decency.

"…on lunch this season, I worked brunch last season. I think I might be ready for dinner next season." Sarah, the woman I always see Reina with, is talking, and it takes me a second to realize that all eyes are on me.

I force my mind to come back to the table and process Sarah's words. Next season, her third season, she's hoping to work dinner. That's why they're looking at me. I'm the gatekeeper of the p.m. shift.

"Oh, yeah, of course you can work dinner next season. We

can get you in for a few shifts this season to get you up to speed. I'll have Jessica talk to Nathan about getting that on the schedule." There. Such a simple thing I can offer to Reina's friend, and I offer it to make up for the fact that I have failed to ask Reina any personal questions.

I realize my mistake almost immediately.

I catch Sarah's look first—her mouth hanging open, eyes wide. Reina has more of a tight-lipped, trying not to laugh, adorable smirk going on. Sam, however, is grinning at me like the game's up.

Sarah recovers first. "That would be great. Thanks, Dominic."

I give her a nod and turn back to my beer. I feel the graze of a toe running up my leg and look up to find Reina looking at me with a secret smile twinkling in her eyes.

All of the concern over my faux pas and Sam finding out our secret washes away in that moment. The only thing I care about is making this girl happy.

Which is a huge fucking problem. I should care about my kitchen. I should be worrying about the dinner menu right now, texting Marcus to make sure someone pulled the stock and checking in on the prep list. Those have been my priorities for so long, I didn't think I was capable of caring about anything else.

How wrong I was.

When the drinks are finally empty, Sam sends the three of them off with a polite refusal of their offer to pay, telling them that he's sorry we won't have room to give them a ride back to the resort. I smile and wave as casually as I can as they gather their things and head back toward the village.

Sam is mercifully quiet about the whole thing as we settle up and make our way toward the cart. We do our grocery shopping and then load up for the trip home.

We're about ten potholes down the road when he finally lets me have it.

"I trust that you are going to let me know when HR needs to be informed about this."

"Shit, Sam," I say, shaking my head. "When is that point?"

"I'm sure it's already long past, but I'm going to give you the benefit of the doubt, considering you have as much at stake here as anyone."

When I don't respond to that, we fall into silence for a moment.

"I'm happy for you, you know."

I let out a snort, and Sam turns his head sharply in my direction. "I am, Dom. You spend too much time at work. We've been on this island seven years, and this is the first time you've shown any interest in anything besides your kitchen and some damn award."

"The kitchen is my life. Those awards are important to me."

"I know. I'm just happy to see you finding something that could be more important. That's what life's about, you know. Not working yourself to death."

"Shut the fuck up, man. You are just as single as I am." That shuts him up for a long moment.

"You know I'm looking for someone to settle down with on the island, it's just complicated. Which you well know. I know it's complicated for you, too. I'm glad you're taking a chance on someone, even if it is a liability nightmare."

"Yeah, sorry about that."

"It could be worse."

We fall into silence, and I know Sam is also thinking about Avery. He was always a playboy, jet-setting around the world with a new model-looking girl on his arm every week, and that behavior didn't stop when he got to Faraday. Problem is, this island is tiny, and most of the available single women work the resort. The reputation he established is not one either of us want to emulate.

I look over at Sam, who is focused on the road now. The guy is just about the kindest, most responsible man on the planet, and I know for a fact that he wanted to settle down before now. He dated quite a bit the first year we owned the resort, mostly locals and expats, but that dwindled off as each and every one of them turned out to not be the one.

He's had a hard time resigning himself to the fact that his future bride is probably a resort employee. He doesn't want to overstep any boundaries as owner and manager.

Something I, apparently, have no problem doing.

Honestly, it wasn't until this moment that I really thought about the possible implications of my little...whatever it is with Reina. I definitely should have checked in with HR, but the idea of going and sitting down with those people and filling out forms about what she and I have...and making her do the same?

It's not exactly the stuff bedroom fantasies are made of.

"I got this, Sam."

He glances back over at me and nods. "I know you do, man. Enjoy yourself. Take some time off."

I grunt in response. Fat chance of that ever happening.

I let my mind drift back to Reina, and how amazing she looked in her little outfit, hair loose, sun kissing all the places I love to kiss. I find myself wondering what kinds of things she'll buy in town, what kinds of things she likes, what I could buy for her.

My last gift, the mattress, was a bit of a stumble on my part. One that cost me a damn fortune. I should have known better than to do something so ostentatious. Something that put her private business out in the open like that.

I suppose a new diamond bracelet would have the same set of problems. Not that I think she wants a bracelet, but my experience with this kind of thing is sorely lacking.

"What do women want?"

Sam lets out a surprised laugh and shakes his head, looking over at me. "You mean in general, like in life?"

I shrug. I suppose if he knows the answer to that, I'll take it, but it's not exactly what I mean. "More like as a gift or a...date?"

"Well, I've only been in a few long-term relationships, but I know that for me, women seem to like it when I get them a new mattress and one for all one hundred of their closest coworkers." He's trying to keep the laughter out of his voice and only partially succeeding.

I crack a smile in spite of myself. "Yeah, I fucked that up."

Sam glances in my direction again before looking back at the road ahead. I can practically hear his mind going through the list of possible HR pitfalls. But finally, he answers. "What do you two do together?"

I let out a snort and leave it at that.

"Okay, have you gone anywhere together or done anything outside of…the house."

"Sam, if I had taken a date anywhere outside of my house, you would have heard about it."

"And this thing is secret. You've talked about not telling people?"

Maybe this is my HR interview after all. "Yeah, we talked about it. She's worried that people will think she's getting special treatment if she moves up in the restaurant, which it seems like she wants to do and is qualified to do. And I'm worried about harming my reputation as a chef by getting involved with a waitress. I mean, a scandal of any kind would hurt my chances of finally getting that Pendleton."

"And you'd rather have the award than the girl?"

"Why do I have to choose?" I snap, more angrily than I expected. "She wants to keep it quiet as well. It's not just me wanting to look good."

"Sorry, man. You're right." Sam, ever the peacekeeper. "All right, well, dates in the house then. You're not going to like this, but I recommend you get a nice bottle of wine and talk to her about what it is she wants, where she sees this going, and what you can buy for her that would be acceptable based on your arrangement."

So fucking sensible, I practically roll my eyes.

Sam must feel my annoyance because he laughs. "Just

because a relationship is secret from the outside world doesn't mean it should be secret from the two people in it."

I cross my arms over my chest and let those words simmer.

He's right, of course. I remember with a flash of guilt the way Reina spoke so easily about her hometown and family back at the restaurant. I want to know those kinds of things. If that means I have to ask her about herself, so be it.

"All right." And that's the end of it.

Sam pulls the cart into The Sands, and I hop out, grabbing my bags from the back. "See you later, man."

"Good luck."

# Rule #17

## RED MEANS STOP. YELLOW MEANS SLOW. GREEN MEANS...WELL, YOU KNOW WHAT GREEN MEANS

### REINA

Sarah and Charles chatter the entire way back from town about Dom's incredible job offer. Sarah can barely contain her excitement as Charles comes up with all sorts of outlandish reasons for Dom's sudden kindness.

"Maybe he was really, really drunk and is just good at hiding it," Charles says as I let my mind drift back to the conversation. "Or maybe he has a secret crush on you," Charles throws one arm around Sarah's shoulder, pulling her in as she laughs. "Maybe he just wants you with him on the late shift."

"Maybe he just thinks you're a good worker, or maybe they're losing staff at the end of the season, and he needs to replace them." As soon as the words leave my mouth, I regret them. They're sharp and even a bit snarky.

I can't help it. It's one thing to have to listen to coworkers complain about that kind, generous, sexy man while I'm on shift. I'm not about to stand by and listen to these two joke about who he has crushes on.

There's only one crush in that man's mind, and it's me.

I'm not usually a jealous person, so the flush of rage I feel in my body is surprising. I must have surprised the other two just as much because they're now walking silently, giving me the side-eye.

"Yeah, that's probably it," Sarah says eventually. "Whatever it is, I'll take it. Moving up to dinner is a huge promotion."

She and Charles continue daydreaming about what Sarah's going to do with all the tips she'll be pulling in at dinner, but my mind drifts back to the table on the beach where I just sipped a virgin margarita with coworkers and pretended not to know Dom.

If we weren't a complete secret from all of our friends, we would have sat next to each other. Dom would have rested his hand on my shoulder or my thigh while we waited for our drinks to arrive. I could have glanced at him when the others were caught up in conversation, catching his eye and smiling, letting him know the pride I felt sitting there with him.

Would he have felt the same way?

This is the problem with secrets. It is hard to get a good perspective on what's actually going on when you can't ask other people for their opinion.

*The sneaking around is only temporary.*

I bring my fantasy back to mind, pushing the uneasy feeling in my gut to the side. It is only a matter of time before I'm sitting next to him at tables with friends, walking beside him through the halls of the resort, and sleeping beside him every night.

*Isn't it?*

I shake my head to clear the worries. I want to be excited about this. It's so new, and so very secret. Sneaking down to the abandoned kitchen the other day to be with Dom in the middle of his workday was easily the craziest, sexiest thing I've ever done. Just thinking about that eerie blue lighting, that storage room, being spanked like a bad girl...it's enough to send a blush high on my cheeks.

The others notice right away.

"You look like you've got a secret, Reina," Sarah chides me from beside Charles. "Are you going to share it with the class?"

"What? Oh, no. I think I'm just overheating a bit." More lies. I'm becoming quite the little actress these days.

We part ways at our apartments with hugs all around.

I'm grateful for the quiet evening in my own apartment, and even more grateful for the leftovers from lunch in town that I have stashed in my bag for dinner. I need some time to myself to be able to think and fantasize, without other people always asking me what's on my mind.

I knew a secret relationship would be challenging, but it never occurred to me just how hard it would be to keep from sharing something I'm so excited about with the people who I'm with all the time.

I strip off my sweaty clothes and take a cool shower, then fall into bed with my phone. I don't have a single picture of Dom to ogle, so I bring up my web browser and Google him, laughing to myself at how silly I'm being as I wait for the spinning wheel to show me the face of my crush.

It never does. The internet must be out again. I toss my phone to the side and close my eyes, bringing to mind an image of his smiling face I know I never would have found online. The one that's just for me.

I can't remember a time when I felt so head over heels about anyone. It's scary, exciting, and completely addictive. I can't even pinpoint what it is about the guy that has me so enamored. Is it his gruff manner that I know is a front for his big heart? Is it his decisiveness, and the way he isn't afraid to order me around?

I love the power imbalance. It's strange, after my whole life of fighting for women's equality, to be craving my boss ordering me onto my knees, but I am. I'm happy to be the waitress so he can be the chef. It's like a real-life role play, and I'm the sassy, sexy, bad girl who needs to be punished.

Just the thought of my first spanking in his office is enough to send my hand between my legs. There's no way around it. I want to be the bad girl. And I want to be punished.

———

My next few days at work pass in a blur of faces, sun, and trying to acclimate to my crazy new sleep schedule.

I am by far the most competent server on the brunch team, so I often find myself running the floor alone while Sylvia works with the other newbies, trying to get them up to speed on espresso drinks and basic table waiting skills.

It's fine with me. I use my newfound freedom to get a real feel for the flow of service, the expectations of resort guests, and the look of all the dishes on the menu. I also use some of my alone time to put myself in situations that could turn into brand-new fantasies, such as taking extra time filling up the mop bucket, hoping a certain chef will find me in the closet and have his way with me.

It's ridiculous, but I'm having so much fun. It's been forever since I've had a crush of any kind, and this one is off-the-charts hot. The secrecy of it and having to interact with him in a boss/employee fashion without letting anyone catch a hint of our relationship keeps my heart racing all through work.

I thought someone might have noticed during drinks in town the other day, but I haven't heard anything from HR, or Sam the GM, so we must have pulled it off.

Sarah's still crazy excited that Dom told her she could work dinner next season. I would be lying if I didn't feel at least a teeny bit proud that my influence probably got her the promotion. I mean, everyone was so surprised by his statement, it seems like something he doesn't offer all the time. And he offered it to my friend. Coincidence? I think not.

It's not that I expect special treatment, but when it comes, damn does it feel good.

When Monday finally rolls around, I get off work and rush

home. I have until nine, but I really need a nap, a shower, and to find the perfect outfit for my first night at Dom's house.

It was a struggle to convince Sarah and Charles that I couldn't join them at pizza night without revealing my secret date, but in the end, they relented and went down alone.

I did a little secret poking around and found out that Dom lives in the large white house at the very top of the hill that my apartment building is on. Just a five-minute stroll up the path through the palms, and I will be at the foot of the long staircase that leads to his front porch.

I tried not to gape at the massive house once I figured out it was his. Two stories with enormous panoramic windows overlooking the ocean view which is unobstructed from so high up.

For the first time, I really internalize what it means for Dom to be so well off. It's one thing for him to buy me a gift or replace all the staff beds. It's quite another to be the owner of a mansion on a tropical island. I know that he owns the resort as well, but this just seems to make it all hit home.

Dom is crazy rich. And I am super-duper poor.

It's funny. I've been considering how the uneven power dynamics of our boss/employee relationship will color our relationship and whether that will make it impossible for us to be together. But this is the first time I've really wondered whether he would actually be interested in something real with someone like me because of the differences in our bank accounts.

And if I can actually trust what he says, since he has so much more power than I do—in more ways than one. That power is hot in the bedroom, but will I always feel like I'm the beggar and he's the king?

It has not escaped me that I managed to latch onto a man who is certainly the richest person on the entire island, but I didn't do it intentionally.

Dom is Dom, and I like him for who he is. He happens to be rich and powerful, but that's just a benefit.

I want to sink into the princess fantasy every girl grows up with, the one where the prince sweeps her away to live in a castle, but my mountain of debt stands in my way.

I need to pay it off to prove to myself that I can stand on my own two feet. That my decisions are my own. That my life is my own. My debt might be a burden, but it's also proof that I took my freedom back.

I'm not ready to give that freedom away again.

Will Dom listen to what I want and what I dream about and help me get there? Or will he be just like my parents and try to use his money to turn me into someone I'm not?

I'm still wrestling with the worry when quarter to nine finally rolls around. I slip out my front door, leaving the porch light off, and disappear into the darkness. I wait until I'm a ways away before turning on my flashlight.

Feeling like a super-spy, I climb the staircase to Dom's house on the hill, glancing around every few steps to make sure no one is watching me. When I tap on the door, it opens immediately.

Dom is there, wearing joggers and nothing else, still toweling his hair from the shower. "You're early."

I flush. "Do you want me to leave—"

With a laugh, Dom grabs my arm and pulls me inside, closing the door behind me. "I'm not sure I'm ever going to let you leave, little one."

His words take my breath away, and I can't think of a single thing to say. Luckily, his lips land on mine a second later, erasing all need to talk.

Our past encounters have been rushed, partially clothed, or in the dark, so this is really the first time I get my hands properly on the bare chest and stomach of this gorgeous man.

*When does he have time to work out?*

I can't help but think of all the chefs I've known in the past, men and women who were wildly out of shape after years of overworking and overeating.

Not Dom. He could be an Olympic athlete with this body of his. I wonder what sport he would compete in.

*Wrestling, perhaps?*

I smile against his mouth and feel him smile back. He pulls away and looks down at me. "Something funny?"

"No, I just…how do you look like this?"

"Like what?"

As if he doesn't know. "Like, so fit. Like you work out all the time."

Without warning, Dom scoops me off my feet and throws me over his shoulder. I scream and pound uselessly on his ass, which like the rest of him, turns out to be rock hard.

"I work out all the time," he says.

"I thought you worked in the kitchen all the time." I dangle over his back, unable to see.

"That too. You ever wonder where the other door in my office leads?"

Now that he mentions it, I hadn't considered where that door led. I shake my head, not that he can see me.

"It leads to an elevator, which takes me straight down to the resort fitness center."

His strong arms pull me off his shoulder and set me down on my feet. When he spins me around, I'm faced with the floor-to-ceiling windows overlooking the ocean. The view is so breathtaking I just stare for a few moments, mouth hanging open.

"Pretty nice, huh?"

"Um, yeah. Pretty nice. Are you ever even here to enjoy this?"

Dom shakes his head. I glance back and catch a hint of sadness in his eyes before it's replaced by the usual desire that always seems to be there when he's looking at me.

"Wine?" he asks.

"Please."

Dom walks into his massive, open kitchen and chooses a bottle from an under-counter wine cooler. He fills two tall glasses and hands one to me. The wine tastes luscious and velvety as it hits my tongue. "The Apolloni Estate Pinot," I breathe. One of my absolute favorites.

I open my eyes and find him watching me enjoy the wine. I bite my lip, realizing my mistake. Why would a brunch server be so knowledgeable about fine wines? Trying to play it off, I set the glass down and take a step toward him. "You were in the village for errands the other day?"

It's a shameless change of subject, and I watch Dom consider carefully before accepting my distraction. "Yeah. We go on supply runs pretty often." He takes a drink of his own wine, watching me. "Did you have a good time in town?"

"I had so much fun. That was the first time I've been there, really. I mean, I came in on the water taxi, but it was pretty late." I'm overcome with the memories of glimpsing the vibrant community for the first time. The brightly colored beach umbrellas and hand-painted signs on the shops. The smell of the ocean and outdoor grills and fresh coconuts being sold with straws at stands along the path. I smile to myself. "We went to the market and walked down every street. I had great tour guides. Sarah and Charles seem to know this place by heart."

"What treasures did you buy?"

Damn. Why did he have to ask me that? I've spent the entire afternoon worrying about him learning the truth of my financial situation, and now I'm going to have to lie to avoid telling him that I didn't have one dollar in my pocket to spend in town.

*I thought you decided no more lying to this man...*

One more isn't going to hurt anything.

"Oh, I didn't buy anything. I don't really need anything. I brought so much with me from the States." My eyes cast downward, and Dom catches my chin in his hand, tilting me to face him as he does so often.

"You didn't find one single thing you wanted in all of Saubry? Not one bikini top or pair of sandals?" His face is in the crook of my neck now, his wine held out to the side. He walks slowly, pushing me backward until I'm pressed against the fridge. "Not one seashell keychain?"

I'm flustered now from the heat of his body so close to mine. I have a hard time focusing on coming up with a believable lie. "I just don't really buy things."

Dom murmurs against my skin. "If I find out there's one thing in that town that you wanted that you didn't buy, little one, there's going to be hell to pay."

"Why?"

"Because you are mine, and you deserve everything in the world that you want."

*Well, this is a new development.*

I push him away and walk back over to the counter, swirling my wine and taking a long sip. "Dom, that's really nice, but…"

He's on me so quickly, I don't have time to react. My back presses against the counter, arching my face up so I have to look him in the eye.

"I know you aren't about to tell me what I can and cannot do."

I take in a rushed breath, my mouth hanging open at his statement. His eyes go straight to my lips, his tongue tracing his teeth.

"Dom, it's complicated."

He steps back with a cocked brow, allowing me the space to stand up straight. "Seems pretty simple to me."

A rush of anger shoots through me, hot and bright. "Oh, really? It's been very simple with all the other women you've kept?"

In a flash, his wine is on the counter, and I'm up against the edge once more, his strong hands spinning me and pressing my chest onto the cool tile counter. He leans over my back, bringing his lips close to my ear. "You know you're the only one." His voice is a purr that I can feel in my bones. "Tell Daddy what's got you so worked up that you thought talking back like that would be okay."

"I'm not trying to talk back."

"Well, you're doing a pretty good job, sweet girl." His hand runs up the back of my thigh and over my ass as he talks, making it even more difficult to form words.

"I'm just trying to make sure you don't think that I need you to pay for everything for me. I want to take care of myself. I *can* take care of myself."

I feel his chest fill and empty slowly, and I prepare myself for what he's about to say.

As usual, no amount of preparation could get me ready for this man.

He spins me to face him and drops to his knees in front of me. I look down at his upturned face, running my hands through his hair.

"What if I told you that nothing would turn me on more than to buy you the things you want? What if I told you that I lie awake at night imagining all of the ways I can spoil you and make you smile and wrap you in luxury? Would it still be so complicated?"

"Dom…" I want to fight, to explain to him how I'm an independent woman who can stand on her own two feet, but those two feet are starting to feel a lot less steady the longer I have his face pressed against the hem of my short dress.

"Tell me what you want, Reina."

The sound of my name from his lips draws me out of whatever stupor I'm starting to sink into. This isn't a game.

How easy it would be right now to let go of the walls I've built. To let him into my world, my worries, my struggles. Hell, he could probably make them disappear with a few taps on his phone.

No. I need to know for sure that we are on the same page first. I can't risk giving control of my life away to someone who isn't going to respect my input on how I live it.

"I…I think it sounds like we need some kind of compromise," I finally manage.

Dom lets out a soft laugh, pressing the hem of my skirt a few inches higher. "I had a feeling it would come to that with you." His fingers are tracing up my legs, sliding ever closer to the lace thong I have on under my dress. "What kind of compromise did you have in mind?"

"Maybe what I meant was a negotiation." My voice is weak, but I manage to get the words out.

"Oh, really. A negotiation, huh?"

"Yeah. And you should start."

Another laugh, one I can feel on my skin as his face draws close to my thigh. "I should start? I seem to remember from business school that the person who goes first loses the upper hand."

"Is that going to be a problem?"

My skirt is around my waist now, my panties fully bared to him. Dom growls and sinks his teeth into my lace-covered flesh, causing me to cry out.

He pulls away with an evil grin on his face and tugs the skirt of my dress back down in one quick movement. Before I know it, he's on his feet and lifting his wineglass to his lips.

It takes me a moment to collect myself and grab my own glass. By the time I do, Dom is across the dining room, leaning on a sideboard and watching me.

When our eyes meet, he speaks. "I want to buy you a golf cart, so you don't have to walk to town. And I want you to have a credit card with your name on it and no limit so you can buy yourself anything you want. I want you to have the management benefits package, and I want you to join me on a trip somewhere no one knows us once a month."

I cough out a surprised laugh. He can't be serious.

First off, how would I explain the sudden appearance of a golf cart in my life? Not that my friends wouldn't appreciate it, but still.

And the credit card. My heart aches at the thought of the bills I get in my email inbox every month from the last five years in Chicago. Swiping my high-interest card for everything from rent to groceries to drinks out on the town, I built myself a tower of problems.

"I see your mind working, Reina. Say it."

I can feel tears start to prick in the corners of my eyes as I try to meet his gaze. I thought I was prepared to negotiate with him. I thought I could be strong and accept next to nothing from this endlessly rich man until he proved himself trustworthy.

But I'm not sure I'm that strong.

Now that I'm faced with asking for—and receiving— anything I want, anything I need. Can I really hold my tongue?

"What do the management benefits entail?" I manage to ask, mostly to buy time.

Dom raises his eyebrows, seeing right through my tactic, but humors me. "Better healthcare, helicopter coverage if you need emergency transport off the island, meal allowance, spa allowance, profit sharing, 401k, paid vacation. Probably other things I'm forgetting."

"I'll take that." I'd be a fool not to, even if I don't deserve it.

"What else?"

"How about a few golf carts that staff can check out or rent to go to town?"

He considers and then nods. He knows as well as I do that we want to keep this whole thing under wraps. Showering me with gifts will draw attention to our little secret. Actually now that I've planted the seed that the best way for him to make my life easier without giving us up is to make life easier for all the staff, I wonder how much will change. And how quickly.

"What else?"

I want the card.

I want it so badly I could scream. But I can't make my mouth form the words. What if he gives me a card to charge anything I want and then things go south between us? Would I be left with that bill to add to my others?

Just the thought of my ever-growing debt makes it suddenly harder to breathe. I bring my hand to my chest and try to take slow, even breaths, but I can feel myself working toward a full-blown panic attack.

Dom is at my side in a flash, close, but not crowding me. "What's wrong? Are you upset?" He steps back, reaching forward but not touching me.

"No, I..." I'm so frustrated with myself right now for ruining this night. For taking a kind, generous offer and turning it black with my stupid past mistakes. "I don't want to talk about money," I manage. After I speak the words, I can finally breathe.

"Okay," Dom replies simply. He fetches my wineglass and holds it out to me. "What do you want to talk about?"

I take a long sip of the expensive wine and close my eyes, savoring the taste. When I reopen them, Dom is watching me with a look filled with care and concern. I'm starting to feel more like myself now, and I want nothing more in the world than to save this night from the train wreck it's threatening to become. I need to change the subject.

If anything can distract this man, it's my body. "I want to talk about what you had planned for this evening, before all this silly talking got in the way."

I walk until my breasts graze across his bare chest, lifting up on my tiptoes to bite his lower lip. Dom still looks like he wants to say something, but in the end, I win.

His lips touch down on mine and all thoughts of money, debt, and unearned gifts fade from my mind. All that's left is the feeling of this man's mouth against my mouth, the gentle glide of his tongue along mine. I sink further into the feeling of peace, the blessed quiet he brings to my mind in moments like this. I'm so distracted by his hands on my body, I don't realize what's coming until it's too late.

Before I can even scream, I'm back over his shoulder, being carried off to another room. He takes me further back in the house, into a room that has the curtains drawn. When I finally hit my feet again, I'm in his bedroom.

The anticipation of what's about to come makes my knees

weak, and I lean back against his chest as I take in the large room.

It's a total man bedroom, everything dark colors and leather. It's neat as a pin, hardly an article of clothing out of place. I can see his watch and phone in a pile on top of the dresser.

The bed must be a California king or something larger. It's comically massive. The head and footboards connect with an iron structure that forms a canopy of sorts over the top. I spot something hanging down from the midpoint of the canopy, but in the dim light, I can't make out what it is.

"Take your clothes off."

I'm surprised by his sudden request, but I'm not going to argue. I quickly pull my short dress up and over my head, leaving only a hot pink lace bralette and matching panties.

"You can leave those."

I toss my dress on a chair and face him. "What's next, Daddy?"

Dom purrs. "Could you be any cuter, little one?"

I shrug, and he laughs.

"Go get on the bed."

I turn and walk toward it, shaking my ass as I go.

"Reina," Dom growls, and I smile to myself.

I climb up onto the bed, crossing toward the center on all fours, giving him one last view of my ass before turning and sitting on my heels, facing him.

"Did you bring your points with you?" he asks.

I'd almost forgotten about the menu quiz in his office, but I nod my head enthusiastically.

Without a word, Dom crosses the room and makes his way to stand beside where I kneel on the bed. He reaches up and pulls something down from the canopy.

It's a strap of some kind.

Anticipation turns to apprehension as I realize I'm about to lose a lot of control.

"Stand up."

I stand on the mattress and face him.

"Hands."

I hold them out. It's not hard to see that they're trembling. Dom takes them in his own anyway. "Yes or no, sweetheart?"

"What?"

Dom uses the hand not holding both of my wrists and tilts my chin up to face him. "Say yes or say no."

"Yes." The answer is automatic. Whatever he's offering, I want it.

"Yes what?"

"Yes, Daddy."

Satisfied, Dom binds my wrists together with a padded leather cuff. It's tight enough that I can't squeeze them free, but not uncomfortable.

"We haven't really talked about boundaries or safety yet, and that's on me. But tonight, we need to have an understanding, okay?"

Boundaries? I can't imagine wanting or needing boundaries with this man, but I nod anyway.

"You are familiar with the colors green, yellow, and red, and what they mean?"

I nod again, this time with more understanding.

"Good. I'm going to ask you periodically to give me a color, and I expect you to do so right away. This is how I check to make sure you are doing okay, even when you're experiencing pain, or you're otherwise indisposed. You don't have to wait for me to ask. If you ever want to say a color, you can do so, and I will be listening."

"Yes, Daddy."

Dom runs his hands down my up-stretched arms, sending a shiver through my entire body. "The colors aren't just for times like this, Reina. You can use them anytime. They coordinate with numbers. One for green, two for yellow, three for red. You can say the number, you can tap the number, you can write the number, and I will know what you mean. Anytime you feel uncomfortable and can't speak up, you can communicate with me in this way. That goes for work, play, home, anywhere. It's my job to look out for your wellbeing, and I want to know anytime you feel unsafe or uncomfortable by anything I'm doing, whether it's in bed or at work."

"Yes, Daddy."

"If you can't use your words because your mouth is covered or full, you tap on my body. Understand?"

I nod, the gravity of his words settling on me. He's making sure I feel safe and in control, even as he plans to do things to my body that will make me feel very out of control. The knowledge that I can tap out at any second makes me feel much better about whatever he's about to do to me. I would let him try anything now that I know I'm the one in charge. I wonder if he knows that.

Apparently satisfied with my answer, Dom takes a step back and picks up the slack of the strap, pulling it taut so that my hands point straight overhead. I look up and see that I'm now secured to a pivot point at the center of the iron bed frame canopy. Biting my lip, I look back to Dom for my next direction.

He's climbing off the bed, strap in hand. I'm cold and nervous without him. I watch as he secures the strap to a peg on one of the bedposts specifically designed for this purpose. It fits right through a hole in the strap like a belt buckle.

"How many points did you have?"

He already knows, but I tell him. "Five."

"Count them out for me, one at a time."

"One."

He moves the strap one notch down, giving me almost a foot of slack overhead.

"Two."

Another notch.

By the time I get to five, the heavy leather is hanging over my shoulder.

"Lucky girl. It looks like you can kneel."

I understand those words as an order and slowly lower myself to my knees. I have just enough slack to place my knees on the bed with my arms held straight overhead.

"Look at you."

Dom's smoldering eyes tell me everything I need to know about how I look. I can only imagine. Naked except for my hot pink lace, kneeling on his bed, suspended by the wrists from above. He can do anything to me.

*I hope he starts doing it soon…*

"What's next, Daddy?" My impatience is starting to eat me alive.

"My dirty girl is eager, isn't she?"

My impatience morphs into embarrassment as Dom taunts me from the end of the bed.

When did I get so eager? I've never been one to beg for sex, and now I find those words on the tip of my tongue near constantly. I must blush because Dom gives me that sly smile he always does when my cheeks turn pink.

"Tell me what you want, little one. And make it nice," he adds with a chuckle.

"I want you in my mouth, Daddy." I know immediately that I said the right thing because Dom's face transforms from teasing to straight up lust. His eyes darken, and the edge of his lip curls as his gaze drops to my lips. I run my tongue over them slowly in a shameless display of need.

In one smooth movement, Dom strips off his sweats and steps onto the bed in front of me, grabbing the overhead canopy bars with both hands. His erection is massive and coming straight at my face. I open my mouth and close my eyes, thinking he's going to bring it right in, but instead, he slaps my right cheek with it and growls.

I open my eyes and look up at him, smiling at the desire I see on his face as he hovers over me. No one has ever looked at me like Dom does—like I'm the only girl in the world.

He shifts his hips to the side and twists to slap me with his cock once more. It's gentle, like teasing, and I turn my head quickly, trying to capture his tip as it goes by. After a couple more rounds of this slap-chase game, Dom lets me get my lips around his gorgeous, engorged tip.

Having him in my mouth is everything I want it to be. Salty, smooth, warm, and so sexy. I slide my head forward to take more of him, working my way up to allowing his tip to touch the back of my throat. I'm dying to wrap my hands around his base, to include the rest of his large shaft in the fun.

I slide him out of my mouth. "Can I have my hands free?"

"You aren't going to need your hands, sweet girl. Keep playing around with that sexy little mouth for a bit, I'll take over soon."

My belly fills with nervous excitement at his words. Images of what's coming flash through my mind, filling my already wet panties with even more liquid desire. I suck and lick greedily while Dom sways his hips side to side, up and down. The chase is infuriating and fun and ridiculous, all wrapped into one.

When he finally brings one hand down from the bar overhead and cups the back of my head to tilt my face up toward him, I'm flushed and breathless. His cock is about an inch away from my lips, and my mouth hangs open in anticipation.

"Have you ever had a man in your throat, little one?"

I nod eagerly, happy to be able to tell him I'm ready for something like this.

Dom looks both glad that I'm not a stranger to the act, but hesitant to fully accept that a man has been there before him.

"Not all the way," I say quickly, wanting his dark look to clear.

"What do you mean?"

"They didn't go all the way down. No one would, even though I wanted it. You will, though, right?" This is a fantasy I've been chasing for years, but I've never had a partner with the bravado to actually go through with it. I can see in Dom's eyes the promise of finally fulfilling this dream as the clouds pass, and he's mine once more.

"Close your mouth, baby girl." His tone is hushed, lusty with anticipation. I know I'm feeling that way, and it turns me on so much to know that I'm doing it to him, too.

I obey.

"Take long, slow breaths through your nose." After I take five breaths or so, I feel much calmer. "Good girl. Now open and stick your tongue out."

I open wide, tongue flat on my bottom lip. Dom uses his hand to tilt my head back once more and guides his cock down my waiting tongue, stopping just when he reaches the back of my mouth.

"Keep breathing through your nose. You're doing so good." His voice purrs over me as his grip on my neck stiffens. His next slide passes farther than before. I can feel his tip start down my throat. There's a soft gag reflex, but I breathe through it just like I've practiced at home on my own. I feel my throat muscles constrict in a pulsing spasm, but I don't pull away. My eyes swim with tears, causing the room to blur.

"Blink one, two, or three times, love, let me know how you're doing."

It takes all of my concentration to hold my teary eyes still enough to give him one solid blink.

He presses farther in.

"Fuck, it feels so good when you gag on my cock. Your throat gets so tight." Dom's voice strains as he presses his tip further down my throat. My tears flow freely now, cascading down my cheeks with every flutter of my eyelids.

"You look so fucking sexy taking Daddy's cock like this."

The thought of pleasing him in this way does things to me, makes me feel things I've never felt before. I'm proud and strong and feel so sexy. I glance down when I feel his body approaching and see that the V of his hip muscles is nearing my face.

*Yes, Daddy. All the way down just like you promised.*

I keep breathing as Dom continues his slow slide. He pauses every few moments to draw his tip back just a bit before sliding it further.

"You are swallowing Daddy's cock like a good fucking girl. Look at you, on your knees, taking it." I can hear the hitch in his voice as he tries to keep himself from coming. I wonder how long he'll be able to hold on.

My throat goes through another series of spasms, trying to do its job and clear the obstruction by swallowing. It's a lost cause, but Dom definitely enjoys it. He tosses his head back with a moan of pleasure before snapping his eyes back to mine.

The one night I decide to doll myself up with lipstick and mascara. I must look like a hot mess right now. But that's not how Dom looks at me. Reflected in his eyes, all I see is desire.

"How about giving me that blink again, little one?"

I blink once.

Dom smiles. "Take a deep breath and give me a hum or a laugh or say something."

I consider this request as I take a long, slow breath through my nose. Laughing and talking seem impossible, so I let the air out of my lungs in a long, low hum.

"Fuuuuuuck," Dom moans as my vocal cords vibrate against his cock where it rests deep in my throat. A thrill of power shoots through me.

I do it again.

That's all it takes to send Dom over the edge. Taking his orgasm down my throat is one of the most intense experiences of my life. He grips the back of my head tightly, pressing my face into his stomach until I can't see light. His cock is pressing as far into me as it will reach, and he spasms and thrusts as best he can without pulling it out. He's so far down there that I don't taste even a hint of his cum as he empties straight into my stomach.

When he stills, he keeps me pressed there for a few long moments. I breathe through it, my eyes squeezed shut. Just when I think I can't take another second, he begins a slow slide out of me. I feel every centimeter of his still-hard tip sliding up my throat and out of my mouth.

When he finally pulls himself free, I collapse my weight into my arm restraints, my knees having gone too weak to hold me. I dangle there, gasping and swallowing over and over.

Dom watches me with a look of wonder in his eyes. I know I did a good job. I can see it on his face. Any discomfort I'm feeling right now is well worth it to have pleased him so much. Especially after the mess I made of what should have been a very straightforward conversation about money earlier.

When my eyes regain focus, I see him reaching up to the tall midpoint of the steel canopy and unhooking my tether. My butt falls onto my heels with a thump. He lays the leather strap gently on the bed, my bound wrists fall into my lap. My arms pulse as blood rushes into them, the relief almost as intense as when my throat was finally freed of his hard cock.

"That was so fucking good, sweet girl. You sucked Daddy's cock right down your pretty throat, and you loved it."

It's true. I finally got my wish, and it was everything I imagined it would be.

"I think you deserve a reward. What would you like that reward to be?"

"Wine." The word flies out of my mouth before I can even think.

Dom gives me one of his dark chuckles and steps down from the bed. He leaves the room and returns with the bottle and both glasses. He hands mine to me. I take it with my still-bound hands.

It takes two long sips of the glorious liquid before I regain the ability to speak normally.

"You know, I'm not going to run away. You don't have to tie me up."

Dom gives me a smirk. "I'm not worried about you running away, little one."

"So why do you have me tied up like this?"

Dom sets down his glass and climbs on the bed in front of me, on his knees so our faces are level. "I tied you up so you can relax. So you can let go."

I consider this for a moment. It's not something I would have thought to ask for, but now that my hands are bound, I can see what he means.

*I can let go.*

I'm not in charge. I don't have to figure out all of the tough things an adult has to face. I can put aside the heap of pressing decisions I need to make about *what I'm doing with my fucking life* and just let Dom guide me.

Somehow, after all of my worrying that his control was going to feel just like that of my parents, I realize why it's different. They were offering me what they wanted, on their terms. This man seems to be offering me what I want, happy to compromise the terms with me.

*I can say one word and stop him anytime we're going somewhere I don't want to go.*

As terrifying as the conversation about money was earlier, there were no visible strings attached to those offers. As long as he wants to keep this thing between us quiet, I hold a lot of the power. I could ruin him with one word to the wrong person. And yet he trusts me not to.

He trusts me.

Can I trust him?

"Okay, what's next?" I'm happy to be led right now while I try to sort out my feelings.

"I think you know what's next, girl. Next, you're getting my cock nestled right in that sweet little pussy of yours. Are you ready?"

I nod, heat rushing up from my stomach through my chest and no doubt coloring my cheeks. I'm so ready.

"I'll be the judge of that." Dom takes my glass from me and sets it on the dresser next to the bottle. I feel a pang of sadness that the soft, velvety liquid is out of reach, but I know I'm about to get something better. Something I dream about every night.

*Something that's also soft and velvety...*

Dom returns to the bed and wastes no time stripping off my fancy bra and soaked panties. He pushes my knees apart where I kneel and slips his hand between them.

"Oh, you're a wet little thing, aren't you?"

I nod, bottom lip clasped tightly in my teeth.

Dom's mouth lands on mine in an instant, capturing my lips between his, licking along the ridge of my teeth before plunging deep into my mouth. Memories of just a few minutes before, when I had another part of him buried deep in my mouth surface and I let out a moan of anticipation.

I need his touch on more of my body, and I need it now.

"Daddy," I say into his mouth.

"Hmmm?" he murmurs, not relinquishing his dominance over my mouth.

"I've been so good."

I can feel him smile against me, and he finally pulls away. Our eyes meet. His sparkle with amusement and lust.

"Have you now?"

I nod enthusiastically, excited by the prospect of getting to prove myself to him.

"And what have you done that you think was so good? I would be happy to reward you, but you'll have to tell me."

I bite my lip, unsure I can make the words come out. Finally, I realize I don't have to. I take a deep breath, open my mouth wide with my tongue out, tilt my head back and let out a long hum.

Dom barks out a burst of surprised laughter.

I close my mouth and then my eyes as my cheeks burn in shame. I wasn't expecting him to laugh at my display, but when he does, it occurs to me for the first time how ridiculous I must look.

"Look at me."

I can't. My eyes stay closed as I try to fight back tears.

Dom's hand grabs my chin tightly and turns my face up to meet his. I allow my eyes to slowly open. His kind expression is laced with desire.

*He loves this.*

And, although I'm just letting myself think about it for the first time, I do too. I love being shamed, then praised, punished then rewarded by this man. It's what I crave when I'm home in bed alone, dreaming of him fucking me. It's not his cock that is the center of my fantasies. It's why I'm bent over in the first place. I've always done something good or something bad to deserve it.

Tonight, I want it bad.

"Fuck me."

My words have the desired effect. Dom's face curls into a snarl. "What did I tell you about using words like that, baby girl?"

"How else am I supposed to tell you to fuck me other than to ask you to fu—"

Dom slams one hand over my mouth as the other holds the back of my head. My eyes go wide in fear and surprise, earning a dark snarl from Dom as he towers over me.

"I think you're looking for punishment, and you've certainly found it."

I'm running out of breath, tears swelling in my eyes cause my vision to grow blurry as I continue to blink in panic. Dom releases my mouth, and I gasp for air.

He stands and moves away from me, the last thing I want.

"You know, I had a pretty nice evening planned for us." He's standing at the edge of the bed with his wineglass, taking a sip. "I was going to make you come so hard you saw stars and then give you wine and cook for you. So many nice things."

I know he wants his words to hurt, but all I can think about is the not nice things coming my way.

*I want them so bad.*

"But instead, I'm going to have to use my point tonight."

It takes me a second to figure out what he's talking about.

*His point? Oh, from the quiz. I got five points, and he got one.*

My five points got me enough slack that I could kneel. His one point—

Before I can finish the thought, Dom has the end of my tether in his hand, and he's climbing back onto the bed. As he pulls, I'm forced to raise my arms and then climb to my feet. It all happens so quickly that I get dizzy and stumble a bit. Luckily, I suppose, my arms are fastened securely overhead, and I can't fall.

After Dom has me hooked back up, he climbs down to where he gave the tether slack before and takes the strap in his hand.

"Would you like to count or shall I?"

"It's your point." My voice comes out bratty and defiant, and I love it. I can tell that Dom loves it too.

"One." He moves the tether one notch down. I feel my arms loosen overhead. It's enough length that I could almost touch the top of my head with my elbows. I'm stuck here in a standing position, and I know damn well I'm not getting any more slack.

The strap is on a pivot point, and Dom turns me to face away from him as he stands behind me on the bed. I feel one of his rough hands smooth over my ass as his face finds the crook of my neck.

"You can never seem to give this pretty little behind a chance to recover, can you?"

I whimper as his grip tightens.

"You know I'm going to have to punish you for that dirty mouth, right?"

"Yes, Daddy," I breathe the words, anticipation shooting through my veins. It is so overwhelming to be strapped up here, completely at Dom's mercy.

I love it.

He grips my hips and walks them backward until my arms are taut, and I have to bend forward a bit. He lands one soft smack on my ass, which is jutting toward him, and uses his feet to move my legs as wide as they will go.

"Look at you."

"What do I look like?"

"You look like a girl who's in a world of trouble."

I take in a quick breath at his words, wiggling my ass as best I can without moving from the position he put me in. Dom smacks me hard on one cheek for my trouble, and I cry out.

"Grab the strap."

I glance up at my wrists and see what he means. I can hold the strap above the wrist cuffs to take some of the pressure off my shoulders. When I do, I let out a sigh of relief.

"Don't celebrate yet, sweetheart."

Dom has me by both hips now, rubbing his miraculously hard cock up and down the slit between my cheeks.

The feeling of his tip coming so close to my clit with every stroke is making it harder and harder to breathe.

I tilt my hips, trying to bring him closer to the place where I need him to touch so badly. "Please?"

"Please, huh? Now you want to talk nicely?"

"Yes, I'll be nice, Daddy."

"Well, maybe I will too, then."

I hold my breath as Dom lowers himself to his knees behind me, my hips still firmly in his grasp. When his tongue touches down right on my begging clit, I scream. "Yes! Right there!"

He licks up and around the little swollen bud, dragging his tongue back to my entrance and sliding into me. I can feel the sensation in every part of my body. I'm on fire with need...and I'm already so very close to the edge.

Somehow, Dom knows.

And my punishment begins.

The cold I feel when he pulls his mouth away is like frostbite.

"Daddy..." I whimper, understanding what my punishment is now, but unable to come to terms with it.

When his open-handed smack lands on my waiting ass cheek, I'm not one bit surprised.

"That's one."

"H-how many?"

Smack.

"Daddy! How many?"

"I was counting the first of your denied orgasms, love,"—smack—"not spankings."

Smack.

I cling tightly to the strap holding me upright and squeeze my eyes closed.

"And the answer is I don't know yet."

He lands five quick smacks on my aching behind. I hang my head between my raised arms, panting with the effort of tolerating the pain.

I'm braced for another spank, but I get his tongue instead. It comes as a surprise...and not necessarily a good one. It's nice to have a break from spanking, but can I even relax into the pleasure of his tongue when I know it's going to get taken away?

*But maybe it won't this time. He has to let me come eventually, right?*

I let my mental shields drop and lower myself into the pool of pleasure that is Dom's mouth. The smooth glide of his tongue, the little flicks to my clit, the way his fingers know just when to join—slipping inside me and tickling my G-spot.

"Yes! More, Daddy!" I regret the words the second they leave my lips.

All movement between my legs halts.

I cry out in frustration, only to hear Dom give a dark chuckle behind me. Color rises to my cheeks at the embarrassment of being at his mercy like this. I want nothing more than to be immune to all of this, but I know it's only a matter of time before I'm begging.

He pulls my hips roughly, causing me to have to take a step back. My legs are now as far back as they can go with the restraint holding my hands firmly in place. He widens my stance.

"That little pussy of yours—of mine, I mean—seems to be needing some attention. Is that right?"

"Yes." I wonder briefly if I could make myself climax with just my mind and the air moving across my blazing flesh.

I don't get a chance to try.

Smack.

Dom's hand lands between my legs hard and fast, smacking my pussy so hard that I scream.

"There she is," he taunts.

"Why are you doing this?" I ask, nearly in tears with frustration.

"Why am I giving you what you want? Because I am here to take care of you, baby girl. I thought I already told you that."

"I didn't ask for this."

"Maybe not with that filthy mouth of yours, but this pussy has been begging for a spanking since the first time I laid eyes on it."

I don't get a chance to argue, which is probably for the best.

Smack, smack, smack.

His aim is perfect, his open palm connecting with the wet, aching nerves between my legs with expert precision.

I want to hate it. For a second, in the heat of my anger and shame, I even want to hate him for doing this to me. I briefly consider using my colors to stop him.

But it doesn't take long, seconds really, before I'm feeling a lot differently. I might even like it.

Love it?

Smack, smack, smack.

The painful pleasure shoots through me like electricity. It hurts, but he's also making such excellent contact with just the right places…

"Daddy, I'm going to come."

*Why, why, fucking why? I shout the swear word in my mind, knowing I can't utter it aloud.*

Dom laughs again behind me, halting his hand midair. He grips my hips and walks me forward until I'm upright once more, coming in close behind me and wrapping his strong arms around my torso.

His mouth grazes my ear. "Oh, no. You're not."

"Please." I'm not above begging anymore. I've never needed anything more than I need this orgasm right now. In the back of my mind, I know that I can just call out red and stop everything, stop this torture, but I'm not sure I want to. It may be painful and frustrating, but it's also the best feeling I've ever had.

Besides, if I call it all off, I won't get my orgasm, will I?

Dom slides his palms up my ribcage, taking one breast in each hand. He grips my nipples, giving a sharp squeeze before twisting them—not too hard, but just firmly enough that I gasp.

He holds tight.

I squirm, trying to get my nipples out of the grip of his fingers, but there's nowhere for me to go. "Daddy!" He twists sharply in the other direction, and I cry out.

"That sound is going to be the death of me, little one." He releases my nipples, sliding one hand down between my legs in the front, and the other hand back to graze down my ass. I flinch at his touch back there, the skin still smarting and red.

He doesn't smack me though. His fingers continue their slide until they're between my cheeks, resting in a very private place. I shift to dislodge them, but between the grip he has on my pussy and my arm restraints, I can't.

"Calm down, little one, I'm not going to claim you back here tonight."

I do calm down, but it's short-lived. Before I know it, he's taken his cock in his hand and presses it between my cheeks. When it pushes right up against my back door, I whimper.

"You said you wouldn't—"

"I said I wouldn't tonight, baby girl. That doesn't mean I'm not going to give you a taste of what it's going to be like."

I squeeze my eyes closed and bite my lip. I do trust him, and he said he wouldn't do that...but I can't help but think about the future. If he says he's going to claim me there, I know better than to doubt him.

Dom has his swollen tip resting right on the dimpled skin of my anus, and he's softly rocking his hips back and forth. The sensation is not all bad, he does have his other hand gripping my pussy, after all, and I feel myself relax into the motion.

Dom must feel it too, and he starts to pump harder. Before I know it, he's slamming his hips against me, his erection wedged longways down my crack, his tip threatening to enter my tight hole at any moment.

"Daddy..." My pleas have fallen on deaf ears so far, but this time, I get my way.

"I should punish you longer, baby girl, but I just can't seem to resist that sweet pussy of yours." With one smooth motion, he lifts my hips, and his cock plunges straight inside my wet, waiting pussy.

I cry out as he hits the end of me, both hands holding me tightly by the hips now. There's no easing into it—not this time. Dom is fucking me with everything he's got. And I'm loving it.

"F—Oh yeah. God, I love it when you do that." I catch myself just before another offensive word escapes my lips.

A smile forms on my lips even as the punishing pace of Dom's cock continues. He's got me bent over just far enough for the slide of his cock to be hitting the right place inside me, while also rubbing over my clit with every thrust.

Between my grip on the strap overhead and his grip on my hips, my feet have nearly lifted off the bed by the time my orgasm overtakes me. It's like I'm levitating, the magic of the moment swirling like an energy I can feel all around me.

My orgasm passes, but I can feel the wetness of it linger, causing the slide of Dom's cock to be faster, smoother. His rhythm starts to falter, smooth and steady turning to punishing and erratic.

"You feel so good, Daddy." I can barely get the words out, but I want him to know what he does to me.

As if my words were a spell, he bellows as he releases into me. Again and again, he pumps into my body, holding me so tightly, I know I'm going to have little fingertip bruises in the soft places below my hip bones. I almost climax again at the thought of him marking my body.

He lets my hands free while still buried deep inside me, and the combination of blood rushing back to my arms and my still full pussy is otherworldly. I start to melt back into his body just so he'll catch me. He doesn't let me down.

This man never does.

# Rule #18

## SECRET FOR A SECRET

### REINA

We lay in stillness, and Dom strokes my hair like he did in the basement. Long, slow slides of his hand over my head and down my shoulders to my back. I follow his movement with my mind, eyes closed, until I finally feel like I can breathe again.

I might nod off for a moment, but Dom never leaves my side. Finally, when I'm starting to feel more like myself again, I roll onto my back and laugh softly.

"You find something funny, love?"

I shrug. "I'm just…this is just so fun. I never thought that I would be able to be someone who got to play these games. I've always dreamed about it, but I didn't know how to make it happen. You just…did it. You knew what I wanted, and you gave it to me."

Dom is watching me with a playful expression on his face. "I'm happy to please."

He hands me my wine as I lie on his bed, still breathless after going to the bathroom to clean myself up.

"Thanks." I sit up to take it from him. As soon as I have the long-stemmed glass in my grip, he reaches below me and lifts me into his arms like a baby.

"Dom." I laugh as he carries me away.

"I've got somewhere else I want you to see." He walks us down a long hallway to the other side of the house. When he turns into a doorway, I'm transported into another world.

Windows line all the walls making the room almost look like an enclosed porch. The ceiling and floor are cedar paneling like the inside of a sauna and a beautiful handmade looking rug in deep jewel blue and cream feels soft under my feet. Decadent cream-colored couches piled high with pillows in all shades of sand and ocean line three of the walls. In the center of the room is a rectangular table that looks to be made of the same wood as the ceiling and holds a small gathering of clear glass candle holders which Dom lights one at a time after he sets me down on the soft sofa. The amber glow of the flames joins the silver of the light from the full moon reflecting off the ocean and makes the whole room glow.

"Dom," I say breathlessly. The view from the living room was incredible, but this is on a whole other level.

"This house used to be a high-end furnished vacation rental. When I bought it, they just left all the stuff here. The whole place looked just like this. I never thought all that much of it, until I started to think about bringing you here. Then all I could think of was what I wanted to do to you in every room."

I laugh. "What do you want to do to me on this luxurious white couch?" I ask, spreading myself out sexily and batting my eyelashes.

"I want to curl you up like this." He settles under my legs and pulls me close. "And hear everything about you."

I laugh again, this time in surprise. "What do you mean?"

"In town the other day…" He pauses, and I swear I see a hint of nervousness on his face. It's such a departure from the man just punishing me endlessly that my heart melts at the sight. "You told Sam some stuff about your past. It made me jealous.

Those are the things I want to know. I want you to tell me about yourself. I don't want to find out stuff like where you're from secondhand while you're telling someone else."

It takes me a second to recover enough to respond. "You just have to ask, Dom."

"I know, it's just...there have been a couple of times when we started to talk about you, like in my office when I was giving you the menu quiz and earlier this evening in the kitchen. You react a certain way to some questions, and I want to respect your privacy. I know how important privacy is. I don't want to scare you off with questions you don't want to answer."

I'm so surprised and taken aback by this little speech that it takes me a full moment and a huge gulp of wine before I can speak. "I definitely know what you mean. I feel like, since coming here, I've been holding tightly to some secrets in a way I never really did before. This thing between the two of us has created a lot of secrets, and I'm not used to lying to people or making up stories all the time. I guess it's made me defensive in other areas."

Dom's eyes are so kind, I could melt into them. "I'm not going to make you tell me anything you aren't comfortable with."

"I know. I'm sorry if it feels like I'm keeping secrets. I don't want to...it's just that...some things are hard to talk about."

"Secret for a secret?"

Fear rushes through me like a cold wave. I want to agree because I want to know this man's secrets so badly, but am I ready for the honesty it will require of me?

I take a deep breath. "Okay."

"I'll start. I haven't spoken to my family since moving to Faraday Island. I reached out a bit at first, but they never responded. Well, some of them responded, but with insults or guilt trips. So I stopped. They all live in New York running the family business and trusts, and I live here. Running a restaurant."

Whoa. That is a huge bomb to drop. I want to process, but I have a couple of questions first. I have no idea how many he'll answer before demanding that I surrender information of my own, but I'm going to push it as far as I can. "Why don't they support you?"

"It's just assumed that everyone will join the family business. I was always the wild card, the youngest. I went off to travel the world, found my way into kitchens, and never looked back. They're all waiting for me to come back into the fold. I guess they figure they can rebuild our relationships when I get back. Or maybe they just don't care. My path has been decided by me and me alone, against the wishes and demands of everyone."

"What's the business?" If it's the mob or something, I'd like to know now.

"Hedge fund management."

I let out a sigh of relief. Dom takes advantage of my momentary guard drop and steps in to ask his own questions. "Why don't you want to talk about money?"

Damn. I thought this game would be him choosing a secret to share and then me choosing my own, but I guess not. I take a deep breath.

*Here goes nothing.*

"I have a lot of debt."

It's the first time I've ever spoken those words aloud. I was expecting it to hurt, but it actually feels like a huge weight has been lifted. I go on. "When I graduated from college, my parents expected me to go back to the town I grew up in and get a job teaching, find a husband at their church, and live down the street from them raising grandkids. But I didn't. I refused to leave Chicago. After a few months, they stopped paying for my apartment and stopped sending money. I went full-time at my waitressing job, taking as many shifts as I could. But it was never enough. I should have moved into a place with roommates, should have spent less on eating out and shopping, should have done everything differently. I just used credit cards to float myself. Until I couldn't anymore. Then I came here. To hide."

Dom is quiet for a moment, his thoughtful gaze resting on my face. I expect him to jump right in and offer to save me, but he doesn't. "Why didn't you go back home with your parents?"

"It's not the life I want. It was never the life I wanted. By making them think I was coming back eventually, I got them to let me go to the city for school. But once I escaped, I was never going back. My debt stresses me out most days, but I don't regret my choice for a second."

"And now you're here living in staff housing and working to pay it back?"

I nod.

Dom nods.

And that's that. My secret shame is out in the open. I bared my soul for another human to see. And it was fine. I didn't have to defend my decisions or my life. I wasn't shamed for my mistakes. I didn't have to turn down his offer of paying my bills for me. It's just…fine.

I snuggle into this chest and cry silently in relief and happiness.

I don't know how long we lay like that before I fall asleep, but the next thing I know I'm being carried back to bed.

It's the same bed I spent the evening getting tied up and fucked on, but it feels so different now. For one thing, Dom has his powerful AC up so high that he can tuck me in beneath a sheet and soft blanket. What a comforting, familiar feeling it is to be snuggled between blankets. My own apartment is so hot I always sleep completely uncovered.

Gone are the leather straps and wrist cuffs. Gone is the man who tortures me for daring to utter the wrong word. If I had any fear about whether Dom would be aggressive and controlling in real life the way he is in the bedroom, that's gone now too. He slips in beside me, and the room goes completely dark. I curl into him as if I've been doing it every night for my entire life. It feels so natural, so ordinary, so domestic. Intimate in a way the sex games never quite reach.

You know that funny feeling when a noise you have become used to shuts off, like your refrigerator or a fan, and you are bombarded with the incredible silence of its absence? You'd been hearing it for so long but now that it's gone, you can't believe how loud it was? That's my brain laying here in bed with Dom's arms wrapped around me.

He didn't offer me money. He didn't say anything at all when I finally spoke my shame aloud. But somehow, he allowed me to free a demon that had been screaming inside my head for years. The quiet is deafening. I drift off to sleep with a sense of peace I haven't felt in so long, I nearly forgot it was possible.

# Rule #19

BE PREPARED TO GET WET

## REINA

> **Dom**
> Be at the east dock in Saubry at 8 a.m.
> tomorrow.

The text comes in as I'm sitting at lunch with Sarah. I peek at my phone and hide it back in my bag. I also have to hide my excited smile.

One handy part about dating your boss is that he doesn't have to ask when you have days off.

He never really bothers to ask if I have plans for those days off, either, but that's okay. There's nowhere else I'd rather be.

I catch a ride with one of the maintenance carts headed into town at seven-thirty the next morning. I wear my bikini, and pack what I need for what I assume will be a day on a boat. Knowing Dom, though, anything is possible.

> **Dom**
> Come prepared to get wet.

I'm always prepared for that.

The east dock is bustling with tourists preparing to board snorkel boats. I make my way through them to the far end, keeping an eye out for Dom. It's the captain of a large catamaran tied to the very end of the dock, however, who finds me.

"Reina Hansen?"

I turn and smile up at him. "That's me."

"We're over here. The boat's ready when you are."

"Oh, I…" I glance around, not wanting to risk sailing away without my companion.

"He's already on board."

Of course he is.

I nod and allow the man to take my hand and help me onto the deck of the gorgeous white boat.

I pass by the benches and tables in the rear of the vessel and make my way around to the helm, where large, flat expanses of pristine white decking call to the sunbather in my soul.

I lay out my beach towel and settle in, knowing Dom will find me as soon as it's safe to do so. I try to spin the whole situation as romantic, but it's hard not to feel a slight pang of disappointment as the captain unties us, and we head out to sea.

That man should be by my side, but instead, he's hiding somewhere under the deck.

"Morning, beautiful."

My glowering thoughts disintegrate when I see the absolute beauty that is Dom, bare-chested in board shorts. He crosses the deck toward me in sunglasses with two glasses of what looks like iced coffee in his hands.

"Morning, Dom. Nice boat you've got here."

"Yeah, it's not half bad."

I stifle a laugh as he settles in beside me and passes me a drink. The boat is definitely not half bad. It's not any fraction bad.

The thing is marvelous.

An ocean breeze playfully tries to undo my ponytail as I

snuggle into Dom's side and take an appreciative sip of my coffee.

"Where are we headed?"

"Just out and around a bit. We can anchor in the marine park if you want to do some snorkeling."

The idea of spending a whole day with my man, outside the confines of his house, is almost too exciting. "That sounds great."

The boat's engines kick into high gear as we pass into deeper water. Dom and I settle in for the ride.

"This is a fun surprise. How'd you get a private boat like this?"

Dom shrugs. "The captain is a friend."

His short answer makes me curious.

Maybe it's the adrenaline from being on this private boat or the joy I'm feeling at getting to spend a full day with this man, but I'm feeling bolder than usual.

"Question for a question?"

Dom raises his eyebrows at me. "I thought the game was secret for a secret."

"Yeah, well. That makes the stakes seem so high. I like this game better." I shrug.

"Sounds good to me. You wanna go first?"

"In this game we get to ask questions instead of just offering up the first thing that comes to mind."

"You sure you're ready for that?"

I'm not at all sure, but I nod anyway. I'm tiptoeing toward real trust for the first time in a while, and I know this man is a great place to start. Besides, answering a question is so much easier than having to think of something about myself to share.

He's not looking very convinced, but he gives a little shrug and a nod. "Ready when you are."

"What did you tell the captain of the boat about us?"

My question surprises him, I can tell. It surprises me a bit, too. I'm not sure why I want to know so badly, but I just can't let go of the curiosity surrounding the arrangement of this private tour.

Our agreement was to keep this whole thing between us, but he let this person in on the secret. I want to know how he made the decision to trust someone.

"Well, the captain, Martin, and I watch soccer together at the sports bar during the season. We've been friends for a few years. He's got a wife and three kids, and he's lived on the island for nearly twenty years. We've had them over to Merit Island a few times for holidays. They're good people." Somehow, Dom understands just what I need from his answer. "I wanted to get you out of the house, on a proper date, without compromising your privacy, so I asked Martin. He promised it would be discreet."

Dom gives a glance over his shoulder, and I follow his gaze. There's no one in sight. "Probably won't see much of him this trip."

"So, we can do anything we want?" I ask with a suggestive lift of my eyebrows.

Dom pulls me closer. "We can always do anything we want, sweet girl. You know that."

"Not at work."

"I have a fond memory of the bathroom in the staff locker room that says differently."

I laugh softly and blush, shaking my head. "I guess you've got me there."

"But don't think you're going to distract me from asking my question."

I take a sip of my coffee, suddenly nervous for his turn. "Go ahead."

He narrows his eyes in consideration. "Hmm. What do I really want to know about Reina Hansen."

His use of my last name sets me on edge. I know for a fact that I never told it to him, which means he knows through other channels. More...official channels.

"Was your apartment in Chicago the first time you ever lived on your own?"

I glance over at him in surprise. "Yeah, it was."

I can't help the smile that sneaks across my lips. Even as poorly as that chapter closed, there's no denying the joy I felt when it was just beginning. "My parents and I drove up to the city the month before I started college and signed the papers. Well, they signed them, really. My mom and I looked at apartments online for a while before we found one that we could agree on. It was a little four-plex surrounded by houses in a residential area close to school and in a nice neighborhood."

I let my mind drift back to the expansive feeling of freedom that I felt those first few weeks in my own apartment. It's no surprise that I refused to leave it.

"I lived on the second floor with a little balcony. It wasn't much, but it was the whole world to me. To be out on my own, buying my own groceries and washing my own dishes. I can't put into words what that freedom felt like after my whole life being the only child of two helicopter parents." I shake my head, remembering how my mom cried as she left me there, promising to visit every weekend and call every night.

"I planted flowers in pots on my porch, and the hummingbirds would come in the morning. I would sit out there and drink my coffee when the weather was nice. Which, honestly, wasn't very often."

"The weather's pretty nice here. Do you still like to sit outside and have your coffee in the morning?"

I shrug. "I don't have a coffee maker in my apartment here, and there isn't really anywhere to sit on the walkway outside my door. I can't sit on your front porch." I laugh at the thought. "Everyone walking by would see me up there, and we'd be caught for sure."

"What you're saying is I need a back deck. Or a privacy screen for the front. Or at the very least a coffee maker for your apartment and some deck chairs?"

I roll my eyes but keep my smile kind. "That's okay, Dom. You don't have to hire a contractor to build a new deck just so I can drink coffee outside. It was just something I used to do. I do different things now."

I narrow my eyes. "Besides, that was more than one question."

He holds his hands up in surrender. "Shoot."

"Why do you work?"

His eyebrows go sky high, but only for a moment. I can tell he knows it's a reasonable question. Maybe one he gets often.

"Well, I have to do something."

I narrow my eyes again, letting him know that he better go on.

"Everyone needs a purpose in life. Restaurant work is how I found mine. I got my first kitchen job right out of college. My father assumed I would move back home, kinda like you, but I stayed in upstate New York and worked as a line cook. It was a little place called Cynthia's. A pescatarian bistro on the water—a favorite with the locals. The crew there was really close, and I got sucked into it. I'd never been on a team where I was so accepted, and everyone was my friend. I had enough money to rent a house, so I let a few of the guys move in with me. That summer was one of the best times of my life. I just got to be a kid. Kinda for the first time. When I was an actual kid, it was always extracurricular activities and parties. The kids I grew up with had this innate sense of competition with other kids. It was bred into us. Prep school was nothing but a giant pissing match. College was no different. But in that kitchen, in that house, we were all on the same team. I never went back to his world."

"And he didn't, like, cut you off or something? I feel like that's what always happens in the movies."

Dom tilts his head to the side and shrugs. "He might have wanted to, but it wasn't up to him. He's the patriarch, but the structure of the family fortune was put in place by generations before him. Each Fuentes kid had his own share set aside at birth to be invested by the company and managed until we're old enough to take over. There's a serious set of legal processes required to change that, and I never did anything heinous enough to trigger those." Dom's looking out over the water, his eyes hidden behind mirrored lenses so I can't quite read his expression. "He had to let me go. And he did. Without much of a fight actually."

*Yikes.*

For all my parents' shortcomings, at least I can say they tried to get me back. They're still trying, for goodness' sake. I know for sure that my mom hasn't given up hope that I'll move back to Ottawa and reclaim my childhood bedroom.

"What about your mom?" I'm pushing my luck with another question, but I try anyway.

"We lost my mom when I was about six. My dad remarried soon after. Martha was always very good to me and my siblings, but she has three daughters of her own, and they took most of her attention. I'm sure they still do."

"Evil stepsisters?"

Dom laughs. "No, no. They're lovely people."

"Just not for you."

A nod.

"So—"

"I'm pretty sure it's my turn," Dom cuts me off.

I give him a teasing glare, pursing my lips. He just laughs it off.

"Do you think you'll stay?"

I open my mouth to answer but close it again, unsure of the real question there. "You mean, on Faraday? After the season?"

He nods.

"Oh. Well, I assume I will. Honestly, I came here with such a firm plan, and you really shook that whole thing up. I haven't had much time to think about the future anymore. The present is always begging for my attention." I run my hand up the smooth skin of his arm to prove my point.

When Dom doesn't respond—or move at all—I pull my hand back. It seems he's waiting for a different answer.

I try again. "I don't have plans to leave. I love it here. My apartment is the perfect size, and it has this amazing bed in it." That earns me a little smile. It's just the confidence boost I need to go on. "And I love my job. My boss is kind of a bear, but I'm learning to work with him."

I expect another teasing look, but instead, I get a serious one. He pushes his glasses up onto his head and pins me with those eyes. "You can still work at The Sands if this…" He gestures between us. "Doesn't work out for whatever reason."

"Oh, yeah. I figured…" I'm just saying what he wants to hear. Fat chance I'm going to stick around and let my ex be my boss.

Dom seems to read that on my face. "Or I can use my connections to find you a similar position and living situation at another resort. Or whatever you need. I need you to know that there's no way this could play out that would end with you being out on your ass or unsafe at work or anything like that."

The words are reassuring, but his tone has me on edge. "Okay." I want to move past this, but suddenly, there's a storm brewing. I have to ask. "Is that why you asked me if I wanted to stay? So you could make contingency plans for what to do with me when you're finished?"

"No, Jesus. Of course not."

"Well, that's what it sounded like."

"I'm sorry. I can hear it now. I just…wanted to know whether this relationship is something I should be thinking as a possible long-term thing. Or if you've got plans to head off at the end of the season."

*And leave him.*

"I don't have any plans to leave, Dom."

He nods. "Well, the other stuff is important, too. I don't want you to feel like you're stuck with me so you can keep your job."

"I don't feel that way."

"I know you don't. But if that ever changes, just tell me. Or tell one of the other guys. They'll all be on your side. We all take the responsibility of helping employees seriously."

"I'll just pack my bags and have Avery fly me out in the dead of night."

I mean it to be a joke, but Dom nods seriously. "Sure. That would be fine. He'd do that."

I start to roll my eyes, but Dom catches my face in his hand, using my chin to turn me to face him. "Promise me."

"I promise."

"You promise what?"

"I promise that if we break up—or if I want to break up with you—I will ask you or one of the other owners to help me get settled somewhere else."

"Okay. Thank you."

"No problem. Actually as soon as we get back, I'll find Avery and ask him for his number. Do you think he'll give it—"

I don't get to finish my thought before I'm tackled to the deck. "Dom! You're going to spill my coffee," I manage to get out through my laughter.

"You've got it coming with that sass, girl."

I just laugh again and surrender. When he stills, I find him gazing down into my eyes once more.

"Is that enough question for a question?"

I nod, stifling a smile.

"Good." He sits up and looks around as the boat engines cut and we start to drift forward more slowly. "I think he's about to anchor." When he turns back to me, his smile is in place, all signs of the heavy discussion gone. "Ready to do some snorkeling?"

# Rule #20

## LIES BEGET LIES

### REINA

The next few weeks pass in a whirlwind of brunch shifts, beach days, late nights, and stomach butterflies—the beautiful kind. I work hard at my job, settling myself into the role. I'm making friends with the whole staff, Sylvia especially. If anything, we are co-running the a.m. shift, and it's going really great.

I'm pretty tired most days from working early and staying up late at Dom's house, but I've developed a schedule splitting my sleep into half at night and half in the afternoon that seems to be working for me. I know my friends think I'm a sleepaholic because I constantly turn down invites in order to be in my bed, but what's a girl to do?

Dom hasn't brought up the subject of us breaking up and me moving away to another resort again after our little conversation on the catamaran. He continues to surprise me with little gifts here and there and always brings home incredible food from the restaurant that we eat in bed after our trysts or cold in the morning.

There has been no mention of money, or any more credit

cards, which I'm grateful for. I keep paying as much as I can on my bills every week, and I'm proud to see the balances all going down. I don't need to spend much, especially not since I got the management benefits package, which has a food allowance. I spend a little of that allowance on my breakfast every morning and use the rest at the grocery store in town. Dom feeds me dinner every night.

I'm happy to get to hold onto my last remaining secret from him, about my work history, having somehow managed to make it through two of our sharing games without being asked. I'm not excited about defending my decision to work brunch when I should be helping him get dinner in shape for the award season, so I haven't instigated the game again, as fun as it was to get to hear his secrets.

"Reina!"

I finish locking my apartment door on my afternoon off and turn to greet Sarah, who is running excitedly up the steps toward me.

"Did you hear?"

"Hear what?" Honestly, I probably have heard, but it's hard to say what she's so worked up about. The amount of gossip I hear on a daily basis between the restaurant and the staff quarters is staggering.

"Look!"

I glance where she's pointing and see a group of maintenance guys setting up a small, rectangular cabana at the top of the path that leads away from the apartment building. There's a central post with cords coming out of what looks like an electrical box or battery of some kind. "What is it?"

"They're putting in a charging station for the new employee golf carts they got us!" Sarah's glee is contagious, and I find myself grinning at her. "I heard that there are going to be four of them, and we will be able to schedule time to use them, and it won't cost us anything!"

"Wow, that's...amazing."

It really is. I was impressed by the speed with which that man managed to find me a new mattress after experiencing the loose springs in my old one, but to procure four new golf carts and get a shelter built for them in just a few weeks?

*Very nice, Dom. Very nice.*

Sarah walks with me down the stairs, and we stroll toward the construction, stopping a few feet away to watch.

"We'll be able to pop into town any time we want," Sarah says, linking her arm through mine and resting her head on my shoulder.

I lean into her, taking a moment to enjoy her presence. We have become pretty good friends, and it feels nice to have someone I'm so close to.

*Even if I'm lying to her about everything.*

That thought comes up more and more.

Back when the story of Dom and me would have been nothing more than hot gossip, it was easier to find justification for keeping it to myself. But now that it's starting to feel like something else, something bigger, the fact that I haven't told her feels like just another heavy weight I carry around.

Whenever I finally tell her, or when she finds out on her own, she's going to know that I've been keeping this a secret for a long time. I pray that our new friendship is strong enough to withstand that kind of betrayal.

"Let's head to the cantina. I have snacks in my cupboard."

I let her lead me away from the construction and down the little sandy path, still worrying about what might happen in the future.

I settle onto the long bench seat at the staff table close to a group of other off-duty employees enjoying their meal and chatting. I recognize some of the women from the restaurant, a couple who work at the front desk who I met at the first staff party, and a group of tightly gathered local women who I know work housekeeping. I often see them driving around in their golf carts, bringing bundles of sheets or buckets of cleaning supplies to and from the main resort building.

Sarah heads over to the wall of plastic, bug-proof food lockers and opens the tiny pink padlock on hers with the combo. When she returns with a bag of the pale round shortbread cookies that I recognize from the bakery in town, I accept one gratefully.

The group of women around us, are, predictably, talking about guys.

"For me, it goes—Nick from the kitchen, Jake from the front desk, and then Juan from pool maintenance. In that order," one of the women is saying, listing her crushes.

"Ooh, the pool guy!" The women break into a chorus of giggles.

"Who do you have your eye on, Sarah?" The whole crowd turns toward us as one of the off-duty servers calls over to her. "I saw you at the bar with Justin the other night. Something we should know about?"

I've already heard the story of the ill-fated drink with Justin, so I place my hand supportively on Sarah's knee as she lets out a sigh and dives into the tale. "He was a little...douchey. I mean, he wanted to talk about other girls at the restaurant he's hooked up with. Which, in itself, isn't too terrible. I mean, I don't mind knowing upfront who he's already dated, you know? But there were so many details, and he wasn't exactly flattering." Groans and noises of disgust echo around the table as the women shake their heads and exchange glances. "I was pretty bummed out. He was my target lay for the season. I was so excited to be getting a drink with him." Sarah shakes her own head, letting out a sigh. "Oh well. Onto the next."

"We need a list where we can jot down the names of all the bad ones and what they did, so no one else has to waste their time," one of the women suggests, and the table agrees.

"What about you, Reina? I thought someone was going to snatch you up on day one. Are you really still single?"

I should have been ready for this question, but it still takes me by surprise. I take a deep breath and prepare to lie, again. "Oh, I'm just taking my time. No need to rush into anything, right?"

The noises around the table are not ones of agreement. I'm going to have to do better than that.

"I...had a bad breakup right before I moved here, and I'm just enjoying some me time." I know they won't ask for the full story, so I'm safe with that lie. At least I think I am until I look up at Sarah to see if she's ready to leave.

*Shit!*

If there was a bad breakup in Chicago, right before I moved here, wouldn't I have mentioned it to her? I'm struggling to keep all these lies straight.

And I don't even want to be telling them.

I want to be building community with these people, not fabricating breakup stories to cover up the fact that I'm living on an island of hot, half-naked single men and not dating any of them.

"We should do a town night soon. Girl, if you thought the selection at the resort was prime pickings, you should see some of the townies. There are a couple of scuba companies that have guides living here full-time, and those guys are hot. Not to mention, they can get you super good hookups on boat rides."

"I would love to hook up on a boat ride," one of the girls jokes and everyone laughs.

Everyone but me.

This feeling of separateness has been becoming more and more pervasive over the last couple of weeks. I'm finally feeling like I might be ready to try bonding with these women and building relationships. Instead, I'm lying, making up stories about my past, and avoiding hanging out with them.

It feels like I'm building walls just when I want to be building bridges.

Crazy but now I can't see a single way around the outcome

that I was trying to avoid by keeping this whole thing a secret. If I tell them about Dom and me, then they might think I was sleeping my way to the top. But if I don't tell them, and they find out later, will I even get a chance to explain myself? Will they give me that chance, or will they just write me off as a liar?

I'm starting to feel the room closing in on me, and I stand abruptly. "You ready to head down to the restaurant?" I ask Sarah, praying she will agree.

"Sure, yeah. I need a coffee anyway. See y'all later."

"Let's for sure do a town night. How about Thursday?" one of the dinner servers offers.

"I work in the morning Friday, sorry," I answer, grateful for once for my early shift.

"Sunday, then. It's karaoke at Kings Sports Bar."

"Sure, yeah," Sarah answers before I can think of another excuse. She turns to me. "You have Monday off this week, right? That will be perfect."

"I'll call my friend Chris and make sure all the hot scuba instructors are there," one of the servers says.

We exit the cantina as the girls break into excited giggles once more.

Sarah and I walk silently for a few feet, but I can feel her questions waiting in the air between us.

Finally, I can't take it anymore. "Sorry about the whole... breakup thing." I don't know whether she will think I'm just apologizing for not telling her, or if she knows I'm apologizing for lying, but it's all I can think of to say.

She's quiet for a moment before speaking softly. "You can talk to me, you know."

"I know."

"I know you are kind of a private person." She holds up her hand to stop me when I try to interrupt. "And that's fine. Really, it's totally fine. I like to blah blah blah all of my personal stuff, but I know not everyone likes to share all their little secrets."

I can barely breathe with the effort it's taking to keep from crying. I'm not trying to be a secretive person. It's just...the whole friends thing hasn't gone well for me in the past. I grit my teeth and force myself to let out some of the words burning holes in my mind.

"It wasn't a breakup exactly. In Chicago." Sarah walks quietly beside me, her reassuring presence exactly what I need to go on. "I worked at a really intense place. It was amazing, and I learned a lot, but the people there were so...cool." I laugh and shake my head. It's the most uncool way to describe it, but I can't think of a better word. "I went into that job with my heart on my sleeve, so young and wanting to fit in with the hip crowd—going to brunch and taking the train and buying all the latest fashions. I figured that if I just acted the part, it was only a matter of time before they would accept me."

Sarah is still listening quietly, giving me all the time I need to share my story. "It didn't end up being real, though. As soon as I started to have problems paying for things after a big fight with my parents when they turned off my allowance, I stopped getting invited out with them. I took out some credit cards and that helped for a while, but I could just never keep up. I don't know how they did it. I mean, I made the same amount of money as they did, how did they manage to sustain those lifestyles when I was sinking into debt? It really did a number on my self-esteem."

Since I've gone this far—and Sarah hasn't gone running for the hills yet—I decide to share even more.

"I've always felt that way, though, kind of. My parents are both schoolteachers, and we lived in a really small town. No one ever wanted to come over to my house. I convinced my parents I didn't want to have birthday parties because some mean kids told me that they'd never come to a teacher's house, and I was too scared to ever invite anyone again." I let out a sad laugh. "It sounds so stupid now, but it was such a big deal back then. My parents just assumed I was shy, but the truth was that I never felt like I fit in with anyone. Anywhere. When I moved to Chicago for college, I was so excited to leave all that behind. But it followed me. Different people, different situations, but it still felt the same. Like I was on the outside of whatever club everyone else was in, and I could pretend for a while, but eventually, they saw me for who I was. Not good enough to be their friend."

After a moment of silence where I try to keep myself from crying, Sarah takes my hand and pulls me into a side embrace as we walk slowly down the sandy path. "People are the freaking worst."

I laugh softly at her proclamation, and a few tears run down my cheeks.

"I'm glad you told me all this. It totally makes sense why you are so hesitant to go out with us all the time now."

It's only part of the reason I don't join them at parties or bars in town, but I nod anyway.

"Well, I've got your back. You know you can trust me. And Charles, of course. And when we go to town with that group of girls to meet up with the hot scuba instructors, I'll be there making sure you find the perfect guy."

I've already found the perfect guy. The words are right on the tip of my tongue. I should just tell her and be done with it.

I mean, what's the worst that could happen?

*The worst that could happen is that you finally find a true friend and then you tell her you've been lying, and you no longer have any friends at all.*

And Charles has been in love with Dom for years. How is he going to react to me swooping in and stealing his crush away?

I'm quiet for too long, and Sarah stops us and pulls me into a full hug. "Really, girl. It's going to be great. I know it can take a lot to trust people after bad experiences, but you're on the right path. You trust me, and pretty soon you'll start trusting other friends. People here aren't like city people. You just got here, but you'll see soon enough. The friends I've made on this island are the most genuine, caring people in the whole world. And you're one of them."

I lean into her hug as the tears start to roll. The last thing I want is to stay silent about all the feelings I'm having right now. All the amazing, unbelievable things that are happening in my bed and in Dom's mansion on the hill. I'm dying to tell her and watch her face light up when I reveal just how much I'm falling for the guy.

But that's not going to happen. And it's not just because of my traumatic past with bullies and mean girls. It's because Dom and I agreed to keep the whole thing secret.

It's one thing to risk Sarah being mad at me—I have a feeling I could make it up to her. But to lose Dom over this?

Not a chance.

I manage to pull myself together by the time we reach the café, and we head to the bar to wait for Sylvia to bring us our paystubs.

It's a funny tradition I'm learning about—all the employees parading down to the resort on payday, even if it's their day off, to grab the envelope containing their paystub. The money is all direct deposited so there's no real reason for this, but everyone does it, so I do it too.

Sarah gives me one more encouraging hug after we order coffee, and it nearly sends me back onto my emotional spiral. I have some serious thinking to do, but this isn't the place to do it.

Sylvia sets two envelopes on the counter with a smile. Sarah rips hers open eagerly, as if it was an envelope of cash, rather than a slip of paper with no value.

I open mine more slowly while I wait for my latte, but when I peek inside, my stomach drops. All of the emotional upset from two seconds before is forgotten as I try to process what I'm seeing.

"Hey, I'm going to go grab something out of my locker really quick. Will you wait here for my coffee?"

"Sure," Sarah says, not even looking up from her phone.

I stroll through the kitchen trying to look calm and cool, when inside I'm anything but.

*How could he?*

By the time I get to the office door, where I know I'll find him, I'm taking deep breaths to steady myself.

# Rule #21

## GOOD WORK DESERVES REWARD...
## AND PUNISHMENT

### DOMINIC

"Come in," I say absentmindedly, not looking up from my computer. When the door shuts a little too loudly, I glance up to find Reina.

And she's pissed.

"Hey," I say, starting to get up and go to her. It's impossible for her to be in the same room without me wanting to have my hands all over her. Inconvenient for a secret workplace relationship, but, hey, what are you gonna do?

"What's this?" she huffs out before I can get to her, tossing an unfolded piece of paper on my desk.

I pause my approach and snatch it up. It's her paystub. It occurs to me that today is payday, and she must have stopped by the restaurant to grab this. "Your paystub?"

I have a feeling I know what's coming next, but I decide to let her tell me.

"Why did you give me a raise? I thought we talked about this."

"Reina—"

"I don't want to be getting raises for,"—she lowers her voice and glances adorably from side to side before hissing out the words—"sleeping with the boss."

I can't help but crack a smile, which does nothing to soothe her. "I'm not technically your direct supervisor, you know. I'm not the one who decides—"

"You had nothing to do with this?"

"I mean, I knew it was happening." I've made it a point to know everything that goes on in this girl's employee file. "But it was Sylvia who requested it and Sam or HR who approved it. I can't give raises to brunch servers. I mean...I could, I guess, but it might raise some eyebrows."

Her face calms as she considers my words. "Sylvia gave me a raise?"

I take that small openness as a sign I can move forward. When my hands touch down on her hips and pull her toward me, she comes willingly. "I told you before that if you didn't knock off the good work, you were heading for a raise. I wouldn't be surprised if those two have a promotion in mind for you."

She blushes and looks away, but I can see that she's pleased.

A pleased Reina gives me nearly as much of a rush as when she's screaming my name in bed. As much as I love bending her over my knee, and to my will, making her happy is just as important.

I may whip her, but I am fully and completely whipped.

"It's a nice little raise, isn't it. You must be doing a very good job."

Reina picks up on the change in my tone and tilts her sexy little head up at me. "Do I get a reward?"

I bare my teeth at her and growl softly. Her body melts into mine. "I don't know about rewards, but I have a feeling there may be some punishment in store for storming into my office, accusing me of things. Be at my house when I get off."

"I didn't mean...I mean, I just..." She doesn't want me to be upset with her, and her backtracking is adorable. "I'll be there," she says finally, not meeting my eye.

She has her own key now. She has a toothbrush and clothes at my house. Her favorite yogurt is in the fridge.

"You better either get out that door or get your hands on that desk and bend over."

Reina lets out a surprised laugh. "I gotta go. Sarah's waiting for me."

I make a noise of disapproval, making no move to let her go. She wrenches her body from my grip, one of my favorite games, and makes it to the door before I can grab her back again.

She turns to me halfway out the door and gives me one of those looks that I love—sultry, sexy, adorable. "See you later," she mouths and then shuts the door quickly behind herself.

I stand alone in my office, leaning against my desk, staring down at the bulge in my pants. I've been this way almost constantly since the first time I laid eyes on that girl. My need for her is nearly uncontrollable.

I should be worried about my stolen focus. I should be looking forward to an excellent dinner service, not praying it will pass quickly so I can get home to her.

As much as I want to chastise myself for my extracurricular activities, there's no denying how well the kitchen is running right now. It's almost as if taking a tiny step back has actually improved things instead of sending the whole place down in flames.

I change the menu less often because my evenings, which I used to spend changing the menu, are now spent spanking the adorable little ass in my bed. In response, the cooks know the dishes better and find new and innovative ways of executing and garnishing them. Every night a dish stays on the menu, it gets better.

I'm in a good mood nearly all the time now, even if I try to hide it behind my gruff exterior. In response, my team feels comfortable sharing their ideas and concerns with me. We've made some changes to the flow of service, the menu, and the order of the courses based on the team's input that upped our game substantially.

As much as I'm still waiting for things to go downhill without my micromanagement and as terrified as I still am to leave the line for one second when the judges could walk through the door at any moment, even I can see how well everything is going.

I'm excited, distracted, and terrified. For once in my life, I feel out of control, and I don't hate it. Even if I have only had the illusion of control all these years, it felt solid in my iron fist. It felt like an anchor that was keeping me from floating off. It felt like reins, keeping me on the path I laid out for myself. Now I'm a tornado of emotions, and I've never felt so alive.

The younger chefs dominate in the kitchen, and I love it. I love watching them change and grow, taking my ideas and my dishes and making them their own. The results are so much better than I've ever accomplished alone.

And now, I have a woman who I really care for. One who rules my every waking thought. I don't know how it's going to go with her. This whole thing is so fresh and new and still a goddamn secret from everyone in my life, except for Sam and Avery. And possibly Sylvia, who has been giving me some knowing looks. That's fine, though. Those three have managed to keep their mouths shut, so my secret is safe.

Our secret.

Reina will stay safe at work, without having to worry about losing her job for sleeping with the boss. And I can manage my team without worrying about people thinking I'm exploiting one of my employees.

I have to admit, I worried about a secret relationship at first, but this could not be more perfect. I'm getting exactly what I want, and I don't have to talk about it with anyone. I don't have to share her with anyone.

*She's mine.*

I want so badly not to fuck this up, and I know that keeping it together—and keeping it completely secret—is the only way. If the whole staff found out, well, I'm fairly certain that would ruin everything. I will protect this secret with everything I've got.

# Rule #22

## DON'T FORGET THE KISS

### DOMINIC

I button up the front of a crisp, clean black chef's jacket and step out of my office. The prep kitchen is in full swing, extra busy at the moment with the changeover between shifts happening. As the daytime prep cooks wrap up their projects and clear their stations, the dinner cooks make lists and set up. The energy of the room is so alive, I can feel it in my bones.

"Marcus, how are things looking?" I cross my arms over my chest and wait for my sous chef to give me the rundown of the night's prep.

Marcus ticks his pen against a clipboard a few times before looking up at me. "We are pretty low on cleaned crab, so that's going to be the priority. Sauté needs to break down steaks, and pastry is going to need almost the whole menu prepped."

"Can you pull someone from pantry to help them?"

"Yeah, I'll pull Suze."

I nod and start to walk up to the front kitchen where the line cooks will be getting their stations ready. I need to check on a gas line to one of the ranges to make sure it got replaced this afternoon.

As I pass by the open door to the staff changing room, however, a certain name on the lips of one of the off-duty cooks inside catches my attention.

"For me, it goes Reina, Samantha, Christine, Raven."

"Fuck you, man, I told you last week I was going to ask Reina out."

"Every man for himself."

"She's not going to go out with your lame ass. She's a sophisticated woman. She needs someone older, more mature."

"Oh, and you think you're mature? Just because you're old doesn't mean shit."

My blood boils as I listen to the conversation, but I'm not sure what options I have. I can't very well burst in there and tell them not to talk about my girl that way—or at all—without giving up what I most want to protect.

But I can't just let it go. "Hey," I call into the changing room. "You guys get changed and get out of here. We need this room for…dinner setup."

The talk falls silent as all the guys turn to look at me. I'm sure they're wondering what kind of setup requires the staff changing room, but I know damn well none of them will question me.

"Sure thing, Chef."

It's the right thing to say, and the guy even said it in a non-mocking tone. But he was one of the worst offenders—the guy telling all of his friends that my girl would go out with him. He's lucky I can't fire him for that because I probably would. "I'm going to need you four in here early tomorrow to do a deep clean on the prep room."

They're silent, but I can feel the confusion and injustice fill the room like a thick fog.

"Can we do that after shift, Chef?" the bravest of the bunch asks. Unfortunately for him, he was the other one speaking Reina's name.

"When we're trying to prep dinner? Not a chance. Two hours early actually. Be here by three thirty a.m. I'll be in early to make sure it's spotless."

Not one of them dares to challenge me. I make eye contact with each of them in turn, staring down their looks of hatred with my own, before storming out of the room.

Unfair…yes. A complete overreaction on my part, also yes, but I can't help it. That's my girl, and no one should be talking about her. They should know better but how could they? No one knows a damn thing. To them, she's just another server. A fucking beautiful, smart, kind, and—as far as anyone knows—single server. Fair game.

I grind my teeth as I walk onto the hot line. The look on my face scares off the dinner cooks working up there, so I have a moment alone to check out the gas lines and think.

There's no way I can tell any of the guys to stay away from Reina without giving up our secret. I briefly consider a blanket no dating policy in the restaurant but quickly dismiss that as insane and impossible.

I can't control the actions of all the men on this island.

If I'm going to get some peace of mind about my relationship with Reina, it's going to have to come from her end. We haven't exactly had a conversation about our relationship and where all this is going. Hell, we haven't even really talked about being exclusive, as crazy as that sounds. I just assume that we're together, she's mine, and she would never be with anyone else.

But has she ever actually said that?

The rage in my blood turns cold with dread. How the hell have I let this go on so long without having some kind of agreement between the two of us? I mean, we have our secrecy agreement, but we have no other commitments to each other. I've always just figured that between her job, her girlfriends, and spending every night with me, she wouldn't have time to be doing something like *dating other people.*

Just those words in my mind bring bile up the back of my

throat, and I have to take a few deep breaths to calm myself down.

There's no way she's dating other people.

No fucking way.

*They sure want to date her, though.*

My mind starts to wander to her at work when I'm not watching, or she's in town or in the staff cantina. How often are guys looking at her or talking to her or even asking her out? Considering the fact she's the most beautiful, charming, perfect woman on the planet, my guess is it's pretty damn often.

I stand up so suddenly, I startle one of the cooks who has bravely made his way back to work at his station. I don't have time to apologize or explain myself. I need to get to my girl.

My phone is on my desk, and I grab it the second I enter my office. I punch out a text and glare at the screen, ordering the gods of phone reception to make the damn thing go through. They obey for once.

**Dom**
My house, twenty minutes.

A text bubble pops up immediately, so I know she read it. I slip my phone in my pocket without waiting to hear what she says. She'll be there, and I'm not interested in any excuses.

"Marcus, I have to run out for a bit. You good in here?"

"Sure thing, boss. We've got it under control."

The funny thing is, I believe him. This time last year, I never would have stepped out for a second, not with dinner service only a couple of hours away. Certainly not during award season. But the kitchen has a different feel to it now, like it can survive without me for an hour.

I make my way up the long, sandy path to my house wearing too many clothes, and I'm sweating by the time I reach my front door. I leave it unlocked and head to the shower.

The cool water pouring over my face doesn't calm me nearly

as much as I hoped it would. I stand there with my eyes closed, taking deep breaths, trying to push aside the thoughts raging through my mind. Trying to replace them with more sane thoughts.

*She isn't sleeping with other guys.*

*She's at your house every night.*

I'm so absorbed with trying to convince myself everything's fine that I don't hear Reina until she's squealing behind me.

"Dom! Why is the water freezing? Are you crazy?"

I open my eyes in the water and smile. My whole body relaxes at the thought of having her so close. She's here. She's safe. She's mine.

I turn and pull her into my arms. "It feels good. It's so hot out there."

Holding her close to me, I take a step back, bringing us both under the stream of water. She squeals and tries to get away, but I hold her tightly. "You get used to it."

"Dom!"

With another smile, I reach back and tip the faucet just a tad, taking the edge off the cold water. Reina relaxes immediately, melting into my arms.

"What's up?" she asks after a moment, looking up at me from inside my embrace. "I had to make up some reason I couldn't go to town with Sarah to rush over here. I thought something was wrong."

"Something is wrong."

I turn our bodies so that her back is to the wall and release my arms so I can press her there with my chest, my hands on either side of her shoulders as I look her right in the eyes.

"I need you to tell me that you aren't...seeing other guys." Even in my anger, I can't bring myself to say the words *sleeping with*.

The look of confusion on her face sharpens at my words. "Wait, what?"

"Tell me, Reina."

"Of course I'm not seeing other guys. Are you crazy?"

I probably am, but I push on. "Not talking to them or going on dates when I'm not around or having them over to your apartment?"

She's pissed now, and I suppose it's justified. I've lost my mind, and I'm taking it out on her.

With a firm push on my shoulders, she frees herself and retreats to the far corner of the shower with her arms crossed. "No, Dom. I'm not sneaking other guys up to my apartment when you're at work. Is that what you are worried about?" She's not only pissed, she's offended.

As I struggle to find the right words, I watch her face change.

"Wait, are you sleeping with other women?"

I scoff. "How could you even ask that?"

Her mouth falls open. "How could *you* ask me?"

"It's different."

"How is it different?"

"I'm…" Now that I'm tasked with explaining myself, I guess it's not all that different. "The owner of The White Sands. Everyone on this island knows me. I can't just sleep around. You, though, are the ripest little peach that ever dropped onto these shores." I take a step toward her, the need to place my hands back on her body burning through my fingertips. "Everyone wants you."

Reina offers an adorable eye roll. "Everyone wants me, huh?"

I nod, taking another step closer. I can feel her shields dropping. She's going to let me back in.

"How do you know who wants me?" Her voice falls to a whisper as I reach her, falling to my knees to press a kiss to her navel.

"I just know."

"The only person I want is you."

Her words flow over me like a balm. I hate myself for needing this kind of reassurance, but I do. I need even more.

"The idea that you walk around this resort, this island, every day looking as perfect as you do, and no one knows you're mine scares me."

"You don't need to be scared, Dom."

I stand back up and bring my mouth to her lips, pressing myself inside. I need to taste her everywhere.

Claim her.

Everywhere.

"This body,"—my hands reach her shoulders and press her back into the solid glass wall—"is mine."

Reina says nothing, but I can hear her breathing rate increase. As I trail my lips down her neck to her breasts, I feel her heart racing.

"These luscious tits." I swirl my tongue around one nipple and then the other. "Mine." I bite down, causing her to jump a little. I hold her tightly in place.

"Mine. Mine. Mine." I trail my lips down her torso, kissing each place I find a tiny freckle.

When I reach the small tuft of hair gatekeeping the place between her legs, I waste no time in sliding my tongue to her clit, giving it a sharp circle. "Mine."

I look up to find Reina with her eyes closed, lip between her teeth. She almost looks like she wants to say something, to argue with me, but she doesn't.

I slide my hand up her wet leg and press three fingers roughly inside her. I press until I can't reach any farther, the warmth and wetness of her body like a home I want to crawl into.

A home I want to claim.

"This right here." I pull out and thrust my fingers back inside her. "Is only mine."

A whimper from her draws my eyes back upward. She's watching me now, expression unreadable.

"Say it, Reina." I pull out and thrust again and again.

"It's yours," she says immediately, her soft voice full of desire.

I pull my hand out and rise to my feet once more, bringing my wet fingers to her lips. She opens without me having to ask, and I push all three of them inside. Her tongue greets my fingers, pressing up to meet them. I push down until I nearly have a grip on her.

"This sweet little mouth of yours, girl. Mine."

I can see her eyes starting to tear up at the intrusion of my hand, but I don't let up. "Say it."

"It's yours." The words sound garbled as she nearly chokes on my hand, but they satisfy me.

I pull my fingers out, leaving her mouth hanging open as she watches me, no doubt trying to figure out what's going to happen next.

I bring my hand up and wrap it in her half-wet hair, pulling her face to mine. I hold her there for a moment, foreheads pressed together, trying to calm myself down. It only half works.

When I can't stand it any longer, I pull her by the hair back into the warm shower stream and press the front of her body into the far shower wall. I step in close behind her, my now raging hard-on finding the crack between her gorgeous pink cheeks.

Still holding on tightly to her hair, I tilt her head to the side, touching my mouth down first on her jawline, then trailing down her neck to her shoulder where I imagine the faint outline my teeth left during our basement tryst. I bite down in the same place again, the squeal it earns me making my already hard cock even harder.

My free hand slides down to meet my cock where it's nestled right over her cute little rosebud. I press lightly on the puckered skin, swirling my finger around.

"I need to claim you everywhere, baby girl."

If Reina knew this was coming, she did a good job of hiding it. A little sound of surprise escapes her lips, and she tries to pull away.

I hold her tightly.

With my free hand, I grab the bar of soap.

It takes me a moment to get a good lather between the soap in my hand and her back, but eventually I have enough suds and slide them down between her cheeks. "Are you ready for me?"

She doesn't say yes, but she doesn't say no. Reina just lets out another little whimper.

"Don't be scared, little love."

"I am."

"No one has ever claimed you down here before?" I ask, finishing my thorough wash of the area and pulling her hips toward the stream of water to rinse her clean.

She shakes her head quickly. "No."

Pleasure at the thought of being the first nearly makes my knees buckle.

I place her hands on the shower wall in front of her and pull her feet back one at a time until she's bent over, hands bracing herself. I slide her feet to the side. She doesn't stop me, but I can feel her resistance.

"What are you scared of, little one?"

"I'm scared it's going to hurt."

"I would never hurt you."

Reina barks out a small laugh and says nothing.

"When have I hurt you?"

"You spank me."

I smile, sinking to my knees behind her. With her bent over like this, legs spread, I have the most glorious view. I can't help but run my tongue around her sweet rosebud, giving it a little swirl.

"The spanking may hurt, but you like it, don't you?"

"Yes..." she replies nervously.

"This will be like that. I'll make sure you like it, even if it hurts a little."

"So it is going to hurt. But you said—"

I stand and press her body flat against the wall with my own, stopping her arguing in its tracks. "What I said was that I was going to claim every single inch of this body. *My* body. Isn't that right?" I speak directly into her ear, my hand fisted in her hair once more.

"Yes," Reina manages in a whimper.

"And I said I'd make sure you liked it. Is that right?"

"Yes," she says again, this time more resigned.

"Yes what?"

"Yes, Daddy."

She has submitted completely, and I could not feel more powerful in this moment. With the desire and dominance rushing through my veins like a drug, I pull her off the wall and into my arms. We walk together out of the shower. Reina stands silently, watching me as I wrap her in a fluffy white towel and dry her off.

When I walk her to the bed and sit her down, she looks so adorable, I can't keep my mouth off her. I pull the towel away and push her down on the bed onto her back.

When I sink to my knees and press hers apart, she relaxes visibly. Good. I want her to relax. I may be dead set on claiming that sweet little ass for my own, but I did promise she'd like it. Relaxing her is a big part of that.

My tongue touches down on her pink flesh and goes right to work. When she's starting to moan in pleasure, I add my fingers, pressing the spot that always makes her sing.

Just as her breath starts to quicken, however, I pull myself away.

I can tell she knew I wouldn't let her come because she doesn't protest. Usually, I live for her bratty defiance, but in this moment, her complete submission is the most satisfying thing I've ever experienced.

I walk over to my dresser where I've been hiding the tiny purple toy I ordered a few weeks back. It's all charged and ready, so I press the on button. The buzzing sound fills the silent room, drawing Reina's attention.

When I glance over and catch her eye, it's curiosity I find there, not fear.

"I got you something," I say, clicking the little buzzer off again.

She says nothing, just watching me as I approach with the vibrator belt in my hands.

"Get on all fours."

She obeys calmly. I wonder if she would be so calm if I was ordering her to all fours with my lubed-up cock coming at her. No, this is a much better way to go. Ease her into it. I will get what's mine, but there's no point in making it a punishment.

I wrap one of the thin purple straps around each of her thighs and one around her hips, securing the little silicone rocket ship in place over her clit. When I click the thing on, she cries out. I click it off again.

Slipping the remote into her hand, I lay down the ground rules. "Don't turn that on until I say you can, got it?"

"Yes, Daddy."

"I'm going to claim this little asshole now, and you're going to like it."

"Okay," she breathes, the hesitation in her voice fading.

"I'm not coming until you do, got it?"

She takes a breath and lets it out slowly before answering. "Yes, Daddy."

I return to the dresser to get the bottle of high-end silicone lube that I bought to go along with the toy—and this particular adventure. Once I'm behind where she waits for me on all fours, however, I set the bottle down.

"I don't think I can manage to not spank this ass when it's just begging me for it like this."

Reina wiggles her ass to agree, making me laugh. I'm so glad she's on board with this, even if it makes her nervous.

"Let's get five good ones, shall we?"

"Yes, Daddy."

I can't restrain myself, so they go quick. Five good, solid smacks on that luscious round ass while Reina screams.

I grab my aching cock with my still smarting palm. I'm not sure I've ever wanted anything more than I want to claim this girl for my own right now. I give myself a couple of firm strokes to take the edge off before taking the bottle of lube back in hand.

Reina is still panting from the spanking when the cold gel hits her bared skin. I rub it over her as she whimpers, a smile forming on my lips. I can't remember ever feeling this happy. I had settled into a life of loneliness. A life of work and nothing else, until this angel appeared in my world. I still can't believe my luck.

Once I have her crack fully lubed, I let my fingers slide to her hole. It's so slippery, I can get one fingertip in without even trying. I press that finger to the first knuckle, bringing in as much of the gel as I can. I slide it out and then back in, this time pressing in as far as my finger will go.

The space is so tight, I'm nearly weak at the knees with the desire to invade it with my cock. Her muscles contract around my finger, bringing all sorts of dirty fantasies to life right before my eyes. I pull my finger out and add a bit more lube, sliding two in right up to their base.

Reina is being very quiet, and I can't see her face, so I check in. "How are you doing down there, little one?"

"Mmm," is her muffled reply from where she has her face buried in the bed.

"Lift your head up and give me three words, baby girl."

She obeys immediately, sending a thrill through me. "I'm nervous."

I nod, even though she can't see me. It's good to know that she's not scared or upset by her current position. Nervous I can work with.

"I'm getting your sweet little body ready for me. How does it feel?"

"Strange."

"Strange good or strange bad?"

A pause.

"Good, I guess."

I pull my fingers out of her and land a smack on her ass. "Good what?"

"Good, Daddy."

"That's right. Are you ready for more?"

"Yes, Daddy. I think so."

I gel up and press three fingers into her body, watching in amazement as her body opens to make room for me. I don't hear any sounds of pain from Reina, which is a good sign. I don't know how much longer I'm going to be able to hold off fucking this perfect ass, and I want her to be ready.

With my three fingers sliding in and out of her in a slow, rhythmic motion, I decide to get the party started. "Go ahead and turn that vibe on, love. Put it on low."

I hear the thing come to life and feel Reina's muscles react from where my fingers are still buried in her body. I cannot wait to feel that vibration in my cock when I'm sliding inside her. Between the lube, my fingers, the vibrator, and the sight in front of me, I'm about to combust. My dick screams at me to let it join the fun.

With the hand that's not inside her, I lube up my cock so well it's practically dripping. I slip my fingers out and firmly grab her hips, while gripping my cock at its base with the other hand.

When I swirl my slippery tip on her tight hole, I swear to God fireworks go off.

"Turn it up a notch," I command.

Reina obeys.

"Give me a color, love."

"Green," she responds immediately.

I press my tip into her, the hole so small that it's a squeeze— in the best possible way. I could stay right there, fucking her entrance in tiny thrusts and be coming in no time. But no. I promised her that I wouldn't come until she did. And besides, that wouldn't be the claiming that I have in mind.

I push in another inch, the gel helping me slide down her tight passage. "How does that feel, sweetheart?"

"It feels...okay."

I push in another inch. "It feels okay..."

"Daddy! It feels okay, Daddy."

"That's my girl."

I slide out until just my tip is inside her and press back in, going even an inch farther. "Turn that thing up a notch."

I can definitely feel the vibration through her body in my cock, and the further I press inside, the stronger the sensation is.

*Am I going to make it until she comes?*

I'm approaching the edge, and I haven't even started properly fucking her.

I slide out and back in, getting closer to fully embedded. "Turn it up."

Reina obeys.

I slide out, adding a bit more gel, and then press inside, holding both of her hips, until my cock is fully seated inside her gorgeous ass. I pause there, savoring the moment, but also trying to get a read on her breathing.

I can hear her breaths coming calmly through her nose, as if she's trying to stay focused. "Does it feel good, love?"

"The vibrator feels good," is her reply.

"What does my cock feel like?"

"It feels like...you're part of my body, I guess."

"I'm going to fuck you now."

"Okay," she says softly, less confident now.

"Okay, what?"

"Okay, Daddy."

"Put that thing on high. Do you remember what I told you?"

"Yes, Daddy."

"Say it."

"You're not coming until I do."

"That's right."

I hear the vibe click into high gear, and I feel its feverish vibrations.

Fuck. This might be the best feeling of my life.

I start to pump. Slowly at first, giving her a nice, steady slide in and out. When it's starting to feel easier, like she's relaxed around me just a bit, I take it up a level.

Before I know it, my balls are slapping against the vibrator tucked between her legs as I thrust into her with vigor. "God, fuck, girl. You feel so fucking good."

I'm nearly blind with pleasure as her tight hole continues to open up and take the fucking.

"Dom!"

Her cry brings my attention back to the present. I freeze. "You okay, love?" It's strange to hear my name at a time like this, when she should be calling me daddy. Something is definitely wrong.

"It's…so much. I don't know…"

"Can you give me a color, love?"

"It's…I'm not sure. Yellow?"

I start to pull out. Yellow is as good as red right now.

"No, not yellow. It's green. It's just so much."

*That's my girl.*

I grip her hips harder, pump into her a bit faster. She'll make it over the edge of fear and into pleasure, I just know it. I need to take her there. She knows how to stop this if she needs to.

"I don't know if I'm going to come." Her tone lets me know she's concerned her words will upset me.

Guilt washes over me as I realize my mistake. I got so wrapped up in claiming her body, in my own indecent levels of pleasure that I left my girl on her own down there. She's too in her head, too nervous to cross over into pleasure. I thought giving her the vibrator would be enough, but I should have taken even more steps to ensure her good time.

I reach down and take her around the stomach with my arms,

pulling her body up to meet mine at the same time as I sink onto my heels. She's now upright in my lap with my cock still buried deep inside her.

The angle gives me a few more inches of depth, a sensation that elicits sounds from both of us.

I wrap my hand around her and find the little vibrator. Pushing her knees further to the side, I press the machine deep into her flesh until I feel bone.

She likes that, there's no doubt in my mind. The change in her pitch is like music to my ears. I hold the vibe there as I find some leverage to pump once more. I'm so deep in her tight ass, the vibrations are so strong at this angle, I'm nearly blind with pleasure.

But I need to get my girl off.

I shift my hand so that two fingers continue to press the vibe deep into her clit while two others find their way to her wet opening. Luckily for me, her G-spot isn't very deep inside her body, and I'm able to reach it while still holding the machine.

Now that I have her in this grip, she's toppling toward her release. I can hear it in her moans and feel it in the stuttering of her breath.

Thank fucking Christ.

It's a feat of epic proportions to keep fucking while holding her like this, but I manage. In and out I slam, my own breathing starting to catch.

Reina comes suddenly, her body buckling at the core. I hold her through it, never slowing my pumping, not letting up on the vibe until she starts to still. When she's limp in my arms, I nestle my cock all the way inside and pull her back up to embrace. My lips find her skin for the first time in what feels like forever.

"If you want to turn that thing off, you can."

She doesn't respond, but I hear the click and feel the vibrations stop.

The room feels so quiet now, her body having stilled its buzzing. It's just her and me now.

I reach up and turn her face until I can see her profile. She looks back and catches my eye. For a long moment, we are frozen, the only movement an occasional blink.

I lean forward and graze my lips up the side of her jaw to her ear, giving the lobe a little nibble. She smiles, and I squeeze her tighter.

This right here. This woman in my arms. The feeling of being inside her body. The knowledge that she allowed me to be here. That she chose me.

I squeeze my eyes closed as my hips start to slowly shift up and down, dragging my tip down her inner walls toward the open air and then pressing it back into her just before it escapes.

Our breathing falls into a rhythm together, as if we are one set of lungs. Our hearts beat together as if we are one body.

My core contracts, and I spill into her silently, our combined bodies folding forward gently as I press deeper into my orgasm. She spreads her knees and takes me.

When I finally slide out of her and release my arms, Reina's body collapses soundlessly on the bed. It takes me a moment to catch my breath before I wipe us both down with the towel from our shower earlier and lay down beside her.

Her eyes are open and watching me. As I curl her in close, they shut.

"How are you, little one?"

"Tired."

"I'm so proud of the way you took my cock. I told you I needed to claim every inch of your body, and you obeyed so well."

She says nothing.

"Did you like it?" I finally ask. I have to know. It's noble of her to have allowed me to take my pleasure even if she wasn't enjoying it, but that's not what I want for our relationship.

"I like parts of it," she answers finally. "No, I guess I liked it."

"Tell me what you liked."

"I really liked the vibrator. I think I might steal that thing."

I smile. "What else?"

"I liked the feeling of you inside me. It's different…back there. Like you are part of my body in a way that I don't usually feel when you're inside me. Like we're one person."

"Do you think it's something you would want to do again?" Not that I'm getting my hopes up, but if she liked it, I could certainly stand to go another round sometime soon.

"Yeah, I could do it again. I know it will get easier. But…"

"But what, little one?"

"I just…I like to see you. This time it felt like you were so far away, with my head shoved into the bed. I didn't get to see you. You didn't kiss me a single time."

I pull her close as disappointment in myself washes over me. I got so caught up in my own jealousy that I lost sight of what's really important—my connection with my girl.

"Sorry I didn't kiss you. I got kind of caught up in my own stuff there."

She turns to look at me, eyes open now. "Yeah, you did. What was all that stuff about everyone on the island wanting to sleep with me? Where did that come from all of a sudden?"

I let out a sigh. It all seemed so important earlier, now I just feel sheepish. "I overheard some guys talking in the restaurant. You appeared on many of their list of girls they wanted to ask out."

Reina laughs. "That's what got you all worked up?"

"It made me think about the secrecy in a different way. I've been happy to have you all to myself, without other people's opinions or judgment to worry about. But then it occurred to me that none of the guys in the resort, or on the island, know that you're taken. They're all planning ways to get you to be theirs when you're already mine."

I can't read the look on her face, but it's filled with so much emotion that I almost have to look away.

"Dom—" She starts to speak, no doubt to tell me that I'm

being silly, that we need to protect our secret, and I'm just being a crazed, possessive fool, so I cut her off.

"I know, I know. The secret is important. We are keeping the secret. I'm not trying to go back on that."

She opens her mouth to speak again, but I need to get these thoughts out of my mind before I lose the nerve. "I was just thinking that, maybe instead of being just...I don't know what to call this, what we've been doing—secret lovers? Maybe it's time you stop being my secret lover and start being my secret girlfriend."

Her mouth opens in surprise, and it takes a moment before the look on her face settles into one that looks happy. I wait nervously for her to answer.

"I would love to be your girlfriend." The word on her lips and the expression on her face tell me everything I need to know. She loves the idea. She's thrilled that I asked. My heart swells with the thought of her being mine, officially.

"Your *secret* girlfriend."

Something about the way she says the word secret makes me pause, but she's already snuggled into my chest and on her way to an afternoon nap, so I let it go.

I glance at the clock and find that I've already been away from the kitchen for over an hour. I can hardly just leave her here, not after what we just did, but I do need to get back to work soon.

I decide to close my eyes for just a moment, but when I reopen them, another hour has gone by.

Shit.

Reina is still asleep in my arms, but this time I have to leave her. I slip out as gently as I can, but she still wakes.

"I have to get back to the kitchen. Stay here if you like. I'll be home around midnight."

"I promised Sarah and Charles I'd go to dinner with them." She starts to get up, stretching and yawning adorably.

"Where are you going to eat?" I can't help but ask.

"I don't know yet. Somewhere in town."

"Come to the restaurant for dinner." The words surprise even me. I had no plans to invite her for dinner. No idea if it's even possible with the night's reservations.

*I'll make it work.*

"To the restaurant? *Your* restaurant?"

"Yeah. The three of you. Come do the tasting menu. I would love for you to experience it."

"How are you going to explain the sudden appearance of three employees at dinner?"

"I'll tell them you are being rewarded for taking my cock so nicely."

Reina barks out a surprised laugh, and I smile.

"I'll tell them whatever. I'll think of something. Come at five thirty."

"Okay…" She's still unsure, but I can see that she really wants to come, so she'll make it work. Hell, it will probably be even harder for her to explain to her friends why they're coming to dinner than it will be for me to explain it to the staff.

"I gotta go, love. See you soon." I place a kiss on her forehead and head off to find my clothes.

# Rule #23

## DON'T OVERTHINK IT

### REINA

"Wait, what?"

Sarah's looking at me like I just sprouted a third arm.

"Charles can come too. It's a reservation for three."

"For doing such a good job as a *breakfast server*."

"Why do you have to say it like that? Breakfast is important. And I love it."

"Well, I guess you'd have to love it to be doing such a good job that Sylvia offered you a dinner reservation for yourself and two guests."

I just shrug. I'm too tired to think up another round of lies, and I'm dying to get back to my apartment to get ready. "Let's just enjoy it, okay? I'm sure it's not the first time resort employees have gotten to go to dinner at the restaurant."

Sarah raises her eyebrows with a look that tells me she thinks it might actually be the first time, but I'm already heading toward my apartment. "Meet me back here at five fifteen? Oh, and will you tell Charles?"

"Sure thing."

Finally alone in my apartment, I heave a huge sigh of relief. It's not that I'm not excited to go down to eat dinner at Raft—I definitely am—it's just that...

More lies.

I don't want to lie and sneak my way to dinner. I want to stroll into that place as Dom's freaking girlfriend. I want everyone to know. I want him to come to our table and kiss me and for the whole staff to see.

I would be lying to myself if I didn't admit that I thought he was going to tell me he was ready to drop the secrecy in our conversation earlier. Instead, he proclaimed me his secret girlfriend. I did my best to hide my disappointment, and I think it worked.

It's not that I'm not happy, it's just that...for a second there, I thought we were on the same page. He was going on about how hard it was to watch me walk around with no one knowing I was his. I thought he was going to tell me he was ready to publicly announce his claim on me. Instead, he claimed me for his own in private—in a very private way—and proclaimed me his secret girlfriend.

I'm thrilled to finally have a title like that to call myself—secretly, in my own mind—it's just...

I've got to stop thinking like this. The last thing I want to do is poison this amazing relationship in my own mind by placing expectations on it, and on Dom, that can't be met right now. I'm happy with what we have, even if it's just between us right now.

I have a billionaire resort owner boyfriend. Officially. That handsome, generous, sexy man is mine. And it was his idea. I'm his girlfriend.

---

I sift through my clothes trying to find something appropriate for the occasion and settle on a blue shift dress and a pair of gold sandals. It may be fine dining, but it's still the tropics, so the dress code will be a little looser. No need to wear heels at the beach...ever.

The temperature has dropped nicely with a bit of cloud cover, and I take advantage of the weather to put on more makeup than I usually dare. Looking at myself in the mirror, nice dress, hair tousled and down, dark eyes, and bold lips, I can't help but feel excitement grow in my chest.

This is what a billionaire's girlfriend looks like. And someday the whole world is going to know it.

When I stroll down to the start of the path at five fifteen, Sarah and Charles are waiting for me, both looking more dolled up than I've ever seen them.

"Girl, you are smoking," Charles drawls, taking one of my hands and spinning me so he can get the full view. "You are going to snag yourself a boyfriend tonight."

I smile and blush at his compliment. He'll never know just how apt of an observation it really is.

*He'll know someday that you were lying to him right now.*

I shake off the thought and link arms with the two of them as we head down the path.

"I've gotten to work two dinner shifts so far, just training at the host station, but still. The food looks amazing. I get to try things here and there, but I can't wait to have the whole tasting menu." She looks at me, her face glowing with excitement. "And the whole thing is paid for, you're sure? Even wine?"

I nod. "Anything we want, on the house." I have no doubt that Dom will take this opportunity to spend money on me.

After our talk at his house a few weeks back where he told me that it would make him the happiest man in the world to be able to buy things for me, I relaxed a bit about gifts and being spoiled. There aren't a huge number of opportunities to buy things or spend money on me, considering we live on this tiny island, and our relationship is a secret.

Luckily, I have everything I need, and the additions that Dom manages to sneak in—fancy wine, lingerie, passes to go on snorkel trips or boat rides—just make life richer and fuller. I'm relaxing into it, though it took me a while. Hell, I didn't even mention it when my rent was never taken out of my paycheck this month.

"Sylvia just told you that you were doing such a good job that you could come to dinner with two friends?"

I sigh softly and nod. "Yup."

I agonized over what to tell the two of them for almost an hour after leaving Dom's house. It's so easy for him to blow into work and tell the staff that three employees are coming in for dinner—because he says so. It's much more complicated for me. I finally settled on telling them that Sylvia offered this little perk to me for helping so much at breakfast while she gets the new staff trained.

It's not totally out of the question that she would do something like this. She tells me all day long how appreciated I am and how she couldn't do this without me. If she had the power to dole out dinner reservations to her staff, I know I would be first on the list.

Fantasy Sylvia happily offered me what real-life Sylvia would have, if she could. It seemed like a totally harmless story.

That is, until we reach the resort, and the first person we see is Sylvia.

There's nowhere to hide, so I continue to walk toward her, arms still linked with the two people who are about to learn what a goddamn liar and fake I am.

"You three look amazing all dressed up," she says, her caring and genuine words making me feel even worse about my web of lies.

"Yes, thanks to you," Sarah says, her voice full of excitement. "We are off to the restaurant for dinner."

I'm the only one who knows what to watch for in Sylvia's face, so I'm the only one who could have possibly watched the tiny flicker of question pass over her face before she replaces it with the biggest smile I've ever seen, even on Sylvia's always smiling lips. And it's pointed directly at me.

"You are so welcome. You three have a lovely time, okay? Reina, I can't wait to hear all about it."

I'm taking deep breaths to try to keep from crying at the woman's words and her kindness for not throwing me under the bus. This woman is a true friend. These two beside me are such true friends. I don't deserve any of them, the filthy liar that I am.

I manage to pull myself together by the time we reach the door to the restaurant.

"Hey, Sarah," the woman at the host station says with a smile as we step inside. "Are you coming for dinner?"

"Yep, the three of us. We should have a reservation."

I'm grateful for Sarah taking the lead here. I thought I was so cool and collected, but now that we're inside, I just feel nervous.

"Oh, the three employees. I wondered who that would be. How'd you guys get so lucky?"

Sarah glances at me but must read my expression because she just brushed the question off. "Oh, just a little perk we earned."

The host leads us to the best table in the whole place, a square four-top situated in front of the large sunset window. "Here we are," she says with a gracious smile.

"Wow," Charles says as he sits across from Sarah and me at the table. "I thought we'd be stuck in the back somewhere."

I nod in agreement, not trusting my voice at this moment. I'm overwhelmed by the whole situation—the beautiful restaurant, the perfect table—and all the lies.

"Good evening, friends," our server, Sally, who we all know, greets us. "Welcome to Raft. Have you ever dined with us before?"

"Ha, ha. Very funny. Bring us the fancy wine, please," Sarah says with a grin.

Sally is grinning as well. "It's not often I get actual friends to wait on. What are you guys doing here?"

"Reina here got us a reservation as a perk for being such an excellent employee," Charles replies, giving me a glance.

"Wow, must be really showing them what's what at breakfast, huh, Reina? I've been an excellent employee for years, and all I ever get is a free staff drink."

I smile and shrug. "We've had some challenges with getting the a.m. crew up to speed, so I guess I've just been extra helpful."

"Helpful indeed." Sally turns her attention back to the whole group, and I relax a bit. "Is it safe to assume you all want the full wine courses that accompany the tasting menu?"

"Yes, absolutely," Sarah says quickly. "Bring it on."

"Just small pours for me," I say before Sally leaves to get our first wine. "I still have to work in the morning."

"Ah yes, we wouldn't want our star employee to show up still drunk to serve breakfast now, would we?" There's a sharpness to her tone that pulls the smile from my lips. I try to force it back up, but I know she sees my falter.

Once she's gone, I take a big drink of my water to try to cool myself off. I'm feeling hot and flustered and a bit out of place. I wanted so badly to just enjoy this evening, but it's off to a rocky start.

Luckily, the rocks are all in my mind.

"This dinner is totally worth you blowing us off almost every night so you can sleep, Reina. I mean, I knew you were dedicated to the job, but I had no idea it would amount to this." Sarah is taking selfies in front of the panoramic window that will never upload to the internet with our pathetic Wi-Fi strength.

"I'm just glad I have you two to share it with. I can't tell you how much I appreciate you both being such good friends, even with my crazy schedule."

"Girl, I get it. I worked brunch last year, remember? I wasn't in bed at nine every night like you are, so I was a wreck every morning. If I had the willpower to skip parties, my life would have been much easier. More power to you. You're a kind of inspiration."

If she knew that I was sneaking out of my house and climbing up to that mansion on the hill to be wined, dined, tied up, and fucked, what would she say?

*She would applaud and congratulate you, dummy. Everyone would.*

Sally appears with three tall flutes and fills them with bubbly. "We are starting tonight with prosecco to accompany our first course."

We all thank her as she disappears with the bottle. There isn't even time to take a sip before a young chef, dressed in perfectly pressed whites, appears at our table, plate in each hand. A second chef stands just behind him with the third plate ready.

"Local lobster, caught this morning, with habanero lime sauce, corn, cucumber, and mint." He sets the plates down in front of Sarah and me, then reaches back for the third, which he places before Charles.

"Ooh, not too spicy, right?" Sarah bats her eyelashes up at the chef, and I really take the man in for the first time since he arrived at our table. He is handsome, in a young, surfer kind of way. I know by now that he is exactly Sarah's type.

"No, my dear. Just the perfect amount of spice," he answers, his tone full of flirt.

Even I have to blush at the smile he gives Sarah as he and the other chef retreat back to the kitchen.

"Screw dinner, I'll just take that chef to-go," Sarah jokes as she finally manages to take a sip from her wine.

Charles and I laugh in agreement.

The food is spectacular. Just as the chef promised, it's not too spicy, but has enough zest to make this wine the absolute perfect accompaniment. I only have about five sips in my glass, and I take them alternating with bites of the succulent lobster, sauce, and perfectly cooked vegetables.

If this was the only dish I ever got to eat for the rest of my life, I would die a happy woman. Once I scrape my plate clean, I lean back in my chair and sigh. I may have started this evening off on the wrong foot, but there's no way to be anything other than content now that the tasting menu has started.

As they clear the small plates and set new wine glasses in front of us, a thought starts to swell in my mind.

If the food is this incredible—and I have no doubts that each and every course on the menu will be just as delicious and perfectly prepared as the first—then why hasn't Dom already won the Pendleton?

I think back to my time in Chicago, during the first season we were going for the award. The chef-owner brought in a consultant from Europe who specialized in award season prep, and that man whipped our little bistro into shape. We went on to win the award three seasons in a row.

What had he changed though? His first suggestion had been to swap the white tablecloths for bare wood tables. The owner was clinging to the white linen look as a way to chase opulence and the feeling of luxury, but the consultant insisted that the Pendleton judges were looking for progressive thinkers. Restaurants needed to show that they could depart from tradition, blaze their own trails, and still hold to the high level of service everyone would expect from starred properties.

I glance down at the crisp white tablecloth below my wineglass and bite my lip in deep thought. I know how much of a challenge it is to keep these tablecloths white and ironed in the tropics. The housekeepers are always complaining about it in the staff cantina. It's a huge priority, though, right up there with keeping the guest sheets looking pristine. A couple of the women have tablecloth maintenance as their full-time job. What would Dom think if I told him that baring the beautiful, polished wood of our maple tables might push him over the edge for that first Pendleton award?

The second course arriving interrupts my thoughts.

"Tuna sashimi, chili tapioca, dragon fruit, and coconut

broth." The same chef from the first course has returned to our table, and I can see him casting sensual eyes Sarah's way. I smile at the little flirtation growing between the two.

As he bows and returns to the kitchen, we turn to our new plates.

"This looks amazing," Sarah gushes as she picks up her clean fork.

There's no argument here. The fish is cut so beautifully thin, and the black and white contrast of the perfectly square dragon fruit is lovely against the hand-formed sea-foam green plate.

It's just…

I take a sip of the crisp white Sally poured right before this course and take my first bite of the dish. It's delicious. The flavors meld so perfectly, the acid of the sauce complements the delicate sweetness of the fish. I have to close my eyes to really savor the fusion of flavors in my mouth.

I want this dish to be perfect, but my mind will not shut up.

*Two seafood courses in a row?*

Another suggestion we received from the consultant back in Chicago was that the judges always want to see a chef's ability to make dishes shine without having to rely on animal protein at every course. This was the biggest fight of all, as the chef-owner of the restaurant was sure that his customers would walk out if every other dish was just vegetables, but exactly the opposite happened when he finally gave in.

Not only were diners raving about the tasting menu, but we won the award immediately.

I wonder if anyone has ever suggested to Dom that he needs to alternate protein and veggie courses for his menu?

The third course arrives to oohs and ahhs around the table, and even more flirting on the part of Sarah and the chef, but I'm left with even more hesitation as I see it. Grilled spring onions and zucchini that came from the rooftop garden, arranged beautifully and drizzled with dressing made from olives that the chefs cure in-house. It smells delicious and tastes just as good.

But...

Perched right on top of the small mound of vegetables is a perfectly seared sea scallop. It was caught by a local fisherman not ten miles off the shore of this very island, but still.

*Stop thinking...just enjoy it.*

Leave it to a career in restaurants to ruin a perfectly lovely meal.

It's not my responsibility to critique this menu, or anything else about dinner. I've taken on brunch as my focus, and I'm doing incredible work there to get the shift up to its highest potential. I just can't stop thinking about how much this award means to Dom. And wondering if he would be willing to take this kind of constructive criticism from me.

*Not unless you finally admit where you had been working the last five years.*

And I'm just not quite ready for that.

The rest of the meal is just as spectacular—thirteen courses and two of the most beautiful desserts I've ever laid eyes on.

By the time we have espresso with house-made vanilla ice cream and amaretto cookies at the end, I'm so full and happy, I can hardly think.

Of course, that's when Dom chooses to finally make an appearance.

After waiting through the first couple of courses, I had all but given up on him coming out to our table and decided it was for the best. It's much easier to pretend you aren't having a secret affair with someone when they're not standing in front of you.

When he finally walks around the bar and takes off his apron, handing it off to a waiting host and smoothing down his chef coat, I'm a little tipsy and practically high from the wonderful culinary experience we've just had.

It's no problem at all to gush to him about the lovely food, and I join right in with Sarah and Charles when he asks how our meal was.

"I had no idea it would be so amazing. It was almost too

much. I mean, I've seen all of those plates go out, but to be sitting here and eating every course with the wine pairing. It's obscene, Dominic. You should have every award on your wall."

I smile at Sarah's proclamation. She has had a bit more wine than I have. I can see it in her cheeks and hear it in her voice.

"Truly a triumph." Charles takes his turn at thanking Dom for the experience. "I'm never going to be able to eat anywhere ever again without comparing it to this."

Dom graciously accepts this praise like he's used to it. He probably is. This is one of his main jobs here at the restaurant during dinner—offering himself to the rich guests so that they can tell all of their rich friends that the famous chef visited their table. He has spoken a bit about how tedious it can be, but he knows the importance, so he keeps doing it.

He's got this part of the judging criteria down to a T. Chef interaction in the dining room is one of the most consistent judging points that we know about on the Pendleton criteria. No restaurant has ever won the award without it.

When the other two finish their praise, Dom's eyes fall on me. There's a question present that I didn't see when he was listening to Sarah or Charles. He really cares what I think of his menu. My chest fills with pride.

"It was incredible, Dominic. The best meal I've ever had." I toss in a tiny smile at the end that's just for him.

My heart swells as I watch him try to hide his own little smile. I have been telling him the very same thing each and every night since I started sleeping at his house, and he consistently brings home dinner. It's become our secret joke. To be making it here, in his restaurant, in front of all of these people, is an obscenity in itself. But it feels so good.

"I have to go schmooze some guests," Dom says to us in a kind, casual tone that I know the other two swoon over. He then turns his attention to Charles. "Can I trust you to get these ladies home safely?"

Charles sits up straighter in his seat. "It would be my honor, sir. I won't let you down."

Dom flashes one more of those killer smiles before heading off to a table of wealthy-looking older people across the dining room.

"Oh my god. Did you see that smile?" Charles looks a little faint, and I know it's not from the wine. "That man is a dream."

I have no problem agreeing with that. My heart glows with feeling for Dom as I sneak glances at his back across the room.

"How much do you think we should tip?"

The question draws me out of my wine-induced daydream and back to the present. I hadn't considered the fact that we would need to leave a tip. I didn't bring any cash with me. Familiar feelings of dread, shame, and lacking pour over me, overtaking the warm glow of our lovely dining experience. "Oh, I didn't think about that."

I can feel tears start to swell inside me, and I will myself to tamp them down. I won't let this feeling ruin my night, even though I do feel really guilty about not thinking ahead and grabbing some cash on my way out the door.

"You, my dear, have done enough. Charles and I will leave a tip."

I open my mouth to express my gratitude and apologize for forgetting cash, but Charles interprets it as me preparing to argue with Sarah about my contribution. "Girl, we just enjoyed a meal worth over a thousand dollars because of you. Let us take care of the tip."

"Oh, yeah. Okay."

His words make me feel so much better, now I want to cry out of gratitude.

The two of them have a quiet discussion about what's appropriate to leave on the table and finally decide that it's all the cash both of them have on them. The pile of tens, fives, and ones looks decidedly out of place on the white linen tablecloth, but I know the staff will appreciate it.

Our walk up through the palms feels like a dream, I'm so full of wine and sleepy. By the time I get tucked safely into my apartment, I know there's no way I'm staying up until Dom gets off.

I shoot off a text before setting an early alarm and crawling into my bed.

> **Me**
> Dinner was incredible. I'm going to sleep, see you tomorrow.

I don't wait for a response before closing my eyes and letting the wine and my full belly carry me into dreamland.

———

The next day is Sylvia's day off, so I'm spared having to deal with my hangover and her prying questions at the same time. I run the shift in her absence, and everything goes great. I know some of the people from dinner last night recognize me from the dining room, but no one mentions it. I leave the café after my shift feeling accomplished and sleepy, excited for my afternoon nap.

Sarah catches me just as I'm slipping into my apartment.

"I know you're off to bed, as usual." Her teasing tone is meant to be lighthearted, but it hits me right in the gut. I lie and tell her I'm going to bed so often that she probably thinks I'm narcoleptic. "But don't forget about tonight, okay? I want to head out at about eight. There are too many of us for a golf cart, so we'll be walking."

Damn. I totally forgot about the plan to go to town for karaoke with the girls. I quickly scan through my mind for excuses to get myself out of it, but Sarah must read that right on my face.

"Don't even think about canceling. It's not happening, girl. I will be here at quarter to eight, and you better be looking as hot as I know you can look. We are going to find you someone to go home with tonight."

Dread fills my stomach as I try to force a smile. I skipped going home with the only person I want to go home with last night after my epic meal and too much wine, and the thought of missing his touch two nights in a row…

I hadn't quite realized until this moment how much I had come to rely on seeing him every day, having his body next to mine, and feeling his words against my skin.

And, after the jealousy I saw flare up in him after his line cooks mentioned wanting to ask me out, I have a whole new kind of dread to reckon with. How is Dom going to respond when I tell him where I'm going tonight—and why?

I can hardly cancel on them. I do far too much canceling already, and Sarah's looking pretty determined. But I'll have to somehow find a reason not to like every single guy they introduce me to. Honestly, it just sounds exhausting.

"I'll be ready," I respond in my most perky tone.

I hope I'll feel better after my nap because right now, all I want to do is crawl in a hole and hide.

# Rule #24

## TROUBLE BREWS IN THE DARKNESS

### DOMINIC

It's been a while since I've been in any kind of relationship. Back in my dating years, I was living in the city and commuting to my chef job on the subway with the other employees, even though I could have hired a car and driver to deliver me. I've been trying to fit in for a long time.

*Trying to pretend I'm something I'm not for a long time.*

I had my feet straddling two worlds. The kind of women who made or came from serious money didn't appreciate the fact I worked such long hours in a hot kitchen. The women from the restaurant, or at the bars afterward with my crew, struggled to get by. I never knew if they were actually into me—or just there for the money.

It all feels different with Reina.

She doesn't seem interested in my money. As a matter of fact, she's hesitant to accept anything from me that she can't share with her friends. She loves it when I spend lavishly to improve the life of the other employees but refuses to accept any help with her own bills.

She has told me a bit about her financial problems but has never gone as far as to name actual numbers. Not that it matters to me what kind of debt she's in. It might be a different story if she was trying to get me to pay for it, but what she's doing is the exact opposite. Somehow, that just makes me want to pay for it even more, but I don't push. What we have right now is so good, the last thing I want to do is screw it up.

If I can keep things going in the direction they currently are, then it's just a matter of time before she's living in my house and spending my money. Letting me take care of her the way I want to.

After the season ends, of course.

For now, we have fallen into a routine that works for us. I arranged my schedule to complement hers slowly over the last couple of months, and no one really noticed. Cell service sucks, but she's always waiting for me when I get home. Anytime during my day that I need a fix of her intoxicating energy, I call her to the office.

And just like that, I end up almost completely reliant on my secret girlfriend in our secret relationship.

I'm a sucker for routine. Ask any of the often-annoyed cooks on my staff, and they'll tell you all about it. I like when things happen in an orderly, predictable fashion. How I got myself into this industry, where some unknown shitshow waits around every corner is beyond me.

Maybe that's why the routine Reina and I have feels so soothing. I always know where she's going to be and when. I don't even need to keep tabs on her. There really just aren't that many places to go, and I know her schedule by heart.

It's one hundred percent due to this delusional fantasy of our domestic agreement that I find myself out of my mind with worry when she isn't waiting for me at my house when I get home. I have wine from the restaurant and one of the night's specials still warm for our customary late-night meal.

She texted me the night before to tell me she was staying

home after her meal at Raft. Understandable, but a bit disappointing. I was looking forward to hearing more about her experience, but I let it go. Tonight, I thought for sure she would be waiting to tell me all about it.

The house is dark when I walk in, but it wouldn't be the first time she fell asleep before my midnight appearance—or kept the lights off to surprise me naked in bed. I flip on a few switches, set down the food, and go looking for her.

I look for a long time before I start to get worried. I keep checking and double-checking rooms, to make sure that I didn't just miss her.

It's not long after coming to the conclusion that she isn't actually here that my brain takes off on its own journey into horror land.

*There's only one reason that she wouldn't be here, and it's because she's lying murdered in the sand somewhere.*

I know there are far more practical explanations for her absence, but I can't convince my terrified mind of that.

I'm out the door in an instant, flying down the steps much faster than I have any business doing in the dark. By the time I reach her apartment door, I'm wild with panic, but trying hard to keep it together.

I knock softly and wait. She's in there, probably asleep, and I rest my forehead against the door while I wait for her to get up and answer.

She never does.

I knock a few more times, but I already know she's not coming.

My logical brain tries desperately to reason with the animal inside me, to calm it down. There are plenty of non-murder reasons that she would have for not being at home or at my house.

*She would have called me.*

She probably tried, I think with a grim shake of my head as I tap my phone to light the screen up.

No service.

The cell service on this island is terrible at best. At worst, they shut down the tower sometimes at night for "maintenance."

My mind is reeling with ideas of where I should go look for her, while my soft, logical voice tells me to just go home.

I'm not sure how long I stand there, hood up, head against her door, listening to the warring thoughts in my mind. Eventually, I can't stay still any longer and decide to take a walk.

I'm about halfway down the path to the resort when female voices drift up to me. I recognized my girl's voice immediately.

She's not alone.

"You are just jealous—"

The two women stop short when they notice me on the path a few feet ahead of them.

"Shit," Sarah exclaims. "You scared me." She laughs it off and slips her arm through Reina's.

She has clearly been drinking. I don't notice anything unsteady about Reina, so I can't tell if she's in a similar state. Her eyes are on mine, a bit wider than usual, a soft smile on her lips.

"What are you ladies doing out so late?" I put on my best concerned boss mask and stand with my arms crossed waiting for an answer.

"We went to town," Reina says simply. Her voice is clear and steady, setting a bit of my mind at ease. At the very least, she wasn't out traipsing all over the island drunk like her friend Sarah.

"Why didn't you take a golf cart?" I know they have four of them to use. I bought the damn things myself.

"We went with a group of the housekeepers and other servers. There were too many of us for the one cart that was left," Reina says calmly.

How can she be so calm at a time like this? Doesn't she know how worried I was?

There's nothing I can say about it right now, not with Sarah here. All I can do is take a deep breath to try to calm down and continue acting like their boss.

Not the concerned boyfriend.

"I can walk you two up to the staff building," I offer.

"Oh, that's—" Sarah starts to shoot me down, but Reina interrupts.

"Okay, yeah. It is pretty dark."

I catch the confused look Sarah shoots her before shaking her head and pulling Reina up the path toward the apartments. I follow behind them, shining my light at their feet.

I can't think of a single thing to say, so I walk in silence, listening to the women whisper to each other. There's a tight knot of feelings caught in my chest. They're unfamiliar, and I can't quite put a name on them. All I know is that they feel terrible.

I want to protect this woman at all times, but I can't.

When she appeared in the darkness after I went out of my mind searching for her, all I wanted was to pull her into an embrace and scold her for making me worry. But I couldn't.

I had to pretend she didn't mean everything in the world to me. And she pretended the same.

I'm finally starting to understand what she tried to explain to me the other night. How she feels like a liar. That part hadn't resonated with me then. I don't have to lie outright to anyone, because no one would ever ask me about my personal life. But Reina does have to lie. She's doing it right now, walking ahead of me, arm in arm with her friend.

It's only a couple more months. Three tops. Then we can start to be more open about all of this. We've made it this far, and we can make it to the finish line together. I'll have my Pendleton, and we will go public about our relationship. I won't have to worry about causing a scandal by dating a waitress because she won't need to waitress anymore. She will never have to work another day in her life.

I stand, shining my light and watch the two of them climb the stairs. Reina deposits Sarah at her apartment first, going in for a moment before coming back outside and continuing down the walkway to her own door.

She glances down at me as she unlocks the dead bolt and swings the door open. I'm much too far away to read her expression in the dark, but the fact that I can't see her lips turn up in a smile sends dread through me.

Without a word, she steps through the door and closes it.

I click off my light and stand in the darkness. I have no idea what the correct next move is here. All I know is that I'm not leaving without touching her. No, I'm not leaving without talking to her.

After a few long minutes, Sarah's apartment goes dark. With a deep breath, I ascend the steps as quietly as I can.

# Rule #25

## BLACKMAIL...BUT THE GOOD KIND

### DOMINIC

Reina opens the door at my first light tap, as if she was waiting just on the other side. Relief pours through me at the sight of her smiling up at me. She steps aside, and I enter, closing the door behind me.

"You scared me, little one," I say, pulling her into a tight embrace.

"I just went out with my friends," she replies in a tone that doesn't sound like she's sorry. "I didn't realize I had to report my every move to you."

I take a step back, still holding her, and look down into her face. She's upset, and so am I. This is not the time—or the place, with the paper-thin walls of this building—to be having a serious conversation. "Let's go up to my house."

"I think I'm just going to go to bed here. It's been a long night." She pulls away from me and walks toward the bathroom, stripping off her little dress and grabbing a pair of shorts from the floor.

"Tell me what's going on."

When she turns, her face illuminated by the amber glow of the bathroom light, I can see that she's crying.

"You want to know what's going on, Dom?"

I nod.

"What's going on is that I just got back from karaoke night at Kings. All the other girls around here dragged me there so I could meet a hot scuba instructor."

My heart explodes inside my chest, but I manage to stay still and say nothing.

"They can't understand why I'm still single. I lied—again—and told them it was because of a bad breakup before I moved here, so they decided what I needed was to hook up with some hot guy and move past it. All I do is lie, Dom. I can't tell them about you and me, so they all want to set me up with someone. And what am I supposed to say?"

She's crying harder now, her soft voice shooting daggers into me. "You think you were scared tonight when for once I wasn't just waiting for you at your house like your dirty secret? How do you think I felt all night at a bar, getting introduced to man after man, having to rank which one was the hottest, worrying that someone would see me there, and you would find out, when all I wanted was to tell them that I—" She breaks off and wipes her face with her hands.

I close the distance between us. Reina doesn't fight me as I pull her into an embrace. "I'm sorry. I didn't know it was like that for you."

"I don't know how much longer I can do this, Dom." The resignation in her voice sends a cold wash of fear over me.

I can't lose her. That's the one thing I know for sure. I didn't even realize how much I needed her until this moment, when, for the first time, there's a threat of her pulling away. Of her choosing one of the many other guys on this island—younger guys—and leaving me to my pathetic mess of a life.

I fall to my knees.

"Reina. Look at me." She does, her tear-stained face looking down at me nearly bringing tears to my own eyes. "I know this is hard, okay? I didn't realize you were going through all of that, and I'm glad you told me. I would never be mad you went out with your friends. I was just worried because I didn't know where you were. Because you are so important to me. If you think for one second that keeping this a secret has anything to do with me not wanting people to know how I feel about you, you're wrong. I want the world to know. I want you to live in my house and walk around the resort holding my hand. I cannot wait for those days to come. And they will come. But I just think we need to hold off a little longer."

She tries to turn away, but I hold tightly to her hips, keeping her in front of me as I look up at her from my place on the floor.

"When we decided to wait until the season ended, we both had very good reasons for doing so. I know you remember. Those reasons haven't changed for either of us. So much else has changed, though. My feelings for you, your feelings for me I'm pretty sure. Your relationships with your friends. This thing between us keeps getting bigger, and so the stakes keep getting even higher. But we have a plan. You and me. We made a plan. We're going to wait until the season ends, and then I'm going to give you the life you deserve. I just need you to hold on a little bit longer."

My eyes are wet as I continue looking up, waiting for her to agree. She has to agree. There's no way I'm letting her go.

*Even if it means giving in and telling people about us early?*

The thought is terrifying—but not nearly as much as the thought of losing her.

"It's so hard," she says softly, her hands landing on my head, her fingers running through my hair. The touch is so familiar, so loving, that I start to calm immediately.

"I know, baby—"

"No, Dom. You don't know. You don't have it like I do. I lie all the time. I'm lying to all of my friends and coworkers and everyone, all the time. Who are you lying to?"

She's right, and there's nothing I can say to defend myself. "I don't have many people to lie to."

"When we finally tell people, they're going to know that I'm a liar. They're going to hate me."

"Reina, most of these people aren't even going to be here next season. When the season ends, and we go on break, they will all leave, and the new people who come will just know that we're together."

"I want to tell Sarah."

I should have seen this coming. Sarah is her best friend, and honestly, I'm surprised the woman hasn't figured it out yet. But Sarah's always with Charles, who has been the resort gossip since day one. If Sarah knows, Charles knows. If Charles knows, everyone knows.

"Reina, I know this is hard. You and I are going to face challenges in our relationship. This is the first of those challenges. But we can get through this, right? Tell me what we have is strong enough to get through this. Because I can't lose you."

There it is. My heart poured out for her to see. She's quiet for a long moment, her hands still in my hair. I squeeze my eyes closed and wait for her to speak.

She never does.

Finally, I look back at her. Her face is unreadable, a mask of sadness and pain. Panic takes over, and I climb to my feet, desperate for her to say everything is okay. That we can get through this.

I take her by the shoulders and lead her to the edge of the bed, sitting her down. "I know this doesn't look great for me, that I need you to keep lying. It kills me to have to ask this of you. Here," I twist the gold band off of my right finger and hold it up. "This was my grandfather's ring. He left it to me in his will, even though tradition stated that it should have passed to my father. He left a note telling the family he wanted me to have it because I was the only one who loved deeply enough to know what to do with it." I hold it up and watch Reina look at it, and then back at me.

I climb to my feet and glance around her apartment, every surface filled with tubes of lip gloss, earrings, discarded clothing. The adorable evidence of her life. The life I want to share. I spot a necklace on her bedside table and grab it, opening the clasp and letting the little pink stone pendant slide off one end. I slide the ring on in its place and walk back over to her.

She stays still, her eyes never leaving my face as I clasp the gold chain around her neck, nestling the ring between her breasts under her shirt.

"I know now what I'm supposed to do with it. This is a promise. My promise to you that we will get through this together. That I'm not putting you through this for nothing. This thing we have, Reina, is real. I promise you that I will make it the most real thing in the whole world."

"In April." Her voice sounds resigned, but kinder than before.

"Yes."

She looks away from me and down at her own cleavage. I watch as she reaches in and pulls out the ring, spinning it on the chain between her fingers. When she drops it and sighs, I know I have her. I was teetering right on the edge of giving in, of throwing caution to the wind and just telling the world. Letting the cards fall where they may.

But she's going to wait for me. I try not to let the relief show on my face as I watch hers soften.

"As soon as the season is over," she repeats, this time with more feeling.

"The second it's over," I assure her.

She drops her hands to her hips and cocks her head to the side. "I wonder how many orgasms it's going to take to keep me quiet for the rest of the season."

A sly smile twists my mouth upward. "My girl thinks that blackmail is the best way to gain sexual favors?"

She bites her lip adorably.

"That sounds like a punishable offense to me."

I stand quickly, slipping my hands under her thighs and sending her onto her back on the bed. I crawl over her, and my lips find hers for the first time today. A warm rush of relief washes over me. As her lips part and I enter her mouth, tasting her sweetness, all finally feels right.

And the bed feels pretty good, as well.

I give a couple of bounces on my knees, making Reina laugh. "This mattress isn't half bad. Maybe we should stay here more often."

"I love it," she says softly, and the thought of her enjoying my gift sends pleasure shooting straight to my groin.

"And your friends? How do they like their new beds?" I never asked, and she hasn't mentioned it.

"They love them. For a few weeks, that's all they could talk about."

I grin. "Do you think they're going to be mad when you tell them the story of how you used your sexual prowess over me to force me to buy over a hundred new beds in a week?"

Reina laughs, and the sound is music to my ears.

"They won't be mad. They might even be a little impressed."

"Or how about when I wanted to buy you a golf cart and instead you made me buy four for the staff to use. Are they going to be impressed with that as well?"

She nods. "But you know what's really going to knock their socks off?"

"What's that, my dear?" I reply, kissing slowly down her neck to her collarbone.

"When I tell them about how the management has decided to offer staff pool hours."

I laugh in surprise, looking up at her from where my mouth was about to pull down the hem of her top. "Oh, really?"

She nods.

With a snarl, I take the hem of her top in my teeth and pull it up sharply, exposing her breasts. Reina laughs and tries to back away, but I sit my hips down and pin her to the bed.

I gather her hands up and hold them over her head, stretching her torso long.

"Look at me."

"Yes, Daddy," she answers sweetly, lifting her gaze from where it had fallen to my chest and giving me a sultry look.

"God, I love it when you call me that." I release her hands and lift my body a little so I can flip her over, my hand landing on her bare ass in a firm slap. The squeak that escapes her lips is pure gold.

The way we can fall right into this little game of ours is so natural, so automatic, it feels like we've been playing these roles our whole lives. As I run my hands up and over the swell of Reina's ass and up her lower back, my heart aches with the need to play this role forever.

I was scared before that someone would think she was available and try to take her from me. On that night, I needed to claim her body for my own. To show her that she was mine.

All I want right now is for her to claim me, but I don't know how to ask. All I can do is fall into her body, enjoy her closeness while I have it. And pray that the ring around her neck is enough to keep her here until I can get one on her finger.

I bring my hand down on her ass once more, gripping the flesh and massaging her until she's wiggling her hips to try to drive my touch lower.

"How wet are you right now?"

"So wet, Daddy."

"Ready for this cock?"

"I'm so ready, Daddy. Give it to me."

"Beg." I can't get enough of her. My hands trail up her sides from her hips to her shoulder blades, sending goose bumps over her soft, pale skin.

"Please give it to me, Daddy. I'm so hot and ready for you."

"I know you've been a good girl. My good girl." I want the

words to express far more of how I feel than they do, but it's going to have to be enough for now.

I take my achingly hard cock in one hand while guiding her to hands and knees facing away from me with the other. Just the word daddy coming off those sweet lips is nearly enough to send me over the edge, but I keep my breathing regular. I will hold on long enough to give her the pounding she's begging for.

"I've been such a good girl, Daddy."

I wonder if she's trying to communicate the same things to me.

I slide one hand between those luscious thighs, finding her so wet my fingers practically fall into her spread pussy. Reina tosses her head back and cries out. Still buried knuckle deep in her, I slap her ass hard with my other hand. I'm rewarded with another soft cry.

*This woman is going to murder me with those cries.*

"I'm about to fuck you so hard, baby. Are you ready for this?" I say, keeping my voice down as best I can.

"God, yes, give it to me." She thrashes a bit, her body twisting to the side and exposing one of her glorious breasts. I can't help but lean around her to take the nipple between my teeth for a little bite before releasing it and taking my cock into my other hand.

I nestle the tip at her entrance, where my fingers have brought her wetness out and made a Slip N Slide for me to glide in. My first thrust goes to the hilt as I squeeze her hips hard. The stifled moan she lets loose is one for the history books.

*I could fuck this woman until I die.*

The sensation of her wrapping tightly around my dick makes my vision go hazy. I lean back, grabbing both hips with my hands and start thrusting harder.

"How do you like my cock, sweetheart?"

"It's so good, Daddy." Her voice is choppy as she tries to get the words out through my punishing thrusts. "Don't stop."

I couldn't stop now if I tried.

I alternate quick, hard thrusts with slow, deep slides, never taking my eyes off the place where our bodies connect. "I wish you could see me fucking you. It's so goddamn hot."

"Tell me."

I let out a small laugh. "You want to know what it looks like from up here?"

"Yes, please," she coughs out as I pound into her.

"I open you up, stretch you wide for my big dick, and your wet pussy swallows it right up." I don't know how to describe what I'm seeing to her. The magic of our union escapes words. "I do it hard, and your gorgeous tits bounce." I give her a demonstration, thrusting as hard as I can into her depths for a moment as her back arches.

"Yes!"

I'm amazed she can get the word out through her gasps of pleasure.

"And then I fuck you nice and slow." I slow my pace down, gripping her tightly as I slide my length out achingly slow until my tip barely teases her entrance before sliding it back in just as slowly. And then I do it again. "When it's slow, I can watch your body begging for me. You don't have to say a word, Reina, your hips and your spread pussy do all the talking."

"God, I love it when you do that."

"I know, baby girl." I give her more of what she's aching for.

As I continue to work her, slow and then hard, it gets more and more challenging to keep my eyes from drifting up to her sweet, puckered hole. I lick one of my fingers and give the rosebud a little swirl. Reina responds with a moan. Memories of the night when I claimed her here come flooding in, and I almost climax just remembering how well her body took me.

"You like it when I touch you there?"

"Yes."

"You liked it when I fucked you there?"

"God, yes."

I grip both of her ass cheeks with my hands, spreading them

wide to give me the most glorious view as I pound her pussy from behind.

"I promise there's more of that coming. Not tonight, but don't you worry."

I pull my cock out and thrust two fingers into her wetness, getting them as deep as I can before pulling them out and nestling my cock back inside her. My now-dripping-wet fingers slide up to that adorable little hole.

My first finger glides right inside, and I hold it there as I fuck her. Her ass is so tight, it makes my mind reel as I remember sliding my hard cock into that hole and that I now get to do that anytime I want to. I can't take my eyes off it. I slide the other finger inside, stretching her as I glide in. She lets out a small whimper but doesn't stop pressing her hips toward me.

"Does that feel good?"

"Yes, Daddy."

"God, you're such a good fucking girl." With my hand in her sweet behind, and my cock balls deep in her pussy, I'm rapidly approaching the point of no return.

But my sweet girl is still holding out on me.

"It's time for you to come for me, little one. What do you need from me?"

"Harder," she manages in her raspy whisper.

I smile to myself. That's always the answer with her.

Sliding my fingers out of her ass, I wrap my hand around to land on her clit. Reina cries out when I press into her flesh, letting me know I found just the right spot.

With my other hand, I pull her torso up and close to my body so I can take her breasts in my hand and give those nipples the attention they have been begging for all this time.

I thrust up and up, keeping my pressure on her clit, twisting one of her rock-hard nipples between my fingers.

"Oh, Daddy…oh…harder, don't stop!"

Upright, she clearly has more lung capacity. I love listening to her dirty talk, even as I try to keep her quiet so the whole building doesn't hear.

"Be a good girl and come for me."

I know she'll follow my directions. She always does.

I don't have to wait long. The moans of pleasure that come out of her mouth are music to my ears. I love them almost as much as I love the sensation of her internal muscles clenching down on my cock as her body rides the waves of pleasure.

"Good girl, keep coming. Don't let go."

My eyes clench shut as I approach the cliff of my own release. With a silent roar, I empty myself into her body, claiming her once again as my own with an animalistic bite of her shoulder.

I nearly black out as the ecstasy spasms through my body, my grip loosening and allowing her torso to fall to the bed in front of me. Her hips are still in the air, and my cock remains nestled deep inside of her as I grip her ass once more, tilting my head back and trying to regain my breath.

"Good fucking girl."

Reina can't answer with her head pressed into the sheets, but I hear her whimper of agreement.

Never in my life have I felt such passion with anyone. Never have I let myself go in this way, let myself feel so deeply.

I sit back on my heels, and my cock slides out of her, still standing stiff and tall, ready for another round. I rub my hands across the swell of her ass as I watch my seed start to drip out of her. Some primal need inside of me drives my hand down between her legs, scooping up the ropey white liquid and sliding it back inside of her body.

As much as I adore watching it drip from her as she runs to the bathroom after our sessions, as much as I get off on the idea that she has to spend her whole shift with my cum drying on her thighs after I fuck her in the office, right now, all want is for it to stay inside her. Fill her up and never empty out.

*Shit, Dominic. You are in deep.*

I can only hope my girl feels the same.

Reina wraps herself around me, and I pull her in close. I know I should sneak out while it's still dark, but the thought of leaving her here is impossible. What we went through together tonight has made our relationship stronger, I know, but it was still so scary. This was the closest I've come to losing her, and it absolutely terrified me.

When have I ever cared so much about whether a person stays or goes? Never. This girl has me wrapped so tightly around her finger, it's hard to take a breath sometimes. When I look at her, I see my future. I see all of the happiness I never thought I'd find. The fulfillment that I started searching for in my work—I have it now with her. I might get to have my own family, my own legacy outside of just my reputation as a chef. Someone to share the big houses and vacations and fortune with.

Reina stirs and looks up at me, her face filled with sleepiness and contentment. Her eyes barely open as she speaks. "Can I ask you a question?"

"Of course, little one. Anything."

"If I were to, hypothetically, tell you that I was falling in love with you...what would you say?" Her voice is barely a whisper, but it feels like a boulder dropped into the ocean of my heart. The splash takes my breath away, and the ripples throw my entire being off balance.

She has given up a lot to be here with me now, things I know she wants. Relationships with her coworkers and friends, the visibility and recognition she deserves. She's putting up with the secrecy for me, so I can get the things I want. And all she wants is reassurance.

I owe her the words even if they aren't true, but they are. I've never spoken a truer sentence in my life. "I would tell you that I was very much falling in love with you, Reina."

Our eyes stay locked for a long moment, and I think she's going to speak again, but instead, she just closes her eyes and nestles her head back into my chest. It's not long before her breathing slows, and she's asleep in my arms.

As carefully as I possibly can, I slip one arm out from under hers and reach to the bedside table where I set my phone. It's not likely that the message will go through anytime soon, but it's officially time to send it.

**Dom**
Sam, I think we're ready for that HR paperwork now.

# Rule #26

## YOU HOLD ALL THE CARDS

### REINA

When I open my eyes the next morning, Dom's gone. I'm surprised he didn't wake me when he left, but after my torturous trip to town with the girls, our fight, and make-up sex, I guess I slept right through him getting up and leaving.

It was the first time he stayed at my place, for obvious reasons, and it meant a lot that he would take that kind of risk to be with me. I understand his reasons for needing to keep us quiet for a while longer. As hard as it all is, I can do it for him. I would do anything for him.

I'm second in for brunch this morning, so I don't have to be there till seven. I take my time getting ready, flashes of the night before constantly distracting me as I try to get my hair and makeup done.

Being with him is so fun, but it also seems to be filling some kind of need in me that I didn't even realize I had. When he takes me over his knee, when he holds me still even as I struggle, it touches something deep inside of me that I think I've been waiting for my whole life.

I love his strong hands on my body. Nothing has ever felt more right. And even more than that, I love that he is able to control my body, control me in the bedroom, but not overstep my boundaries by trying to control my day-to-day movements or take charge of my finances like my parents always did.

Things will change when the season ends, and Dom and I go public. People are going to have different expectations for me, but I'll cross that bridge when I get to it. This time, I won't be alone. I'll be with Dom.

I told him I loved him last night.

I was crazy to say it.

It was like an out-of-body experience, my memory of the words sound like someone else speaking.

But when he said them back, when he told me that he was falling in love with me...that changed everything.

I reach into my shirt and pull out the gold chain with Dom's ring hanging on it. It's warm from my skin and catches the light with a glint. I press the smooth metal to my lips and close my eyes.

He gave me his grandfather's ring and told me it was a promise. And he told me he was falling in love with me.

I squeeze my eyes closed as a jolt of excitement shoots through my body. I'm so happy I could cry. I am actually crying a little. I laugh as I dab my smeared makeup for the millionth time this morning. My heart almost hurts with love and joy and elation. I feel ready to take on the world. No challenge is too large.

With a deep, calming breath and a sigh, I tuck the ring back safely in its hiding place between my breasts and switch off the bathroom light. I let my smile stay out for everyone to see. I couldn't hide that if I tried. I may not be able to share the reason for all of my happiness yet, but I'm still going to allow myself to enjoy every second of it.

---

The restaurant is already bustling when I get there.

"Glad to see you, Reina," Sylvia calls to me from the coffee station.

I glance around in confusion. "What's going on?"

Brunch doesn't open for another half hour and already this place looks like it's deep in the weeds.

"We've got an early expedition this morning. One of the groups staying here is going out big game fishing, and they need a full day's worth of meals for fourteen. Somehow, they saw fit to wait until six this morning to tell anyone." Sylvia sounds annoyed but determined.

That's how it goes in this industry most of the time. You never quite know what's going to hit or when. Lots of the job is preparing for the unknown.

"On top of that," she goes on, talking to me over her shoulder as she switches the coffee pots. "The owners are all on island, and they're taking a trip to Merit, the island next door, for a retreat or getaway of some kind. They need lunches and meat prepped for them to grill. The dinner guys are supposed to be here getting ready for that, but only two of them have shown up so far. God only knows what happened to the rest of them."

Wait, an owner's trip to another island? Why hadn't Dom told me about that? "All of the owners? Even Dom?"

Sylvia laughs and rolls her eyes at my eager question. "Not likely. That man would never walk away from this restaurant during award season, especially to an island a plane ride away with zero cell service."

Relief pours through me, allowing my mind to click back into gear. "How can I help?"

———

Insane. That's the only way to describe my shift. I loved every minute.

Our brunch guests can feel the hustle and extra energy all

around, and they give us plenty of grace. I truly love serving people brunch. They're just so much more relaxed than dinner guests. We manage to get the big game fishing expedition off with a full day of gourmet meals and lattes, and they show their appreciation with a tip so large that it leaves us speechless.

While the staff celebrates with mimosas during cleanup, Sam comes in through the dining room and walks right up to me.

"Hey, Reina," he says casually, leaning against the bar. "Can I borrow you for a second?"

A moment of panic goes through me, the normal feeling when a big boss wants to talk to you, and he must see it on my face because he smiles. "Just a bit of paperwork, no biggie."

"Sure, yeah, let me just tell Sylvia I'm leaving."

I don't offer her any details, but I don't need to. Her eyebrows go up when I start talking and don't go back down until I'm done. After a moment of silence, she pulls me into a tight embrace. "You are the best employee I've ever had, Reina, and I will not lose you to some ridiculousness. I trust the owners of this resort deeply. I've worked for them for years. I know they will be fair. But if you need anyone on your side on this, that's me, okay? Just say the word, and I'll be in there with you."

I can hardly breathe through my swelling tears at her emotional admission and the way she jumps right on my side, even after all the secrecy. "Thanks, Syl," I manage to whisper.

She pulls away and looks me right in the eye. "You have all the power in this situation. Don't ever forget that. Anything they offer, make them give you double that."

I laugh in surprise and wipe my eyes. "Okay."

Syl gives me one more reassuring smile before heading back to work.

I follow Sam out the dining room doors and down a few halls and staircases until we reach the door I know leads to the large HR offices. I haven't been here since I filled out my new hire paperwork. Once we pass through the doors, I feel extra conspicuous, especially as he leads me past all of the people working at their desks and through another door into some kind of conference room.

It's not until the doors close behind me that I realize Dom's already in there.

"Morning," he says from his seat at the huge white table.

"Hey," I reply, the word leaving my mouth before I realize that I should have probably addressed him differently, less familiarly.

But who am I kidding? If he and I are in a room together in HR, someone already knows.

"Reina, we just have a couple of forms that I need both you and Dominic to sign. I want to make this as comfortable as possible, but I know it's bound to be a little awkward, so my apologies for that."

I can tell I'm blushing already, so I say nothing as I take a seat across the table from Dom.

Sam sits between us, pulling papers out of a folder. "This is pretty standard workplace relationship stuff—agreements and disclosures." He passes copies of the papers to each of us with pens. "This one is a bit more specific and outlines some of the legal complications with one of the parties being an owner." He passes another form my way. This one is a fat stack of stapled papers.

"Now, you can take as long as you need to read over the forms, there are places to initial, and a couple of places where you will need to write out your answers and a few personal disclosures. If you don't feel comfortable with any of it, just let me know. And if you would prefer to have Celeste, the head of HR, here to discuss any of this, that is well within your rights. I just thought that since privacy seems pretty important to you both, it would be better for me to handle it." Sam is speaking directly to me. When he's finished, I look up from the papers and find both him and Dom watching me.

"Okay," I say, feeling a bit overwhelmed by the suddenness of the whole thing. "I'll just look these over and let you know?"

"Take your time," Sam says with a smile.

I start with the big one because that's the one I have a feeling will be the most interesting. Sam said that there were extra legal complications because Dom was the owner, which I expected, but to see them laid out in black and white now, it makes this whole thing so much more real.

It's mostly legal mumbo jumbo, outlining the parameters of how Dom can interact with me at work, that he can't have any say in my pay, schedule, etc. Not exactly the juicy documents I was imagining, but still pretty engaging. I don't know how long it takes me to get to the last page, but when I look up, the guys are still watching me.

"Everything looking okay? Any questions?" Sam asks casually.

I start to say no, but then something from the last page catches my eye. "Bently Adams? Isn't that one of the other owners?" His name is at the bottom of the page, under Preparer.

"Yes, he is. He's a lawyer, so we had him draw up the paperwork for this."

Just then, the door flies open.

"Hey-o!"

Even in the subtle tension of the task at hand, I have to smile as Avery struts into the room, dressed like he just rolled off a yacht.

Hell, he probably did.

"We leave in forty. You guys ready?"

"Avery, we're in the middle of something," Dom says impatiently.

Avery stops and takes in the scene. "Holy shit, paperwork, huh? Making it official?" He strolls over to where I'm sitting, my cheeks burning under his attention. "Welcome to the family, love." He places a kiss on the top of my head as I sit frozen, pen in hand. "You coming to Merit with us? It's going to be a blast. We never convince your old bore of a boyfriend to join us, but you would be welcome. We can all get to know each other. I'll be happy to answer any of your burning questions about why that asshole is the way he is—and do I have some stories for you…"

"Get out, Avery," Dom says, his jaw tight and eyes blazing.

"All right, all right. I'm going." He turns back to me as he's slipping out the door and winks. "That invite still stands. Plane leaves at four."

The sound of the door closing echoes through the silent conference room.

"Reina, I'm sorry about that interrup—"

"The owners are your friends," I say, cutting Sam off.

Dom looks up at me. "What?"

"When I first got here, Sarah told me that you didn't have any friends, but Charles said that the other owners were your only friends. You've been friends since childhood. Those are your friends."

Dom is on his feet, but he doesn't approach me. I can see him holding his breath from where I sit. The look on his face tells me he understands perfectly, but I'm not done.

"Sam." I point to him with my pen. "Bently." I jab the paper in front of me. "And Avery." I use my pen as a weapon, stabbing the air between myself and the door. "Your friends all know."

"Reina—"

"When you told me that we had to keep this a secret, you were only talking about *me* keeping it a secret from *my* friends. You already told your friends. Last night, when I poured my heart out to you about how difficult it was for me to live a life where I had to lie to everyone around me all the time, you told me that you understood. That it was hard for you too. But your friends already know. It's not a secret for you. The only person you were lying to was me."

Dom is coming around the table now, and Sam is on his feet, a look of concern growing on his features.

"Reina, I didn't really think—"

"That much is clear," I retort, holding his gaze. There's a lot of sadness and regret in those hazel eyes, but I'm in no mood for apologies.

"Can we just get these papers signed, and then we can go somewhere private—"

"Oh, don't worry, Dom. I have no intention of causing a scene in HR and exposing your dirty little secret." I toss the pen down on the desk. "You can keep your papers."

I reach behind my neck and unhook the tiny clasp on my gold chain, the action finally causing the tears that have been building to spring into my eyes. This chain, this ring, it meant so much to me just moments before. And now I see it for what it was.

Hush money.

He was just telling me what I wanted to hear to keep me quiet. He would have said anything to keep me from exposing him. He wants so desperately to win this award, to be seen as the top chef in our industry, and I'm just a potential scandal standing in his way.

Even his words from the night before, the ones I had carried off to sleep with me, the ones I thought meant he and I were walking toward the same future together, now sound so hollow.

*"I would tell you that I was very much falling in love with you, Reina."*

I took those words to mean that he loved me as much as I loved him. But in this new light, I can see that's not what he said at all.

I drop the chain, and the ring hits the table with a tiny thud. For a moment, all three of us stare at it. I know I've shocked them both with my outburst because I'm the first to recover.

Without another word, I walk out the door, closing it gently behind me. I keep it together all the way through the HR offices, all the way down the long hallway that leads to the emergency exit stairs.

Once I'm inside the stairwell, however, I completely lose it. I make it to the first landing before collapsing into a heap in the corner with my face in my hands.

What a damn fool I've been. I allowed that man to spin me a tale of our future together, when in reality, he was stringing me along. Without the feedback from my friends to help me gain perspective on the whole thing, I just fell for it.

How could I have been so stupid?

My sadness quickly transforms into anger.

What an asshole. I can't believe all this time he has been talking about this with the people closest to him while insisting that I stay quiet around mine. Well, that garbage ends right now.

As I storm up the hill toward staff housing, I shoot off a group text to Sarah and Charles, which mercifully goes through right away.

They're both waiting on my doorstep when I get home.

# Rule #27

## WHEN IT RAINS, IT POURS

REINA

"I'm trying so hard to be angry at him, but all I feel is rage toward you that you don't have a single goddamn dick pic to show me," Charles says when I get done laying out the last few months for them.

Sarah throws a pillow across the bed, hitting him square in the face, but I can tell she's trying to hold back laughter. "The guy deserves to rot in hell," she assures me.

I crack a smile. I'm still very angry and hurt and sad, but I feel a million times better just having told them. A hundred-pound weight has been lifted off of my chest, and I can breathe.

The problem is that the weight didn't start today with Dom's betrayal. I've been carrying it around all along.

Tears spring back into my eyes for the hundredth time today. "I just feel so stupid. I should've told you guys from the beginning."

"Umm, yeah. You could have saved me the trouble of perfecting my Charles Fuentes signature in my manifestation journal," Charles says bitterly. "But seriously, girl. We all get pulled under by feelings sometimes. Love makes people do crazy things."

"Yeah, like sitting through an entire night of scuba instructor speed dating when you have already bagged yourself a billionaire boyfriend," Sarah chides.

"I'm so sorry for all the lying. Can you forgive me?"

"Obviously," Sarah says immediately. "It's already forgiven. Are you kidding me? I one hundred percent would have done the same thing. I mean, I love you guys, but if one of those owners offered me a secret affair, I'd lie my ass off."

My tears start again as the relief her words bring settles over me. "I was so worried you were going to hate me when you found out."

"Girl, you are going to wish Charles hated you after a few days of the questions he is going to be badgering you with."

"She's not wrong there. I want to know everything." Charles snuggles up to where I'm sitting, resting his head on my thigh. "All the juicy details."

I laugh, stroking his hair affectionately. These two are the best friends I've ever had. I feel silly now thinking they would abandon me over this. "You get one question for now, better make it good."

Charles bites his lip in concentration. "Okay, does he ask you to call him chef in the bedroom?"

Sarah and I break out into a fit of laughter.

"No! I've never called him Chef, but…" I pause for dramatic effect, the two of them waiting with their mouths hanging open. "I do call him Daddy."

"Stop! You do not!"

I purse my lips and nod. "Sure do."

"Well, I'm dying to unpack all of this, but I want to wait until I can get a few margaritas in you," Charles says, turning to his phone, which has been pinging nonstop over the last few minutes. "What's the rumor mill up to?" he wonders aloud, eyes focused on the screen.

"Tell us," Sarah begs him. "We need a distraction."

"Reina's daddy bomb wasn't enough of a distraction for you?"

"It was for me, but not for her." Sarah cocks her head in my direction, giving me a look that lets me know she's sending love my way.

"Okay, here's one for you. One of the prep cooks just sent me a pic of tonight's dinner books, and look at this name on the reservation list." He holds his phone out so we can both see the picture.

I have to squint to make out the tiny writing where he is pointing, but when I finally read the name, I gasp.

*Quinlin X. Fairchild.*

"I mean, as if Quinlin Fairchild wasn't enough, they had to throw the X on there," Charles jokes.

"What the hell could their middle name even be? Xavier? Xena?" Sarah's laughing at the possibilities, but she stops short when she looks at me. "What's wrong?"

I can feel the blood drain out of my face as I try to remind myself to breathe. "That's the judges."

"What?"

"The Pendleton judges." I'm on my feet now, searching for my phone. "That's the same name they used when they came to eat at Bon Vivant in Chicago."

"Wait, you worked at Bon Vivant?"

"Charles, I don't have time to explain right now. Where is my freaking phone?" I'm frantic now, tossing clothing piles around the room.

"It's here," Sarah calls from the bathroom.

I run to her and grab it, dialing Dom's number as quickly as I can. His voicemail picks up right away. I hang up and call again. Same thing. With a frustrated cry, I shoot him a text.

> **Reina**
> The judges are coming in for dinner tonight.
> Their reservation is under Quinlin X Fairchild,
> party of four.

I hit send but the message fails to deliver. Charles's phone is still pinging like crazy, so I don't think the reception problem is on my end.

"Where is he?" I ask, exasperated.

"According to the rumor mill, he got on that plane with the other owners half an hour ago. My guess is he's sunning his toes on Merit Island," Charles answers, still staring at his screen.

I stand statue still with my mouth hanging open, taking in the news.

"There's also a lot of chatter about a full-on restaurant crisis happening down there. Apparently, there was some bad ceviche at a party last night. None of the dinner servers have made it in, only two of the cooks are there, and zero dishwashers."

I squeeze my eyes closed for a moment and take a long, slow breath. After I let it out, I try calling Dom one more time. Still no luck.

With a resigned shake of my head, I dial Sylvia.

# Rule #28

## ASK THE RIGHT QUESTIONS

### DOMINIC

I only get about two minutes of processing, and not a single encouraging word from Sam, between the time Reina closes the door behind her and Avery opening it.

"You guys done yet?" He glances between Sam and me, and then to Reina's empty seat. "Good. Plane is getting loaded now. I'm about ready to do the same." He laughs at his own joke, his laughter echoing off the walls of the otherwise silent room. When neither of us join in or react at all, Avery falls silent. "What's wrong?"

I shake my head. "I fucked it all up."

Avery balks. "Come on, man. That girl was completely doe-eyed for you. Not even you could have fucked this one up."

"I've been insisting the whole time that it stays secret from the restaurant, thinking that was what was better for both of us. But what I failed to grasp was that the restaurant is her world in a much different way than it is mine. She has spent the whole time lying to her closest friends, while I've just been keeping my private life private from my employees. All of my closest friends knew about her."

The room is quiet for a few moments before Avery pipes back up. "Well, that is pretty fucked, Dom, but par for the course for your socially awkward ass. Let's go to Merit, get drunk, and we can sort it all out."

"Avery, I don't think—"

"No, he's right," Sam says suddenly.

Both Avery and I look at him in surprise.

"Go get on the plane."

"Sam, I have a restaurant to run."

"Not today, you don't. Today, you are going to give that woman the space she deserves to process what went on in this room. The last thing she needs is you running up to her apartment trying to make things right or hovering over her as she tries to do her job. You need to give her time, and I know you won't, so you're coming to Merit."

Every single part of me is screaming to run from the room, get to Reina at all costs, make her understand how sorry I am, how stupid a mistake this was.

But deep down, I know he's right.

I walk down the runway and board the plane like a man walking death row.

"Did you get the papers signed?" Ben asks as the pilot closes the door behind us.

"Uh, no. They did not sign any papers. The girl got to see the man behind the mask before he could get her name on the dotted line," Avery jokes, and I scowl at him.

"What's that supposed to mean?" Ben asks me, his tone sharp. "All you had to do was sign that goddamn paperwork, and the property would have been legally protected. I thought I made that very clear."

"She changed her mind."

"About the paperwork?"

"About me."

I try to speak the words as calmly as I can, but my tone must give away some of the feelings I'm trying to keep inside. These guys know me too well for me to hide it for long anyway. The plane falls silent.

"Sorry, man."

"Yeah," I reply, grateful for the finality of that statement. We all look out the windows for the rest of the short flight, saying nothing.

Max, the caretaker, meets us when we climb off the plane. He and his family have lived on Merit Island for generations, and we were lucky to get them to agree to take care of our place. He is a gem of a man and treats us well when we visit.

I haven't been here during the on-season for years, my apron strings far too short, so I see the look of surprise in the man's eyes when I climb out of the cabin.

"Dominic!" He greets me with both arms open. I allow him to pull me into an embrace. "What a surprise to have the chef on island. I have dinner all set up on the beach for you, fire hot, drinks ready. Maybe you would like to do the cooking tonight? Or I can still do it if you need the night off." He takes our bags and loads them into a golf cart driven by his wife, Petunia, who offers us a smile and a wave.

He ushers the four of us onto a different cart and drives us straight to the beach.

Merit Island is exactly what you would picture if you imagined washing up on a deserted island after a shipwreck. Enormous white sand beaches, interior jungle, and a tall mountain right in the center. It's gorgeous, mysterious, and just wild enough to be a good vacation spot for men who already own a piece of paradise.

If it wasn't for the complete lack of bedrock, we may have opted to build another resort over here. Instead, we contracted the locals to build us a luxurious three-story house. Our spacious mansion hideaway waits on the other side of the tiny island. For now, Max is taking us to the absolute best swimming beach where he has a pit barbecue set up with coals already glowing.

I hate to admit it, but Sam was right. This is exactly where I need to be right now.

The guys all crack a beer as Max and I drag the heavy steel grate over the hot coals.

"How's the kitchen going over there, Dominic? Must be running very smoothly if you could get away on a Friday night."

I let out a sigh and pass him the grill oil. "It's been a tough day, so the guys convinced me to take the night off."

"No point in holding back now, Dom. I fly over here and have Max solve almost all of my personal problems for me. The man is a sage. Lay it on him," Avery calls over from his lowrider beach chair.

Max carefully wipes oil over the grates with a blackened towel attached to a long stick in silence. I can tell he is giving me space to speak.

I shake my head in resignation as I drag the cooler over to the pit. I may as well let these guys help me. If there's any way I can get Reina back, I want to know about it. My tortured brain can only come up with worst-case scenarios and sob stories right now, so I would be a fool to pass up advice from this group.

"I met a girl. A brunch server who came in with the new crew. She was different from the others, right from the start. And I know she liked me. We started...a thing. And we agreed that it was better to keep it just between us. I know it looks bad now because I'm trying to win an award, and I made her keep our relationship secret, but at the beginning, she was just as eager to keep it quiet. She has ambitions to move up at the restaurant and didn't want people thinking she was sleeping her way to the top." I pause and hand Max the metal pan containing a fat T-bone steak for each of us. We also brought enough chicken and pork chops to feed his entire family and some of the strays. The meat sizzles as he lays it on the hot grill.

"It was a few weeks in before she started expressing

concerns about lying. I kind of brushed it off, which was a mistake, I realize now. I'm just so used to keeping everything in my life private. I didn't understand what it all meant to her. Last night she came home from a trip to town with some of the other female employees. Apparently, they were trying to set her up with one of the scuba guides from town. They all thought she was single, and she couldn't say anything to the contrary. She told me that she needed to tell her friends, but once again, I convinced her to wait." I don't want to say the rest, so I pause, the words stuck in my throat. The guys know the story isn't over, and they all wait in silence, sipping their beers.

"Last night she told me she loved me. Well really, she asked what I would say if she told me she loved me." I let out a bitter laugh, remembering my pathetic answer. "I told her if she told me that, I would say it back. I should have just told her I loved her right then and there because I did. I do." I accept the tongs from Max and walk around the grill, poking the steaks to check if they're ready to flip.

"I texted Sam and told him it was time for HR paperwork. He'd been letting it slide for a while, but I knew we crossed a line, and it was time. The three of us met up just a couple of hours ago, as you all know." I gesture with my head toward the group of guys around the firepit, each of them looking at their bottle of beer, giving me space to pour my heart out. "But she realized during the meeting that everyone important in my life already knew about us. You guys all knew. She had been lying to her best friends while my friends knew. Not that I talked to any of you assholes about it, but I could have. I just didn't feel like I needed to. But she did. She needed to talk to her friends. When she found out that I was making her lie when I didn't have to, she walked. Dropped the ring I gave her on the table and just walked out."

"Ring?" Ben asks.

"My grandfather's ring. I gave it to her on a chain to wear

hidden under her shirt. A promise that someday things would be different."

"Holy shit, man. I can't believe you gave that ring away. I've never seen you without it since the day he gave it to you," Avery said.

"He gave it to me because he thought I would be the one to know when it was time to give it away. He thought I was the only one in the family who understood what love was. If he could only see me now, he'd roll over in his grave."

"I don't know, Dom. Your grandfather was the best judge of character I ever met. He knew you were the lover of the family, and he was right. You knew when to give it away, didn't you?" Ben asks.

"Yeah, but she gave it back."

"Do you still want her to have it?" he asks gently.

"Of course. I just don't know how I'm going to get her to trust me again after this."

"Have you considered just buying her a house or flying her to Paris or something? That kind of shit always works really well for me," Avery chimes in from the table set up in the sand, where he's setting out forks and steak knives.

"Oh, really, Ave, it's worked so well in all of your many relationships?" Sam jokes, joining him at the table.

"Seriously, which of your one-night stands did you buy a house for?" Ben asks with a laugh.

"You know what I mean. The house thing was for Dom. That's totally the kind of thing he would do. I'm more of the fly 'em to Paris guy."

"She doesn't want me to buy her stuff," I say, carrying the tray of steaks over to the table. "It's a whole thing. If I bring up money at all, she kind of freaks. The only big things I've been able to buy for her have been things that the whole staff gets. After I slept one night in her terrible staff bed, I had a new mattress delivered for her. The next day, she made me order one for all hundred thirteen other staff beds." I pause as the guys break into laughter, Max included. He's been quiet during this discussion, but I can almost hear his mind working. I can't wait to hear what advice he will offer me.

"I wanted to buy her a golf cart so she wouldn't have to walk to town, and she instead wanted a fleet of employee carts for everyone to use. Money is an even worse topic. One time I tried to offer her a credit card so she could buy things in town, and she nearly had a panic attack." That much is true enough, but the part about Reina's debt feels too personal to share, even with these guys.

We all settle at the round table, looking eagerly at the dishes laid out before us. To go along with the platter of steaks, Max prepared a bowl of slaw, roasted potatoes, cut melon, and steaming beans and rice. It's the perfect island feast.

All talk switches to admiration for the gorgeous food as we heap our plates and pass dishes around the table. When we're all served, Max sets down his silverware with a solid thunk. We all look over at him, mouths full.

"You aren't asking the right questions, Dom."

The table falls silent, and I struggle to process his words. I don't get there before he speaks again.

"Our quality of life depends on the quality of questions we ask. If you aren't getting the answers you need, the clarity you need, it means you aren't asking the right questions."

As if that explanation was satisfactory, Max lifts his fork and knife once more and starts cutting into his meat.

It takes me a full moment to recover my voice. "How do I know what questions to ask?"

"What is it that you want to know?"

"I want to know how to make her forgive me."

"Then you need to ask why she's upset."

"I know why she's upset."

"It sounds to me, Dominic, like you know nothing at all."

The words floor me. I look down at my plate, unable to breathe.

He could not be more right.

With a deep sigh, I lift my eyes back up to the men sitting around the table. "You're right. I don't know anything. I've just been pushing forward with this thing as if it's a given, as if I'm the boss of the situation, and it will continue to go whatever way I want for as long as I want. I lost sight of the fact that there's another person involved, one with a whole world of feelings and past experiences and hopes for the future."

"What's the question you want to know the answer to, Dominic?" Max asks into the silence that follows my admission.

"I want to know how I can be better…a better man for Reina. Be a better role model for my kitchen. Be a better person for my future children." I glance down again, not sure if the next words will make it out of my mouth. "Be a better father than my father was."

I look up to see Max nodding. "Now that you know the question, do you have a better idea of what the answer is?"

I nod back at him. "Yeah, I think I do."

# Rule #29

## STAY CALM...IT'S JUST CHAOS

### REINA

When I arrive at the restaurant, Sylvia is already there.

"It's not looking good. All of the servers are out with whatever this stomach thing is, and we have four of the six cooks."

I nod grimly. "Sarah's on her way. She's been through two dinner training shifts, so that's a plus." I take a deep breath and let it out. "And I ran the dining room at Bon Vivant in Chicago for their dinner service for almost five years. I can do this."

Sylvia gives me a sly look that doesn't contain a single drop of surprise. "I knew there was more to your résumé than you let on."

"Sorry, I just really didn't want to get promoted to dinner."

"For more reasons than just the handsome chef who seems to follow you around like a puppy dog?"

I can feel myself blush but smile through it. "I got really stressed out working fine dining and late nights in the city. I may have narrowly escaped a nervous breakdown by coming to Faraday Island."

"You don't have to convince me, girl. Dominic can steal you for dinner over my dead body."

I'm grinning now. "Let's check in with the kitchen."

Just then, Sarah and Charles arrive with Jess in tow.

"Let's do this. Dinner service anarchy," Charles sings out. He's dressed just like I told him to—in clothes he doesn't mind getting dirty.

I roll my eyes but smile. "Get in the dish pit, Charles."

He bows and heads off to his fate.

I turn to the girls. "I'm going to go check in with the kitchen, will you ladies get the dining room set up?" The two nod and walk back out toward the empty dining room.

When I step into the kitchen, it's much less calm.

The dinner cooks who did show up are clearly feeling under-prepared—lost without their full team and the prep that should have been done by the afternoon staff. Luckily Marcus is here, although he's not looking his best. I wonder if he would have stayed home in bed if circumstances were different.

"Hey," I start, knowing I have a big hill to climb to gain the trust of these people. "I'm Reina, I know we haven't really talked much this season—"

"You spilled cranberry juice on our game," one of the guys chimes in from across the line.

I nod and sigh. "Yup, that was me. Anyway, we have kind of a motley crew here, but I know we can pull this off."

Marcus is shaking his head, looking over his clipboard which no doubt contains the night's prep list. "I don't know. I think we might be better off closing for the night or maybe just serving pizza."

"No." My voice is firm, and all the faces turn to me. "The judges are coming in tonight. We are doing the full tasting menu, and we are going to do it perfectly."

"How could you possibly know that the judges are coming?"

I grab the night's reservation book from the pass. "See right here?" I point at the name and the closest cooks lean over to see.

"This is them. I know it is. I worked at Bon Vivant when they came in, and that was the same name they used. With any luck, it will be the same judges I met before. They were really nice, and they liked me."

"Wait, you worked at Bon Vivant? What are you doing serving breakfast?" Marcus asks.

"I don't have time to explain right now. Do you have enough prep to run the menu tonight?"

"It's gonna be tight, but we have everything except the scallop dish. The fisherman didn't show up today, and besides, the spring onions are not looking their best."

I bite my lip and consider. "What else do you have that we could put in that slot?"

"What about the cauliflower?" one of the young female cooks asks from behind Marcus. We all watch Marcus consider.

"It's prepped and ready to go. Chef Dominic approved it. But it's a shared dish, and he wasn't sold on sending one of those out on the tasting menu. Besides, we don't have time to train the servers on how to set it up, and we don't have dishes picked out to serve it on," he says nervously.

"No, no. That's perfect," I say quickly. "Let's run with the cauliflower instead of the scallops. Marcus, can you get the plates picked out for it? I can present it to the judges' table. That's not a problem."

The man nods, and I nod back. Sometimes, that's all you get from the kitchen guys, but somehow, it's enough.

I turn to find Sarah behind me, breathless. "Reina, the table-cloths haven't come down from laundry. We looked everywhere. Want me to send Jess up to housekeeping to see what's going on?"

"No," I say quickly. "Just set the tables without them."

She nods and rushes off.

When I get back to the service station, I find Sylvia preparing the wine for the tasting menu. This is going to be the biggest feat. With none of us servers familiar with the coursing of the wines, there's going to be a steep learning curve.

"Will you make a note for each bottle with the course it goes with and the glass it needs and put them in front?"

Sylvia nods and heads off to find notecards.

I spin slowly in place, a familiar dance from my days running the dining room at Bon Vivant.

The kitchen is giving off a bit of anxiety, but all in all, they look okay.

The dining room looks great—the bare wood tables change the whole color scheme of the room, and the place now looks a bit darker, more dramatic.

The dish pit is well in hand, the reservation book is in the host station, which is being manned by a front desk employee who hosted at Raft the season before. The wine is going to be a challenge, but not one we can't rise to.

I nod to myself as I come full circle. It's by no means an ideal situation, but we are going to make it. I pull my phone out of my pocket and send the millionth text to Dom.

*We are set up and getting ready to open. Things are hectic but okay. We got this.*

I hit the send button knowing damn well he won't see it until it's much too late, but it just feels right to keep him in the loop.

We have some personal problems to work out, ones that might be insurmountable, but when it comes to work—I can put all that aside. All of the people in this room, and the ones at home sick, have worked too long and hard to see it all go down in flames. We will pull together and kick ass tonight.

Tomorrow is another story.

# Rule #30

## NEVER LEAVE CELL SERVICE

### DOMINIC

It's a bumpy golf cart ride back to the house, and we ride mostly in silence. I only had one beer, so I'm able to hold on pretty well —Avery, on the other hand, isn't faring so well. I see Ben holding tightly to him, keeping him from falling out the side as we take corners on the narrow jungle path.

Max is going on about his son who is visiting after graduating from engineering school. I'm only half listening, my own worries about the future of my relationship taking the front-row seat in my mind.

"...installed a couple of upgrades to the whole island, but there is one in your house that you are going to be so excited about."

"What are you talking about up there?" Avery calls from the back.

"I'm talking about the secret surprise my son installed in your house," Max explains patiently. The man really is a saint. "You are going to be so pleased."

I smile at him, noting the look of pride on his face. Max's son is an only child, and I've spent many an afternoon listening to him and his wife talk about his progress through school, his job prospects, really everything about the kid. They're so proud of him for accomplishing what he has, and their love shines through each and every story they tell.

We should all be so lucky.

I know plenty of people would groan at the fact that I consider a poor kid from a Caribbean island who is the first in his family to go to college luckier than me, a billionaire trust funder, but in some ways, I do.

That kid has something I will never have—the unconditional love and support of his family.

I gave up on my family of origin long ago, but I did think that someday I would have a family of my own. Over the last few months, that dream was starting to look more and more realistic.

Then I went and fucked it all up.

I put work before my feelings for Reina, and that turned out to be an offense so bad, it might be unforgivable. I don't care what the guys say. I saw the look on her face as she realized my betrayal. I'm not sure there's any coming back from that.

Even if I manage to step up the way I plan to and show everyone I care about them as people rather than just warm bodies in my kitchen, a means to an end, it might be too little too late.

I'm determined to do it anyway. Even if I never get the girl back.

I see now that my crew deserves better from me. The whole resort deserves better. I've been living this laser-focused mission for far too long, and I've lost sight of what we've already accomplished here.

The White Sands rose from the ashes of its past to become the most unique and in-demand resort in this half of the globe. It's the standard that other properties now strive toward, with our commitment to sustainability and our relationships with the land and the local people. We provide an experience that allows our guests to really get to know the island, instead of just lying beside a pool behind concrete walls.

For the first time in the last five years, I'm able to see the resort as a whole. All I see is accomplishment. All I feel is pride. I lost myself to thinking that this award would gain us something that we were lacking. All I needed to do was open my eyes and realize that we already had it all.

Those days are over. I have a new mission. I will show up every day and celebrate the life I have. I will work toward melding my creative pursuits with the rest of The White Sands and create something even better—for the guests, but also for the employees, the people who have given up everything to move here and live with us. I was blind not to see the richness already at my fingertips, and I know I have a lot of making up to do.

As we pull up to the house, pings and dings start coming from every pocket in the vehicle.

"What's going on? It sounds like we're at the club or something," Avery jokes as he pulls his phone out.

I don't bother with mine. It's a well-known fact that there's zero cell service on this island. We are lucky to have a landline in the house.

"I have bars," Avery says excitedly, climbing out of the golf cart and heading toward the house. "Do you guys?" He tosses a look back at me, and I narrow my eyes.

"Yes, this is the secret I was waiting to tell you," Max says eagerly. "My son has installed a signal boost device that will make your phones work perfectly."

Now that is a surprise.

I told Marcus to text me with a prep update, so I pull my phone out to check. I'm not expecting to have any messages from Reina, although I'll be damned if my heart doesn't hold out hope.

What I see when the screen lights up takes me a full moment to process.

Twenty-three missed calls, almost a hundred text messages. They've been coming in for hours, from my cooks, my front of the house manager, even housekeeping. Most important of all, many of them are from Reina.

I feel my heart lift with hope—until I start reading the messages.

Apparently, food poisoning has taken out sixty percent of my staff, and the judges are coming in for dinner.

Of course they are.

I glance at the clock. It's six twenty. Reina said that the judges have a seven o'clock reservation.

I can still get there in time.

"I need to get back to the airstrip." The lone pilot will have settled into his dinner by this time, but I'm sure I can talk him into one more flight.

Max starts the cart immediately.

"Wait, what? No, Dom. We are here for the night. Come in, let's hang out," Sam says, getting out of the vehicle.

"The judges are arriving for dinner in forty minutes. Half of the staff are out sick. Reina is running the service."

Sam climbs back into the cart. "To the airport, Max."

We leave Ave and Ben at the house and speed off into the night.

# Rule #31

## THE SHOW MUST GO ON

### REINA

Working a dining room is like riding a bike in a lot of ways. For one, you never forget how to do it. And two, if any part slows down, the whole thing crashes.

There's no risk of slowing down tonight. With four servers doing the job of seven, we don't have a second to pause between tables and courses.

When seven o'clock rolls around, the four of us have settled into a nice flow, dividing up the tables and getting used to the wine service. The chefs still have enough staff to deliver most of the dishes, so it's mostly a matter of keeping the water filled, the right wines on the right tables, and the courses fired in the correct order.

I see them before they see me. My heart soars when I watch them walk through the doors of Raft. It's the same judges I waited on three years back at Bon Vivant for the winning meal that year.

I wait until the host has shown them to their table before walking over.

"Good evening, old friends."

All four faces turn to me, and I watch each one break into a smile.

"Reina," one of the women greets me. "What are you doing all the way out here? I never imagined Sebastian would let you go."

I return her warm smile. "I needed a change of pace. The city was getting too busy for me. And besides, you can't beat the weather on Faraday—or that view." I subtly draw their attention to the pink sky outside the panoramic window adjacent to their table as the sun starts to set.

"Well, I can't wait to see what you have in store for us tonight. If this is the place you chose, I have officially raised my expectations," one of the older men, the stickler, teases me.

"Stop, Frank." His wife, one of the other judges, slaps him playfully on the arm. "I'm surprised you got your already high expectations through the door."

The whole table laughs good-naturedly, and I join in, but the conversation has a pit forming in my gut. I knew this would be hard to pull off, but now that the actual people are in front of me, shit just got real.

I'm happy they remember me and seem to consider me a friend, but I know just how critical these four diners are. They're the official judges for the most prestigious culinary award on the planet. No amount of goodwill toward me will sway them if we don't deliver the greatest meal of the year.

I excuse myself to grab the first wine. Sylvia and Sarah are both waiting for me in the service station.

"Same judges?" Sarah asks eagerly. I can see all eyes on me from through the kitchen pass as well.

"Yup," I say, loud enough for the guys in back to hear. "Same judges, they remember me. It was really friendly out there, which is a great start. But we have to deliver, you guys. One thousand percent. Clean coats in the dining room." I direct that statement straight to the kitchen. "Perfectly polished glasses for every wine course," I say to the women beside me.

Everyone nods and looks solemn. This is the moment we have all been waiting for.

"Okay, let's do this," I say, and everyone springs into action.

It's been decided that I will take care of the judges' table exclusively, while the other ladies run the rest of the dining room. I instructed them to quietly let the guests know what's going on and tell them their full meal will be on the house, just in case something isn't perfect. I can tell by the excited looks around the room that the other guests love being in on the secret —and the comped meal doesn't hurt either.

Marcus will deliver each course to the judges' table, with the exception of the cauliflower dish, which apparently is the brain-child of one of the female cooks, so she's going to take that dish out herself.

There's no substitute for Head Chef Fuentes making an appearance at the table, but what we have to offer will have to be good enough.

The first wine and first course hit the table. I can feel the energy of the whole staff coming together as one as we all try not to get caught watching them eat. It's challenging to look away, but we have to let them have their dining experience.

As the lobster plates are cleared, I pour the wine for the sashimi. I can see the kitchen preparing to sear off the cauliflower dish as I line up the glasses I will need for that course.

I know it's a risk sending out this untried dish, and in a style of service we don't usually do at Raft, but I know in my gut it's the right move. Not everyone likes getting a shared plate at such a fine restaurant, having to pass it around and serve themselves from the communal dish, but these people do. I clearly remember the dishes that got the highest marks on our scorecard at Bon Vivant, and both of them were shared plates.

When it's time, I bring out the wine I selected to accompany this new dish, an orange wine from Gerard Bertrand. The faces of the judges all show a bit of surprise and delight as I splash the unexpected beverage into their crystal wineglasses.

When the female cook enters the dining room carrying the handmade plate with the round of homegrown cauliflower on it, I know we made the right decision.

These judges are culinary critics second—they're parents, grandparents, and lovers of the industry first and foremost. This cook is the ultimate representation of where we can go as an industry, and she's hamming it up like she knows it.

I lean against the counter and watch as she masterfully fields question after question about her background and education, what she loves about cooking and Raft specifically. Her answers would win her the goddamn Miss Universe sash, and the judges are practically eating out of her hand by the end of it.

I squeeze her shoulder as she passes by me to head back to the kitchen. "Great job," I whisper. She responds with a tight-lipped smile that I can tell is the only thing holding her excitement in.

I watch the judges ooh and ahh over the cauliflower before passing it around and filling their clean share plates. A commotion in the kitchen has me turning to look through the pass.

And I make eye contact with Dom.

He just rushed into the kitchen. I can tell by his casual attire and the breathless look on his face. He comes to a dead stop as our eyes meet. There's so much emotion in that glance, it's all I can do not to look away.

It breaks my heart to have to shut down at the sight of him, instead of lighting up, which I would have done yesterday, or any of the other days since I met him. My heart is still so full of love.

But now it's also full of questions.

Can I trust him?

How could he have put me through this?

Is it really over between us?

I have to look away, as I'm in no position to break into tears at this moment.

I feel him come up behind me. When I turn, he's leaning on the counter a few feet away.

"Give it to me," he says.

"They're on the third course. We went with the cauliflower shared plate, as there weren't scallops. Seems to be going very well. Not a hiccup so far. The rest of the dining room is in on the secret and have been informed that their dinner is going to be comped. Sylvia, Sarah, and Jess are working those tables. We have six more tables to seat tonight, all of them in the next hour." I walk over to the dinner chart that maps out each table and where they are in the tasting menu. "We have three tables going into mains together, which seems like a lot for sauté, but I didn't catch it in time to slow one of them down."

"I'll take care of it," Dom says. "Anything else?"

I shake my head.

"Thank you for doing this, Reina. You don't know what it means to me."

"I do know, Dom. This isn't just about you. This award means everything to all of us. We're all in this together."

My words hit him just where I intended, and I watch as he bows his head and nods. Then he walks back toward his office to change.

I head back out to the judges' table to see how they're enjoying the cauliflower. They gush over the dish, and I can't wait to tell the young cook.

"You know, I was starting to wonder when we were going to lay eyes on the elusive Chef Fuentes, but honestly, that young chef could bring out every course for the rest of dinner, and I would be happy," one of the ladies says with a smile. "I hope she's in line for a promotion."

"She's one of our rising stars," I assure the judge, even

though I have no idea what the ladder in this particular kitchen looks like. The truth isn't important right now.

"There he is," one of the male judges says, looking behind me.

I turn to find Dom, in full chef regalia, strutting toward the table. I smile broadly and take a step to the side, allowing him to walk right up to the judges.

"Welcome to Raft," Dom starts in his chef voice. I have to stifle a smile at his impeccable acting abilities. You'd never know that both his kitchen and personal life were currently in flames. It looks like the man doesn't have a care in the world.

I excuse myself and start preparing the next wine course at the server station.

"Are you going to forgive him?" Sarah hisses as she comes up beside me, as if I have time to think about such things right now.

"I'm not sure."

"He really is very handsome," she says, eyeing his backside at the table.

"You were the one who told me to stay away from the guy in the first place."

"Yeah, but that was then. Things are completely different now."

"You think I should forgive him?"

"I mean, make him earn it, but yeah, probably."

I roll my eyes and turn back to polishing glasses. If only it were that simple. The hard part is—this isn't really about forgiveness. It's not like Dom did something wrong, per se. He just didn't prioritize our relationship the way I wanted him to. No amount of forgiveness on my part can change that.

That's something he needs to figure out on his own. If I somehow rise to the top of his priority list, then maybe we have a shot.

If not, well, I just hope I can keep my job.

The rest of the evening goes smoothly, all things considered.

Everyone leaves the restaurant happy, and the judges' table gets every ounce of attention it needs to deliver the most perfect dining experience.

As I watch Dom and Marcus tour the dining room at the end of service, saying thank yous and goodbyes to all the guests, I'm satisfied that we did the absolute best we could.

I just hope it's enough.

# Rule #32

## THE TRUTH WILL SET YOU FREE

### DOMINIC

Nothing in the world could have prepared me for the service we just completed. In all my years of training, in all my months of planning, having every single thing go wrong that could possibly have gone wrong and still pull off the most perfect meal for those judges…

I know exactly who I have to thank for that.

Reina may have just won us the award I've been working toward my whole adult life. And she did it pissed as hell at me after I betrayed her trust and broke her heart.

Maybe I don't deserve her.

Something she said earlier keeps coming back to my mind as I walk the last of the guests out of the dining room.

*This isn't just about you. This award means everything to all of us. We are all in this together.*

She couldn't be more right. This team is more than just a group of people working together. These people are my family. They understand me in ways my family of origin never even tried to. On levels I've not even considered sharing with my parents or siblings. I'm a fool to have thought they would be anything but supportive of me finding happiness in my life, no matter who brings me that happiness.

It doesn't even matter if we win that award or not, we've already won. I've already won. My life is exactly what I wanted it to be. Everything I've dreamed of is right within my reach. All I have to do is hold out my hand.

"Hey," I call loudly enough that the cooks in the back can hear. "Can everyone come out here, please?"

I just locked the front door and stood waiting for my team in the middle of the empty dining room. All around me is the glorious mess of a perfectly executed service, the thrill of pulling it off still hanging in the air.

One by one, the crew joins me, gathering around in a semicircle. Reina stands with the other servers next to the bar with her eyes on me.

"This was incredible, you guys. Some smart science guy once said something about how everything that can go wrong will go wrong, and he was damn right. This was a perfect storm of problems that could have taken us down. But they didn't. You all pulled together and made this happen. You ran a service better than I ever could have asked for. Hell, better than I would have done if I'd been here the whole time. We have a good shot at placing for that award, we might even win it. And it's all because of you." I pause and take a deep breath, trying to keep my emotions in check. This may be a celebratory bonding experience, but that doesn't mean I need to get all teary-eyed in front of everyone.

"You all know Reina, and you know things about her and her work experience that until tonight none of us, myself included, knew. She really stepped up and made this happen. I don't know what would have happened if she wasn't here." My eyes lock on Reina's as I speak. I watch her fight off her own emotions. She's successful so far, but I know it's a battle she's going to lose soon enough.

"But there are other things you don't know about Reina." I see her tense and shake her head, but there's no stopping me now. "First and foremost, you don't know that she's the love of my life."

Gasps and whispers flow through the group, but they all sound excited and supportive. I continue.

"I've been selfishly keeping her a secret from you all, even though you are the most important people in the world to me. My family, if you will. All of you. And I apologize for that. I got caught up in the idea that in order to do this job well, I needed to maintain a certain image. I can see now how wrong I was. Reina…"

The crowd moves to the side as I walk over and stand before her. "I don't know how this award thing will go, but it doesn't matter anymore. I can see now that all I ever wanted, I have. I have my restaurant, my team, my home, my island. My family is right here. And that family is you. If it takes me until my last day on earth to convince you to forgive me, I will consider my life well spent."

I fall to my knees and take her hands, looking up into her now wet face, locking my gaze onto her tear-filled eyes. I can see the love in those eyes, and it helps me gather the courage to go on. "I don't have the ring I want to offer you yet, and not because I'm unsure about marrying you—I'm not. I'd marry you right now with these people as our witnesses if I could." I hear some quiet words of emotion from around me, but I can't take my eyes off of Reina. "But I want it to be right. I only have this ring to give you."

I pull out my grandfather's ring and hold it up, the gold chain still dangling through it.

"I know I offered it to you before as a promise in bad faith, and I would do anything to go back and change that. But I want to offer it again, this time for real. I promise that you will never be second to my job, or anything else in my life, ever again. I promise that I will bring the world to your feet. I will work for the rest of my life to create the world you want to live in. I promise that as soon as I can get off this damn island, I will have the biggest rock you have ever laid eyes on mounted on a band for you and slip it on your finger. And I promise that I will love you for the rest of my life."

I stop speaking and hold my breath, my hand holding the ring still hovering in the air between us. After a torturously long moment, Reina nods, and I slip the much too large ring, complete with dangling chain, onto her finger.

She makes her hand into a fist to keep it from sliding off.

Tears are rolling down my cheeks now, and I reach up self-consciously to brush them away, but as I do, I catch sight of all of my staff members around me. There's not a dry eye in the place. I laugh softly at the sight of all my line cooks and my sous chef trying to look stoic as they rub tears from their red eyes.

How could I ever have thought these people would be anything but happy for me?

I stand and pull Reina into my arms, the small crowd breaking out in applause. She and I share a teary laugh, the emotions of the moment a palpable thing I can feel in the air all around us. It's so special to get to share this moment with all of these people. I guess that's why people get married—to have this kind of connection with their friends and loved ones.

Up until now, I thought I needed to keep everything to myself. I thought family was only there to criticize and let me down. I can see now how wrong I was. As long as I have the right family around, my chosen family…if I have that…I have everything.

I have more love now than I ever thought possible. And it's all because of this woman.

Reina and I slip away without helping with cleanup—pushed out the back door is a more accurate way to describe it—and we make our way up the path to my house hand in hand. I know it's probably just the adrenaline still running through my veins from dinner service, or possibly the exhaustion from the crazy day I've had, but it almost feels like the night air parts for us to walk through. Like the stars have lined up to light our path.

Nothing has ever felt so right.

# Rule #33

## SOME LESSONS HAVE TO BE LEARNED THE HARD WAY

### REINA

"Dining room manager at Bon Vivant, huh?" Dom asks as he closes the front door of his house behind us.

I knew this was coming. Honestly, I'm surprised it took him this long to bring it up. "Cat's out of the bag, I guess," I say with a small sigh.

It's not that I didn't want him to know, it's just that…

I can't go back to the dinner shift and try to be one of the cool people on a day-to-day basis again. The friends I'm making at breakfast are so genuine, and I need the sense of calm I feel when I'm there. I couldn't risk having to give that all up.

I can see now that it was a fool's plan. Keeping my relationship secret almost ended it, and keeping my work history secret just means that now I have a lot of explaining to do.

"We've talked about the Pendleton how many times? And you never thought to mention that little tidbit?"

I watch him settle into the living room with a sheepish feeling. It sounds ridiculous now, but it was important to me. I only hope I can make him understand.

"I didn't want to work dinner."

Dom nods. He knows as well as I do that if I had sent the restaurant an honest résumé, I would never have been considered for breakfast. They wouldn't have passed up my kind of talent for the dinner crew. "Do you want to tell me about it?"

I walk over to the large gray sofa and sink into his arms. The answer is no, but also yes. I've gotten so used to lying over the last few months that it almost comes naturally, but I learned today how good it can feel to get things off your chest. Telling the people you love and trust the truth is the best feeling in the world.

"I came here with a lot of debt, like I told you before, but also a lot of anxiety. That job in the city, running that high-end dinner service—it was too much for me. I was really good at it, and I needed to make as much money as I could to try to stay afloat on my own, but it wasn't good for me. The stress, the competition, the people. I thought those people were my friends, but it turned out they only liked the me I pretended to be. And once I was working at that high level, and the restaurant started winning award after award, it just felt like there was no escape. I couldn't go back to just enjoying food and serving. It was all award season, all the time. Meetings and standards and getting chewed out by the chef when a fork was one millimeter out of line. I started worrying about it all the time, even when I wasn't at work. I would dream about working dinner service and everything going horribly wrong."

The memory of those days can still send a chill down my spine, even in this heat.

"Then I came here and got the breakfast job, and it seemed so freeing. With the low rent in staff housing, I could make less and still work to pay down my debt, and I didn't have to deal with the dinner stress. But...I still ended up hiding the truth about myself from a lot of people, so I don't know if I was any better off. Honestly, this whole secret relationship thing has been just as stressful as working dinner in the city. I'm really glad the secrecy is over."

"I wouldn't have made you work dinner if you didn't want to."

I roll my eyes. "Of course you wouldn't have made me, but if you knew that I could have helped you win that award, and I chose not to, it would have changed things between us. I know it would have. You were so focused on winning. I was scared of what it would do to us."

Dom pulls me into a tighter embrace. I curl my back into his chest, my knees curled into his. He's quiet for a long moment.

"Reina, I made a lot of mistakes these last few months. Hell, these last few years, but let's just start with this season. I should never have put that award before you. I put it before everything —my staff, my health. I've been watching everything in my life suffer for that stupid award for years, and I've done nothing about it. I know it's no excuse, but this is exactly what I watched men do my whole life. Fuentes men have every award on the planet. They have achieved great things. But none of them have good relationships with their wives or children. They just work all the time. I know my father thinks that he's doing what he does to provide, that it's his responsibility, but the truth is that he never needs to work another day in his life. My grandfather and great-grandfather took care of that. The investments would easily support generations to come. Work is his way of avoiding the real challenges in life—other people. He's the boss at work and that feels easier than coming home and dealing with his family. I hate that I got to that same place. But I'm going to do better. I acknowledge it now, and I can change it. That's my new project."

I take a moment to process Dom's heartfelt words before glancing up at him. "You're doing a great job, Dom. Your crew loves you."

"Well, it's time I loved them back."

I nod with a smile, tears threatening the corners of my eyes once more.

"Same goes for you. I love you, Reina. You swept into my life and left me a changed man. I owe you a debt of gratitude."

I groan. "Ugh, can we just keep on with the nice things and leave the word debt out of all of this?"

Dom smiles. "You know you're about to be a very rich lady, right?"

I shake my head. "We're not married yet. And besides, I'm going to pay my debt. I need to, and I need you to understand how important that is. It's not medical bills or student loans, or something honorable like that. Mine is credit card bills. It's money I owe for things I bought. It means a lot to me to make those payments every month."

"You'll be writing those checks every month with a million-dollar diamond on your finger," he teases.

"Dom, seriously. How old are you? No one writes checks anymore."

"I do."

"Stop. You do not."

We're heading for lighter territory, and I allow it. I'm happy to be putting the heavy conversations aside for the night. A lot has been said, a lot will still be said, but for now, I think we are in a good place.

"You know, I don't appreciate being called old. Thirty-nine is actually pretty young, all things considered. I'm not even over the hill."

I glance up and see the glimmer of mischief in his eyes. I'm willing to play along.

These little games always end well for me.

"I don't know, Daddy. Over the hill is something an old person would say."

I get just what I'm asking for with my sass. Dom lifts me easily with the arm wrapped around my middle and tosses me over his shoulder as I laugh in surprise.

As he carries me through the house toward his bedroom, something he's done countless times over the last few months, I start to see the place differently. This is going to be my home. The reality of this whole thing starts to sink in.

This man loves me. He has vowed to take care of me. He made a promise with the ring that's now back around my neck. He promised that it would only be a matter of time before there was one on my finger. I love that he knew me well enough not to have to ask, really. He knew my heart. He knew that I was just waiting for him to step into his truth, our truth, the truth of this relationship and our life together.

As soon as he did, our future together clicked into place.

He tosses me on the bed, and I look at him with tears in my eyes. They're tears of happiness and relief, wetting my cheeks as they run down toward my chin.

Dom sits down beside me, taking my face in both hands. He uses his thumbs to wipe the tears from my cheeks. "Are you okay?"

I nod.

"And we're okay?"

"We're better than okay, Dom. I'm better than okay. I'm…the best I've ever been." The words bring a whole new flood of tears to my eyes, and a sly smile to the lips of my lover.

"If you think you're crying now, little one, just wait until you get your punishment for calling me old."

"Not for lying to you about my work history?"

Dom's face expands into an evil smile. "I forgot about that, sweet girl. Thanks for reminding me. Double punishment. I like the sound of that."

I'm on my knees before I even know what's happening. Dom flips up my work skirt and pulls my panties down around my knees. His first spank comes without warning.

I scream and start to crawl away across the bed. He catches me with two fingers sliding straight into my wet pussy, curling up and pulling me back toward him. As I squeal and struggle, he nestles his thumb right into my tight back door, giving himself a firm grip to pull me back and hold me in place.

As the next round of spanks comes, I thrash and buck against his hand, the pain of my spanking only working to enhance the crazy pleasure I get from having him inside both of my holes. I'm going to come so quickly. I can already feel the first one building.

"You look like you're enjoying your punishment a bit too much, baby girl."

"No, Daddy," I manage to get out, even though I'm currently holding my breath, teetering on the edge of orgasm.

Dom knows me too well to fall for that. He withdraws his hand, leaving me cold and desperate. I press my hips back toward him, begging for more of his touch.

I get my wet pussy smacked hard three times in a row for my trouble.

"I know you like it when I fuck you here." Dom works his fingers back inside my wet entrance, giving me a few hard thrusts to prove his point. I can't hold back my moan as I start to climb the cliff of pleasure once more.

But then he pulls them out. I cry out in frustration. Dom only chuckles behind me.

"And I know you like it when I fuck you here."

His thumb goes back in my ass. It feels so different when he goes inside there without all the lube. It's so tight he can barely get his thumb in. I'm so turned on by this point that I'm happy for any contact I'm given, so I graciously accept this penetration, rocking my hips back to try to get more.

But then he pulls out, landing a hard smack on my ass.

"I think tonight you're going to get both."

His words send a chill over my hot skin. I know he always takes care of me, that I never go without my pleasure, but this is going to be something I've only fantasized about. I'm so happy I get to experience it for the first time with this man I love.

Usually, my punishment lasts until I'm screaming in frustration, so I'm surprised when I feel his mouth land on my pussy as he drops to his knees behind me. His tongue goes straight to its favorite place—swirling my clit.

I nearly come with all the contact, it might happen right now from the soft, sweet swoops of tongue up and around my clit. When his fingers enter me, all of me, and start rocking my body back and forth against his mouth, my orgasm erupts.

I barely have time to utter a moan before my breath catches in my lungs, and I squeeze my eyes closed, trusting Dom to work me all the way over the edge.

He doesn't let me down.

I'm still gasping to recover when I feel the tip of his cock dipping into my pussy. He's just wetting it, teasing me—and himself. I press my hips back, greedy to get the full slide sooner, but he pulls back.

"Patience, patience, little one."

We both know I have none of that.

"I think I might strap you down for this one."

"I don't need to be strapped down, just fuck me."

Dom lets out a dark laugh. "Oh, you're definitely getting tied up, baby girl. And you know you just earned yourself more punishment."

I don't fight him as he takes me by the wrists and drags me across the mattress to where the leather strap with soft cuffs from the top of the bed lies waiting for me. Dom clicks the cuffs closed and secures the strap so that my arms are held tightly, straight out in front of where I lie face down.

Then he climbs back over me.

I get one hard slap and a bite on the ass before he lifts my hips up to bring my knees to the bed, opening me wide before him.

"So fucking beautiful. I could stare at this pretty pussy all day long."

I moan and shake my hips, desperate for the promised penetration to begin. I know better than to speak, however. That will only prolong my torment.

"Which hole should I fuck first, sweetheart?"

I hold my tongue. Any answer I give right now will only lead to me getting the opposite. Besides, I want to be surprised. Both have their own pleasures waiting, and he promised me both. I can take what I'm offered.

The cold lube hits my exposed back door, making me gasp. Dom spreads it all around, and then inside me. His fingers feel so good sliding in and out of me. When his tip joins the party, pressing once again into my pussy, I squeeze my eyes closed and breathe deeply.

I don't want to come too quickly this time. I want to make this last.

When the full length of his cock is inside my pussy, I know I have at least three fingers in my ass. This may be the closest I ever get to having real double penetration—Dom isn't likely to share me—so I want to enjoy it as much as I can. The fullness feels so complete, right on the edge of too much. The overwhelming feeling takes over my mind, heightening my senses—which is just what I need right now.

Then the pounding I've been waiting for starts.

In and out he slams, getting into a rhythm with his hips and his fingers, making sure my back hole gets fucked just as well as my pussy. I tilt my hips up just a bit to catch the action of his swinging balls against my clit and from there, it's only a few punishing thrusts before my second orgasm crashes down.

I moan and clench down all my muscles as I contract and spasm. Dom cries out behind me as I bear down on him. He doesn't let up, though, if anything, he fucks me harder.

"Goddamn, you feel so fucking good. You are such a good girl coming for Daddy again. You like this, huh?"

"Yes, Daddy," I say when I can finally manage to get a word out. My release has passed, and I'm starting to relax.

It's then I feel the lube hit my backside once more.

I breathe slowly and steadily, keeping myself calm as I feel the smooth tip of Dom's cock circling. I don't have the vibrator to distract me this time, but I'm confident I can take him. I'm so open and turned on right now—and I'm dying to feel one of Dom's powerful orgasms inside my body.

As he slides himself into my tight channel, I relax further, taking him in.

"Oh god. Good fucking girl." The praise hits me right in my chest, and my eyes swell with tears. It makes me so happy to please him like this. And all of his pleasure is giving me orgasm after orgasm, so I can hardly complain.

Dom grips my hips with one hand and with the other he reaches below me and finds my pussy entrance. I feel him circle it with his fingers, and then I feel something cool and smooth enter me.

"Dom?"

"What do you call me, girl?"

"Sorry, Daddy. I just…what is that?"

"I had more toys hidden for you, little one. I think you're going to like this one."

I try to settle my breathing, to keep myself calm, but it's harder now. I thought I was getting all the double penetration I would ever get just a moment ago, but my generous daddy had other surprises up his sleeve.

As the dildo slides inside me, nestled right up next to where Dom's huge, hard cock is filling my back channel, I can hardly breathe. The sensation is so raw, so real. I'm so full right now I don't know what to think. I can't think at all.

Dom starts his slide in and out of me, easing me into the motion. He holds the dildo tightly in place as he pumps.

"How do you like getting fucked in both holes, little one?"

"I love it, Daddy," I reply.

It's true.

"You look so amazing from up here. Do you want me to tell you?"

317

"Yes, please."

"With your arms tied up so tightly, you can't move a muscle. Your hands clenched in little fists and your arms straining against the cuffs—so fucking sexy—like you're trying to get away. You're not trying to get away, are you, little one?"

"No, Daddy."

"You arch your back and tilt your beautiful, round, red ass into my hands as I push my cock into it. You like that, don't you?"

"Mm-hmm."

"I can just see your wet pussy down there. I get a little glimpse of it every time I pull out." He pauses with just his tip nestled in my asshole before slamming it back in. "I can see how well your pussy swallows up the new toy I bought you. I can feel the toy inside you against my cock. Can you feel my cock rubbing up against the toy?" He pauses halfway down my tight channel and runs the tip of his cock against the tip of the dildo cock through the thin layer of skin that separates them. The sensation is so incredibly alien and overwhelming, so punishing and yet so pleasurable, it makes me moan in response.

"I think I'm going to come in your ass, baby girl. Would you like that?"

"Yes, Daddy." I work up the energy to get a few words out this time. The idea of him pounding my ass until he spasms and empties into me almost pushes me over the edge again. I just need some contact with my clit. Then, I would certainly come with him.

"I want to come too," I call out as he starts fucking me harder.

"My girl wants to come on two cocks at once, huh?"

"Yes, Daddy."

"What do you need?"

"A finger holding my clit."

Dom gives it to me immediately, reaching his hand down from my hip and pressing one strong finger down on my tight bundle of nerves. He doesn't let up the pace of his cock in my ass and even manages to get the dildo pumping in and out of me as he holds that finger in place on my clit.

My breathing stops for a moment. I let the sensation take me. It's so much, it's all so much, but somehow, it's just right. I come suddenly, my body contracting around the two foreign invaders, the extra friction of having them both inside me prolongs and enhances my orgasm. It's so strong that I'm somehow screaming through my held breath.

Dom is coming right into the center of my orgasm, my tight contractions drawing out a scream of his own. I can feel him pause deep inside me, losing control of the dildo and just keeping it pressed deep inside me as well. His body pulses, filling me with his seed.

I must hold my breath for far too long, because when I'm finally released from the claws of pleasure, I see little stars in my periphery.

Dom pants above me, hunched over my back, his hands still holding tight to my pussy, his cock as deep in my ass as it goes.

We are joined together now. The feeling is both familiar and foreign. I lose track of where my body ends and his begins.

When he finally lets the dildo and his cock slide out of me, the emptiness is breathtaking. I'm already craving the feeling of him inside me again.

I lie reveling in the feeling for a moment before Dom lifts me and carries me to the bathroom, where he sets me gently in the tub and turns on warm water. With the handheld sprayer on low, he gently washes me from where he kneels on the rug next to the tub. He tucks me back into bed, and I can hear him taking his own shower.

I just start to drift off when I feel the sensation of being pulled into his arms.

"Reina," Dom starts.

"Hmm?"

"Did I ask you to marry me? Or did I just assume that you would?"

I smile, my eyes still closed. "You assumed. But I'll let it slide this time because you assumed correctly."

"I'm happy to hear that, but in the future, I want you to let me know when I'm making assumptions about what you want instead of asking. You may be my girl, but I need you to know that you have full say in our life together."

"Don't worry. I'll let you know if you're making incorrect assumptions."

"Like, for instance, when I assume that since you did such an excellent job running the dining room at dinner tonight, you'll be my dinner front of house manager now—"

"That would be an incorrect assumption. Yes. Good example."

Dom growls and pulls me closer. "Reina, you were marvelous tonight. You belong on dinner."

"That's not what I want."

"You don't want to work the tasting menu?"

"No."

He's quiet for a few long moments, holding me tightly. The silence gives me a chance to process what he said—and what I said. I've been very worried about how I would turn down that offer if he ever found out about Bon Vivant and wanted me to join his shift. Turns out, all I had to say was no.

*Could have saved myself months of lying and worrying and just said my peace in the first place.*

Oh, well. I guess I have to learn some lessons the hard way.

"Have you considered a date for the wedding? We could have it anywhere in the world you want and as soon as the season closes."

Just when I thought I was ready to stand up for myself, this man throws me another curveball. It's so hard to turn him down, but I guess this is a muscle I'm going to need to strengthen to survive a lifetime together with him.

"Dom, I'm not going to be ready by the end of the season."

That gets his attention. He lifts his body and props himself on an elbow, looking down at me in confusion. "Why not?"

I let out a sigh. "Because when we get married, I will have too much income at my disposal. I need to pay off my bills before that happens."

Another growl escapes his lips, and I glance up to see a look of exasperation.

"Dom, I told you it was important for me to do this."

He flops down next to me, pulling me back into his arms. "Okay, so you are going to keep working until you pay off your debts and then we can get married."

"That's right."

"You are about to get one hell of a raise."

I can't help myself and let out a laugh. "Don't you dare."

I'm pulled so close that we share the same air. With his forehead pressed to mine, Dom pulls the sheet over our heads, creating a little pocket of darkness, like a fort under the kitchen table.

The feeling of closeness between us grows as we stare into each other's eyes. There's no one else in the world but he and I.

"I love you, Reina. I'll wait forever."

"I love you, too, Dom," I say, realizing it's the first time the words have actually left my mouth. They feel good. Right. I say them again. "I love you. And you aren't waiting, not really. I'll be right here."

I drift off in our secret fort, with Dom's arms wrapped around me. I'm safe and happy, content to be following through on my obligations, while at the same time getting the future I never even dreamed possible.

That's the win-win I've been waiting for.

# Rule #34

## NEVER GIVE UP ON WHAT YOU WANT

### REINA

Four Months Later

"All right, all right! I'm coming!" I set down the stack of plates I just carried in from the dining room and wash my hands.

Dom, the other owners, and the whole restaurant staff gather in the dining room, along with a few straggler guests. They all wait impatiently for Dom to open the envelope in his hand, but he won't do it until I'm there.

I hurry back to stand beside him, brushing a lock of hair out of my eyes and smiling up at his stoic expression. He's been a ball of nerves the past week, since he started getting word from his chef friends that the Pendleton announcements had started arriving. The mail takes a bit longer to reach us out here, but ours finally showed up in the mailbox this morning.

The envelope is creased and worn from being in his hands for hours as he waited for breakfast to be over so we could all gather together.

"Open it," someone shouts from the crowd, followed by a chorus of laughter and agreement.

"I think you should do it," he says, trying to pass the envelope to me.

"Dom, open the envelope," I whisper.

With a sigh, he carefully opens the seam and slides the paper out.

I can feel the whole room holding their breath as we watch him read. Finally, after what feels like ages, he lowers it and looks out over the crowd, expression unreadable.

"We won."

There's a full beat of silence before the room erupts into chaos. There's cheering and clapping and screaming and hugging and crying. Everyone pulls someone into their arms.

I snatch the paper from his hands and read the handful of lines twice. We took the top spot. They were very impressed. Ceremony and award to follow after the official announcement.

The moment feels surreal, all the excited energy around me where I stand in a little bubble with Dom. He's looking down at me with gratitude and love in his eyes. I smile back up at him. "Congratulations, Chef."

"Hmmm," he growls softly in my ear. "I could get used to you calling me that."

I laugh and take a step back. "I think you'd miss your old nickname too much."

He watches me walk into the crowd with a smile on his face. I'm embraced by so many happy people that I nearly lose sight of him, but when I glance back, I can see his staff, his family, bombarding him with attention as well.

This award means a lot to everyone here, and I am ecstatic that we won it. The White Sands—and Faraday Island—is about to be on the lips of every foodie in the world. We have a lot to prepare for next season, but luckily, some of the changes are already underway.

I feel Dom's arm slide around my waist as he comes up

beside me. "I gotta get back downstairs, but I'll see you at home in a few hours? You probably want to nap before the party."

The owners are planning an all-staff bash to celebrate the end of season, and now there will be extra cause for celebration.

"I definitely need a nap. I should be done here by three, I'll just head up."

"Come get me first."

I smile at the back of him as he heads toward the door that leads to the elevators in the lobby. He knows damn well that he will never make it out of work on his own, but if I come down and demand that he go home with me, he always obeys.

Turns out, he's not the only one who can give orders.

I head back to the server station, Sarah close on my heels.

"So exciting!"

I smile at her and nod in agreement. "Well deserved."

"I can't believe I'm going to be working dinner next season at a Pendleton restaurant! Do you think the prices will go up? Probably. The tips will be insane! I'm definitely getting a place off property next season."

I'm so happy for Sarah. She has really bloomed in her new position as lunch server by day, dinner host and assistant server by night, preparing for her full transition to Raft dinner server next season. She deserves her own place off property. I can't wait to help her move in.

Turns out, transitioning to girlfriend of the chef wasn't as rocky as I was expecting it to be. People forgave our secrecy, if they were ever upset to begin with, and accepted me as part of management with open arms. Everyone is going to be sad to see me leave breakfast, but the work we've been doing downstairs to get the new restaurant—aptly named Reef Café—has everyone eagerly awaiting next season.

I finish up one of my last shifts at Raft and head toward the elevator. A lot has changed downstairs since my first time exploring the abandoned kitchen and dining room—and mattress storage closet. The place is nearly unrecognizable.

They pulled down the facade that was covering the walls to reveal large windows that look out over the pool area, with the ocean in the background. The old-fashioned tables with fake flower vases have been replaced with bar seating and stools, as well as booths and couch seating. Construction happening right now will create a door through the dining room wall so that they can add outdoor seating poolside.

I find Dom hunched over a stack of menus on one of the prep counters. He and Marcus are deep in conversation, but they look up as I approach. "You about ready to head up?" I ask Dom, giving Marcus a friendly shoulder squeeze in greeting.

He really stepped up in the aftermath of our crazy judging night. When Dom decided that they would be opening the casual restaurant downstairs regardless of whether the Pendleton was ours or not, he promoted Marcus to Head Chef of the new space so Dom could focus on getting Raft ready for the onslaught of foodies who were about to bombard the resort. The young chef from the dinner crew, Suzie, who was dubbed The Cauliflower Queen, was promoted to sous chef of Raft.

It's been great for everyone involved, myself included. I've been getting to use my keen restaurant eye to help design both the dining room and the new menus. The place looks great, and I can't wait to finally see it in action.

Dom and I will also get to align our schedules a bit—no more staying up until midnight waiting for him to get off work when I have to be up for work at five. With breakfast and lunch moving downstairs to Reef, he'll be able to work a lot less, focusing on menu design, presentation, and schmoozing the guests.

He still keeps me up late, but it's for other reasons.

The happiest people of all are probably the almost entirely local crew who worked breakfast and lunch in the cramped quarters upstairs at Raft. When the announcement was made that Reef would be opening downstairs next season, taking over breakfast and lunch service, a cheer went up through the crowd. I can't blame them for the excitement about leaving behind the dinner hotshots and claiming the enormous new kitchen of Reef. When the new staff arrives in the fall, extra hires will be added to the crew to make opening day as smooth as it can be.

Dom smiles at me but makes no move to wrap it up. "Yeah, give me just a few minutes, okay? Why don't you go check out the door progress. I think they're putting the big overhead door on its tracks today."

"Five minutes?" I ask. I don't want to rush him out of his work, but I'm more tired than usual, probably because of all the excitement from the award. After tonight's party, I am not scheduling anything for at least a month. I need a break.

I get a second wind as I pass through the kitchen doors into the dining room. The place is gorgeous. With these windows letting in natural light and the shimmery glow of the pool reflected in the wood-framed mirrors on the walls, it's a truly magical space.

One that I had a heavy hand in creating.

This place is going to be everything I dreamed a restaurant could be. It brings together my love of great food and service with the quick, easygoing flow of casual fare. I picked out most of the furniture in here myself, spending long nights unpacking stool after stool with the maintenance crew. And Dom, of course. He loves this space just as much as I do.

It's fitting, in a way, that we each have our own restaurant. We have been working side-by-side shifts since day one of our relationship, now we will get to do it forever.

*Forever.*

The word has been coming up more and more in our house, slipped into conversation by my—apparently hopelessly romantic—fiancé, who doesn't seem to take my need to wait for the wedding as any reason to wait on dreaming about the big day. He will casually bring up friends who had epic destination weddings or toss out ideas for dinner menus.

It's sweet, and I don't feel any kind of pressure from him, which is nice. Even with my new salary as restaurant manager at

Reef, it's going to be another full season before I'm ready to walk down the aisle.

The construction crew working on the new garage-door-style slide-up that will connect Reef to the pool area stand aside and wave me through the hole. I tiptoe through their debris and thank them with a smile and wave. Once outside, I walk over to the pool and turn back to admire the new space.

Where there used to be a faux stucco wall covering these giant windows, there's now an almost fully formed restaurant. My restaurant. It's amazing how much can change in a few months.

The same is true for my own life. Like this restaurant, I felt like I was living behind a wall I put up to hide my past. Dom helped me take that wall down, and now look at me. The future is everything I never allowed myself to dream was possible.

My eyes have gone a little blurry while thinking about how far we've come so I don't notice Dom until he's right beside me.

"Ready to go home, sweetheart?"

I wipe my eyes and smile up at him with a nod. "Yes, Daddy."

# Rule #35

YOU ARE THE QUEEN

REINA

Two Years Later

"Girl, you're a princess!"

I turn to smile at Fran as she enters the bridal suite, arms overflowing with my veil and flower crown. "Is it too much?"

Staring at my own reflection in the full-length mirror, long, flowing white lace dress filling the frame, I already know how she's going to answer.

"No way. It's perfect. He's going to die when he sees you."

"I hope not," I respond. I know she's only joking, but I can't help biting my lip in concern.

Fran flicks my cheek lightly. "None of that. We just spent twenty minutes on those lips."

Her face softens beside mine in the reflection, tucking in close to mine as she pulls me into a side hug. "I meant die in a good way. Like melt into a puddle of joy that his princess is finally, finally walking down that damn aisle."

I relax into a grin. "It hasn't been that long."

But it's been far longer than anyone expected. People really thought I was going to cave the first year and sign on the dotted line to secure my handsome, rich husband. But I was serious when I decided to work off my past debts first.

It took two full years, but I did it.

Now, when Dom and I take that first walk as husband and wife, we'll be stepping into a new life together. Starting fresh.

A knock at the suite door makes us both jump.

Fran cracks the door and then slams it shut. "Dominic Fuentes, you know damn well you can't come in here."

"If I want to open this door, there is very little you can do to stop me," comes Dom's stern, muffled response.

Fran clicks the flimsy knob lock into place. "It's bad luck to see the bride before the wedding."

"You're too young for those old wives' tales, Franny," I tell her.

She spins to face me, eyes wide with surprise. "I'm not letting him in."

"Why don't you blindfold him?" I suggest with a shrug.

I'm not going to pretend I don't want to touch my future husband. To absorb some of the powerful, unconditional love that radiates off him every time he's near me.

Fran narrows her eyes at me but turns back to the door. "Put your tie over your eyes."

Dom grumbles something we can't make out through the door, but I can hear him rustling around out there. A small thrill shoots through my stomach when I realize he's going to comply.

Usually, I'm the one who's blindfolded.

Fran must read my mind because, after cracking the door to check that he's securely blinded by the silk tie, she slips out. "If you mess up one inch of her with your kinky…whatever, I swear to god, I'm going to have you killed by assassins, Dom."

He holds both hands up in surrender, far more agreeable now that he knows he's getting his way.

Still grumbling, Fran slips past him through the doorway and down the hall.

I cross the room, holding my dress up with one hand, and reach down to take Dom's with the other, leading him into the room. He looks magnificent and regal in his champagne slacks and vest over a white dress shirt with sleeves rolled to reveal strong forearms, the ocean blue tie that was secured around his neck just moments ago covering his eyes.

"Can you really not see me?"

He shakes his head. "I am imagining you naked, though."

I close the door behind him and step into his arms.

Dom finds my lips with practiced ease, then trails his mouth softly down my neck.

"Low-cut dress," he murmurs as his lips find the textured edge of the sweetheart neckline. He follows the curve as it dips low in the center, growling softly when he finds the swell of my breasts. "Who needs a wedding?"

I laugh and take a step back, hands on my hips, although he can't see me. "You do, Daddy."

And it's true. Although I'm over the moon about our gorgeous, elegant Bora Bora wedding, my first vote was for something small, in the dining room of Raft, where we first fell in love. I was worried Dom was trying to prove something to the world with all this excess. He assured me he just wanted to make sure I got the pictures I would want hanging in our living room as we grew old together.

And, well, it's hard to argue with that.

"I didn't think there were going to be so many people," he answers, closing the distance between us to trace the bare skin of my arms with his fingers.

"You and I wrote the guest list."

It's Dom's turn to smile. "True. But I forgot there would be moments when I would be without you."

Perfectly on cue, Fran taps at the closed door. "Ten minutes until we walk down there, Reina. Dom, you should be at the altar right now."

"Tomorrow we'll be on a plane, and you'll have me all to yourself," I remind him.

"Wife," he whispers.

"Go on then," I whisper back with a little shove, trying to be strong, even as his single word nearly brought me to my knees.

There will be plenty of time for that in Japan.

After all the planning and decadence of this week in Bora Bora, we agreed on a much simpler month-long honeymoon in Japan. Nice but normal hotel room, long days spent wandering through gardens and shops, eating from the small vendors in the local markets.

"See you down there," he answers, but makes no move to exit.

With a smile, I turn him and march him to the door, letting Fran inside as I close it behind him.

"Ten minutes, love," I tell him as the door clicks shut.

Fran secures my tiara of plumeria, tiare Tahiti, and bougainvillea flowers across the crown of my head and pins the long veil in place behind it.

Stepping back up to the mirror, my breath sucks sharply into my lungs at the sight.

I'm no princess.

I'm the queen.

Time fades as Fran leads me down the hallway and the wooden steps to the wide garden doors that lead to the aisle.

She takes Sarah's hand and steps up to take her turn walking before me, turning to blow a kiss as she disappears around the corner.

"You look lovely, Reina," my father tells me as I step into his embrace.

My relationship with both my parents has improved a lot over the last two years, as I grew into my independence and started seeing them for who they are—adults just like me who are doing their imperfect, messy best. We've never been closer, and they adore Dom, of course.

"Can't Help Falling in Love" plays softly from garden speakers as my father leads me around the corner to begin our march.

The aisle stretches before me, soft sand lined with orchids, ferns, and ti leaves.

Someone must announce my presence because the crowd filled with family and friends rises from their chairs and turn my way.

But I hear nothing.

As I lock gazes with Dom, standing proudly at the end of the aisle, the whole world fades away.

I've become accustomed to the reverence in this man's gaze whenever he looks at me, the love akin to worship that I strive to live up to every day in our dream of a life.

But this is something else.

The passion still smolders there. The love still echoes. But it's softer. Rather than a bonfire, this love feels like a warm embrace, welcoming me home.

I walk toward him, never looking away.

Dom leaves his post to meet me at the head of the aisle, accepting my hand from my father and taking the other one as well, holding me close like he does so often...but this time it's different.

I thought marriage was just a couple of legal documents.

I put this off for years thinking it wouldn't change anything between us.

If I had known this is what it would feel like to finally claim this man as my own in front of the world, to let him choose me forever...

Well, I would have done it years ago.

Dom leans down to kiss me, and the crowd swoons in unison. I smile against his lips and pull back, glancing up at him.

"Hi," I whisper.

He smiles back, a soft, secret smile. The vulnerable one he only shows to me. "You look beautiful."

"Beautiful enough to marry?"

His smile turns to a playful little smirk as he gives my hands a little tug. "Come on, then."

Avery, Ben, Fran, Vic, and Sarah wait for us on either side of a massive arch of flowers, misty-eyed and clearly trying to keep it together.

Sam officiates the short, romantic ceremony with his easy charm, drawing laughter, sighs, and misty smiles from the small crowd.

When it's time for the vows, I know I'm not the only one grateful for waterproof mascara.

"Reina, my love," Dom starts, speaking only to me, "I should have married you that first day at the server station of Raft. Just dragged Sam in there and handed you a table bouquet."

I smile as my first tear escapes, memories of that day feeding the growing storm of happy emotions swelling inside me.

"But you would have shot me down so fast." Dom chuckles, and the whole crowd laughs softly as well. "I've always followed your lead. Even when you look to me for guidance, know that I'm taking mine from you. I've never had a partner like this, a real partner. An equal. Someone I respect and whom I want to earn the respect of. I planned to say that you make me a better man, but it's more than that. You make me a man, period. I feel so grateful and blessed that you chose me. And that you made me wait. Because now I know what it is to want. And I will spend every day for the rest of my life wanting you."

He slips the ring onto my finger, nestling the rose-gold band engraved with waves above the ornate diamond and turquoise engagement ring I've been wearing since his heartfelt proposal two years ago. We had the band custom-made from his grandfather's ring by splitting the old ring into two.

Fran steps up beside me to slip the little velvet bag

containing Dom's matching ring into my hands. I take a deep breath, knowing it's my turn.

"Dom," I start, pausing to clear my throat and try to calm my voice. "Dominic. My love. My life. I never let go of anything before I met you. I dragged every hurt, every grudge, around with me, desperate to prove I was right. That I could do it alone. I never imagined how safe it could feel to tell the truth. With you, I feel safe for the first time in my life. I love that I can learn from you and that you let me teach you. You allow me to let go. To be my true self. I will love you always for so many reasons, but for that most of all."

The gold wave ring, twin to the one I now wear, slips easily onto his waiting finger.

Dom leans in, twinkle in his eye, to press a kiss gently to my forehead before taking my lips with his own.

And just like that.

Forever begins.

*A Look At Book Two:*

## SHAMELESS

**He's my stepbrother, my last mistake… and the only man I can't say no to.**

I came to this island to launch my dream wedding planning business—not to fall into bed with a masked stranger at a masquerade ball.

One night. No names. No consequences. Until I find out exactly who he is.

He's a billionaire. My new stepbrother. And now he's decided to stick around… offering help I didn't ask for, and stirring up feelings I can't afford.

He's reckless, irresistible, and everything I'm not. I've spent my whole life trying to prove I'm more than a disappointment. I can't risk my one shot at success—not for a fling that was never supposed to follow me past sunrise.

But every look is a dare. Every touch, a promise. And on an island where secrets don't stay buried, falling for him might just ruin everything.

***AVAILABLE JANUARY 2026***

*Acknowledgments*

This book is in no way autobiographical…but, as to be expected, there is quite a bit of me in the story.

Long before I became a real grown-up with bills on autopay and vacations to do things other than visit family, I worked at a resort on a small island. It was the opposite of tropical, and I lived in a tent. When I first got the idea for this series, I set the story in that resort. Later that year, Chipp and I flew to Belize, and everything changed.

I decided to set the series on a tropical island so I would get to spend more time in the fabulous sun. Goodness knows, I get enough rain in real life. The resort and the island and the town exist as an amalgamation of places I've been and things I've seen during my travels. People ask me all the time if The White Sands is a real place, and the answer is…kind of.

What is real, however, are the feelings. Maybe you're like me and would prefer to keep your entire life secret from everyone around you, with the exception of a few choice details. I've grown out of this a lot, but I can still remember the ripped open wide feeling of coming to live in a tiny, close-knit resort community where everyone knew everyone, and it was impossible to screw up (or screw, for that matter) without all of your coworkers finding out. It was a paralyzing feeling, to say the least.

I'd love to tell you that I learned and grew during those years, but I don't think that's the truth. What I did was close even deeper into myself, perfect my 'everything is fine' mask, and protect the real, imperfect me from the world. It was much later in life that I figured out how to share my stumbles as well as my wins. That vulnerability is what brings people closer, what helps us understand that we're all human.

So, as one does, I dragged a few poor, unsuspecting characters through my own shit. I think it worked out okay for them, and it really helped me. If you see a bit of yourself hiding in here somewhere, just know that you're not alone. It's hard and scary to tell people the truth. People are scary! But you've gotta find a few good ones and let them love you. It makes all the difference in the world.

This book would not be what it is today without Karen Washo. When I first sent this to her, completely rough, her reply text to me read: It needs some work, but we'll get it there! And bless her heart, we did.

Thanks to Morgan and Cathy, my ride-or-die partners in all this madness. I tell you what, if you ever find someone willing to read and re-read your butt-sex scenes over and over until they're just right...well, do whatever you gotta do to keep those people on your team.

Thanks to my ARC readers, the ones who've been with me since day one, and all the lovely friends who've joined us over the years. Releasing books with you all is what I look forward to most. Here's to many more.

And thanks to the Love N. Books team, Ellie and Kayla, and to the kind folks at Wolf Pack for taking a chance on me. I've come a long way from that scared 20-something hiding in her tent, and I can't wait to see what kind of magic we make together.

Until next time, love!

Lore

You can learn plenty of normal things about me in my various platform bios, so here's some things you can only learn in the back of this book:

**Q: Which scene was hardest to write—and why?**
A: Ooh, this is a good question. For me, the hardest was the scene where Reina shows up at the staff party Dom told her not to go to, and approaches him when he's sitting at the campfire with his guy friends. The subtle rejection of that moment is one that really got to me while writing, and I almost took it out. I am, first and foremost, a conflict avoider in real life, and I find myself always wanting to coddle my characters in the same way. Stories need the drama, though, so instead of taking it out, I made it worse! You're welcome.

**Q: If you could have dinner with one of your characters, who would it be and what would you eat?**
A: I'd love to have dinner with Chef Dom…and I'd eat anything he was cooking.

**Q: What book changed your life—and how?**
A: As a lifelong reader, there are so many books that have been pivotal in my development as an author and a human, but I think two that are feeling really relevant to my art right now are The Invisible Life of Addie Larue and A Court of Mist and Fury —both of them for the same reason. I'm obsessed with the idea of falling for the shadow daddy who swoops in and upends your entire life. And I love when the narrative of a book—especially the romantic arc—can surprise me. Like, I'm a 40-year-old woman. It's hard to surprise me these days. Both of these books succeeded in doing just that.

**Q: What's your ideal writing setup? Chaos and caffeine, or quiet and candles?**
A: I write first thing in the morning—literally straight out of bed —standing in my silent office with my coffee. I write for as long as possible before I have to go do something else, like go to work or eat. And after that first interruption, it's almost impossible for me to get any more words in. Sometimes that writing time in the morning lasts 40 minutes, sometimes it's a solid 4 hours. I type nonstop until I'm forced to quit. And then I do it all again the next day.

**Q: What's something about being an author no one warned you about?**
A: One of the things I didn't quite understand when I started all this was how much it would take over my life. I started publishing during covid, and chose a pen name, assuming I could keep it all to myself. Fast forward five years, and I've got stacks of my own books on my shelves, I've got my Publisher's Marketplace deal announcement framed on the wall, it's just impossible to keep it a secret. My family is happy and proud of me, of course, but I do get the comments from all three of my parents about how they ordered copies of my books and find them very…interesting. My mom asked me if I was planning to

write any books about dragons. I've been forced to face the fact that members of my family wish I was writing books they could read and recommend to their friends. One of the reasons I kept it to myself in the first place was the desire to create without worrying about my parents (or co-workers or ex's, etc.) reading it and judging me. They all know now, and it's been a struggle to keep myself focused on creating for myself and my audience, without worrying what everyone I know is going to think when they read it.

The best place to find the most current info about my books and events is here:

linktr.ee/authorloretownsend

www.loretownsend.com

Join Lore Townsend's Romance Club